Zeb AND Bel

A CASE OF BIRD PROBLEMS

CITY SCOUTS BADGE DAY

DEDICATED
TO SIBLINGS
OF ALL KINDS.

PERPLECK PASS
Metro

WHOSE CAT?

HAZEL

QUEEN

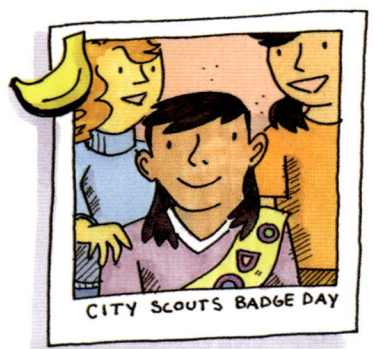

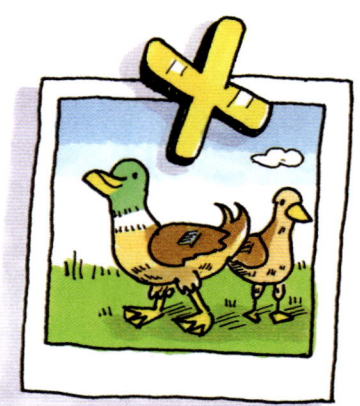

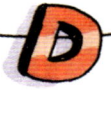

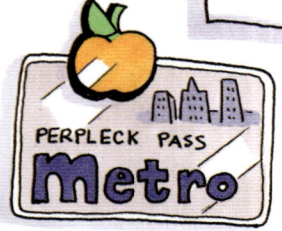

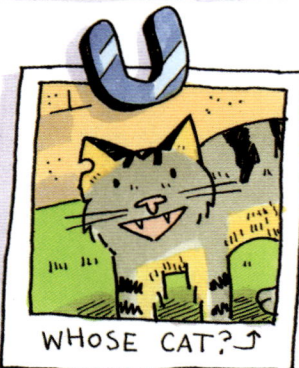

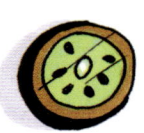

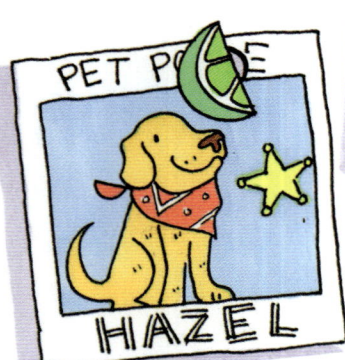

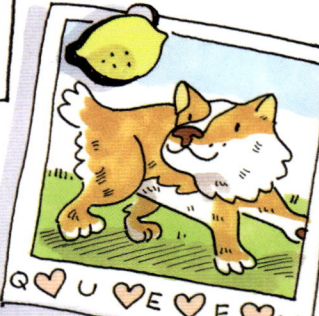

Zeb AND Bel

A CASE OF BIRD PROBLEMS

RACHEL ELLIOTT

HARPER alley

An Imprint of HarperCollinsPublishers

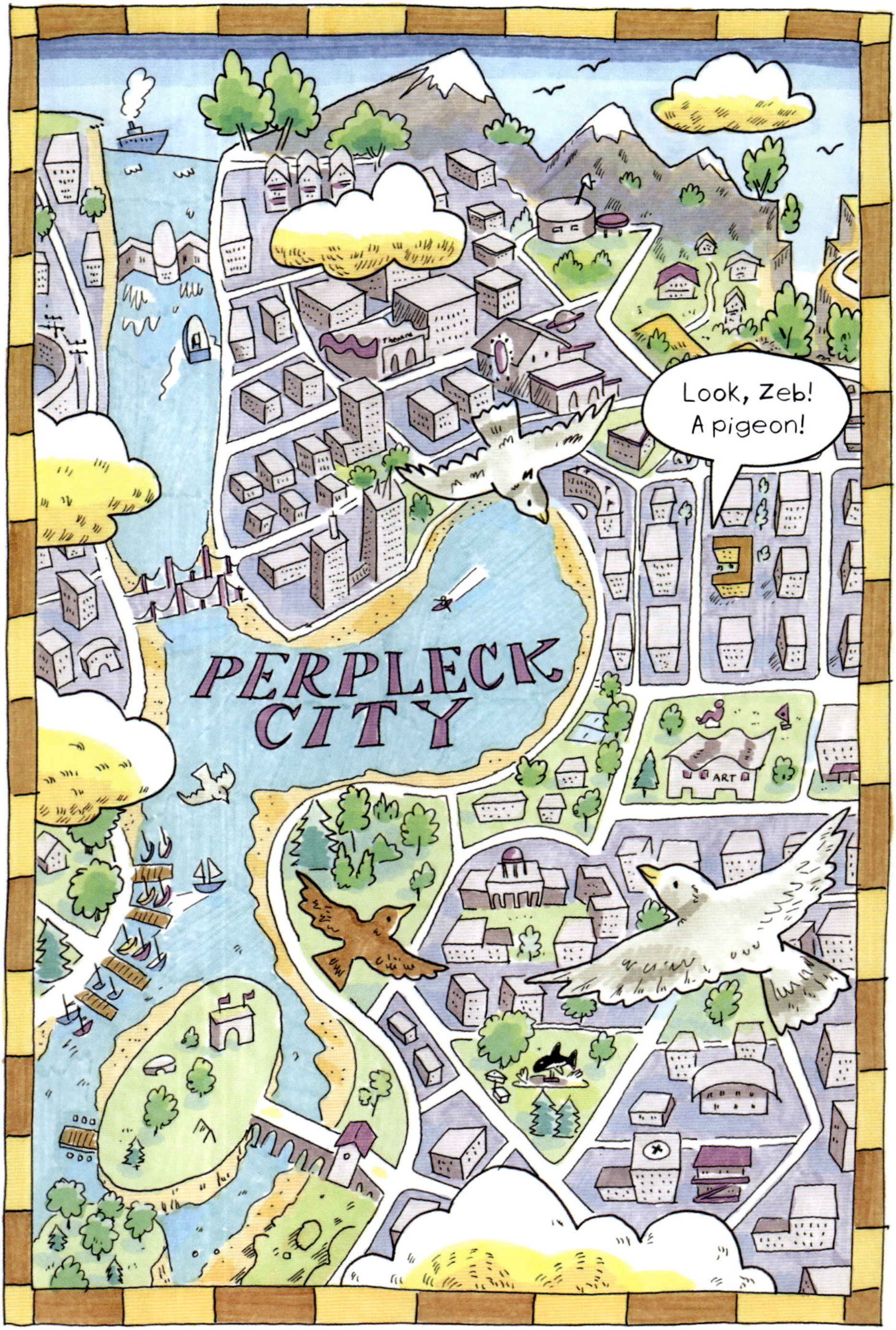
PERPLECK CITY
Look, Zeb! A pigeon!
ART

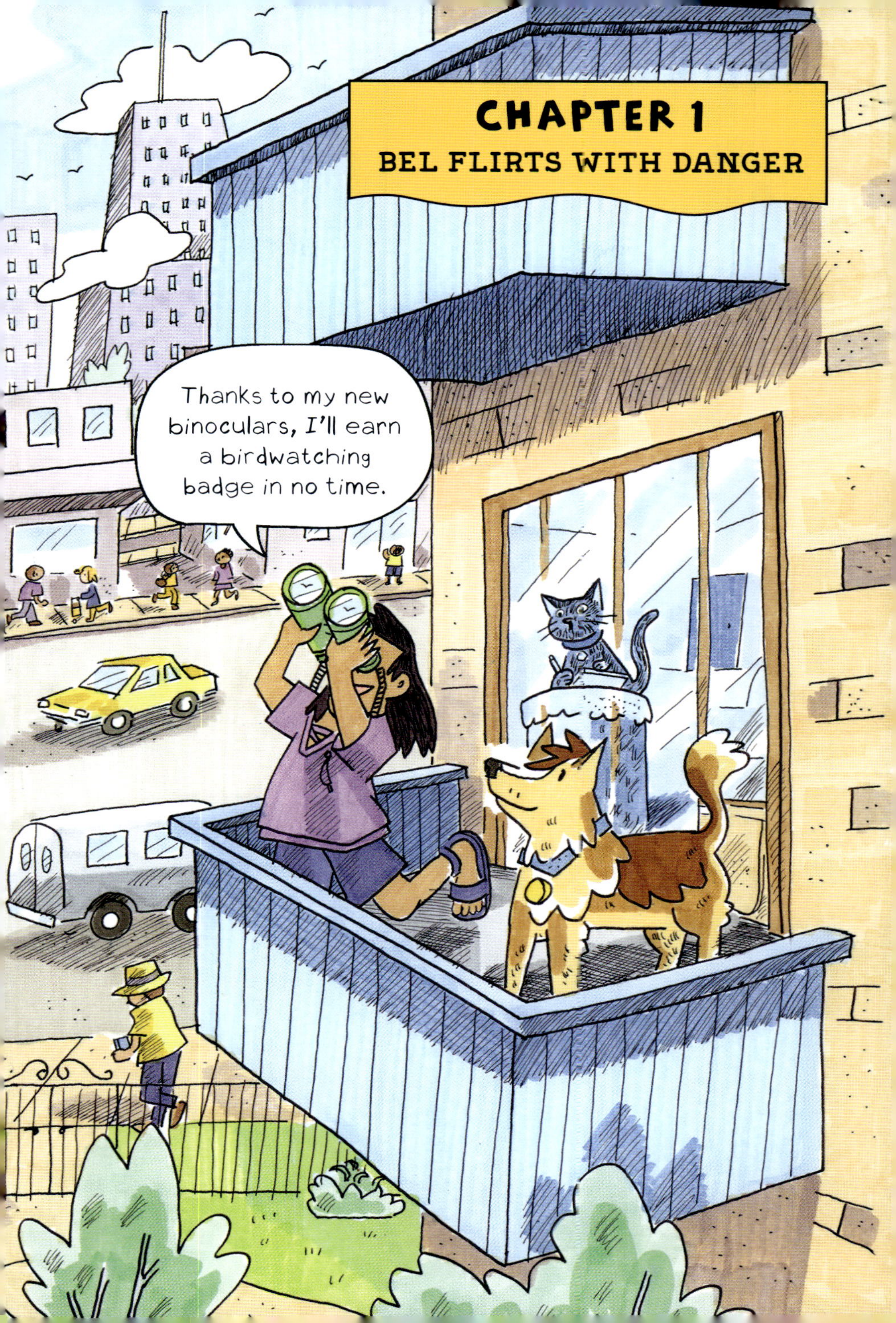
CHAPTER 1
BEL FLIRTS WITH DANGER
Thanks to my new binoculars, I'll earn a birdwatching badge in no time.

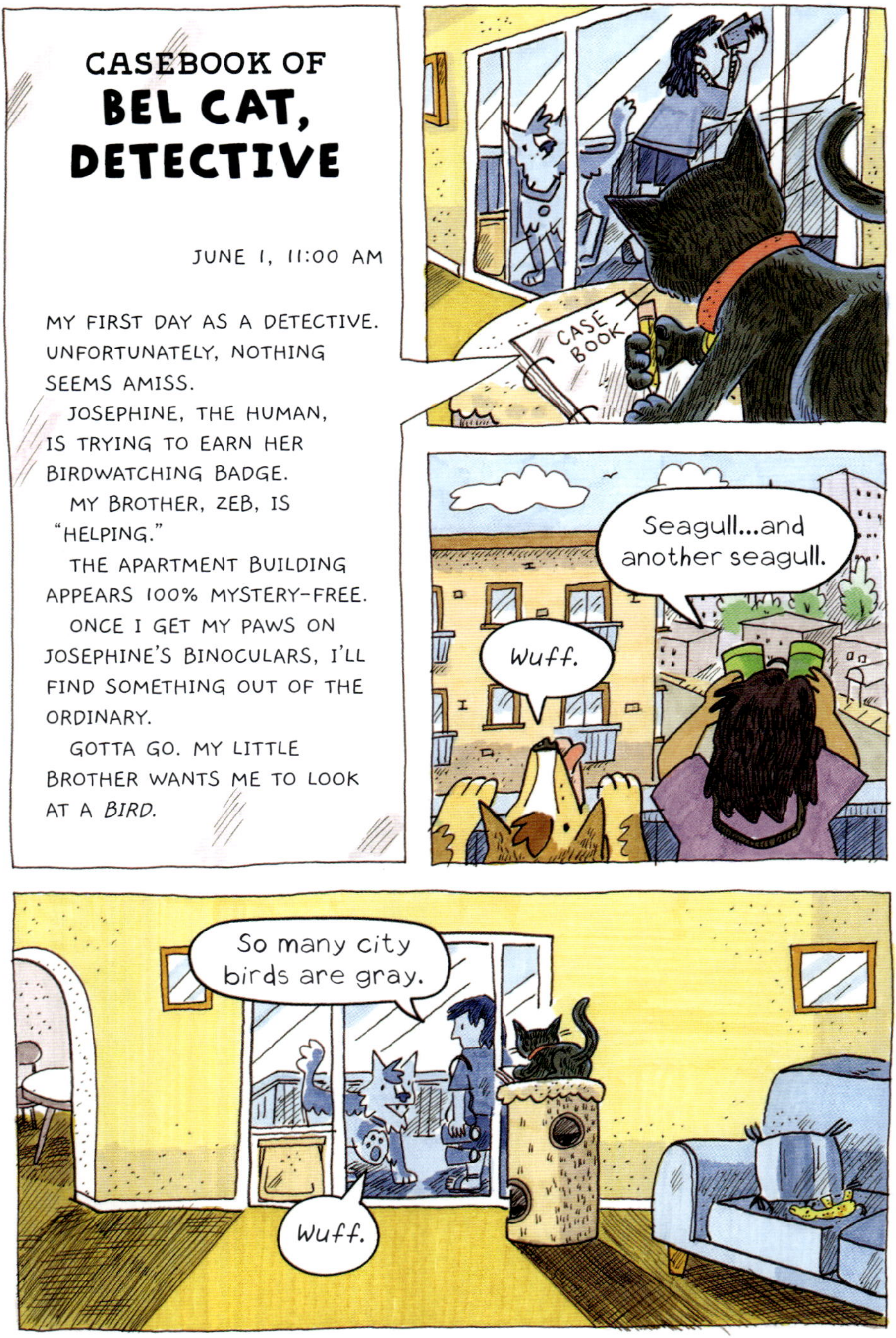
CASEBOOK OF
BEL CAT, DETECTIVE
JUNE 1, 11:00 AM
MY FIRST DAY AS A DETECTIVE. UNFORTUNATELY, NOTHING SEEMS AMISS.
JOSEPHINE, THE HUMAN, IS TRYING TO EARN HER BIRDWATCHING BADGE.
MY BROTHER, ZEB, IS "HELPING."
THE APARTMENT BUILDING APPEARS 100% MYSTERY-FREE.
ONCE I GET MY PAWS ON JOSEPHINE'S BINOCULARS, I'LL FIND SOMETHING OUT OF THE ORDINARY.
GOTTA GO. MY LITTLE BROTHER WANTS ME TO LOOK AT A *BIRD*.
CASE BOOK
Seagull...and another seagull.
Wuff.
So many city birds are gray.
Wuff.

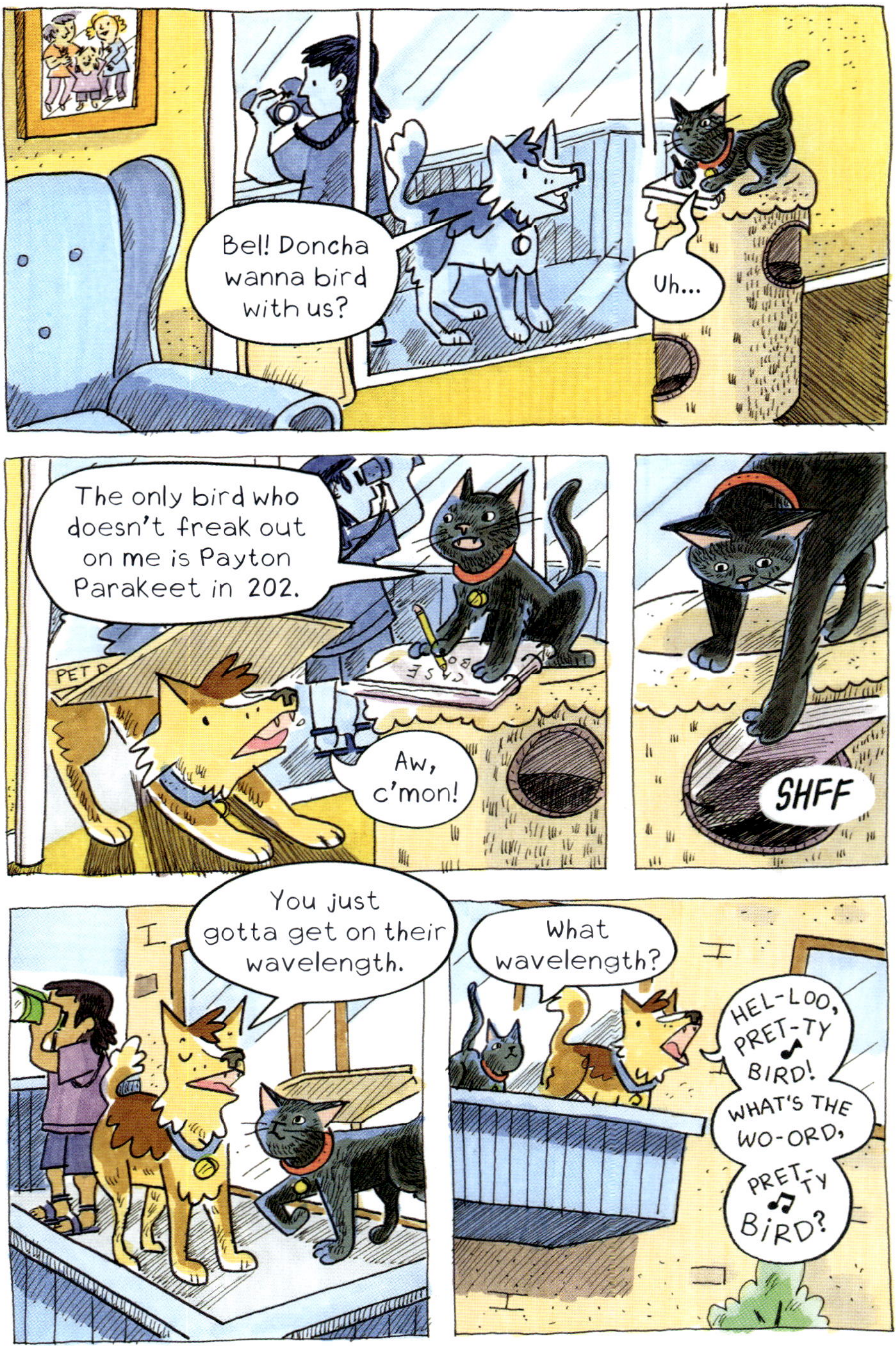
Bel! Doncha wanna bird with us?
Uh...
The only bird who doesn't freak out on me is Payton Parakeet in 202.
Aw, c'mon!
SHFF
You just gotta get on their wavelength.
What wavelength?
HEL-LOO, PRET-TY BIRD! WHAT'S THE WO-ORD, PRET-TY BIRD?

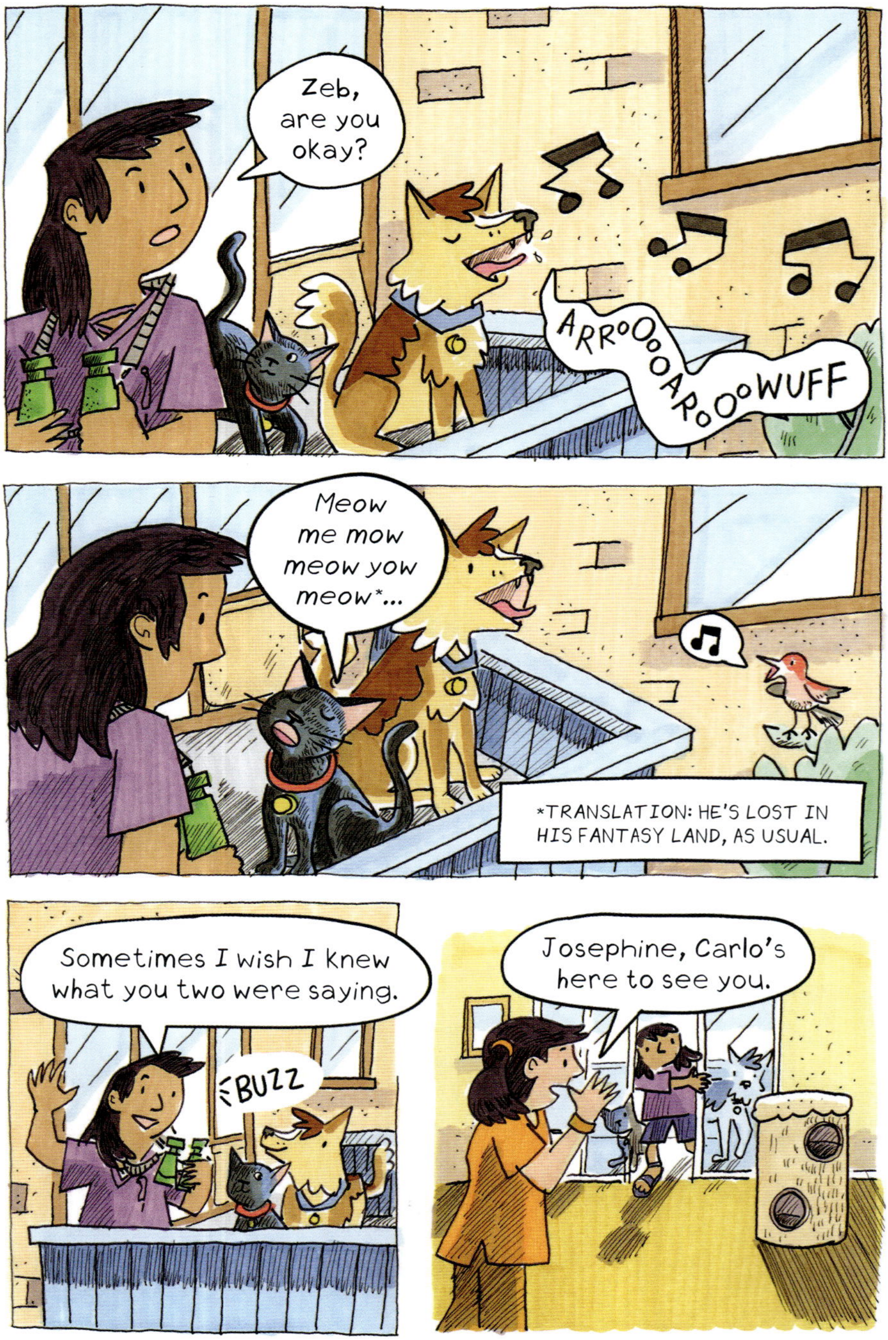
Zeb, are you okay?
ARROOOOAROOOWUFF
Meow me mow meow yow meow*...
*TRANSLATION: HE'S LOST IN HIS FANTASY LAND, AS USUAL.
Sometimes I wish I knew what you two were saying.
BUZZ
Josephine, Carlo's here to see you.

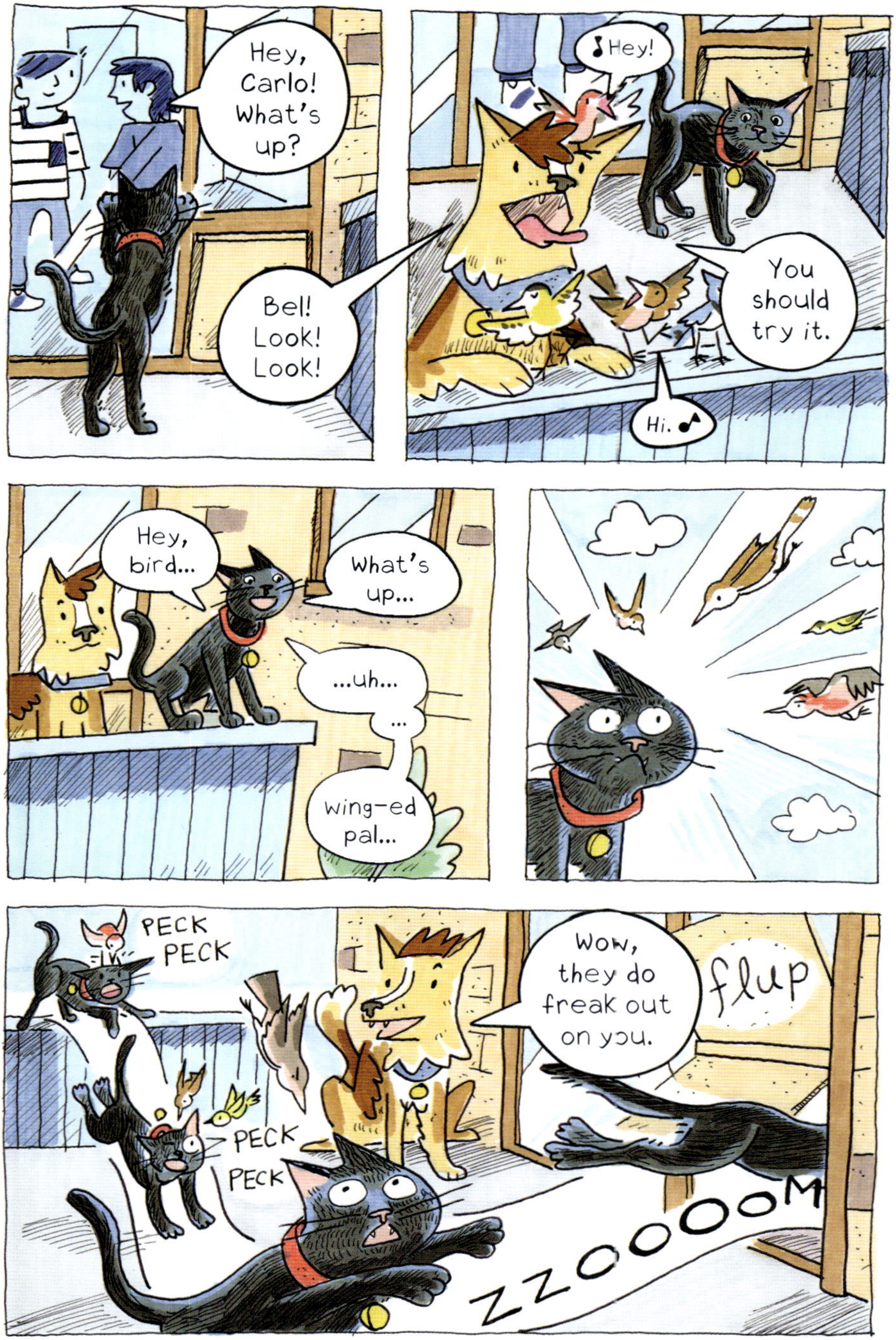
Hey, Carlo! What's up?
Bel! Look! Look!
Hey!
You should try it.
Hi.
Hey, bird...
What's up...
...uh...
...
wing-ed pal...
PECK PECK
PECK PECK
Wow, they do freak out on you.
flup
ZZOOOOOM

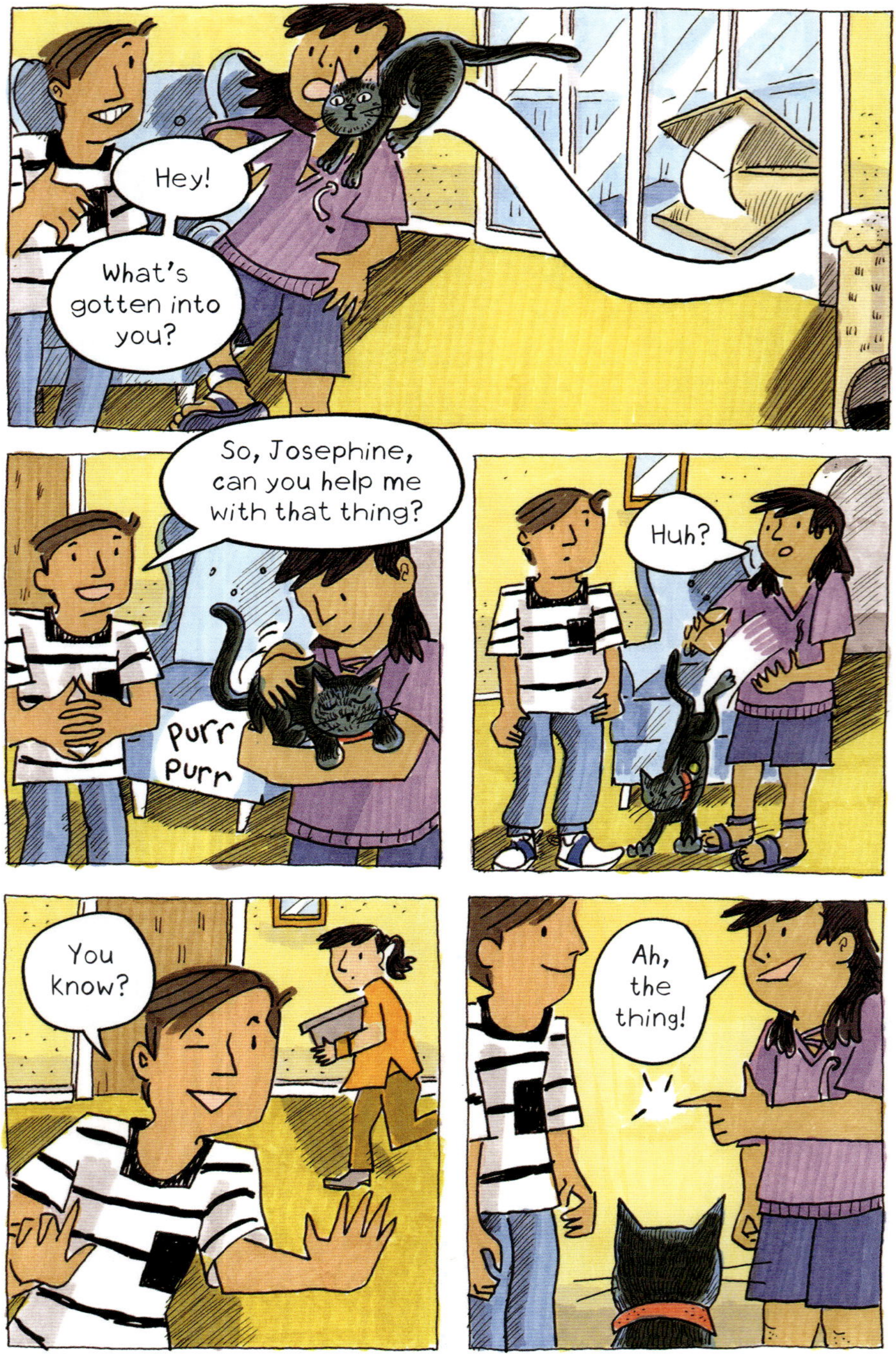
Hey!
What's gotten into you?
So, Josephine, can you help me with that thing?
purr purr
Huh?
You know?
Ah, the thing!

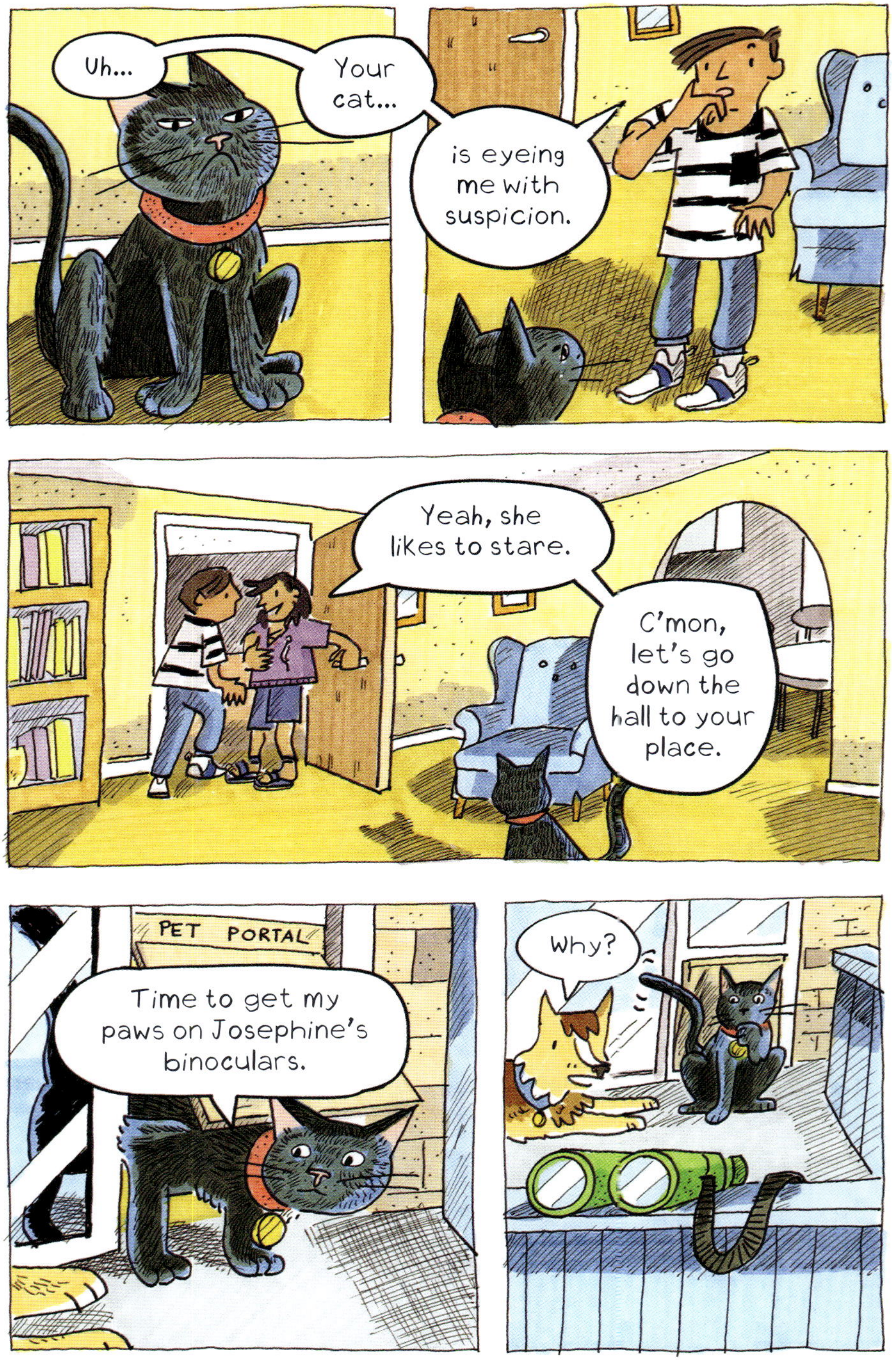
Uh...
Your cat...
is eyeing me with suspicion.
Yeah, she likes to stare.
C'mon, let's go down the hall to your place.
PET PORTAL
Time to get my paws on Josephine's binoculars.
Why?

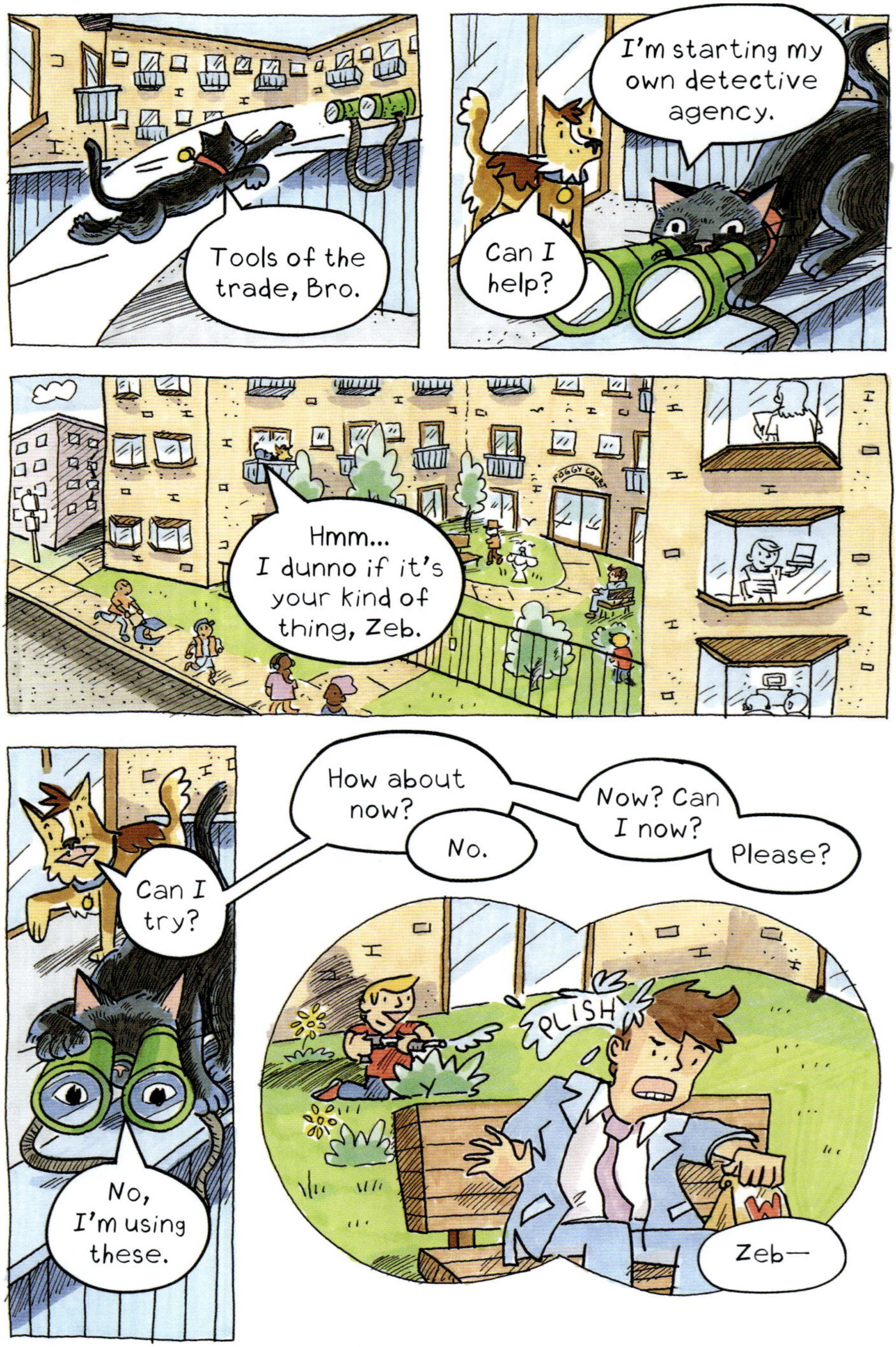
Tools of the trade, Bro.
I'm starting my own detective agency.
Can I help?
Hmm... I dunno if it's your kind of thing, Zeb.
FOGGY COURT
Can I try?
How about now?
No.
Now? Can I now?
Please?
No, I'm using these.
PLISH
Zeb—

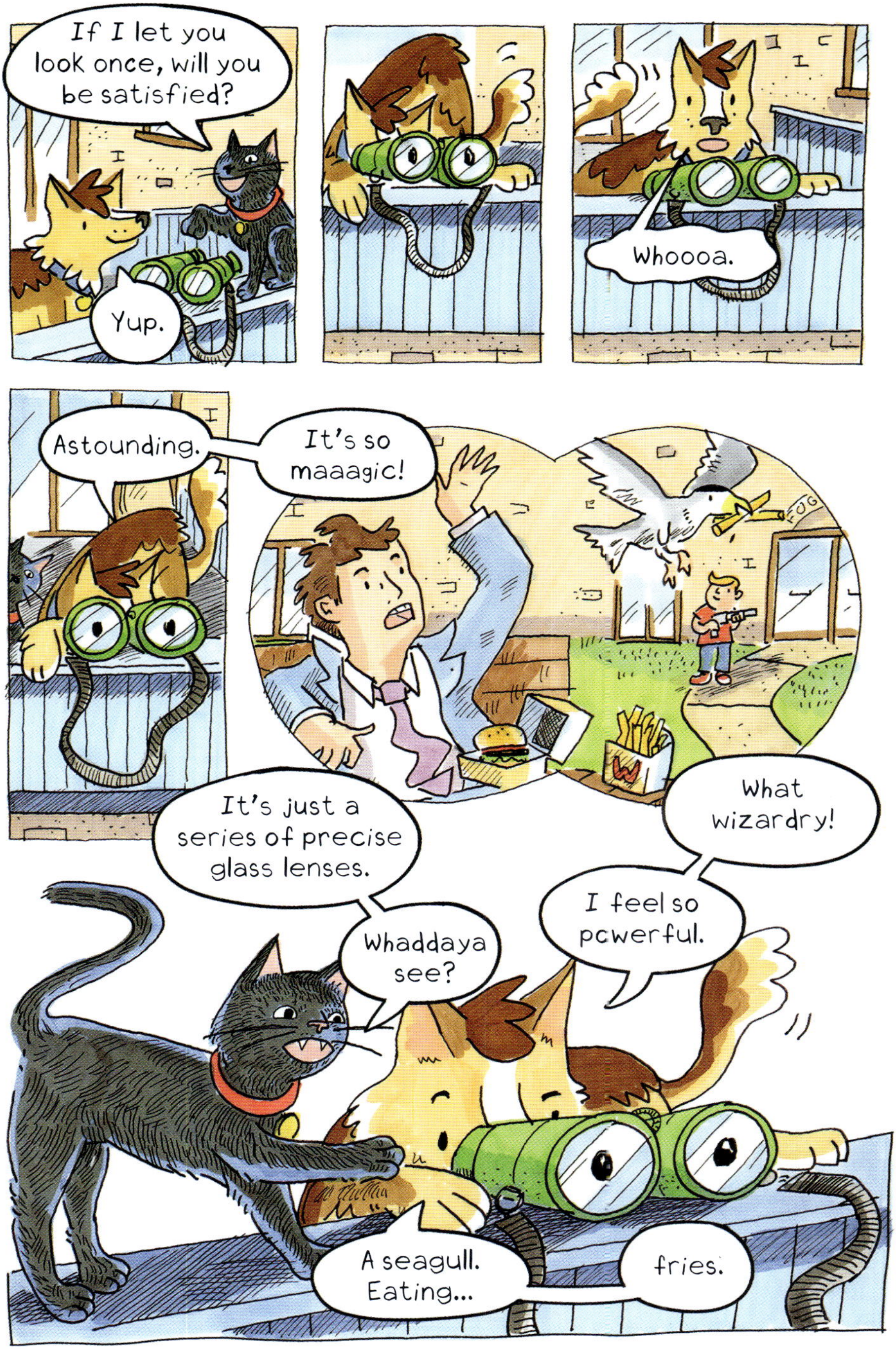
If I let you look once, will you be satisfied?
Yup.
Whoooa.
Astounding.
It's so maaagic!
FOG
It's just a series of precise glass lenses.
Whaddaya see?
What wizardry!
I feel so powerful.
A seagull. Eating...
fries.

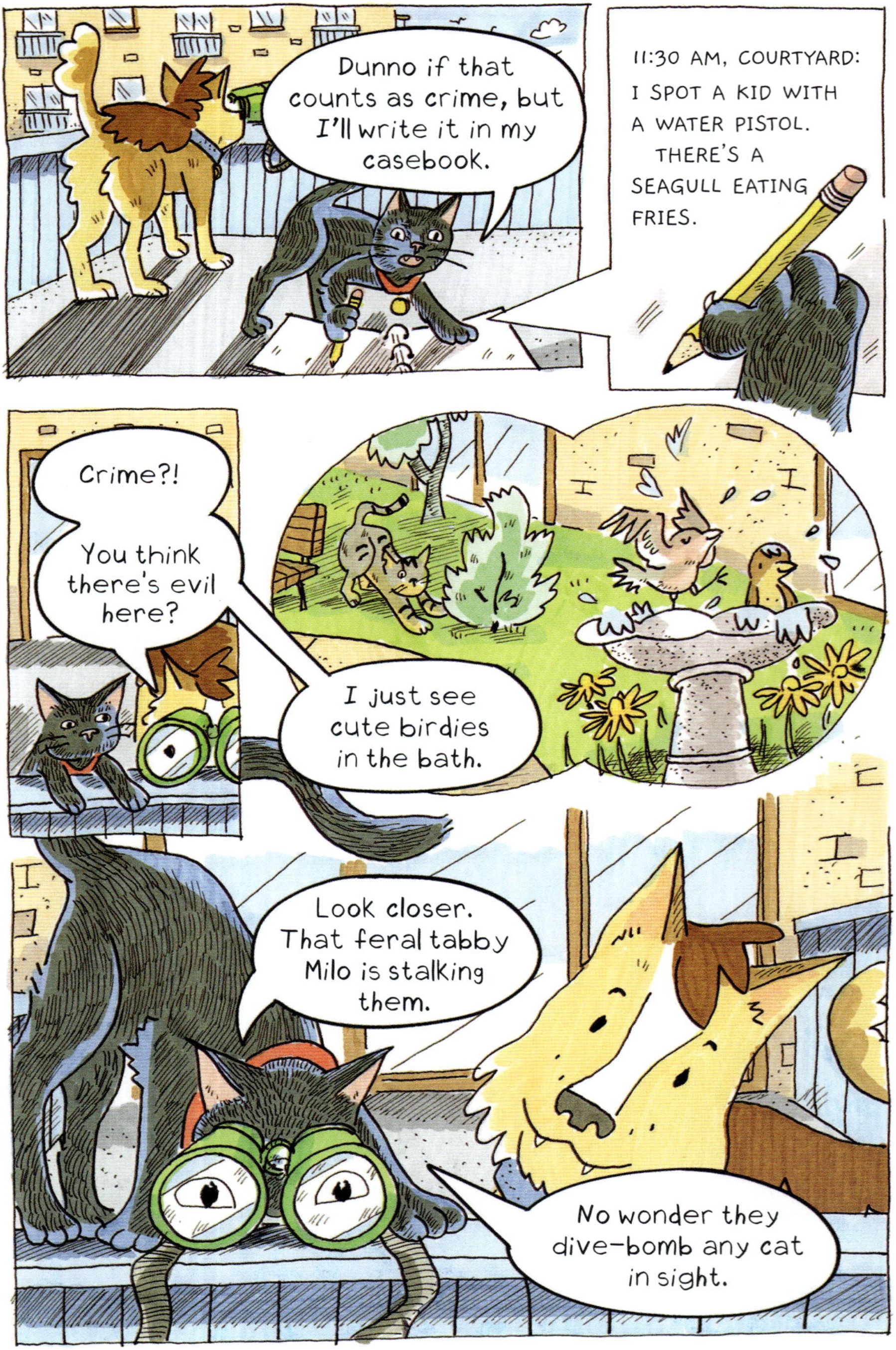
Dunno if that counts as crime, but I'll write it in my casebook.
11:30 AM, COURTYARD: I SPOT A KID WITH A WATER PISTOL. THERE'S A SEAGULL EATING FRIES.
Crime?!
You think there's evil here?
I just see cute birdies in the bath.
Look closer. That feral tabby Milo is stalking them.
No wonder they dive-bomb any cat in sight.

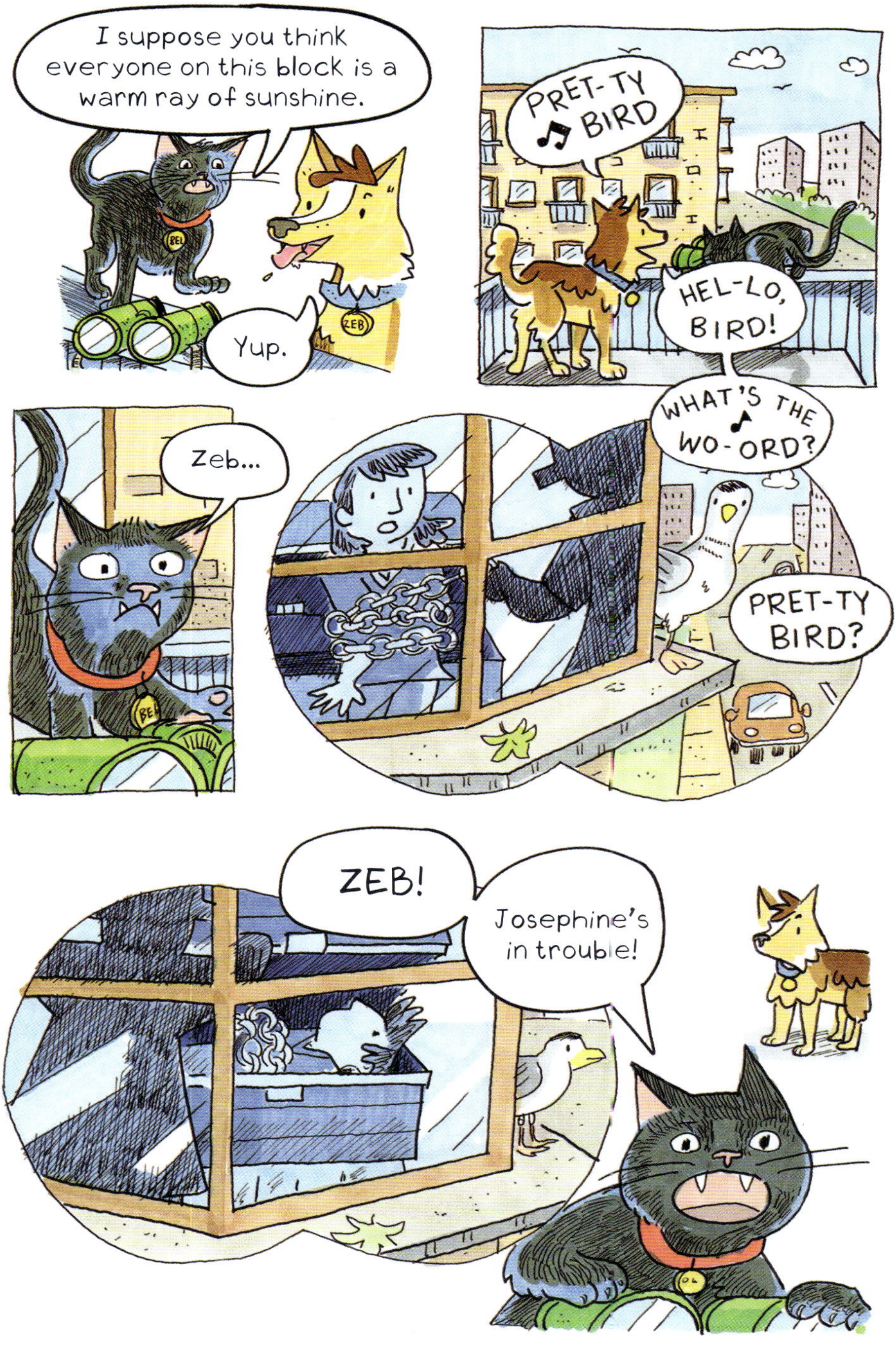
I suppose you think everyone on this block is a warm ray of sunshine.
Yup.
PRET-TY BIRD
HEL-LO, BIRD!
WHAT'S THE WO-ORD?
Zeb...
PRET-TY BIRD?
ZEB!
Josephine's in trouble!

CHAPTER 2
ZEB BELIEVES IN MAGIC

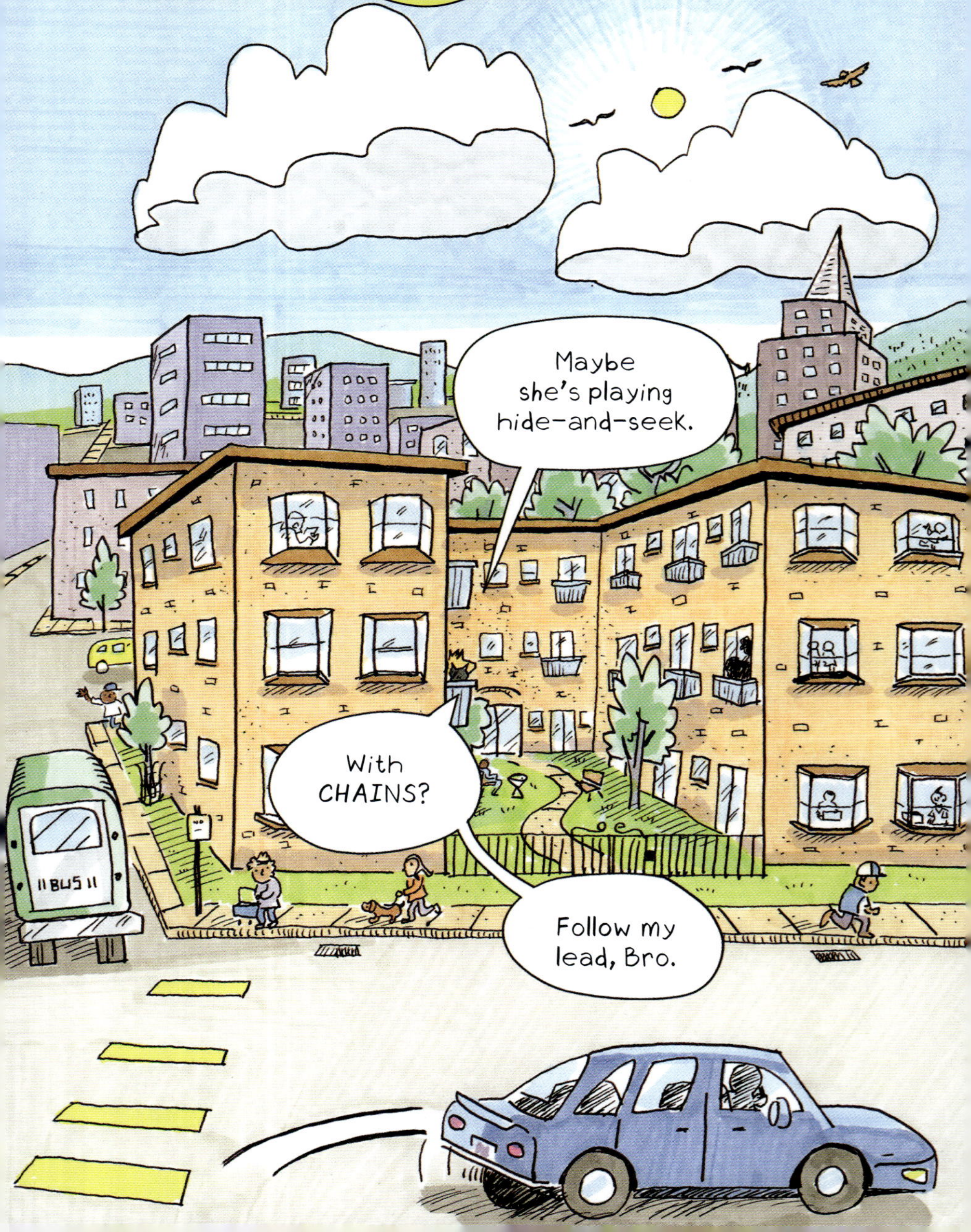
Maybe she's playing hide-and-seek.
With CHAINS?
Follow my lead, Bro.
"BUS"

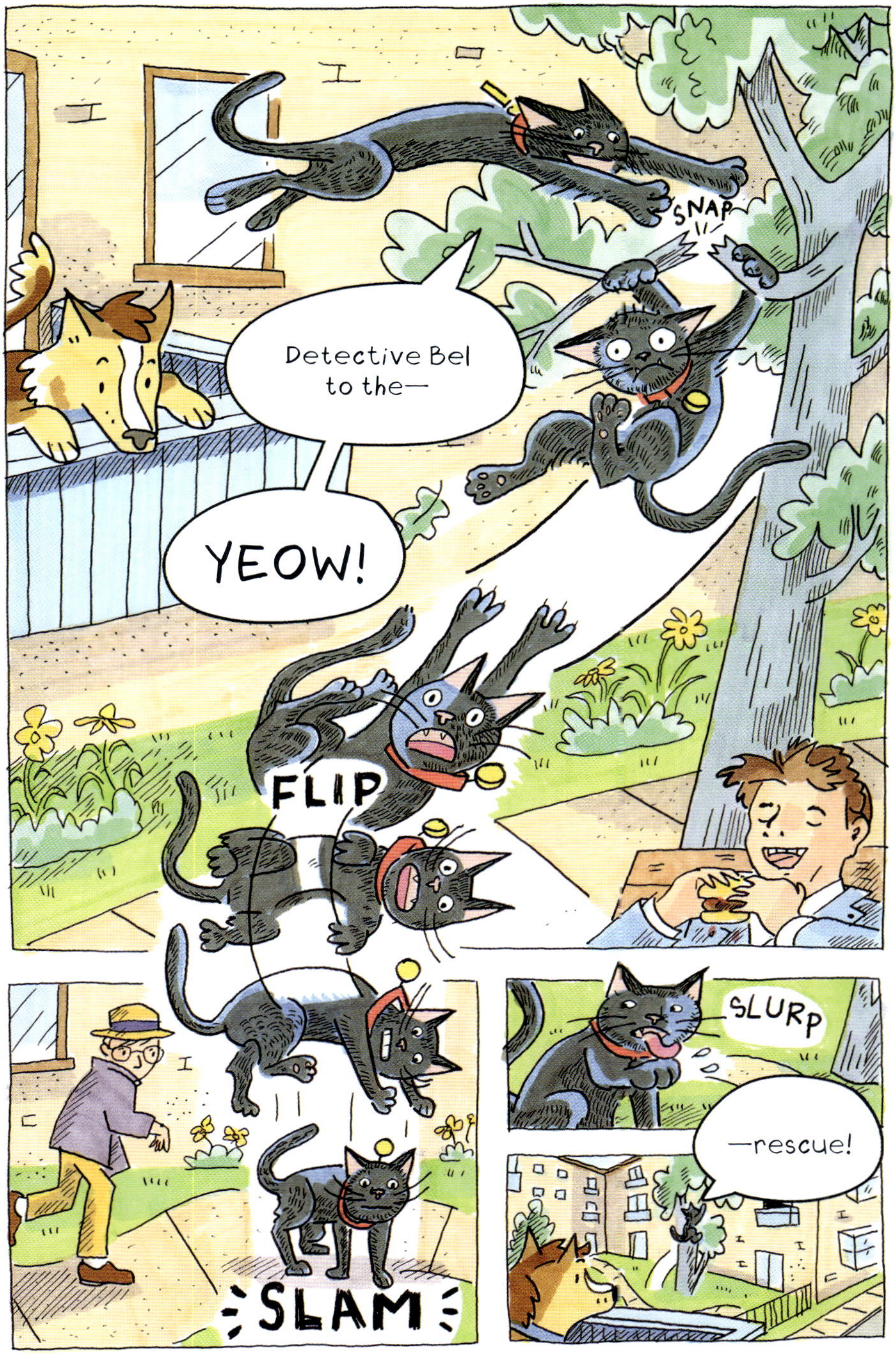
SNAP
Detective Bel to the—
YEOW!
FLIP
SLAM
SLURP
—rescue!

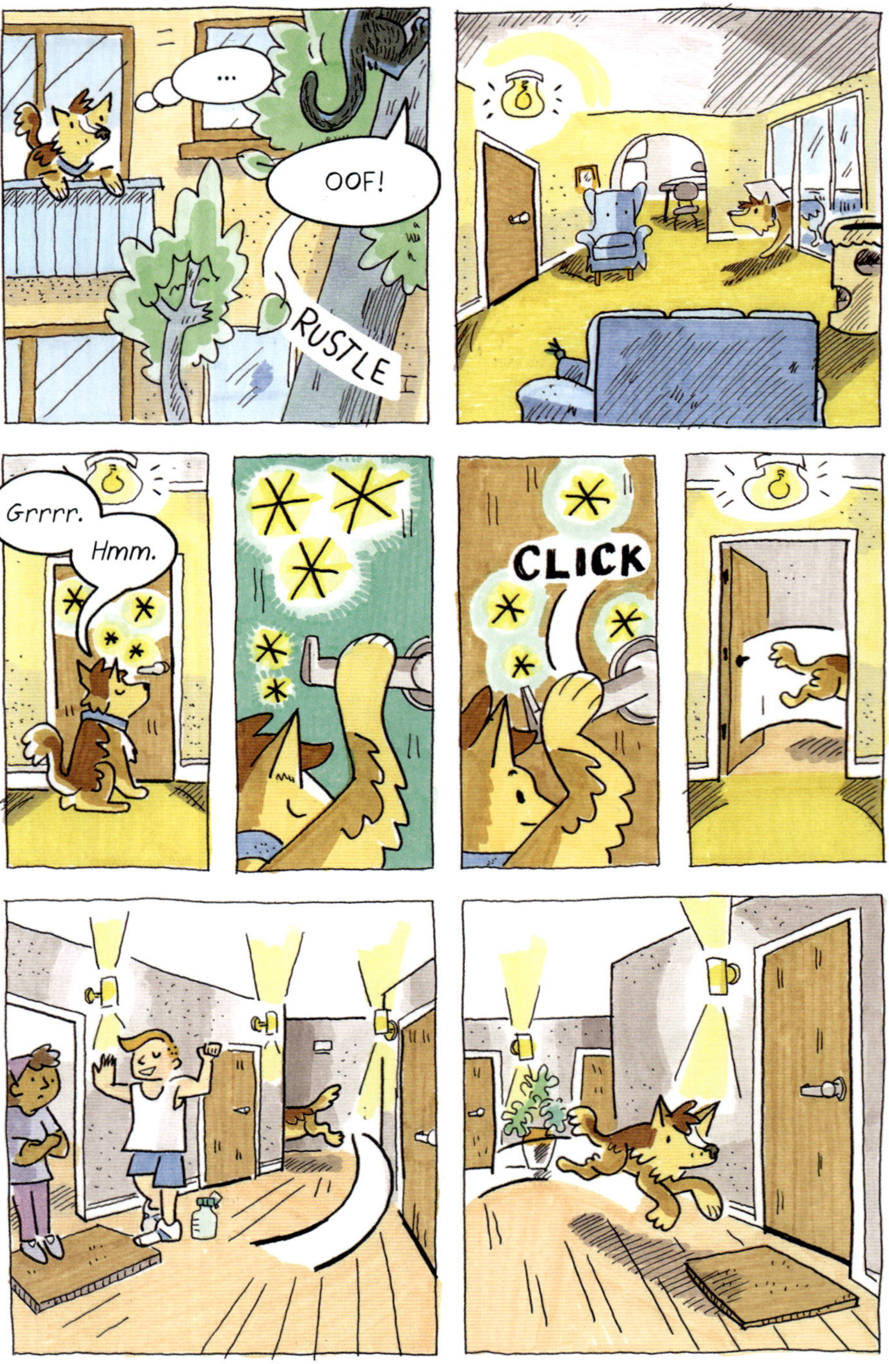
...
OOF!
RUSTLE
Grrrr.
Hmm.
CLICK

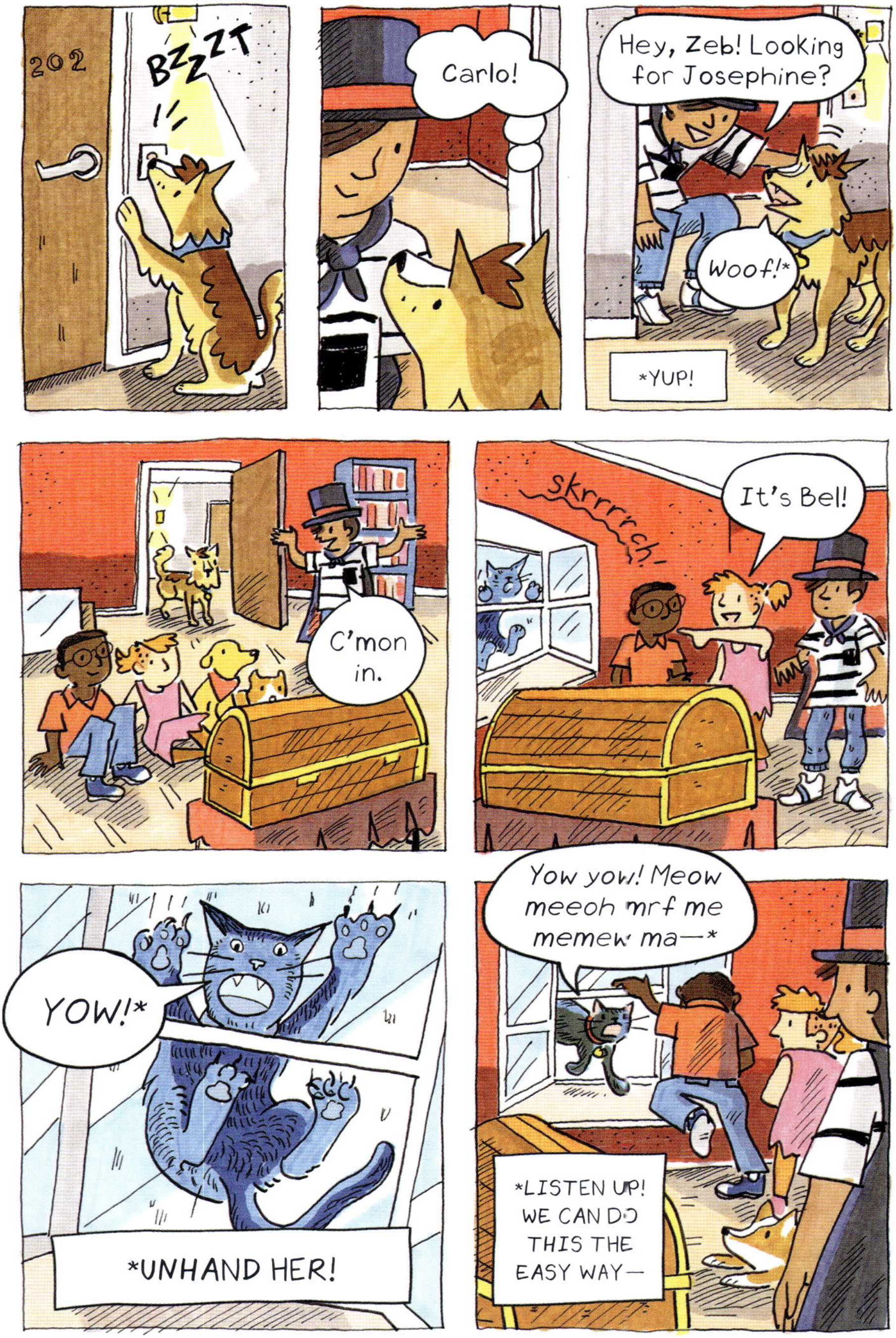
202
BZZZT
Carlo!
Hey, Zeb! Looking for Josephine?
Woof!*
*YUP!
C'mon in.
Skrrrrrch!
It's Bel!
YOW!*
*UNHAND HER!
Yow yow! Meow meeoh mrf me memew ma—*
*LISTEN UP! WE CAN DO THIS THE EASY WAY—

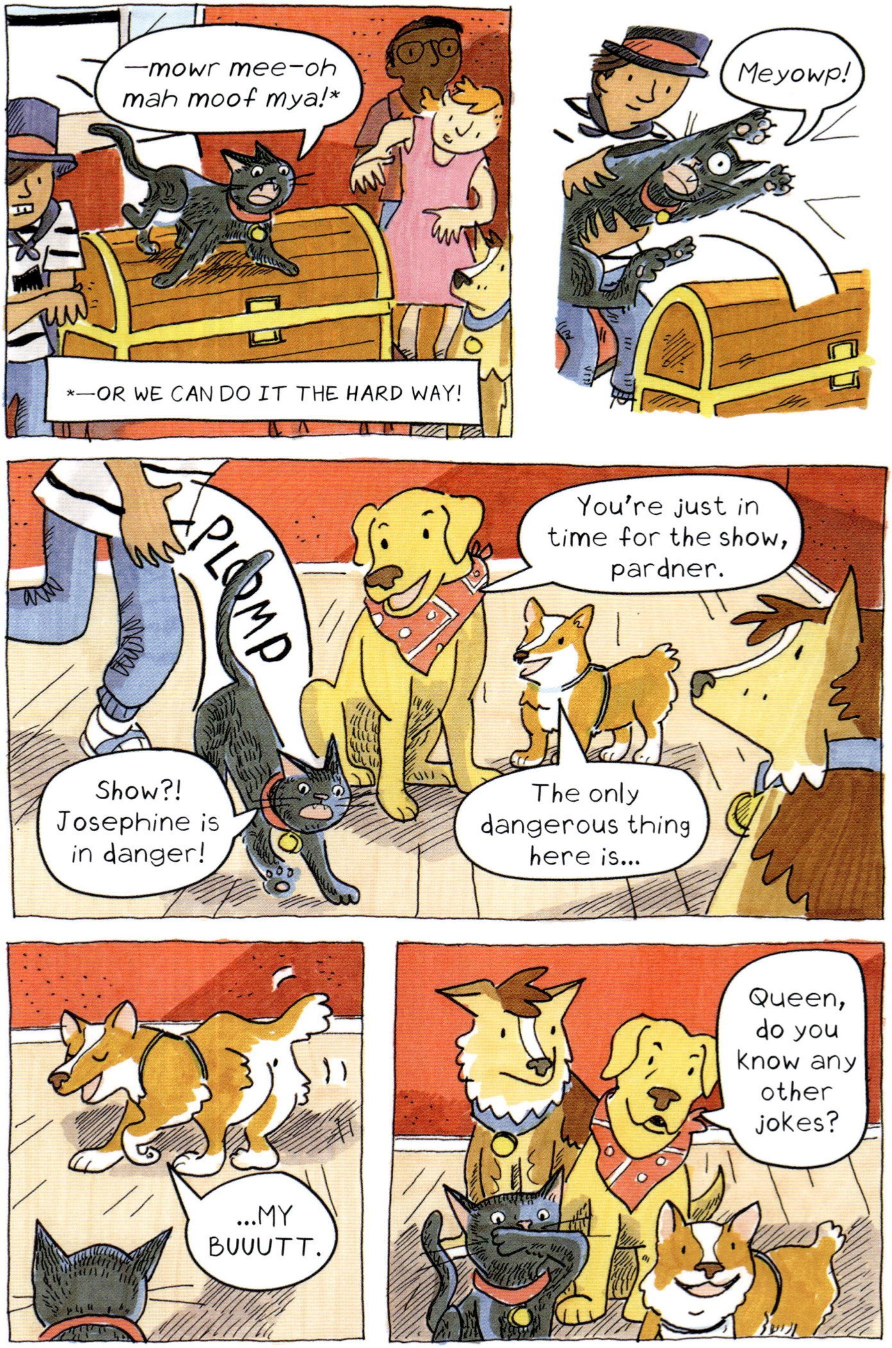
—mowr mee-oh mah moof mya!*
*—OR WE CAN DO IT THE HARD WAY!
Meyowp!
PLOMP
You're just in time for the show, pardner.
Show?! Josephine is in danger!
The only dangerous thing here is...
...MY BUUUTT.
Queen, do you know any other jokes?

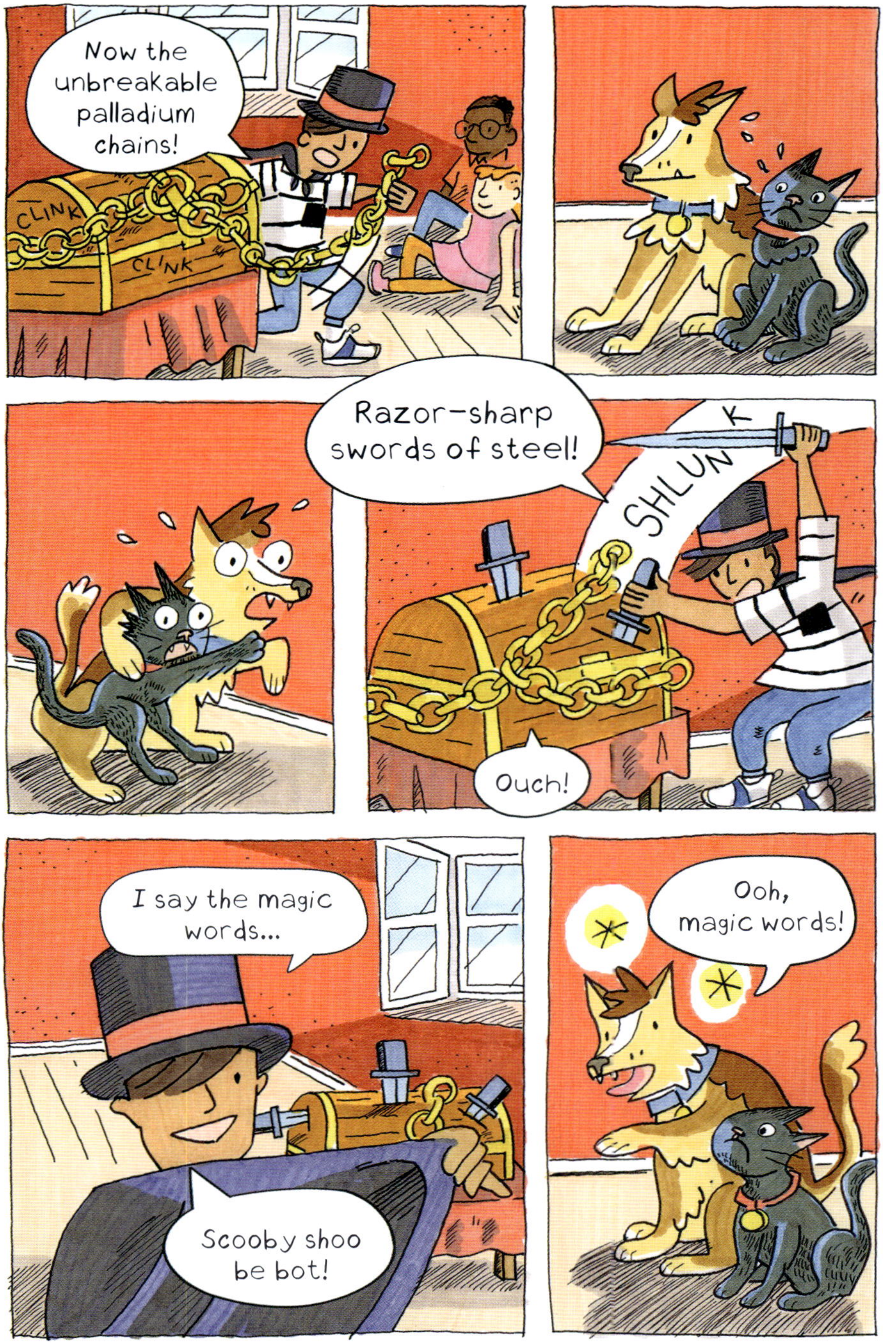

Now the unbreakable palladium chains!
CLINK
CLINK
Razor-sharp swords of steel!
SHLUNK
Ouch!
I say the magic words...
Scooby shoo be bot!
Ooh, magic words!

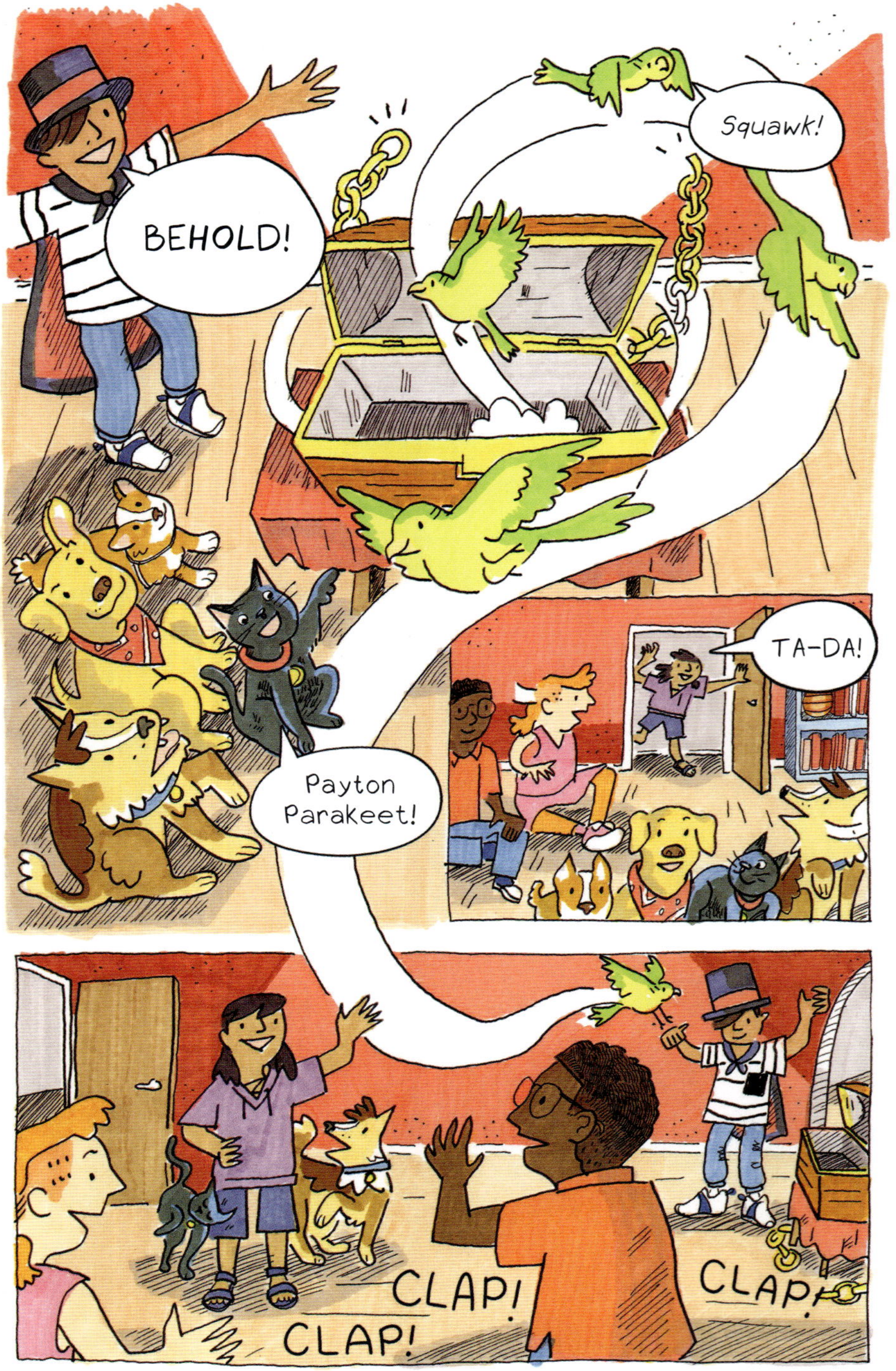
BEHOLD!
Squawk!
Payton Parakeet!
TA-DA!
CLAP!
CLAP!
CLAP!

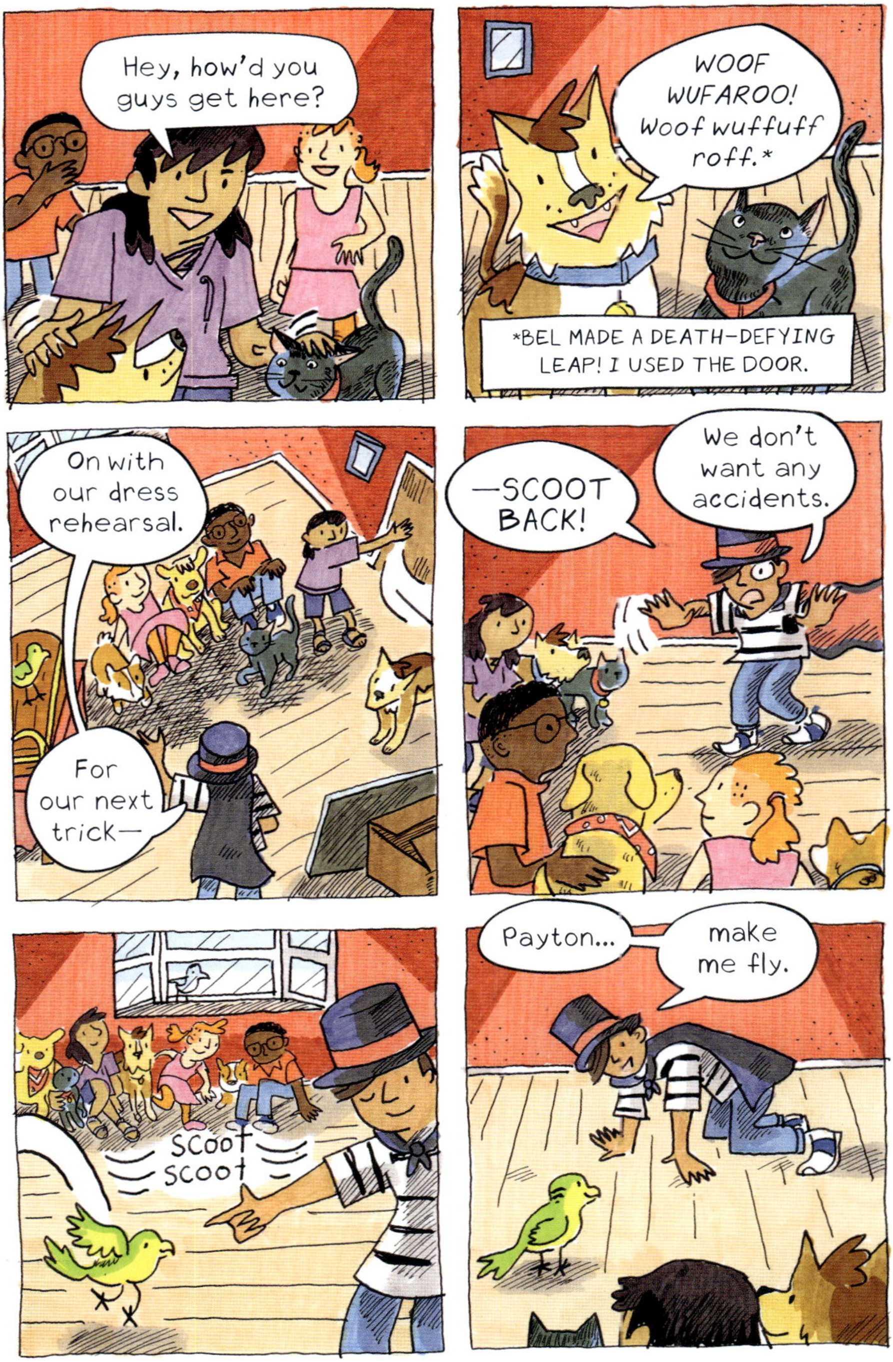
Hey, how'd you guys get here?
WOOF WUFAROO! Woof wuffuff roff.*
*BEL MADE A DEATH-DEFYING LEAP! I USED THE DOOR.
On with our dress rehearsal.
For our next trick—
—SCOOT BACK!
We don't want any accidents.
SCOOT SCOOT
Payton...
make me fly.

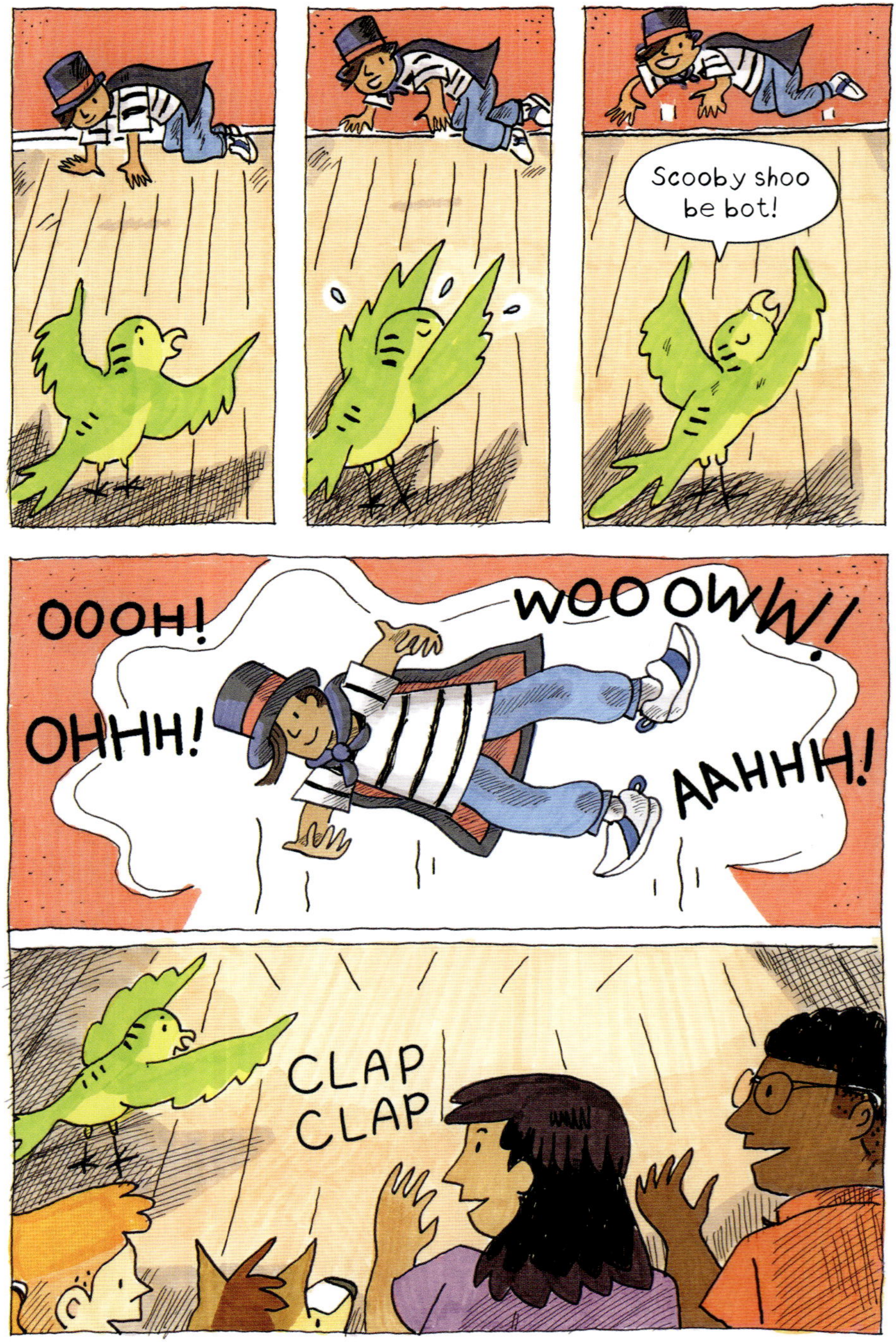
Scooby shoo be bot!
OOOH!
WOOOWW!
OHHH!
AAHHH!
CLAP CLAP

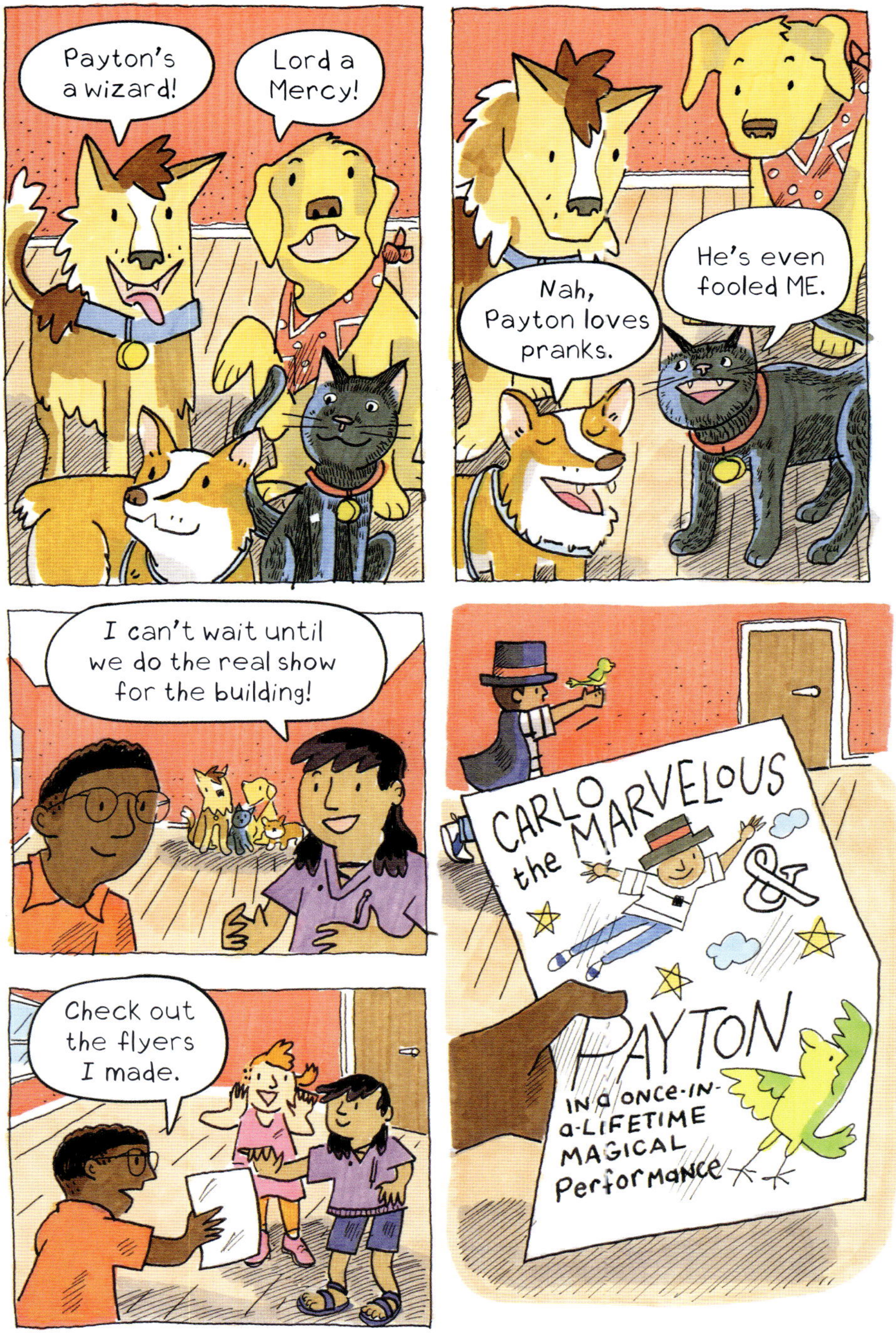
Payton's a wizard!
Lord a Mercy!
Nah, Payton loves pranks.
He's even fooled ME.
I can't wait until we do the real show for the building!
Check out the flyers I made.
CARLO the MARVELOUS &
PAYTON
IN a ONCE-IN-a-LIFETIME MAGICAL Performance

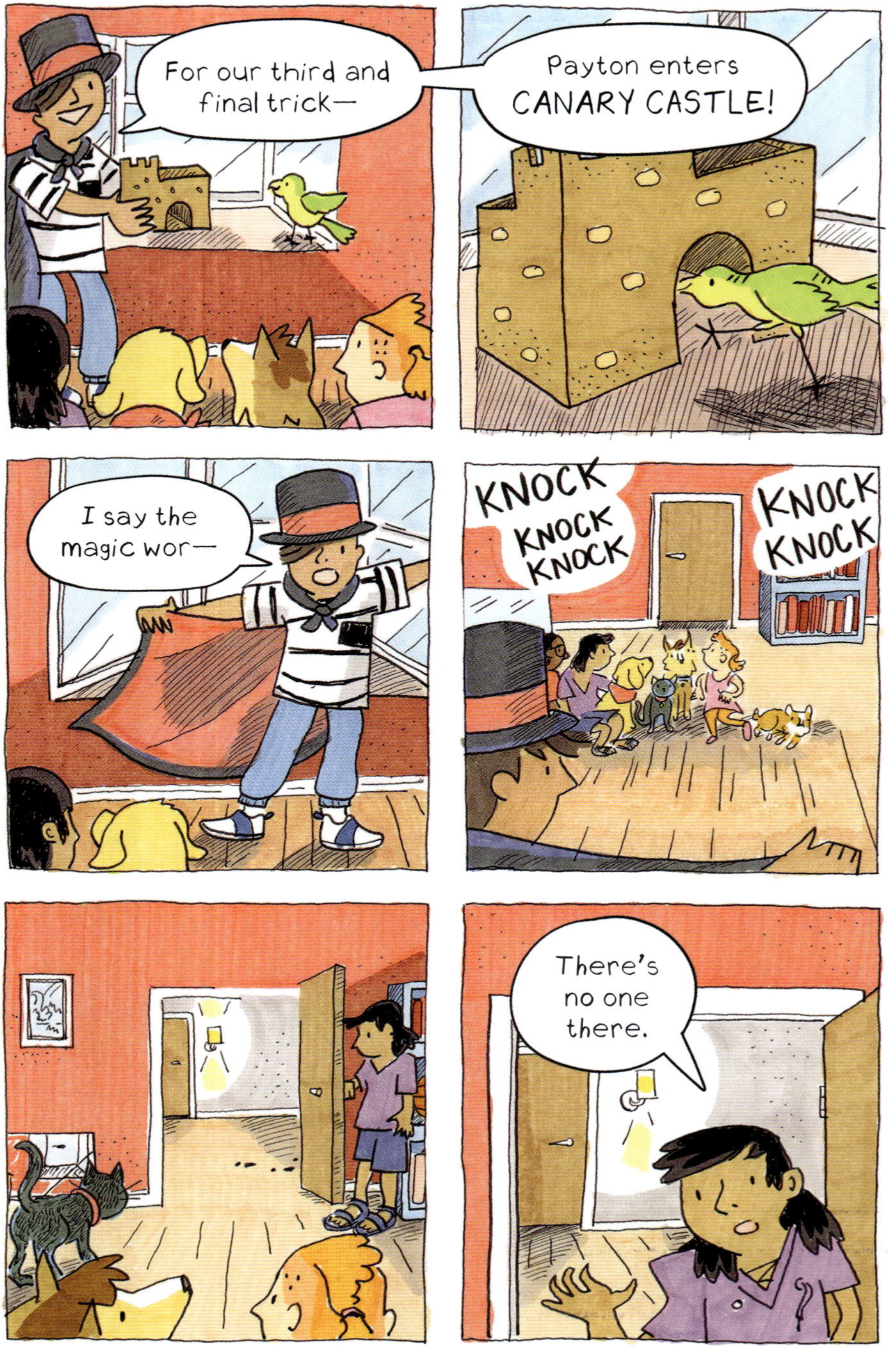
For our third and final trick—
Payton enters CANARY CASTLE!
I say the magic wor—
KNOCK KNOCK KNOCK
KNOCK KNOCK
There's no one there.

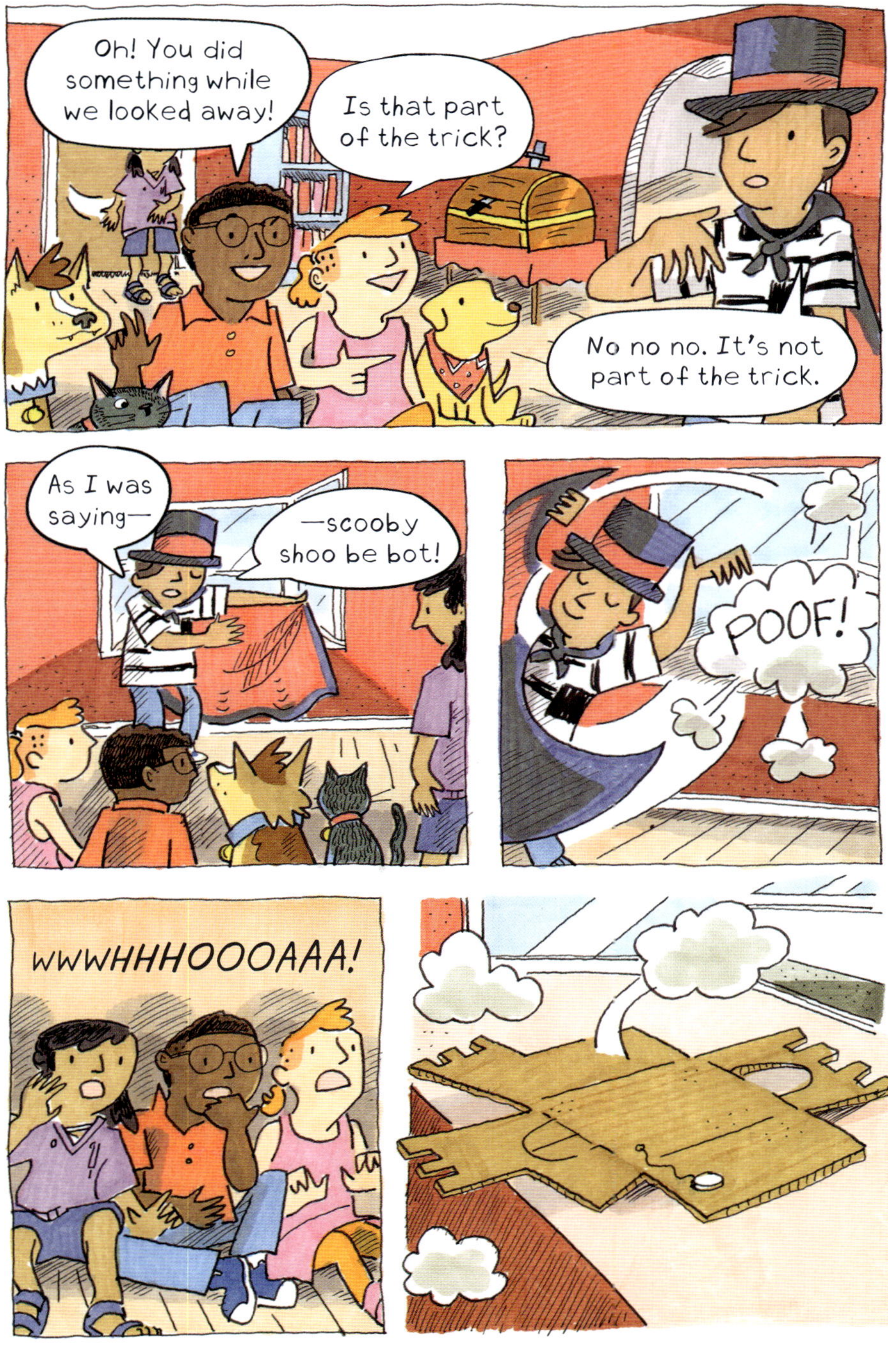
Oh! You did something while we looked away!
Is that part of the trick?
No no no. It's not part of the trick.
As I was saying—
—scooby shoo be bot!
POOF!
WWWHHHOOOAAA!

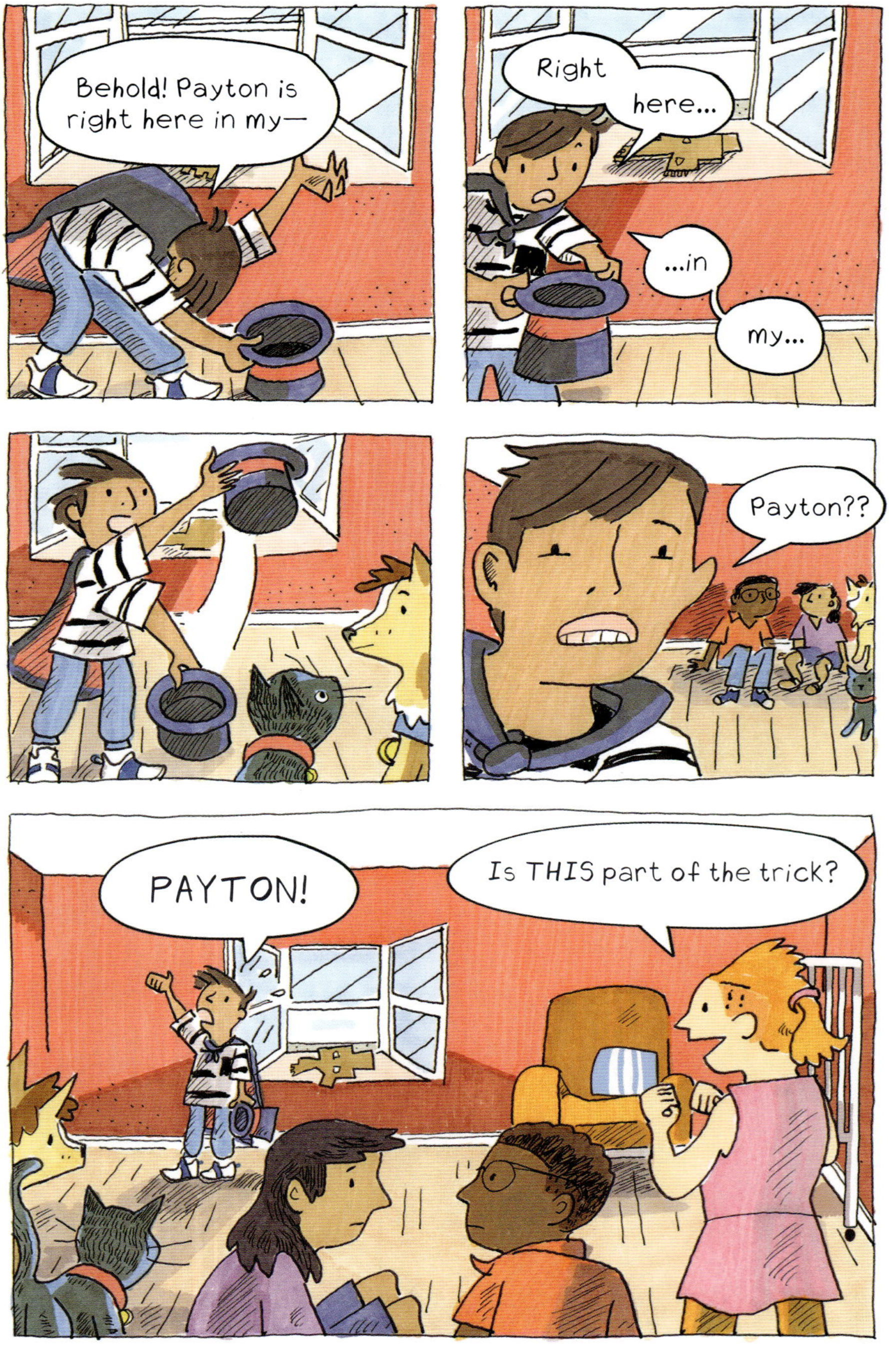
Behold! Payton is right here in my—
Right
here...
...in
my...
Payton??
PAYTON!
Is THIS part of the trick?

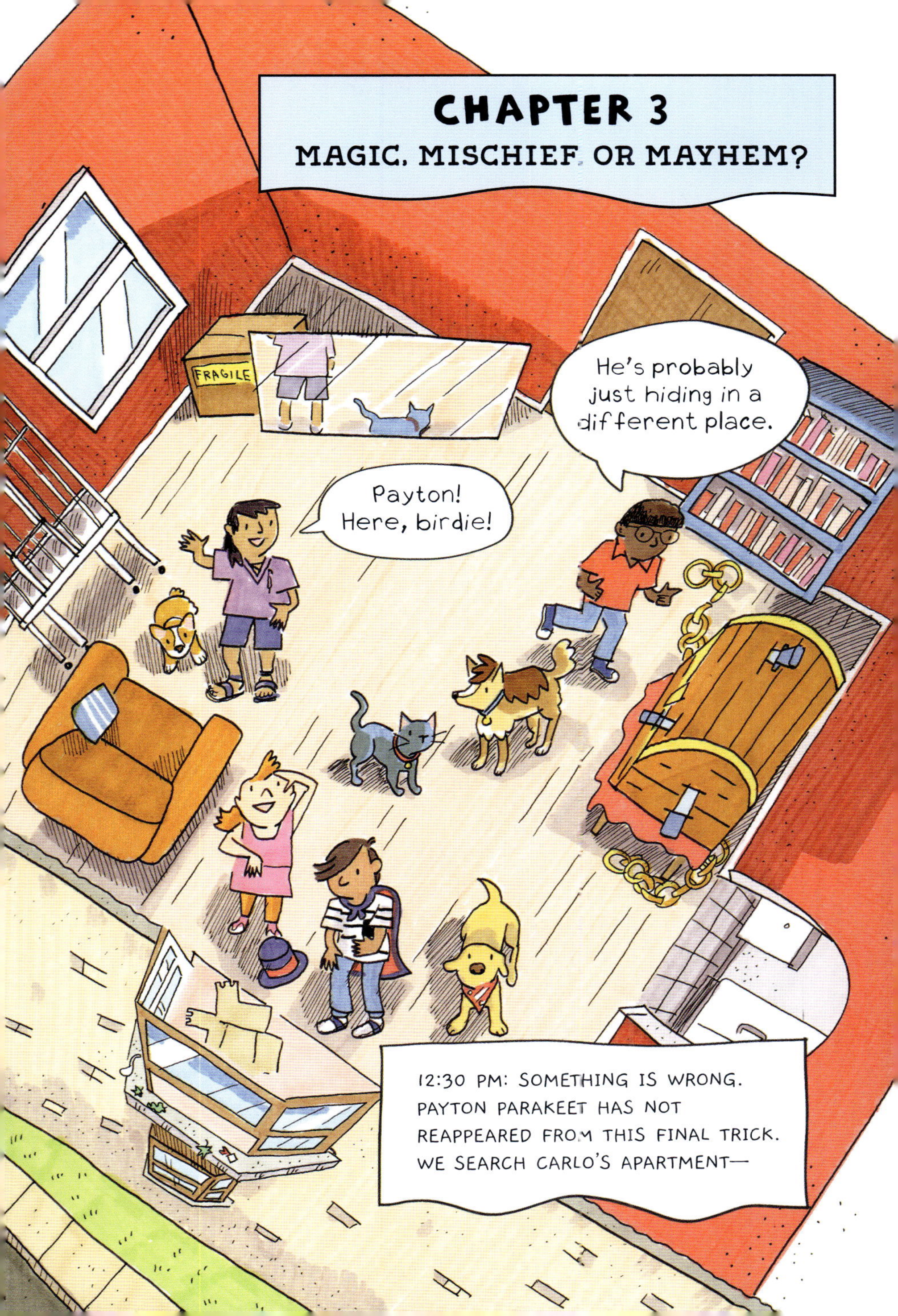
CHAPTER 3
MAGIC, MISCHIEF, OR MAYHEM?
FRAGILE
Payton! Here, birdie!
He's probably just hiding in a different place.
12:30 PM: SOMETHING IS WRONG. PAYTON PARAKEET HAS NOT REAPPEARED FROM THIS FINAL TRICK. WE SEARCH CARLO'S APARTMENT—

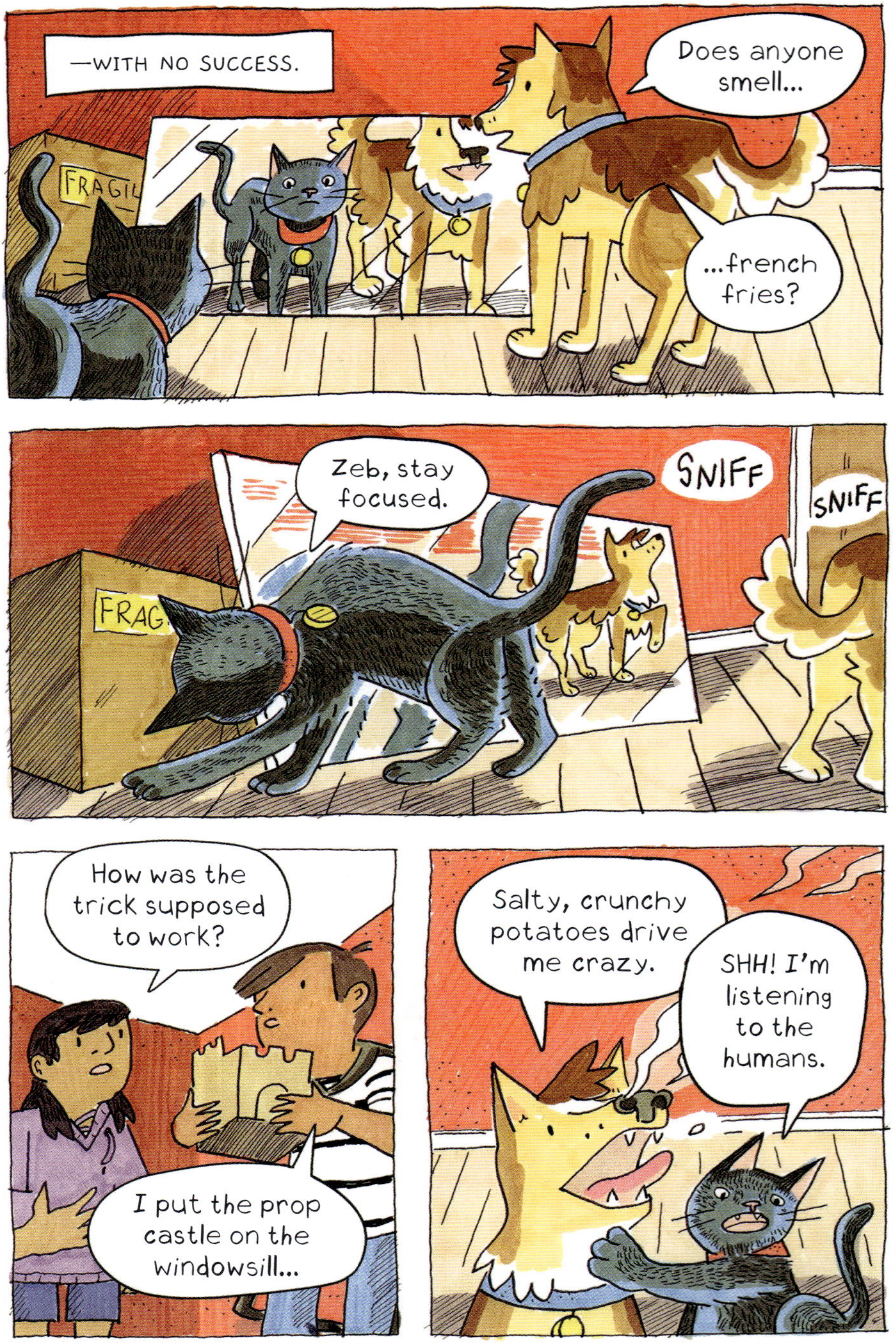
—WITH NO SUCCESS.
Does anyone smell...
...french fries?
FRAGIL
Zeb, stay focused.
SNIFF
SNIFF
FRAG
How was the trick supposed to work?
I put the prop castle on the windowsill...
Salty, crunchy potatoes drive me crazy.
SHH! I'm listening to the humans.

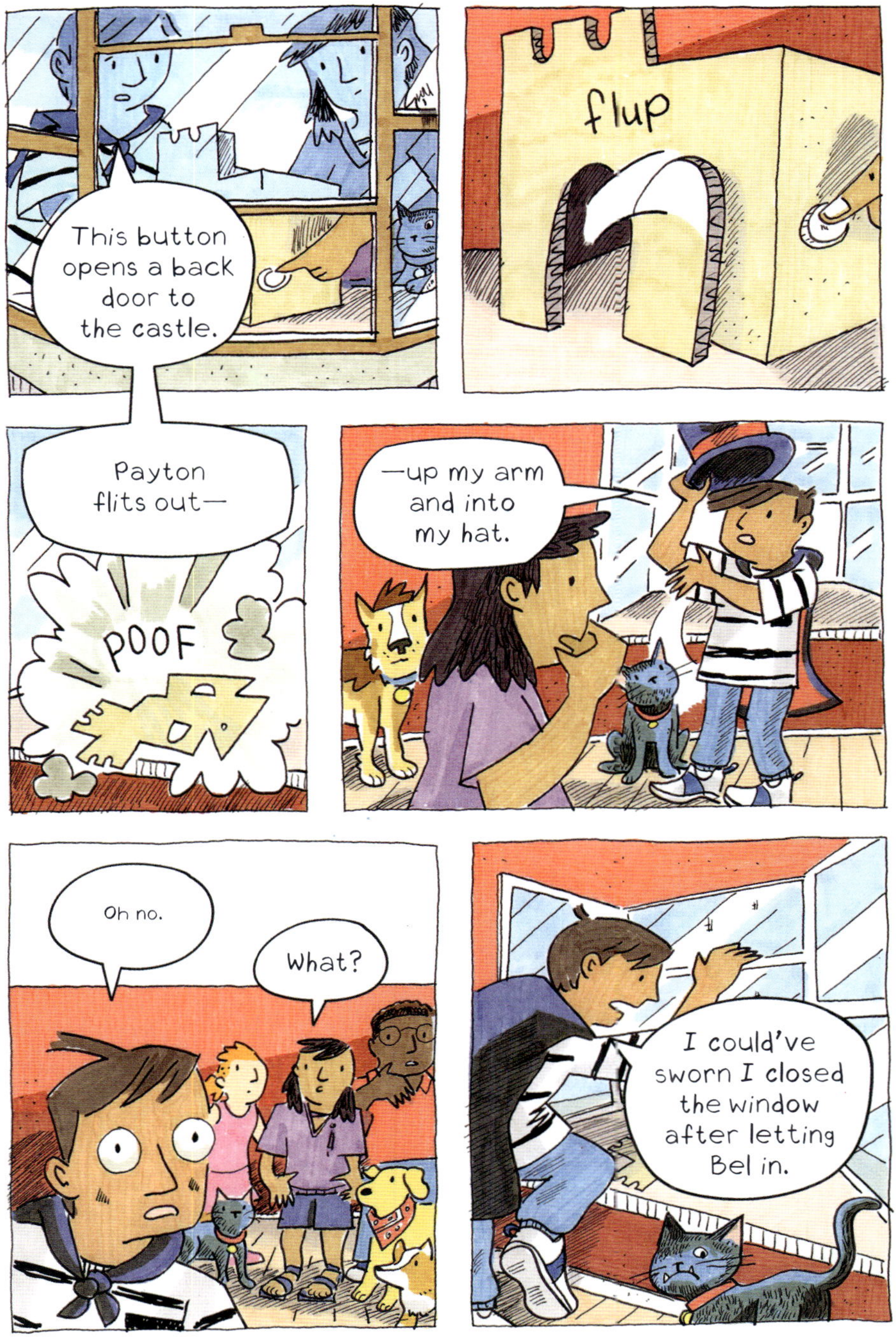
This button opens a back door to the castle.
flup
Payton flits out—
POOF
—up my arm and into my hat.
Oh no.
What?
I could've sworn I closed the window after letting Bel in.

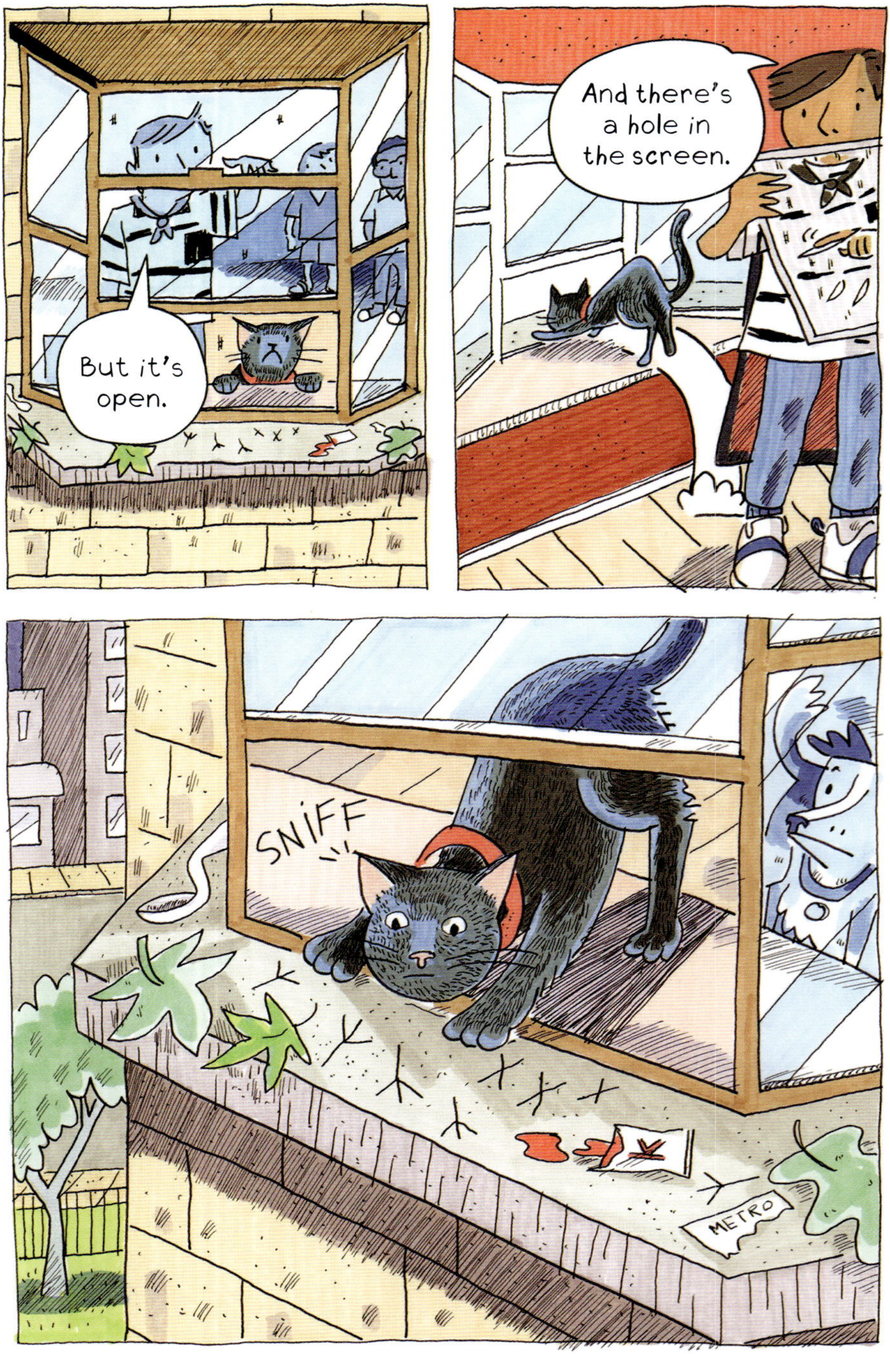
But it's open.
And there's a hole in the screen.
SNIFF
METRO

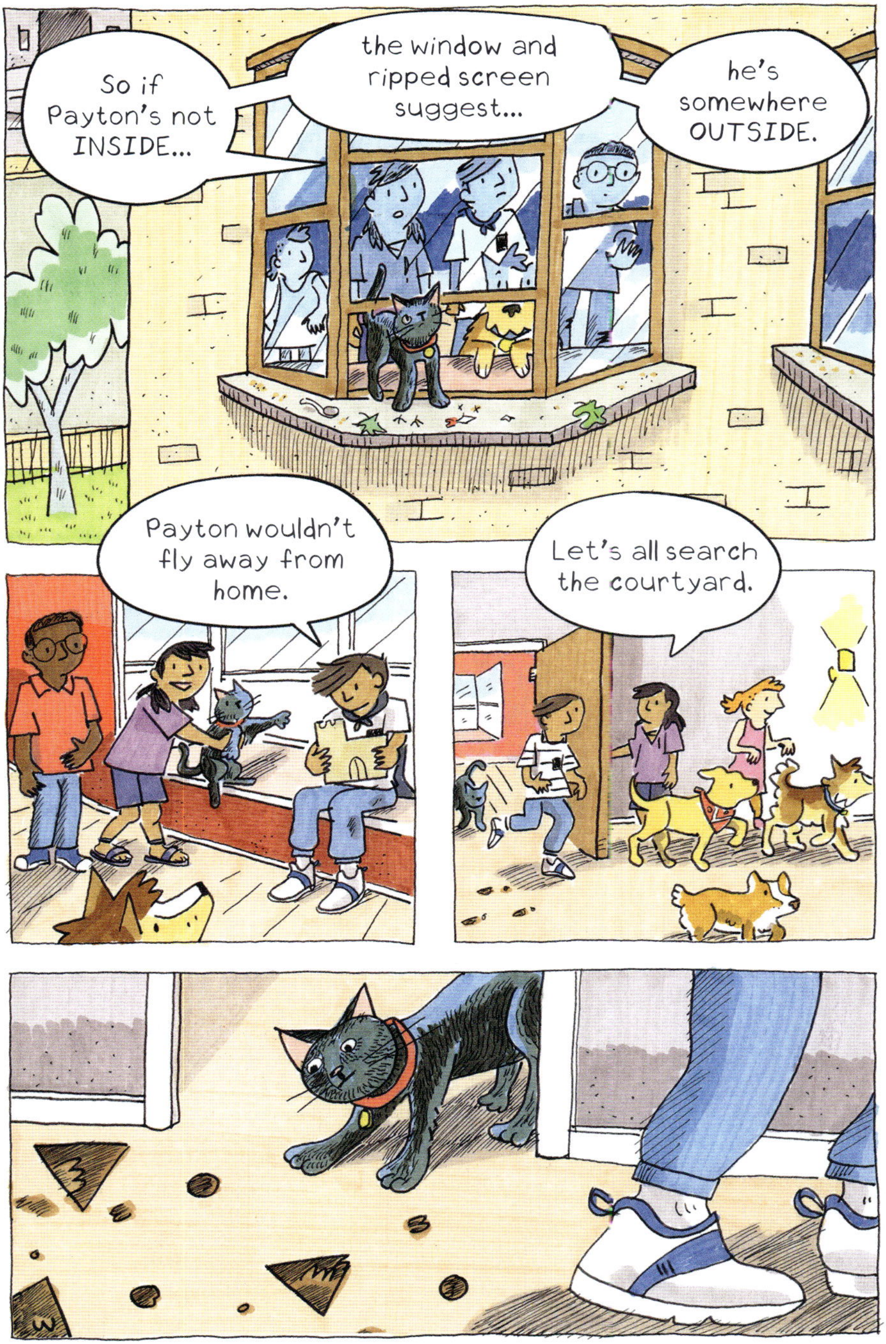
So if Payton's not INSIDE...
the window and ripped screen suggest...
he's somewhere OUTSIDE.
Payton wouldn't fly away from home.
Let's all search the courtyard.

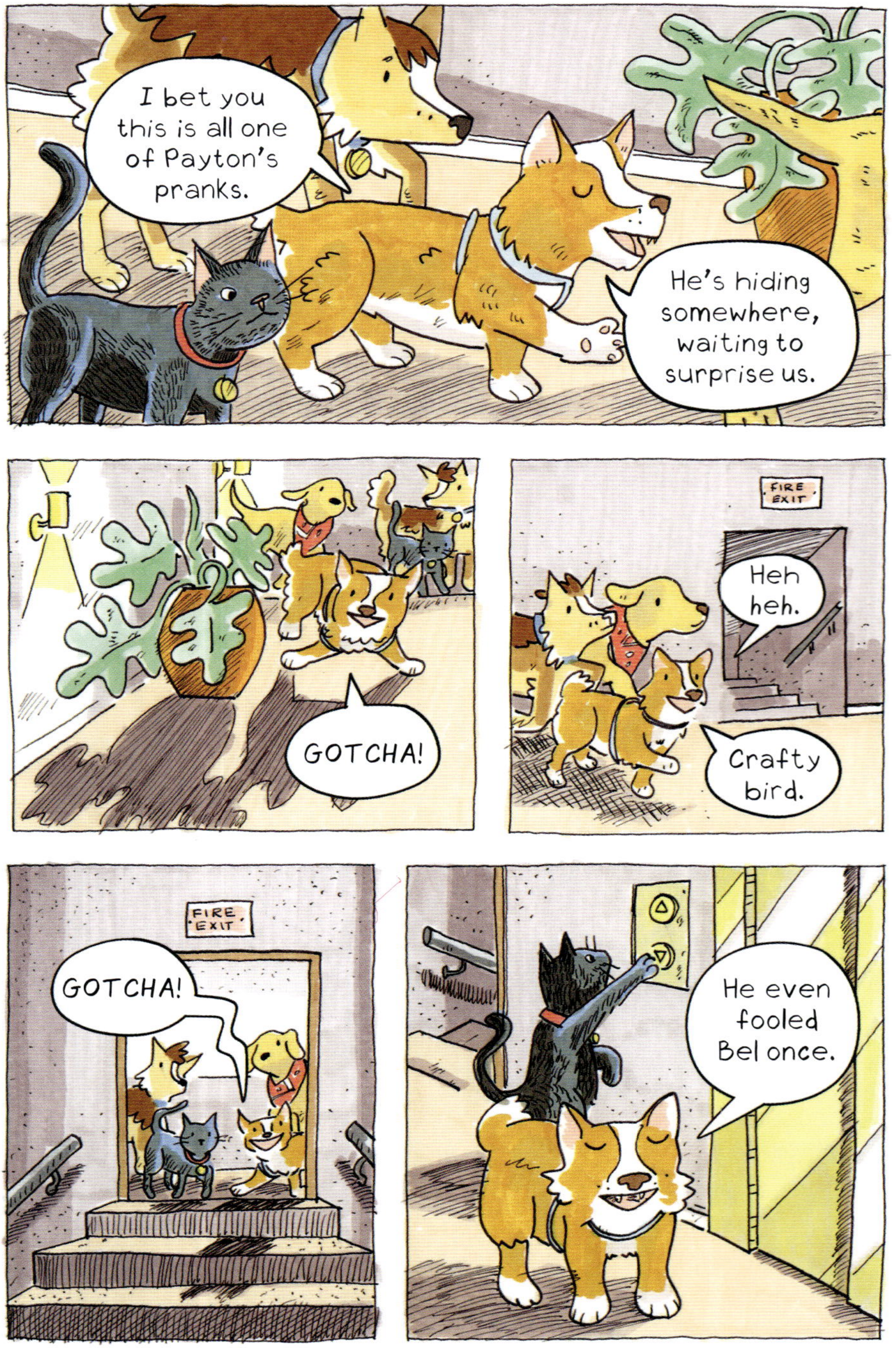
I bet you this is all one of Payton's pranks.
He's hiding somewhere, waiting to surprise us.
GOTCHA!
FIRE EXIT
Heh heh.
Crafty bird.
FIRE EXIT
GOTCHA!
He even fooled Bel once.

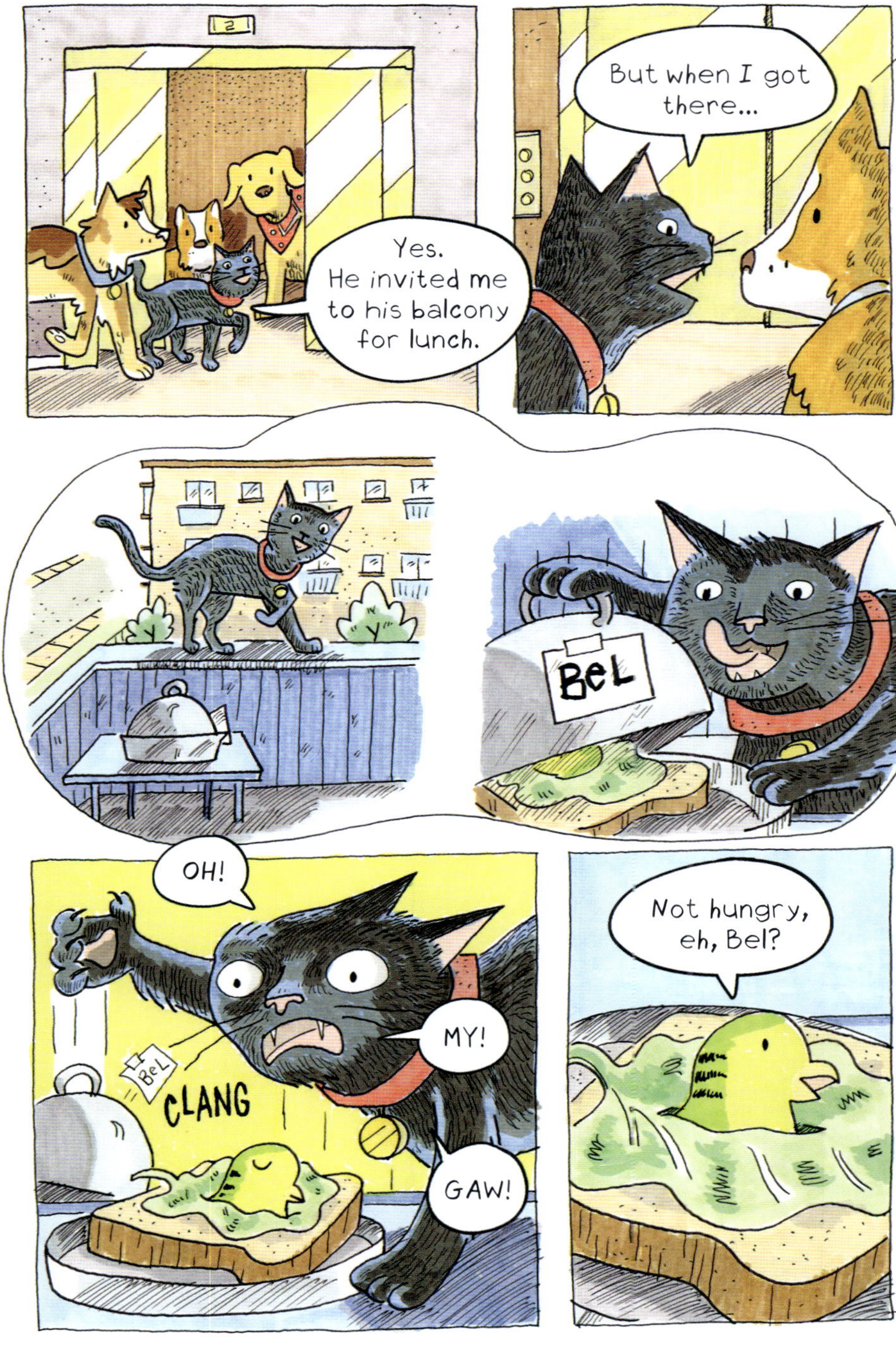
Yes.
He invited me to his balcony for lunch.
But when I got there...
BeL
OH!
MY!
GAW!
BeL
CLANG
Not hungry, eh, Bel?

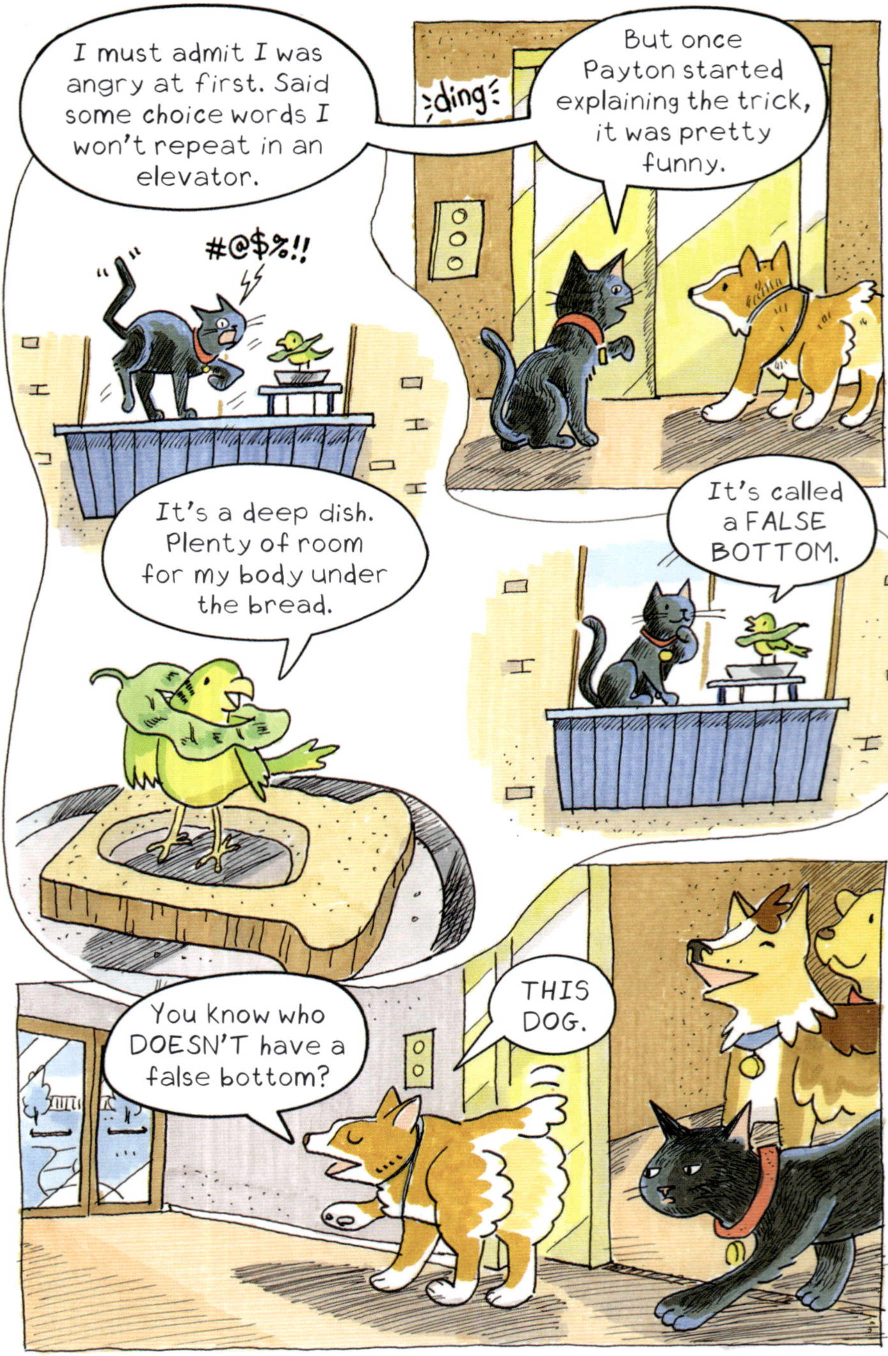
I must admit I was angry at first. Said some choice words I won't repeat in an elevator.
ding
But once Payton started explaining the trick, it was pretty funny.
#@$%!!
It's a deep dish. Plenty of room for my body under the bread.
It's called a FALSE BOTTOM.
You know who DOESN'T have a false bottom?
THIS DOG.

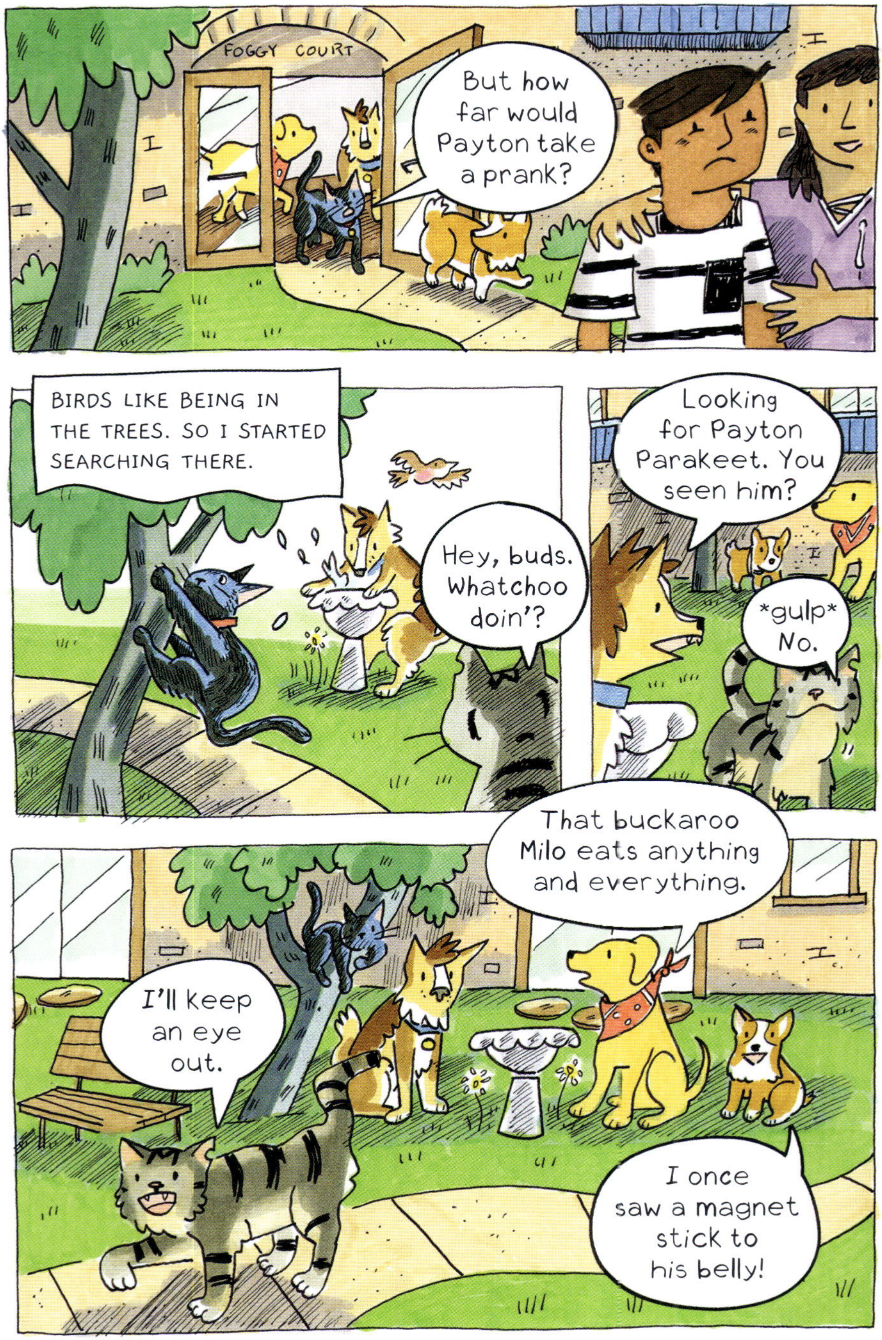
FOGGY COURT
But how far would Payton take a prank?
BIRDS LIKE BEING IN THE TREES. SO I STARTED SEARCHING THERE.
Hey, buds. Whatchoo doin'?
Looking for Payton Parakeet. You seen him?
gulp No.
I'll keep an eye out.
That buckaroo Milo eats anything and everything.
I once saw a magnet stick to his belly!

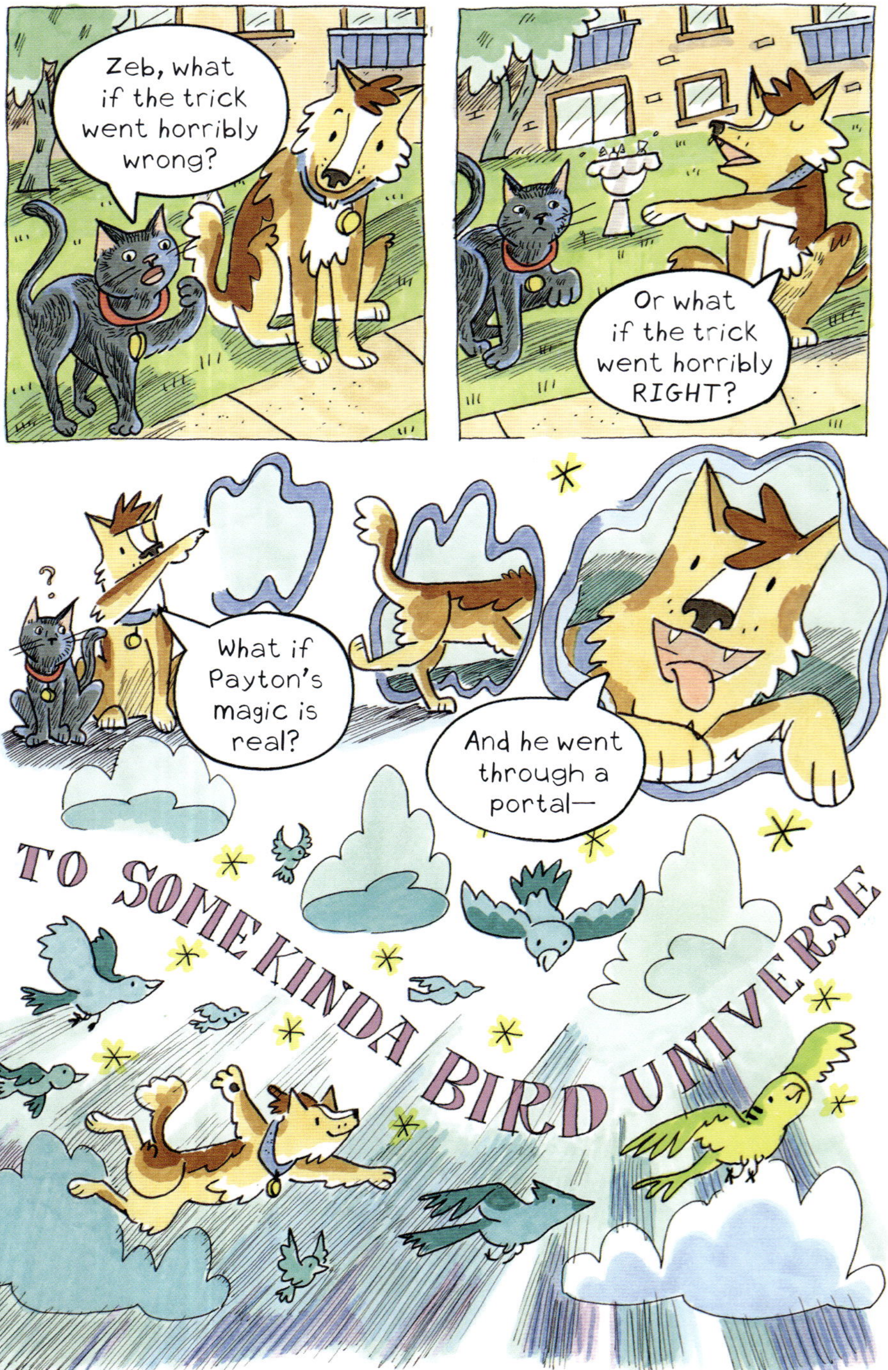
Zeb, what if the trick went horribly wrong?
Or what if the trick went horribly RIGHT?
?
What if Payton's magic is real?
And he went through a portal—
TO SOME KINDA BIRD UNIVERSE

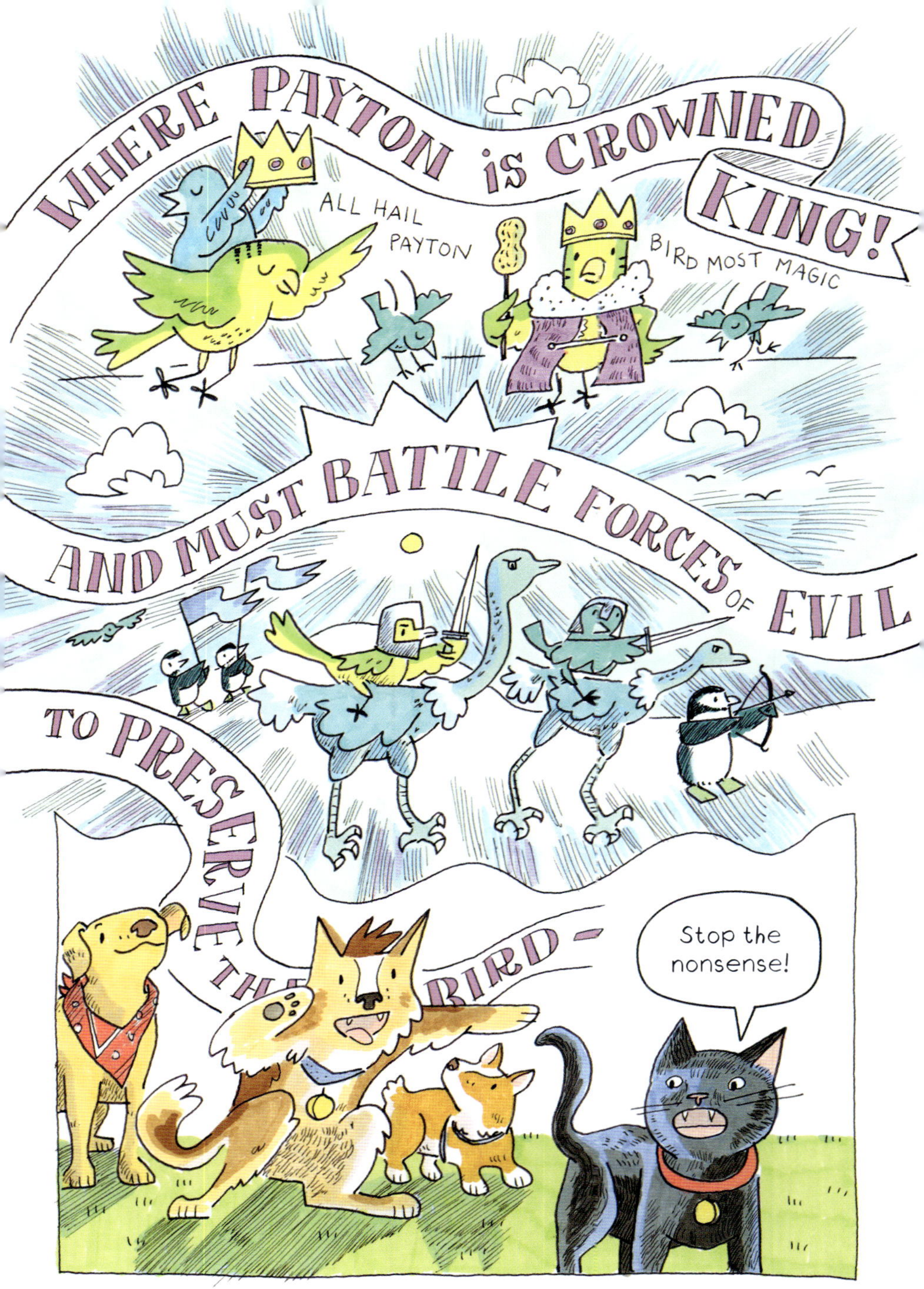
WHERE PAYTON is CROWNED KING!
ALL HAIL PAYTON
BIRD MOST MAGIC
AND MUST BATTLE FORCES OF EVIL
TO PRESERVE THE BIRD-
Stop the nonsense!

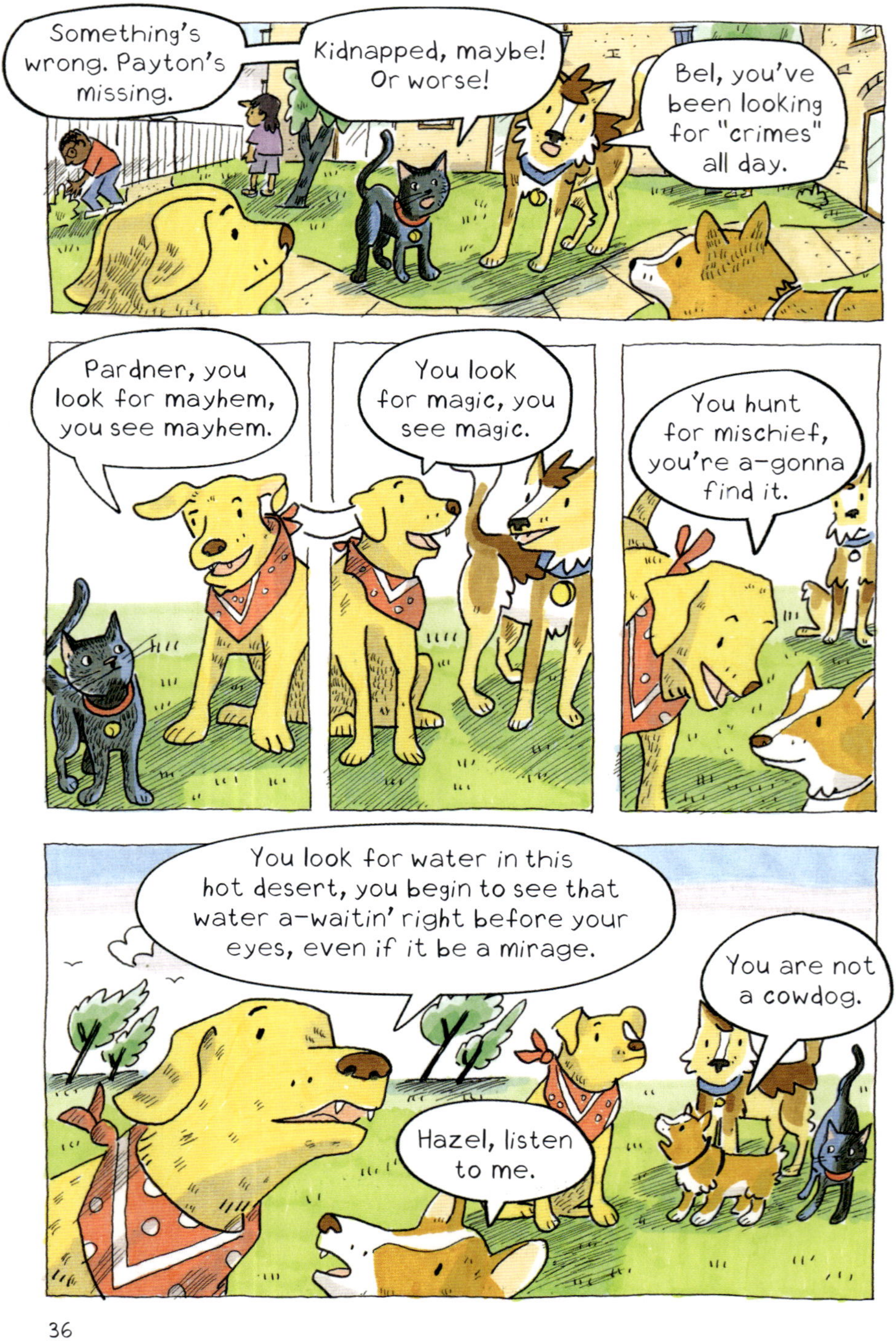
Something's wrong. Payton's missing.
Kidnapped, maybe! Or worse!
Bel, you've been looking for "crimes" all day.
Pardner, you look for mayhem, you see mayhem.
You look for magic, you see magic.
You hunt for mischief, you're a-gonna find it.
You look for water in this hot desert, you begin to see that water a-waitin' right before your eyes, even if it be a mirage.
You are not a cowdog.
Hazel, listen to me.

2:00 PM: NO ONE FOUND PAYTON IN THE COURTYARD. THE LAST SIGN I SAW OF HIM WAS BIRD TRACKS ON THE WINDOWSILL, NEXT TO SOME TRASH.

QUEEN THINKS THIS IS A PRANK, BUT PAYTON WOULDN'T HIDE OUT WHILE CARLO WORRIES.

ZEB THINKS PAYTON WENT THROUGH A MAGICAL PORTAL.

DO MAGIC PORTALS REALLY EXIST IN THE WORLD? I DOUBT THAT VERY MUCH.

WOULD PAYTON LEAVE FOGGY COURT BY CHOICE? RUN AWAY FROM HOME? HE SEEMED HAPPY WITH LIFE HERE, SO WAS HE KIDNAPPED?

I WILL INVESTIGATE FURTHER.

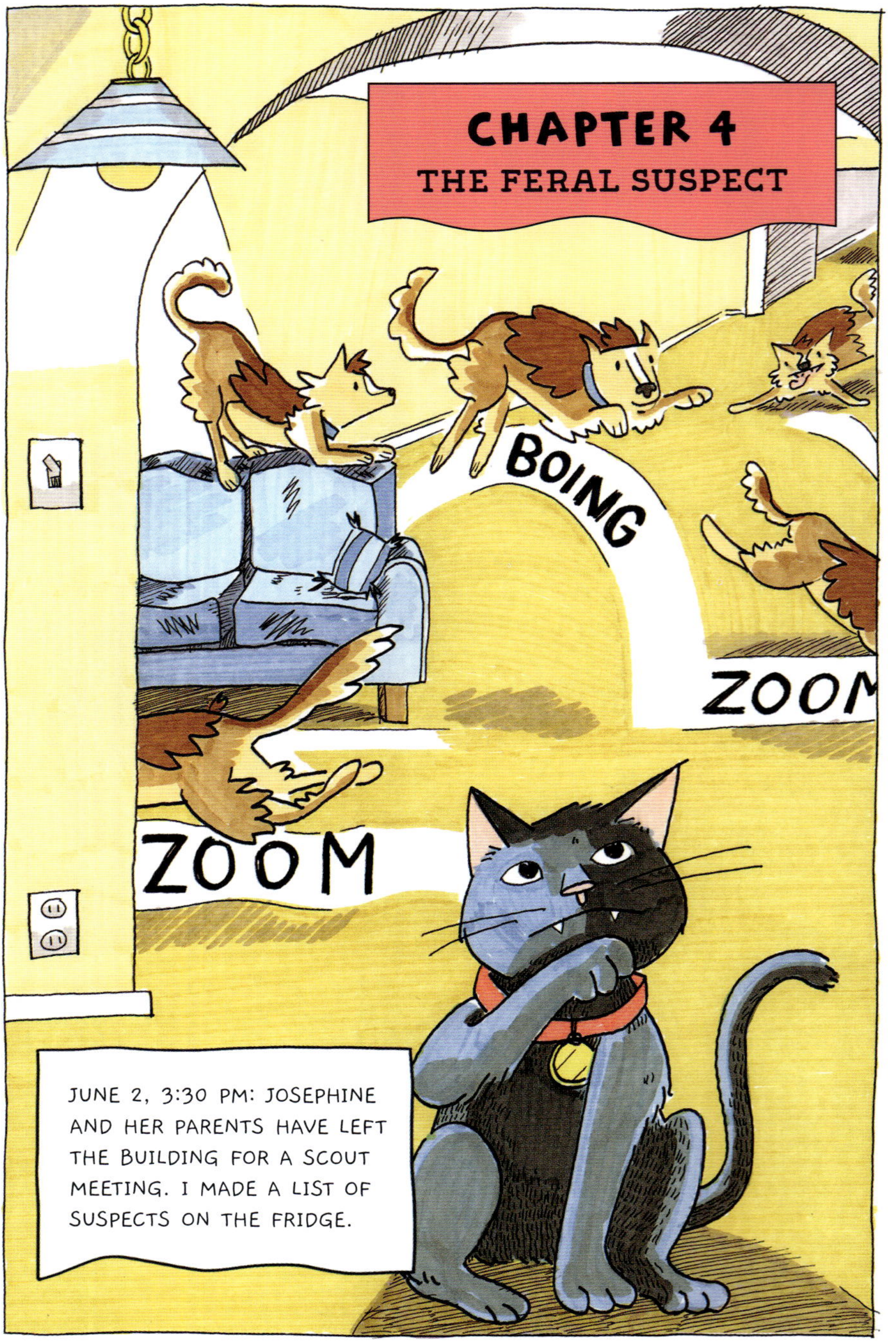
CHAPTER 4
THE FERAL SUSPECT
BOING
ZOOM
ZOOM
JUNE 2, 3:30 PM: JOSEPHINE AND HER PARENTS HAVE LEFT THE BUILDING FOR A SCOUT MEETING. I MADE A LIST OF SUSPECTS ON THE FRIDGE.

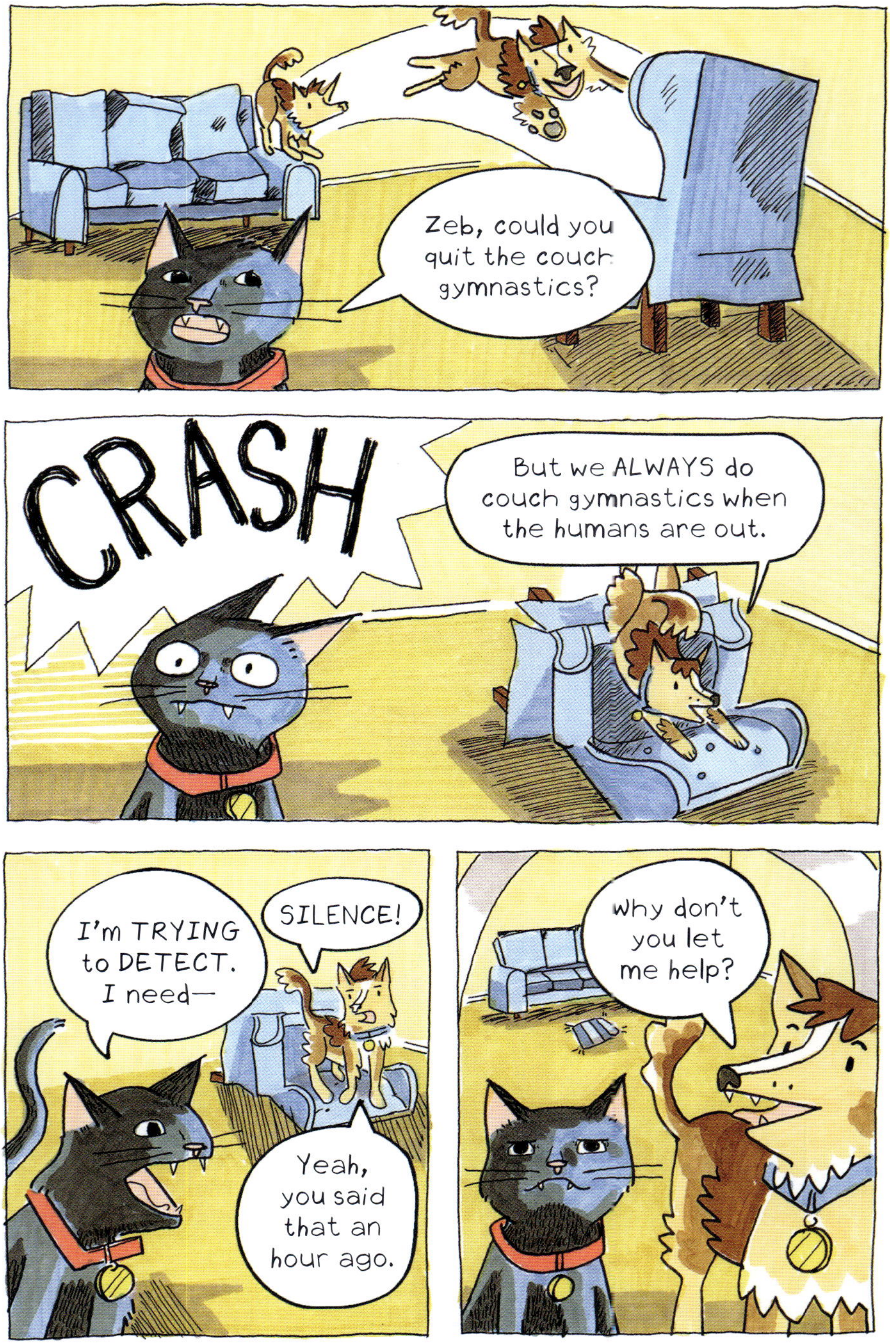
Zeb, could you quit the couch gymnastics?
CRASH
But we ALWAYS do couch gymnastics when the humans are out.
I'm TRYING to DETECT. I need—
SILENCE!
Yeah, you said that an hour ago.
Why don't you let me help?

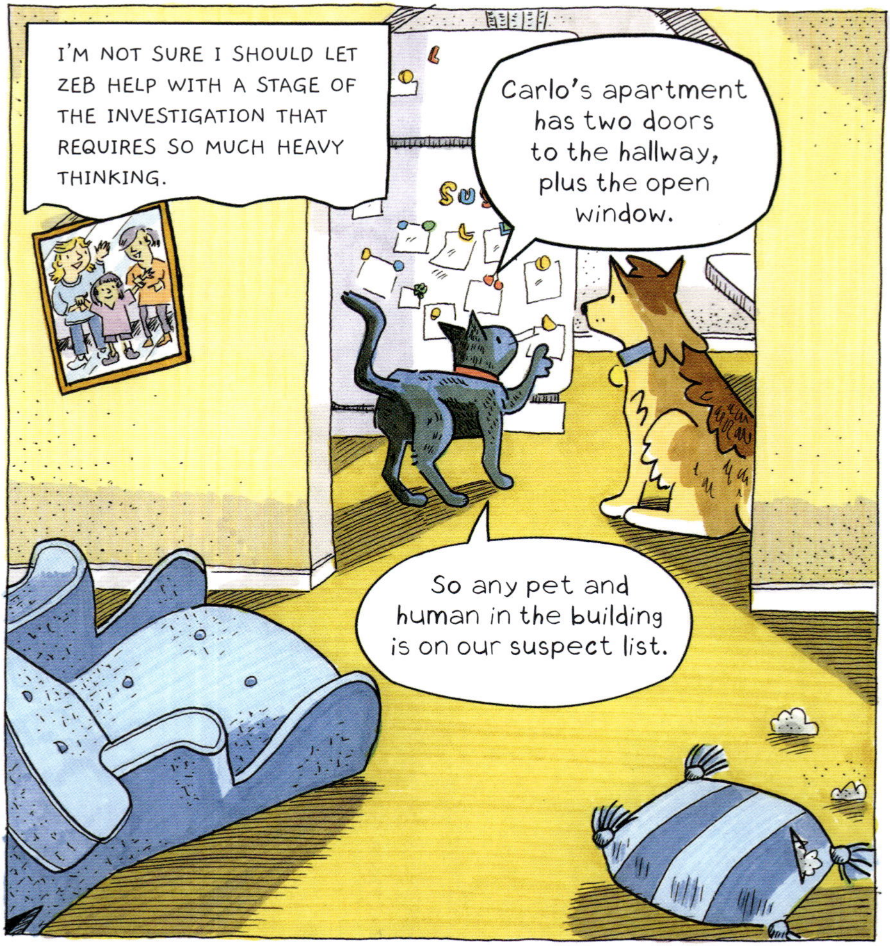
I'M NOT SURE I SHOULD LET ZEB HELP WITH A STAGE OF THE INVESTIGATION THAT REQUIRES SO MUCH HEAVY THINKING.
Carlo's apartment has two doors to the hallway, plus the open window.
So any pet and human in the building is on our suspect list.

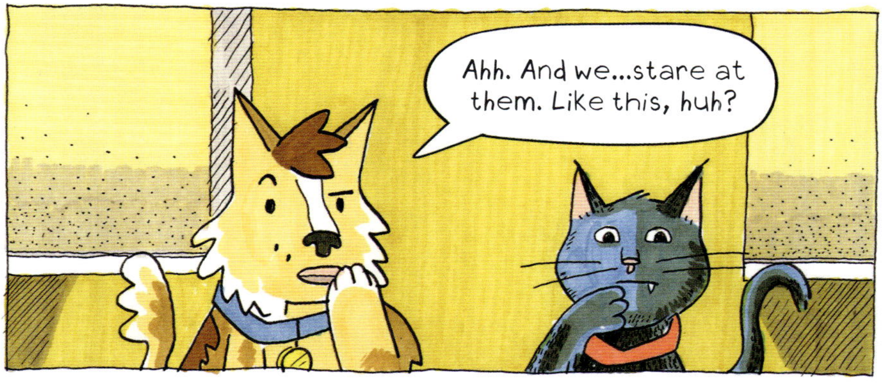
Ahh. And we...stare at them. Like this, huh?

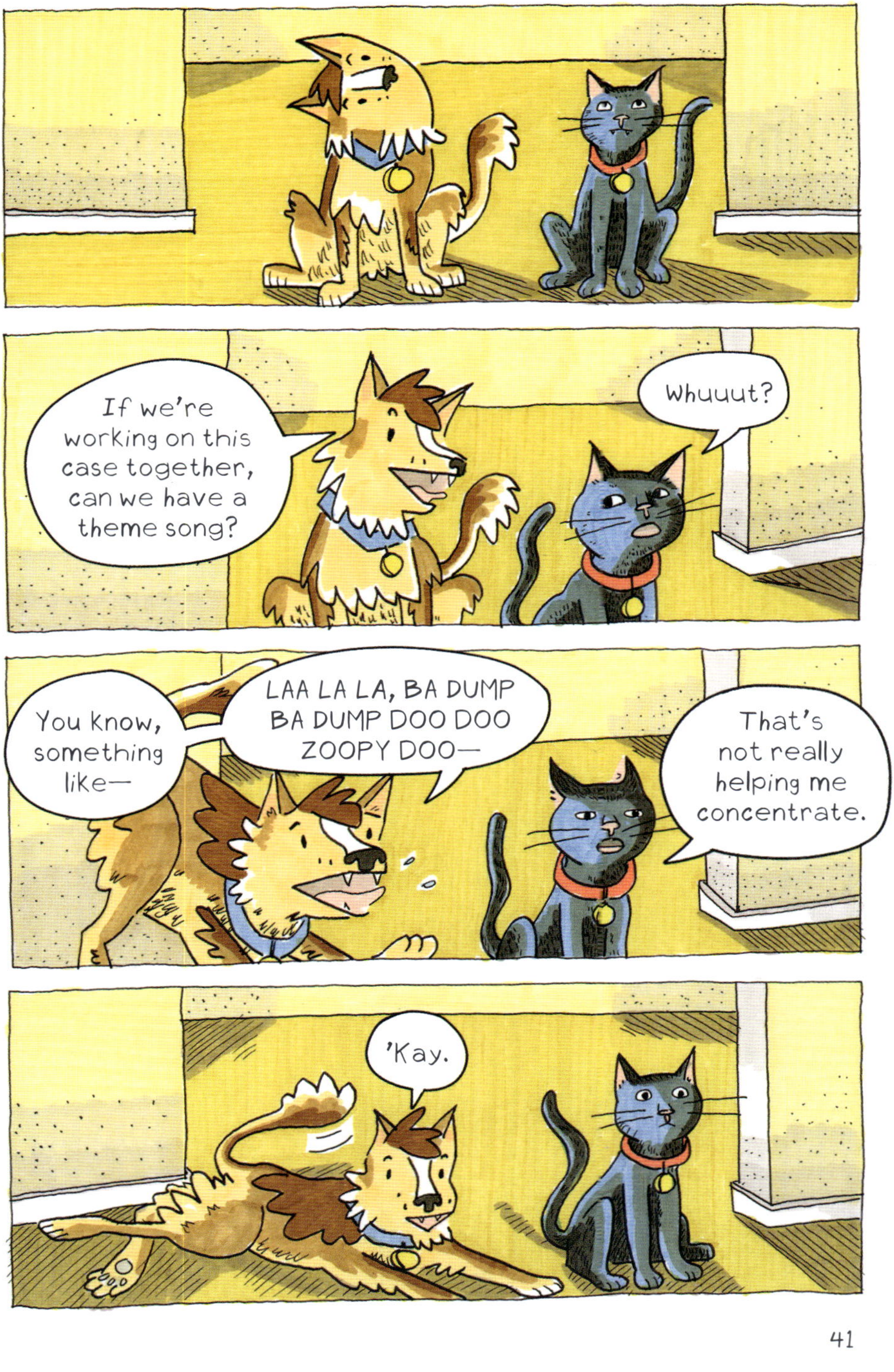
If we're working on this case together, can we have a theme song?
Whuuut?
You know, something like—
LAA LA LA, BA DUMP BA DUMP DOO DOO ZOOPY DOO—
That's not really helping me concentrate.
'Kay.

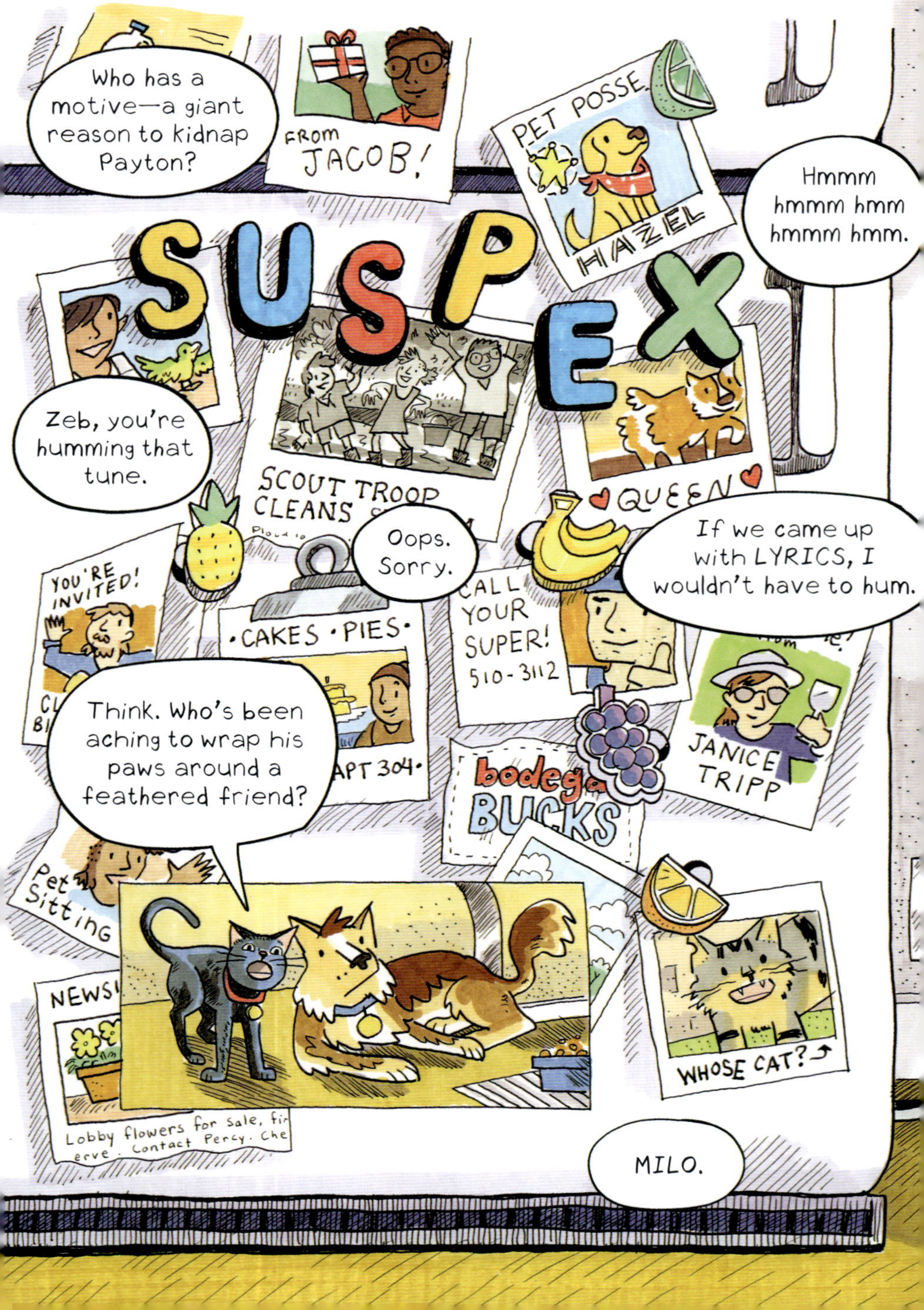
Who has a motive—a giant reason to kidnap Payton?
FROM JACOB!
PET POSSE
HAZEL
Hmmm hmmm hmm hmmm hmm.
SUSPEX
Zeb, you're humming that tune.
SCOUT TROOP CLEANS
QUEEN
Oops. Sorry.
If we came up with LYRICS, I wouldn't have to hum.
YOU'RE INVITED!
•CAKES •PIES•
CALL YOUR SUPER! 510-3112
JANICE TRIPP
Think. Who's been aching to wrap his paws around a feathered friend?
APT 304•
bodega BUCKS
Pet Sitting
WHOSE CAT?
MILO.

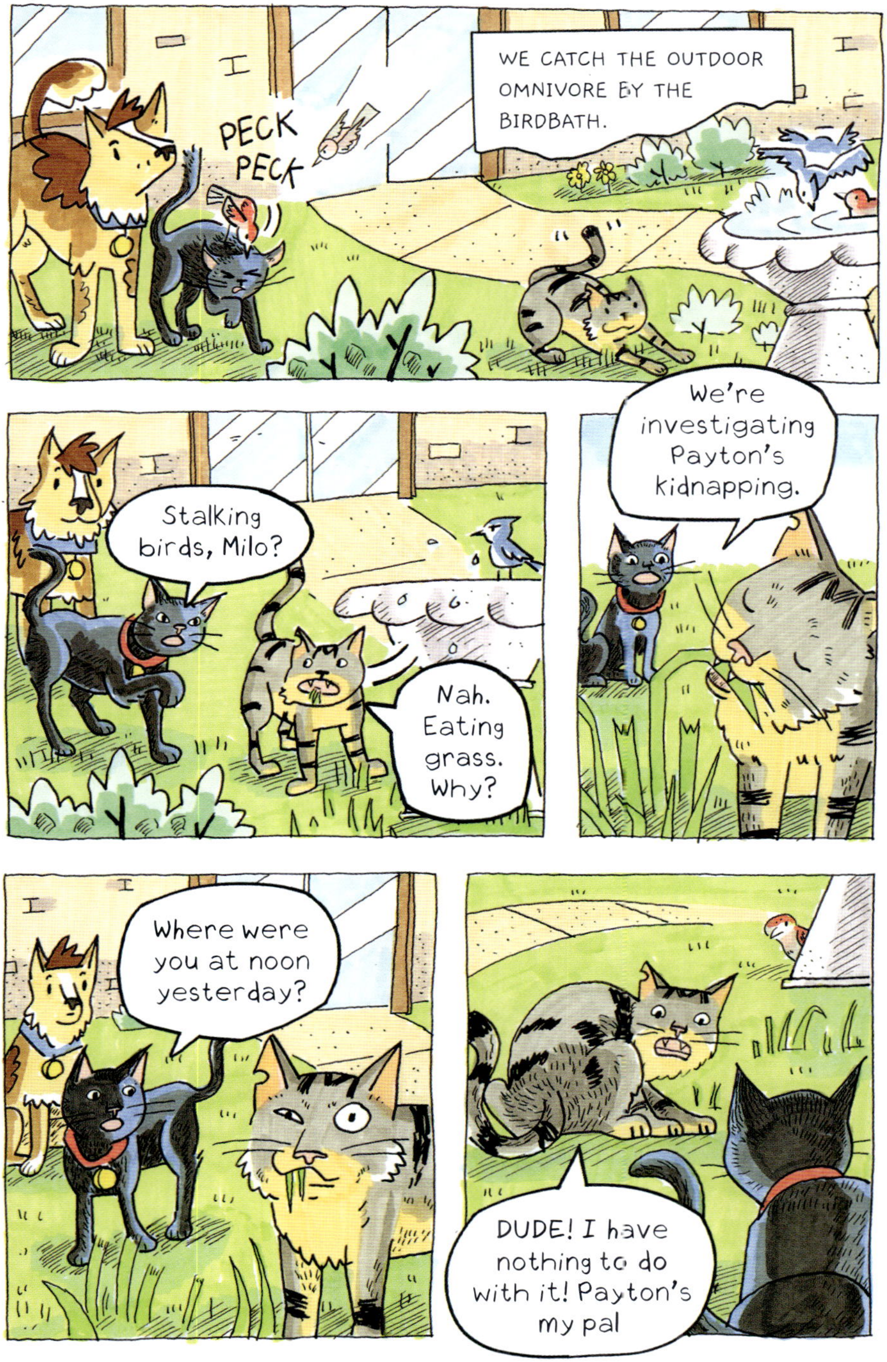
WE CATCH THE OUTDOOR OMNIVORE BY THE BIRDBATH.
PECK PECK
Stalking birds, Milo?
Nah. Eating grass. Why?
We're investigating Payton's kidnapping.
Where were you at noon yesterday?
DUDE! I have nothing to do with it! Payton's my pal

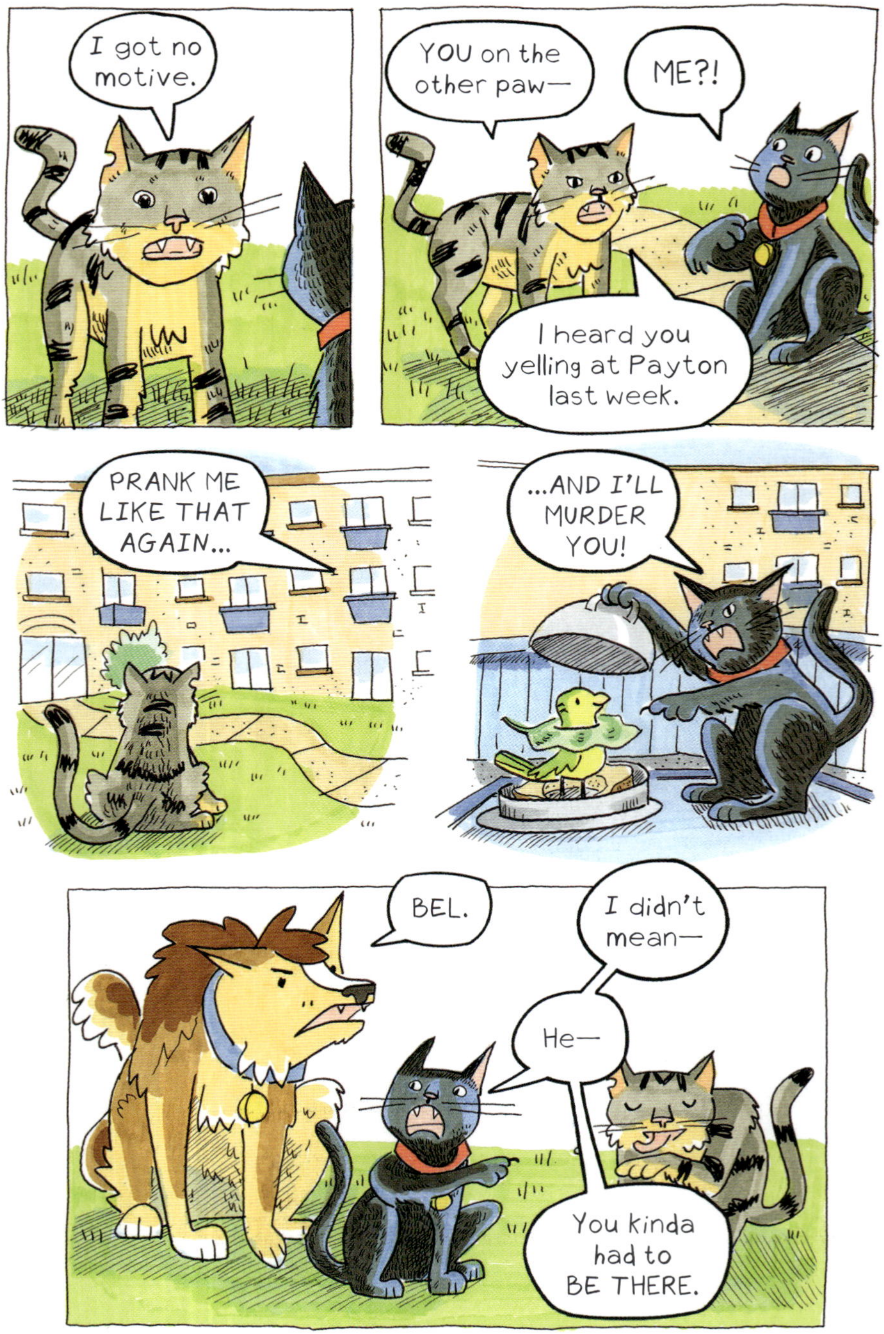
I got no motive.
YOU on the other paw—
ME?!
I heard you yelling at Payton last week.
PRANK ME LIKE THAT AGAIN...
...AND I'LL MURDER YOU!
BEL.
I didn't mean—
He—
You kinda had to BE THERE.

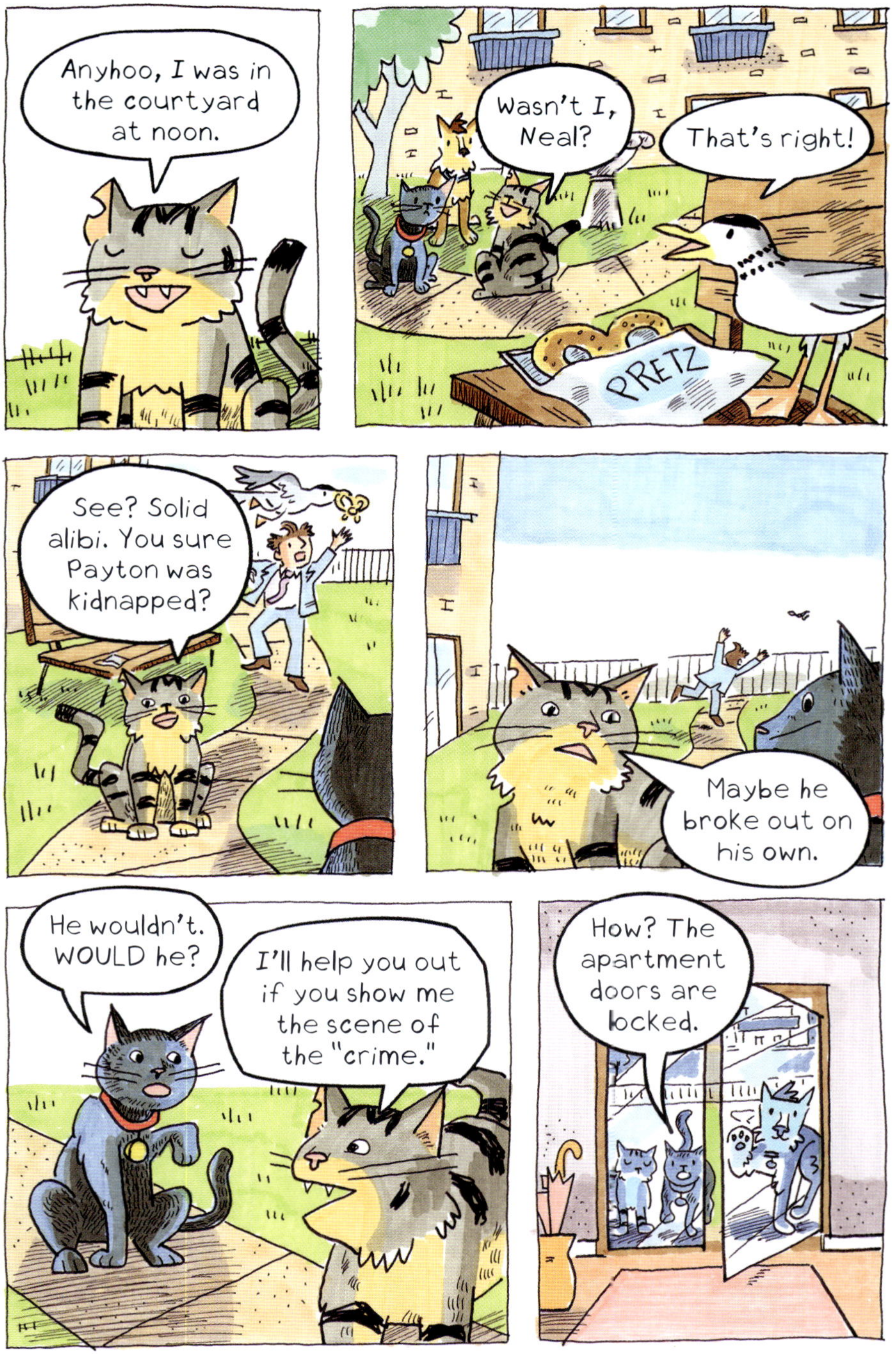

Anyhoo, I was in the courtyard at noon.
Wasn't I, Neal?
That's right!
PRETZ
See? Solid alibi. You sure Payton was kidnapped?
Maybe he broke out on his own.
He wouldn't. WOULD he?
I'll help you out if you show me the scene of the "crime."
How? The apartment doors are locked.

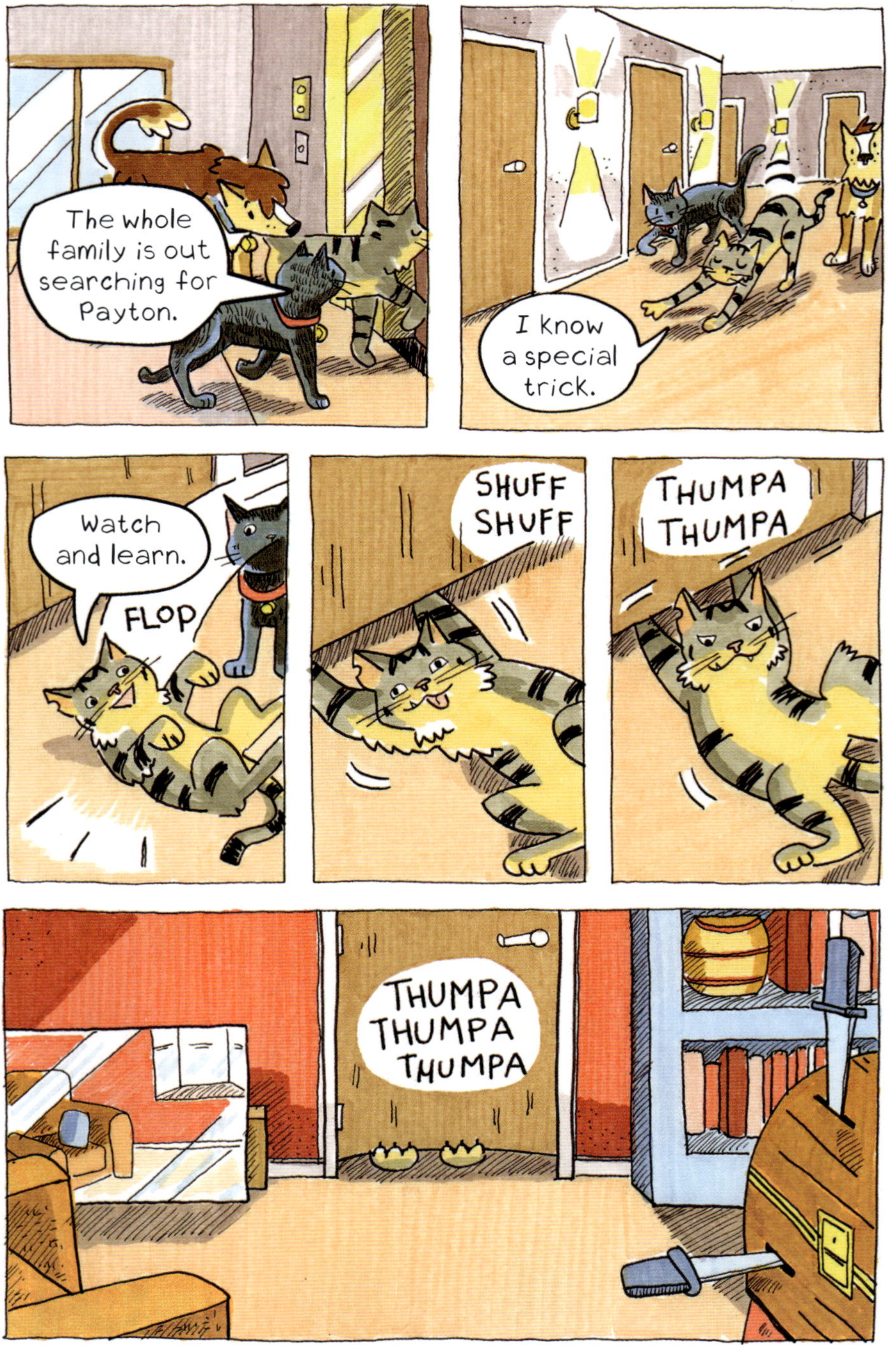
The whole family is out searching for Payton.
I know a special trick.
Watch and learn.
FLOP
SHUFF SHUFF
THUMPA THUMPA
THUMPA THUMPA THUMPA

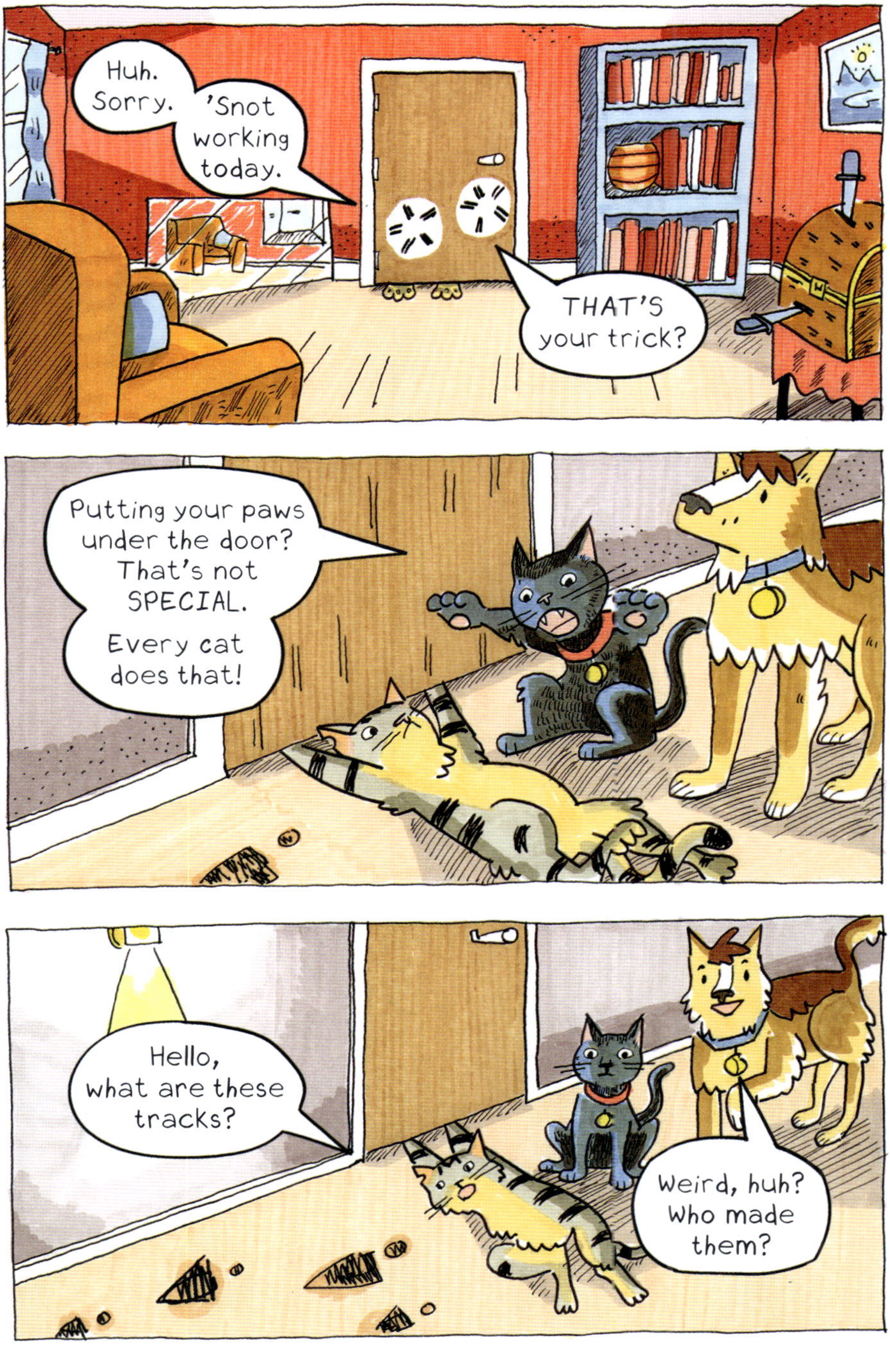
Huh. Sorry.
'Snot working today.
THAT'S your trick?
Putting your paws under the door? That's not SPECIAL.
Every cat does that!
Hello, what are these tracks?
Weird, huh? Who made them?

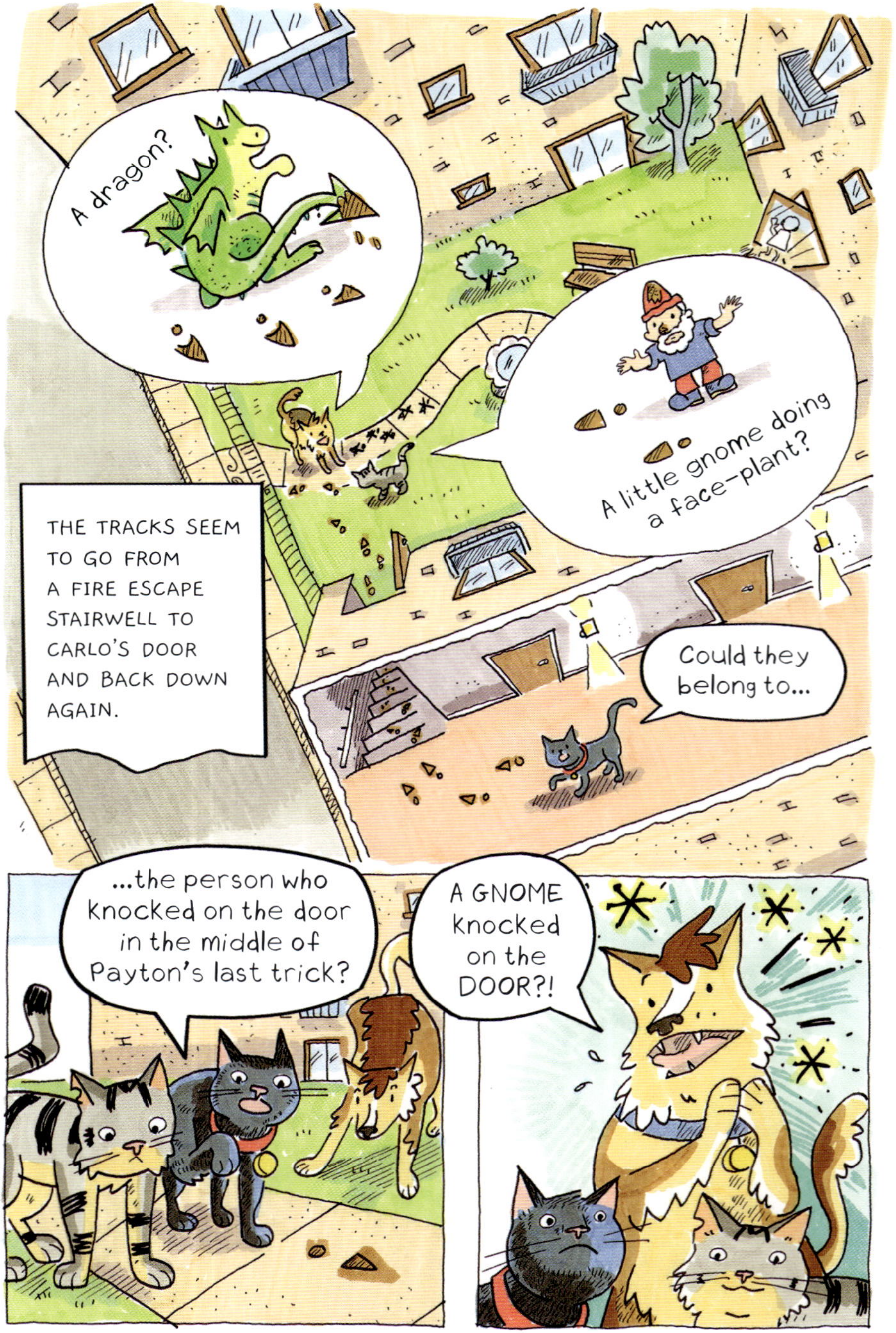

A dragon?
A little gnome doing a face-plant?
THE TRACKS SEEM TO GO FROM A FIRE ESCAPE STAIRWELL TO CARLO'S DOOR AND BACK DOWN AGAIN.
Could they belong to...
...the person who knocked on the door in the middle of Payton's last trick?
A GNOME knocked on the DOOR?!

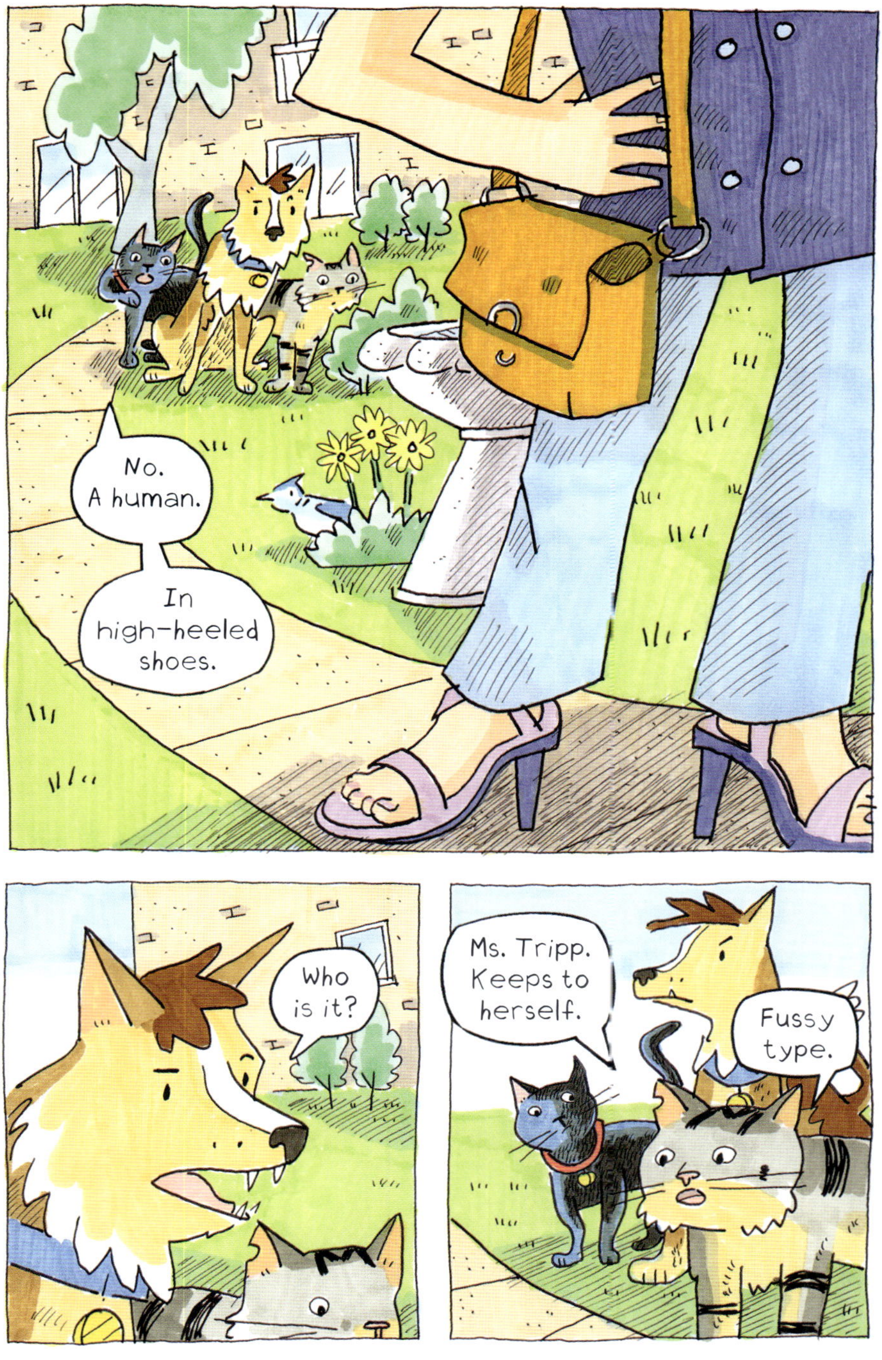
No. A human.
In high-heeled shoes.
Who is it?
Ms. Tripp. Keeps to herself.
Fussy type.

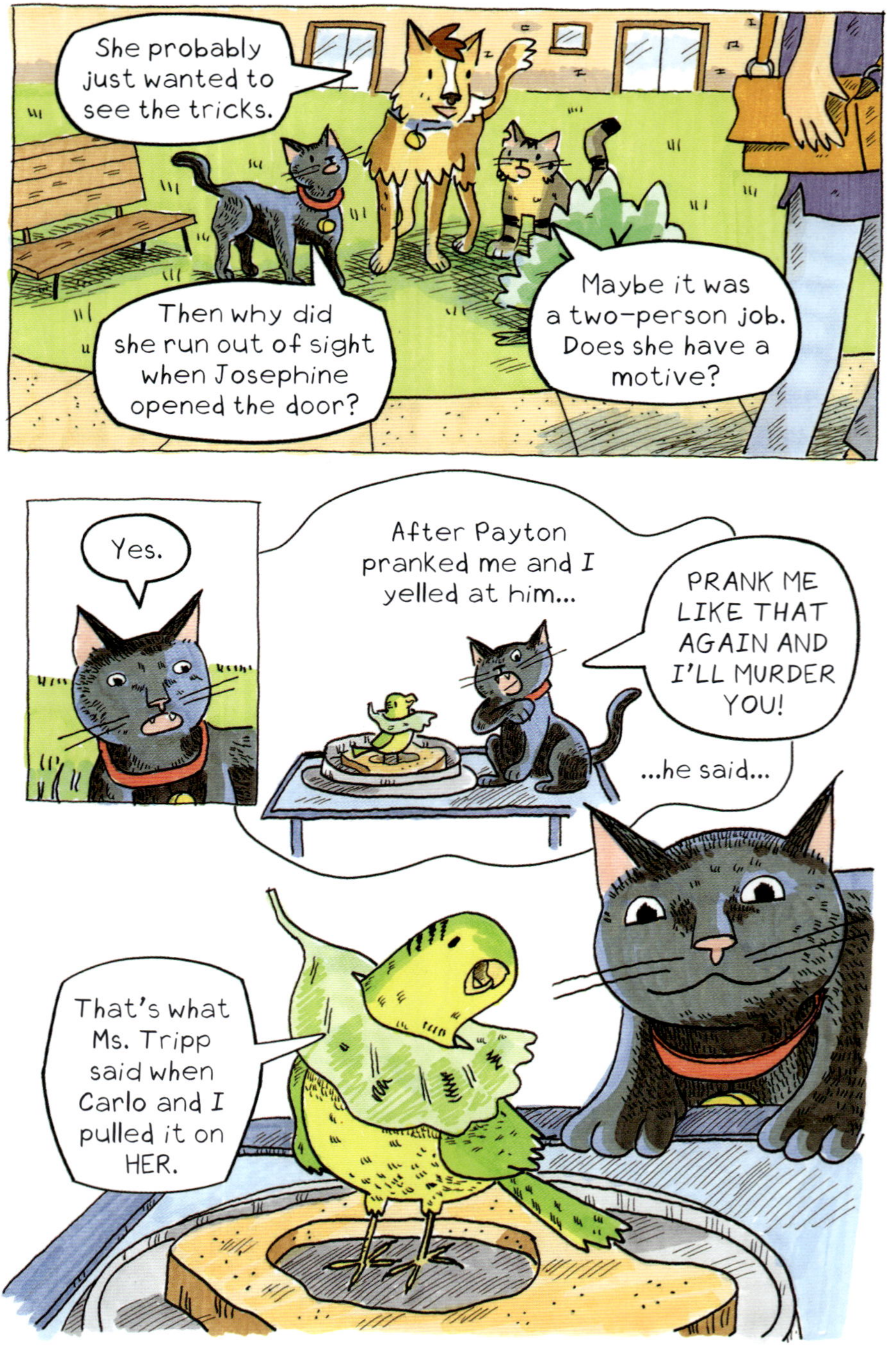
She probably just wanted to see the tricks.
Then why did she run out of sight when Josephine opened the door?
Maybe it was a two-person job. Does she have a motive?
Yes.
After Payton pranked me and I yelled at him...
PRANK ME LIKE THAT AGAIN AND I'LL MURDER YOU!
...he said...
That's what Ms. Tripp said when Carlo and I pulled it on HER.

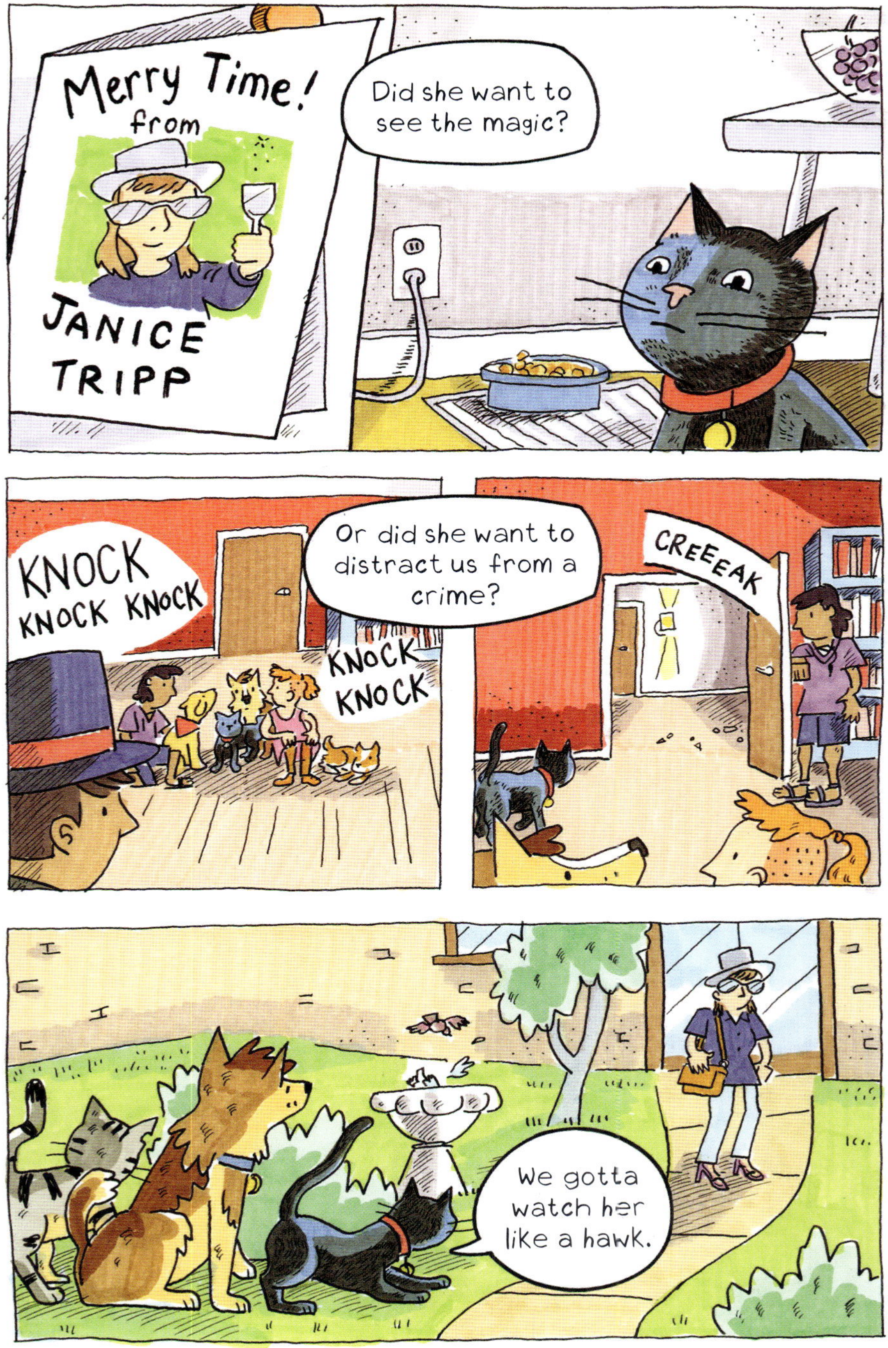
Merry Time! from JANICE TRIPP
Did she want to see the magic?
KNOCK KNOCK KNOCK
KNOCK KNOCK
Or did she want to distract us from a crime?
CREEEAK
We gotta watch her like a hawk.

CHAPTER 5
ZEB TAILS A SUSPECT

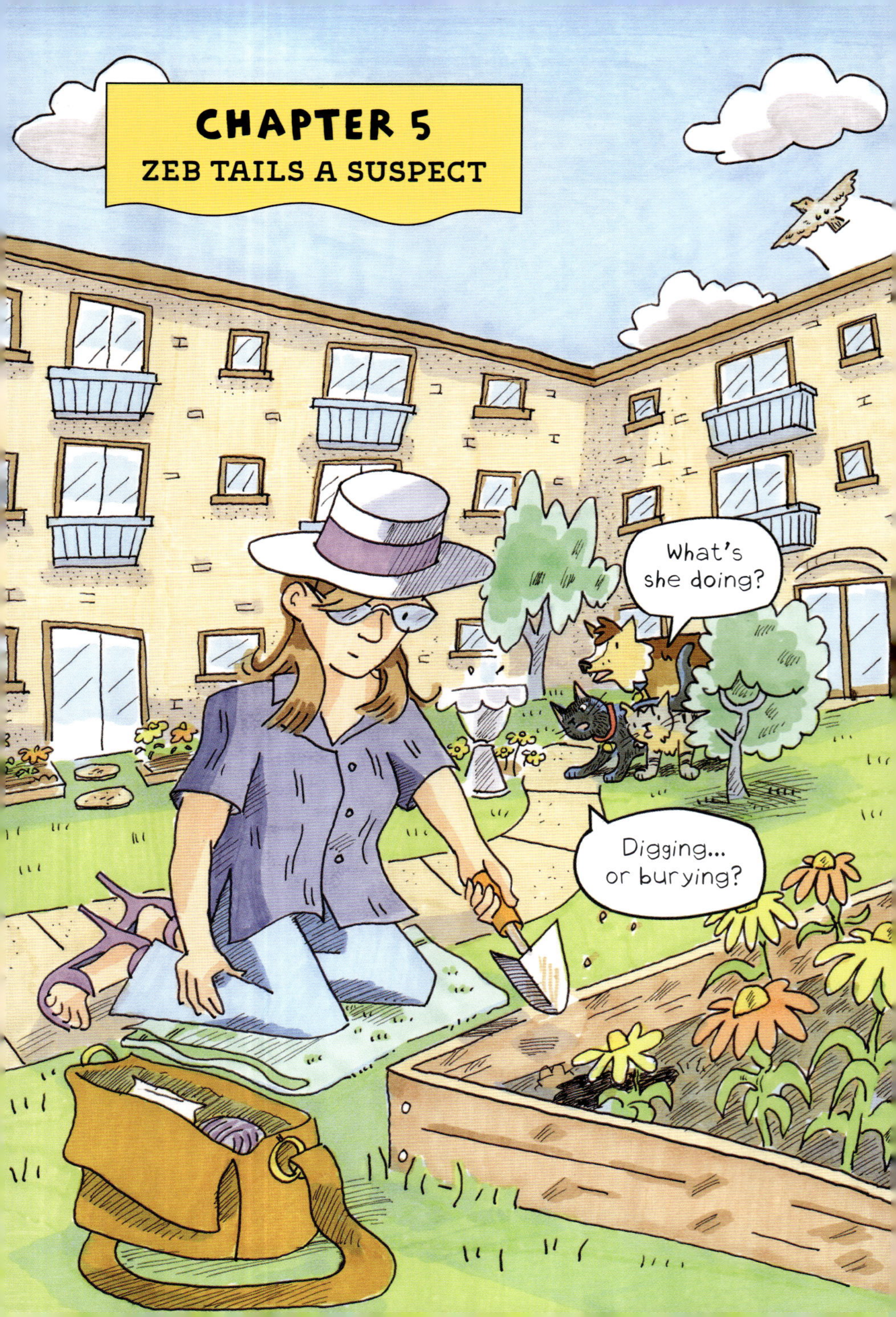
What's she doing?
Digging... or burying?

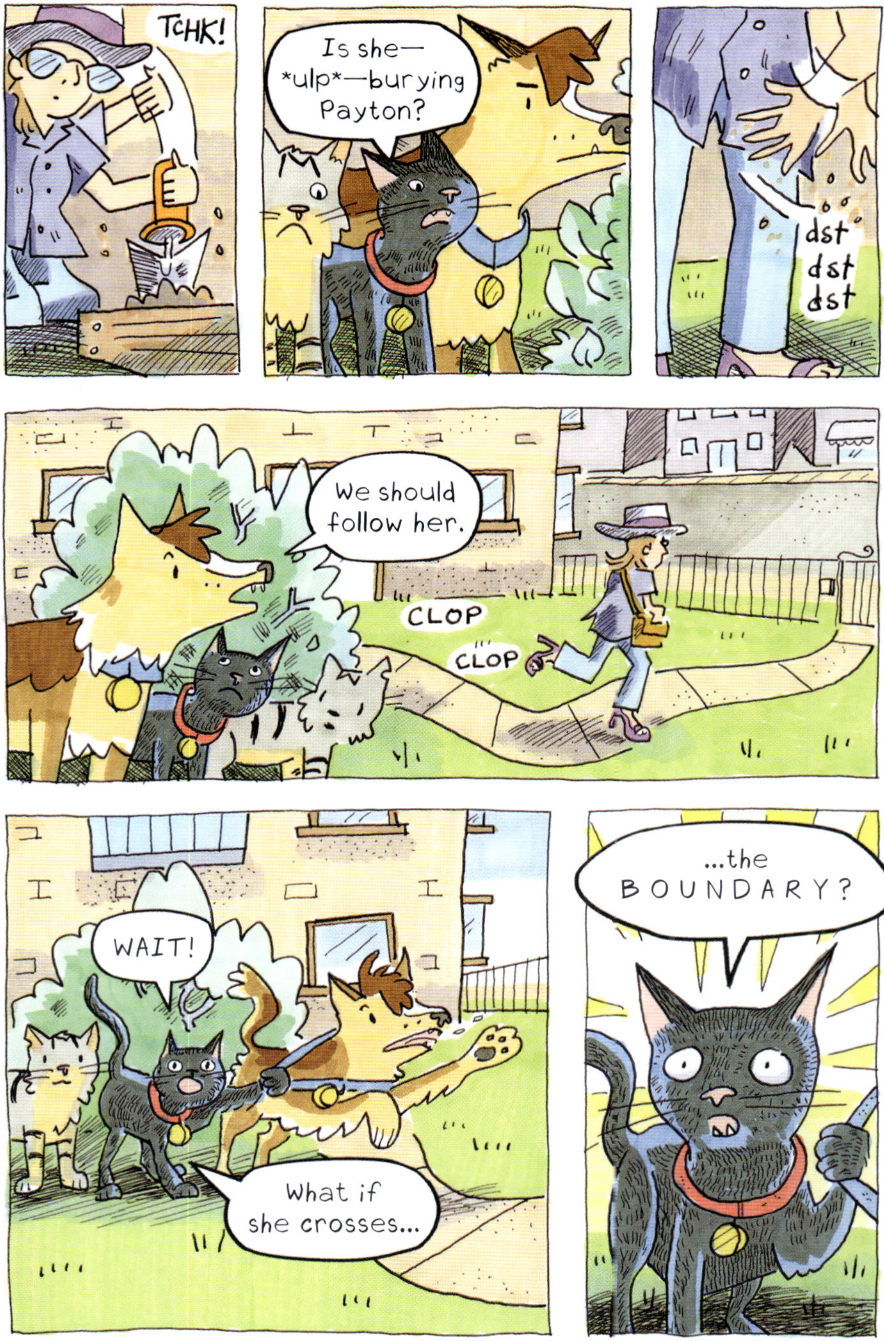
TCHK!
Is she—*ulp*—burying Payton?
dst dst dst
We should follow her.
CLOP
CLOP
WAIT!
What if she crosses...
...the BOUNDARY?

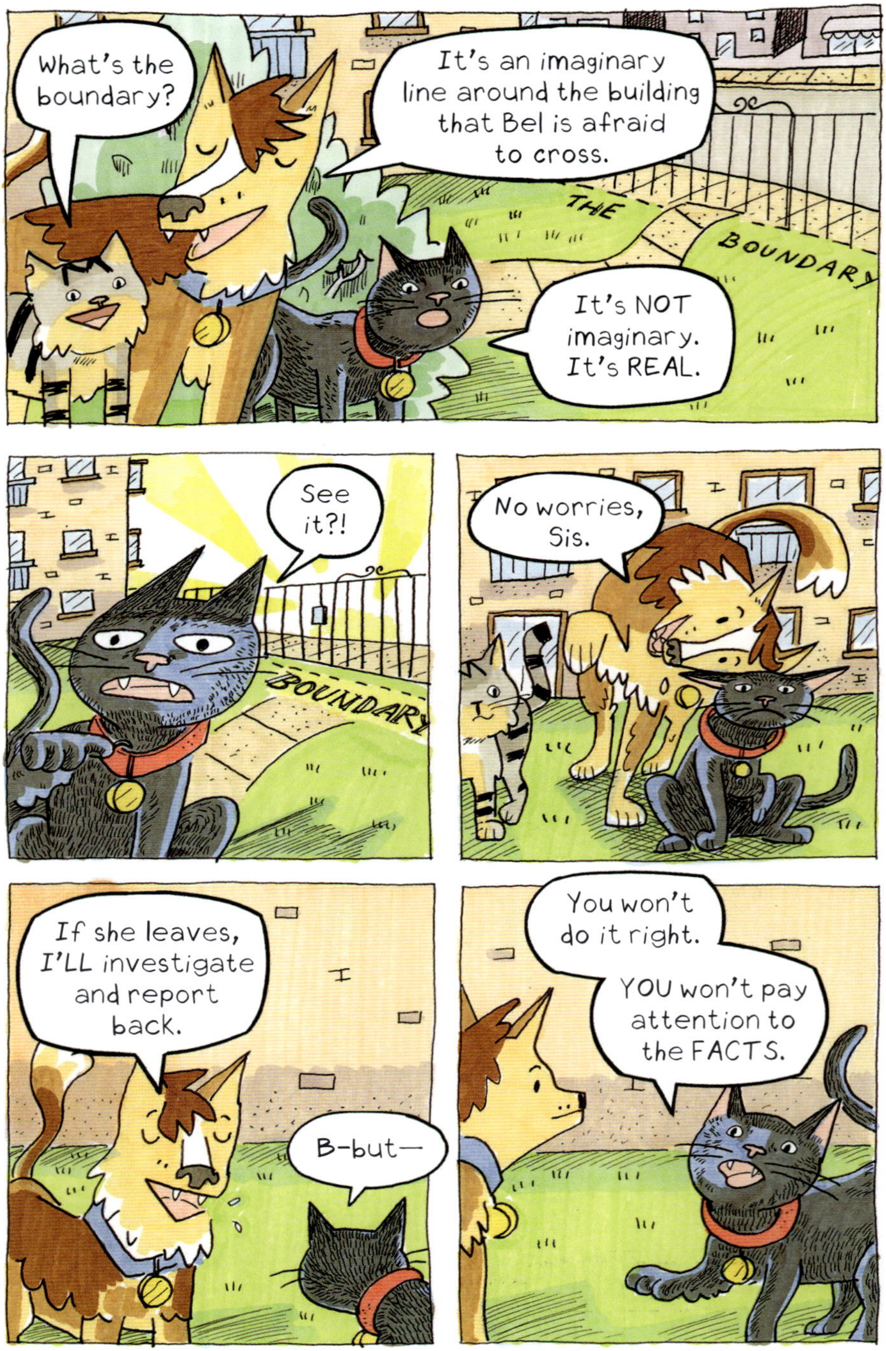

What's the boundary?
It's an imaginary line around the building that Bel is afraid to cross.
THE BOUNDARY
It's NOT imaginary. It's REAL.
See it?!
BOUNDARY
No worries, Sis.
If she leaves, I'LL investigate and report back.
B-but—
You won't do it right.
YOU won't pay attention to the FACTS.

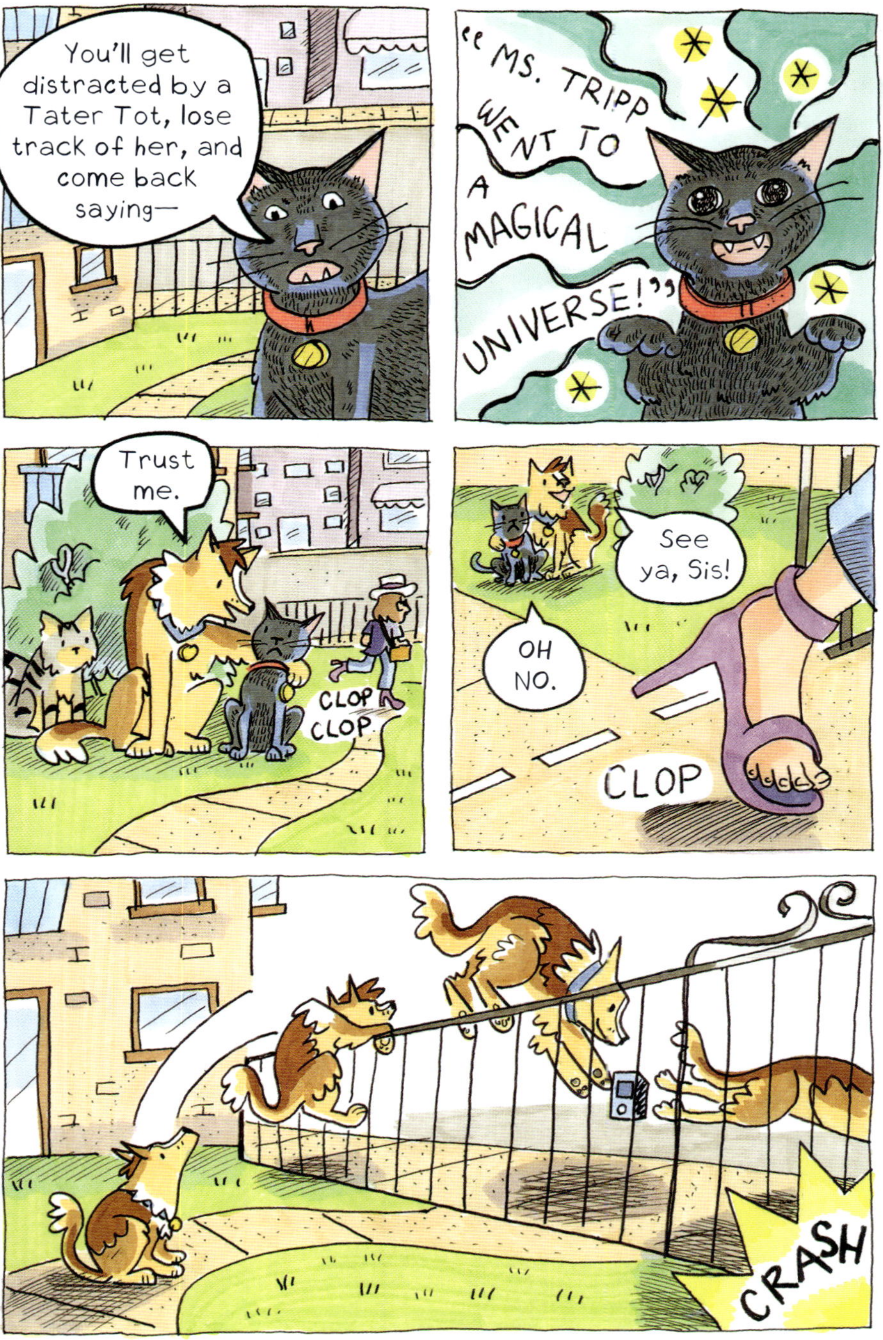
You'll get distracted by a Tater Tot, lose track of her, and come back saying—
"MS. TRIPP WENT TO A MAGICAL UNIVERSE!"
Trust me.
CLOP CLOP
See ya, Sis!
OH NO.
CLOP
CRASH

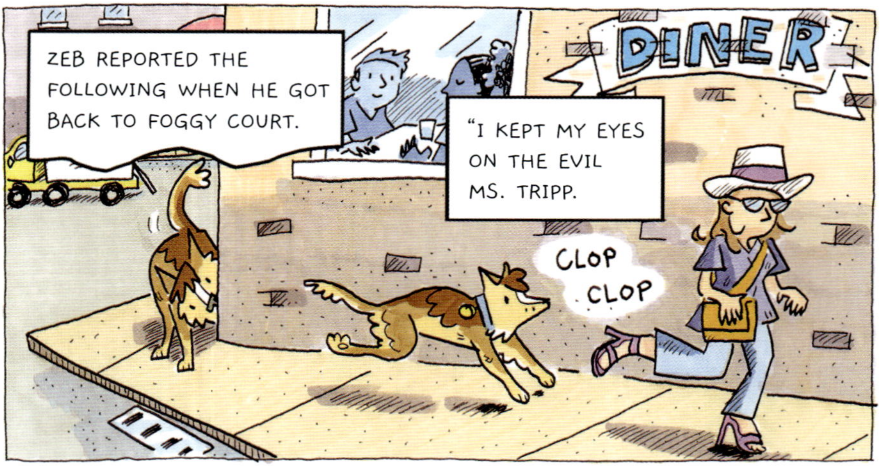
ZEB REPORTED THE FOLLOWING WHEN HE GOT BACK TO FOGGY COURT.
DINER
"I KEPT MY EYES ON THE EVIL MS. TRIPP.
CLOP CLOP

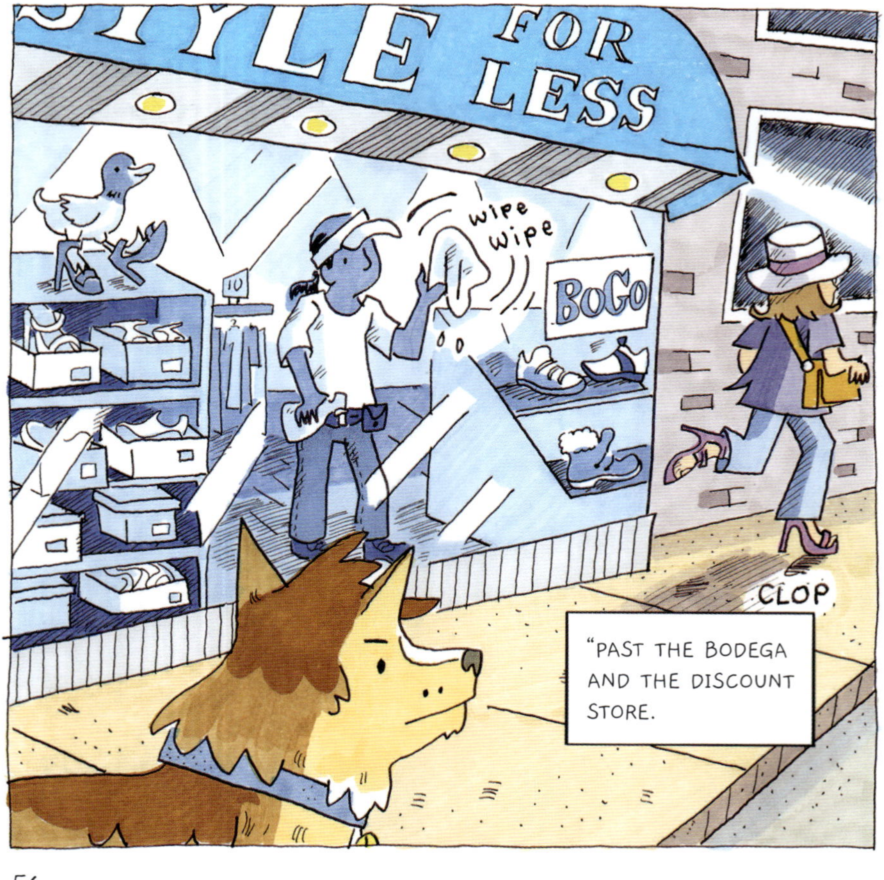
STYLE FOR LESS
wipe wipe
BoGo
CLOP
"PAST THE BODEGA AND THE DISCOUNT STORE.

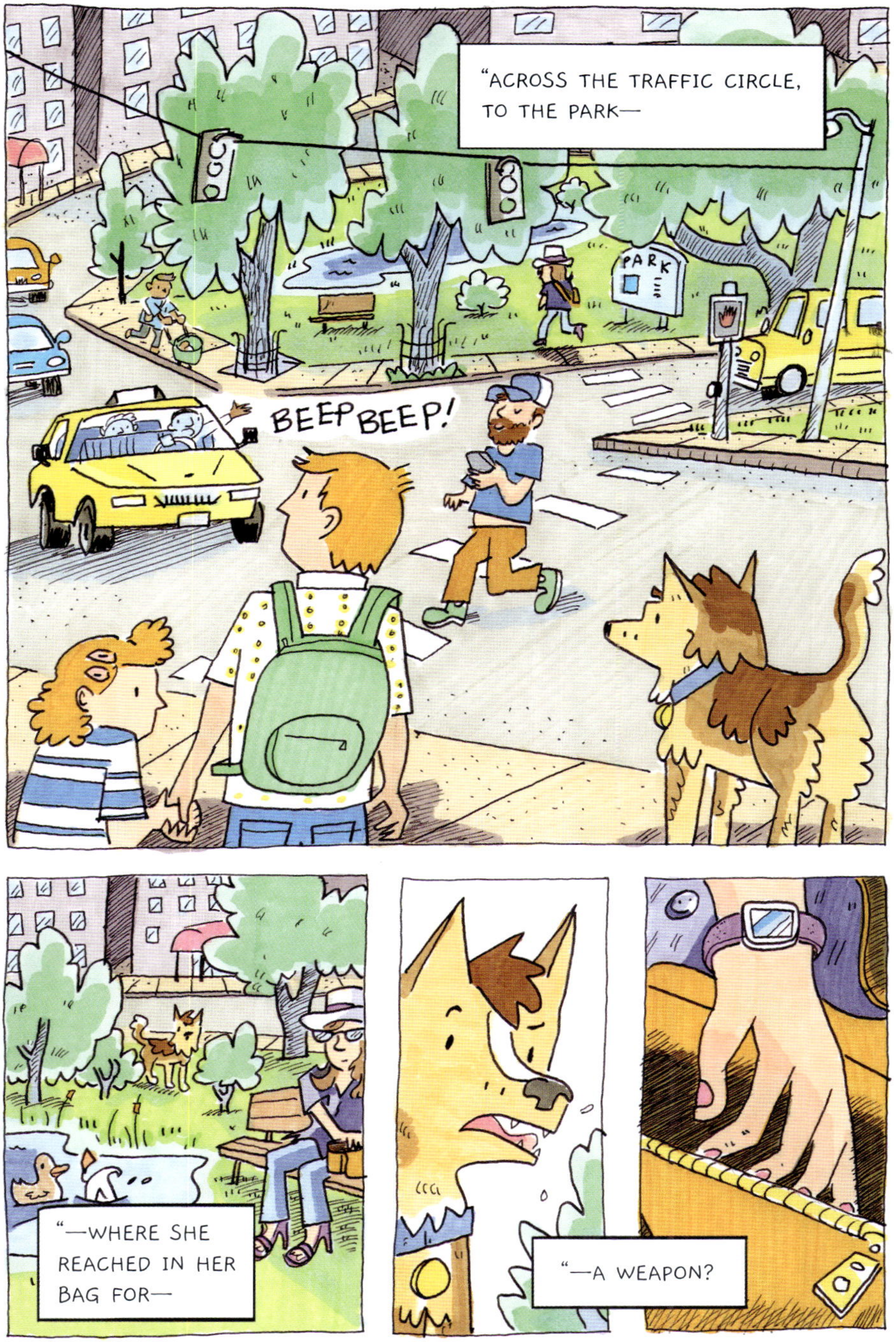
"ACROSS THE TRAFFIC CIRCLE, TO THE PARK—
PARK
BEEP BEEP!
"—WHERE SHE REACHED IN HER BAG FOR—
"—A WEAPON?

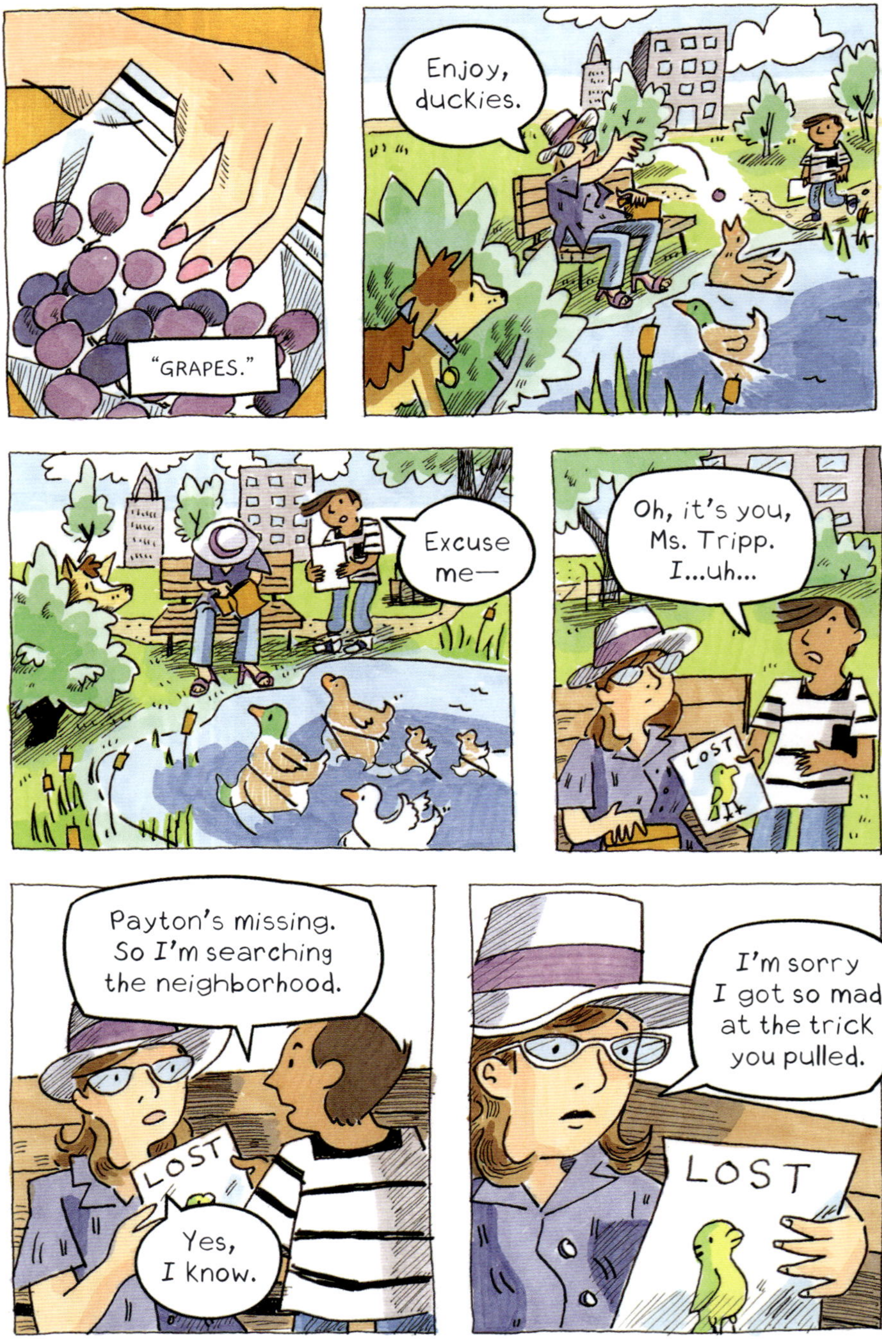
"GRAPES."
Enjoy, duckies.
Excuse me—
Oh, it's you, Ms. Tripp. I...uh...
LOST
Payton's missing. So I'm searching the neighborhood.
LOST
Yes, I know.
I'm sorry I got so mad at the trick you pulled.
LOST

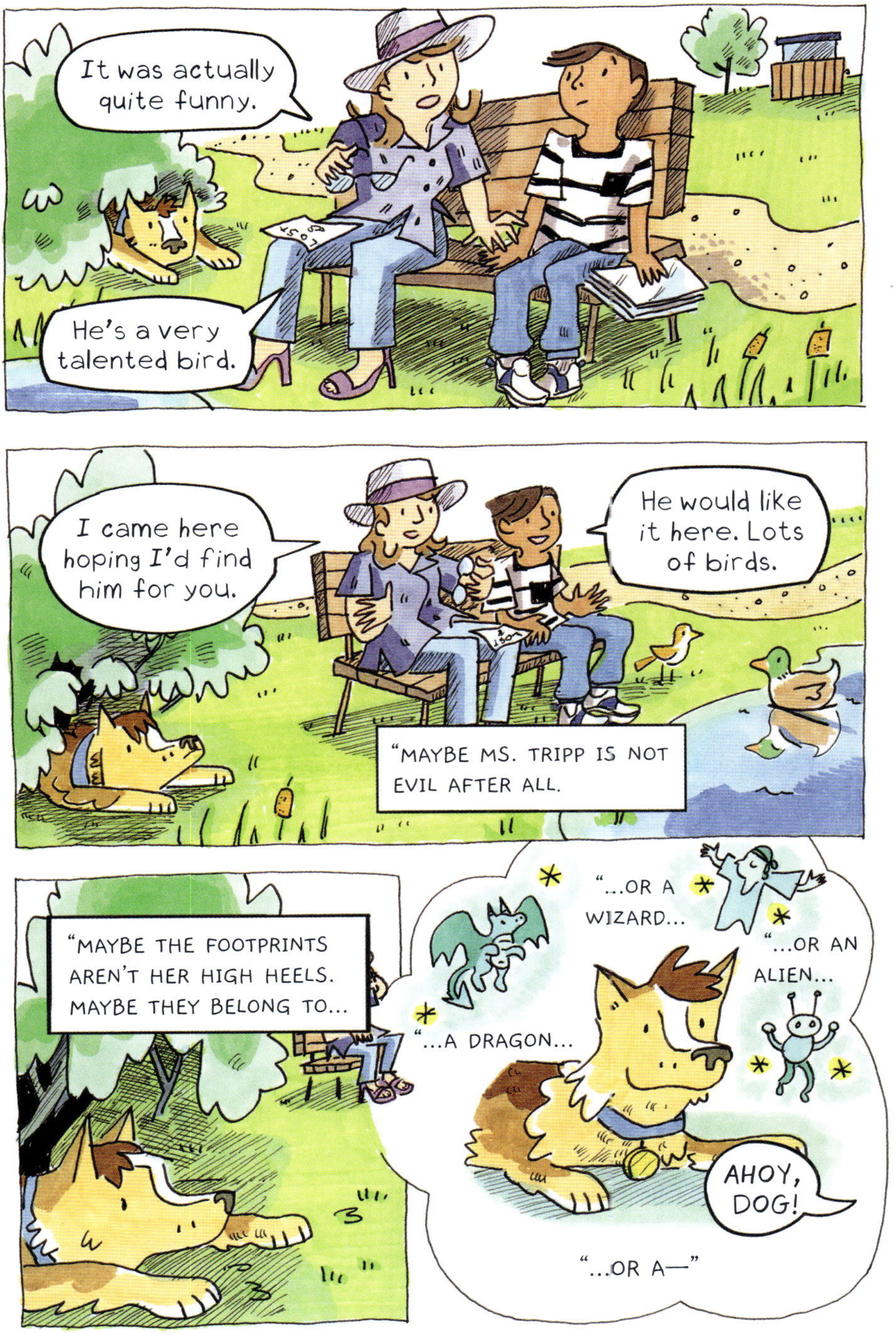
It was actually quite funny.
He's a very talented bird.
I came here hoping I'd find him for you.
He would like it here. Lots of birds.
"MAYBE MS. TRIPP IS NOT EVIL AFTER ALL.
"MAYBE THE FOOTPRINTS AREN'T HER HIGH HEELS. MAYBE THEY BELONG TO...
"...A DRAGON...
"...OR A WIZARD...
"...OR AN ALIEN...
AHOY, DOG!
"...OR A—"

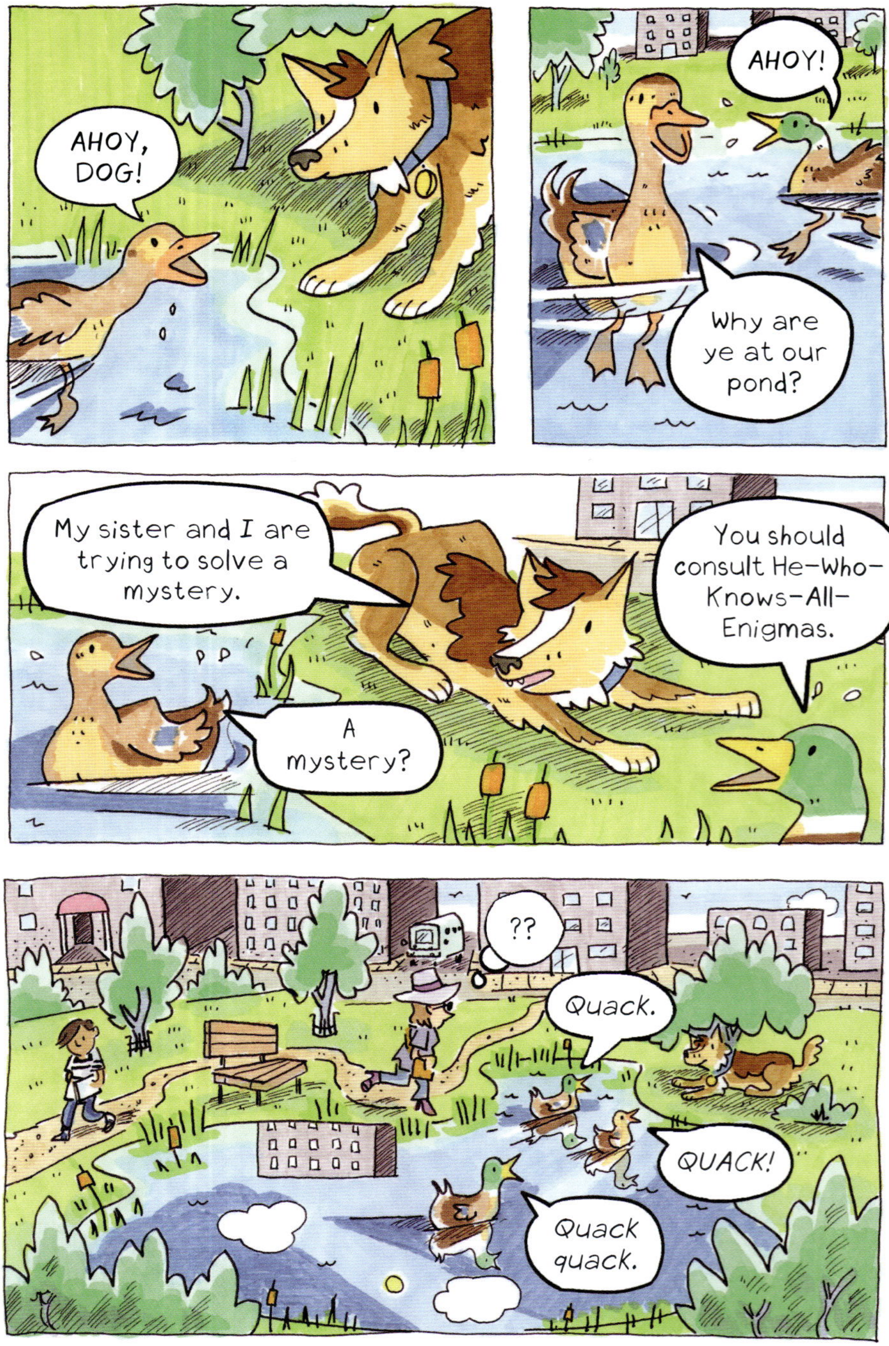
AHOY, DOG!
AHOY!
Why are ye at our pond?
My sister and I are trying to solve a mystery.
A mystery?
You should consult He-Who-Knows-All-Enigmas.
??
Quack.
QUACK!
Quack quack.

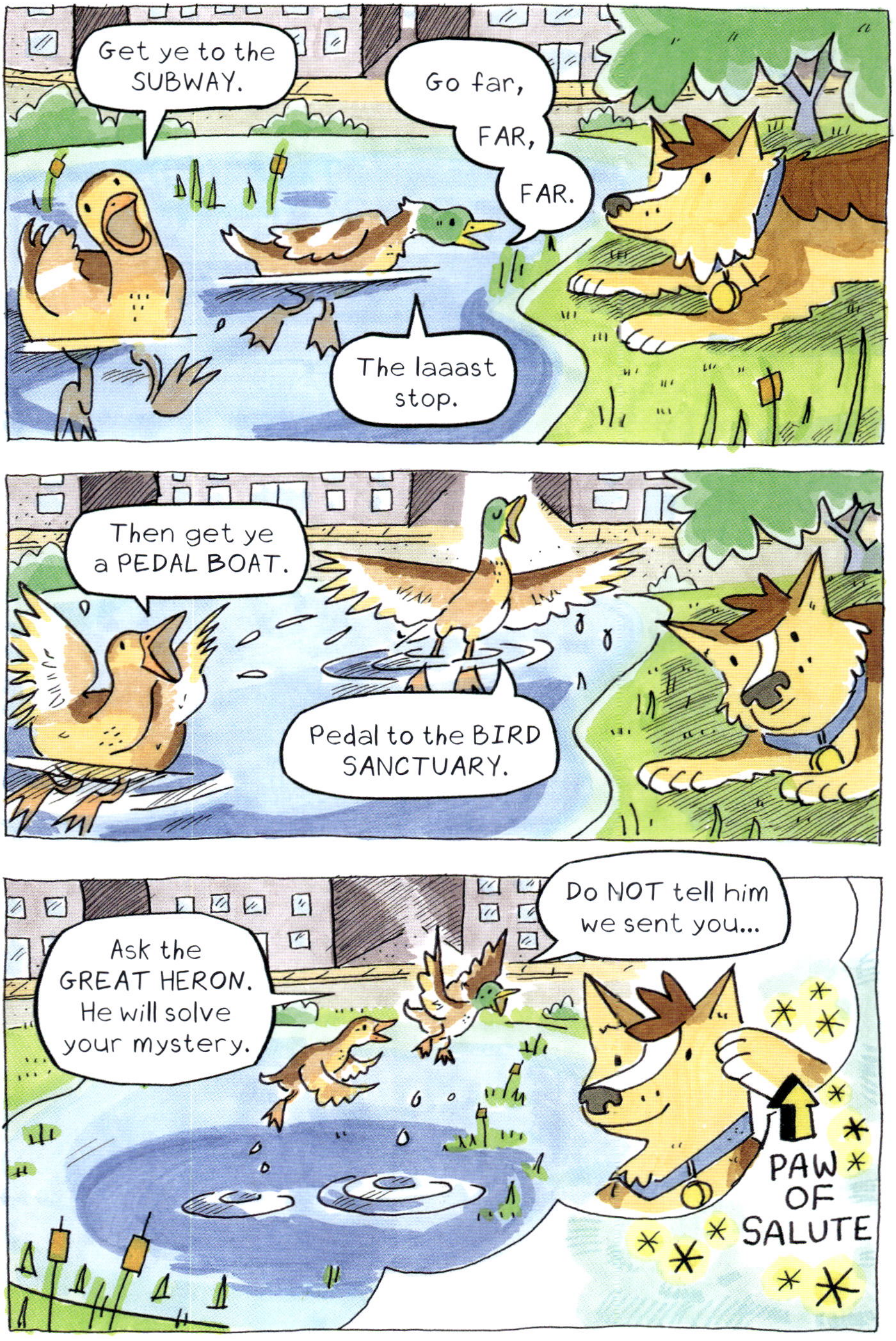
Get ye to the SUBWAY.
Go far,
FAR,
FAR.
The laaast stop.
Then get ye a PEDAL BOAT.
Pedal to the BIRD SANCTUARY.
Ask the GREAT HERON. He will solve your mystery.
Do NOT tell him we sent you...
PAW OF SALUTE

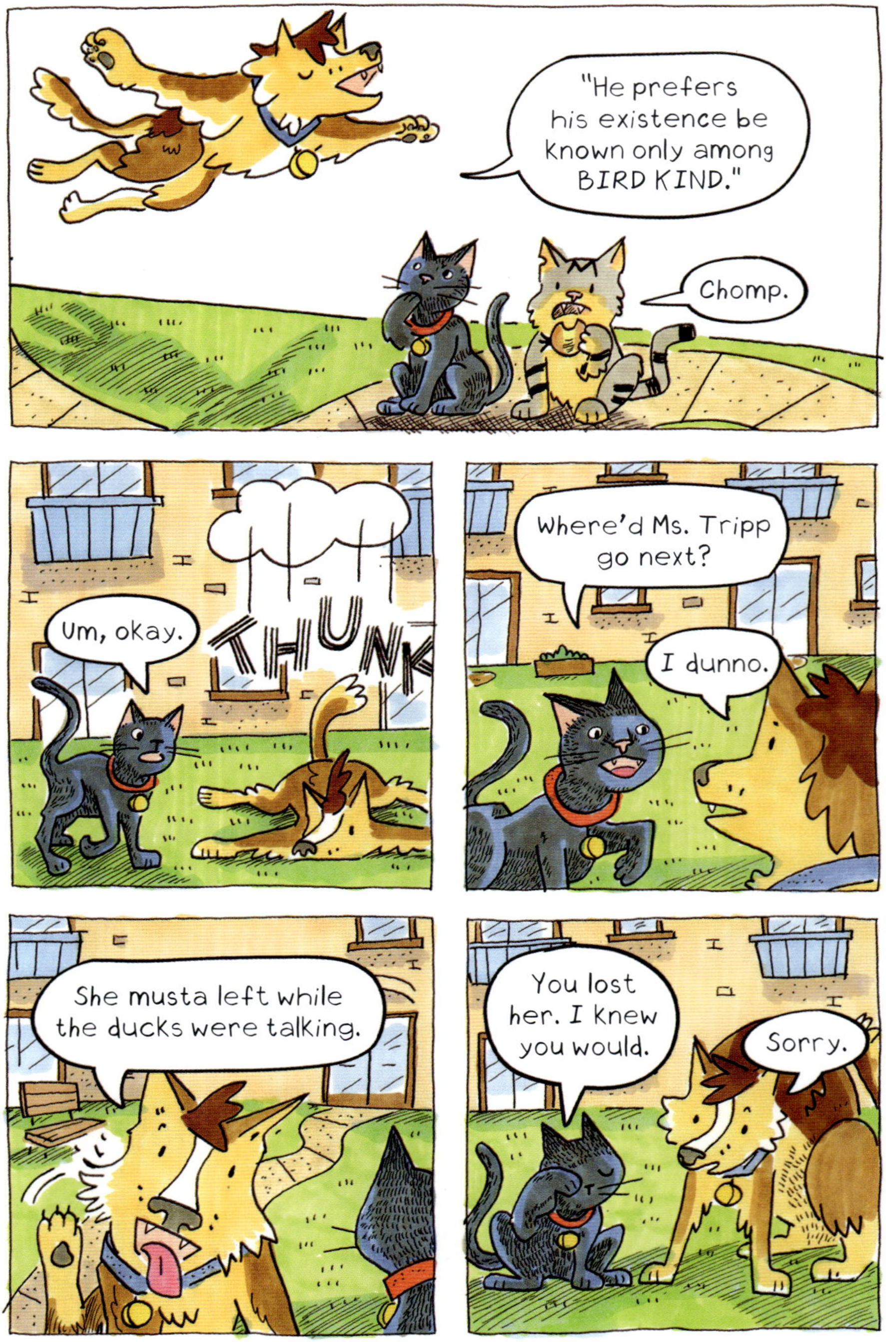
"He prefers his existence be known only among BIRD KIND."
Chomp.
Um, okay.
THUNK
Where'd Ms. Tripp go next?
I dunno.
She musta left while the ducks were talking.
You lost her. I knew you would.
Sorry.

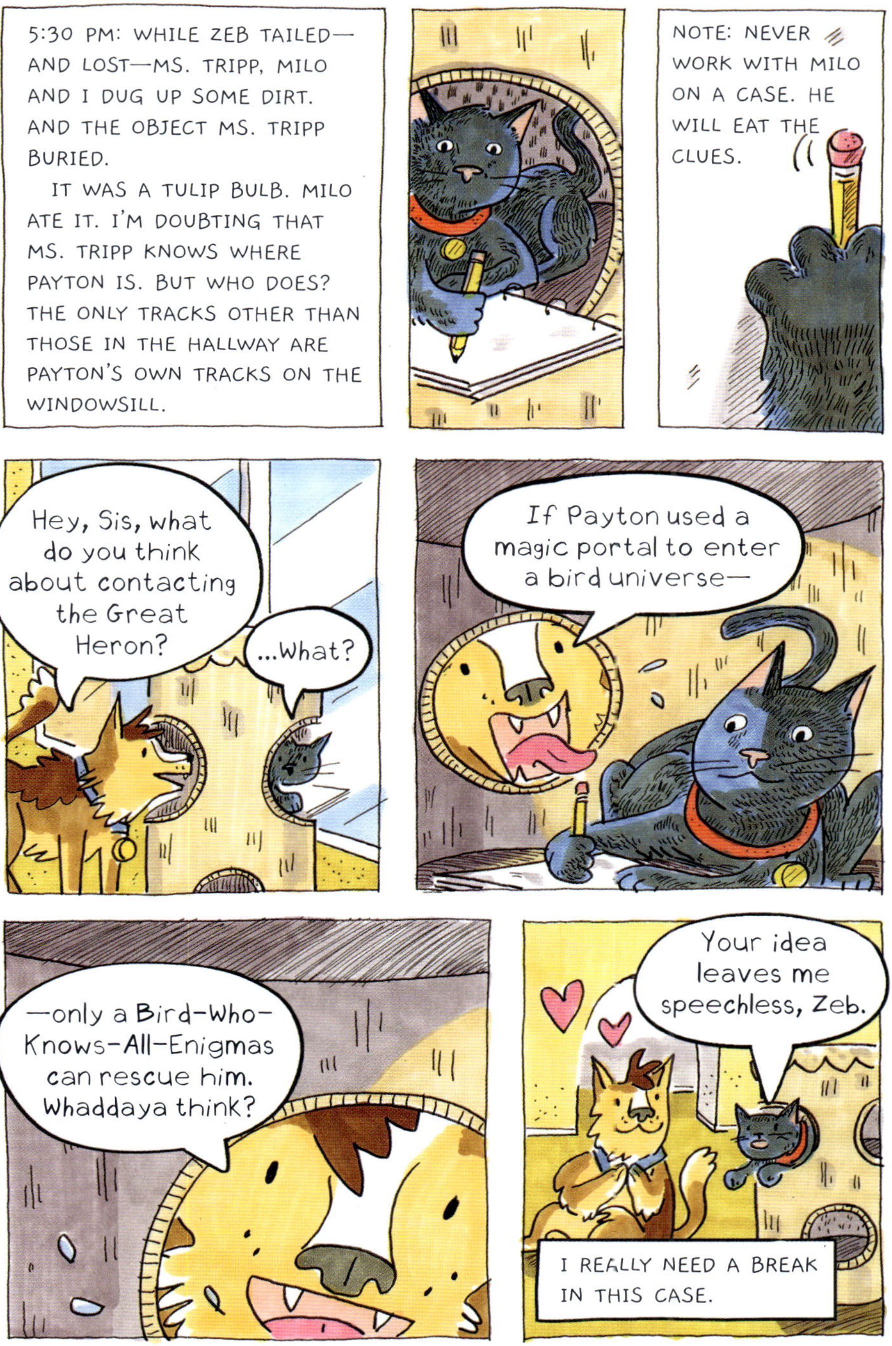
5:30 PM: WHILE ZEB TAILED—AND LOST—MS. TRIPP, MILO AND I DUG UP SOME DIRT. AND THE OBJECT MS. TRIPP BURIED.
IT WAS A TULIP BULB. MILO ATE IT. I'M DOUBTING THAT MS. TRIPP KNOWS WHERE PAYTON IS. BUT WHO DOES? THE ONLY TRACKS OTHER THAN THOSE IN THE HALLWAY ARE PAYTON'S OWN TRACKS ON THE WINDOWSILL.
NOTE: NEVER WORK WITH MILO ON A CASE. HE WILL EAT THE CLUES.
Hey, Sis, what do you think about contacting the Great Heron?
...What?
If Payton used a magic portal to enter a bird universe—
—only a Bird-Who-Knows-All-Enigmas can rescue him. Whaddaya think?
Your idea leaves me speechless, Zeb.
I REALLY NEED A BREAK IN THIS CASE.

CHAPTER 6
A MUSICAL BREAK

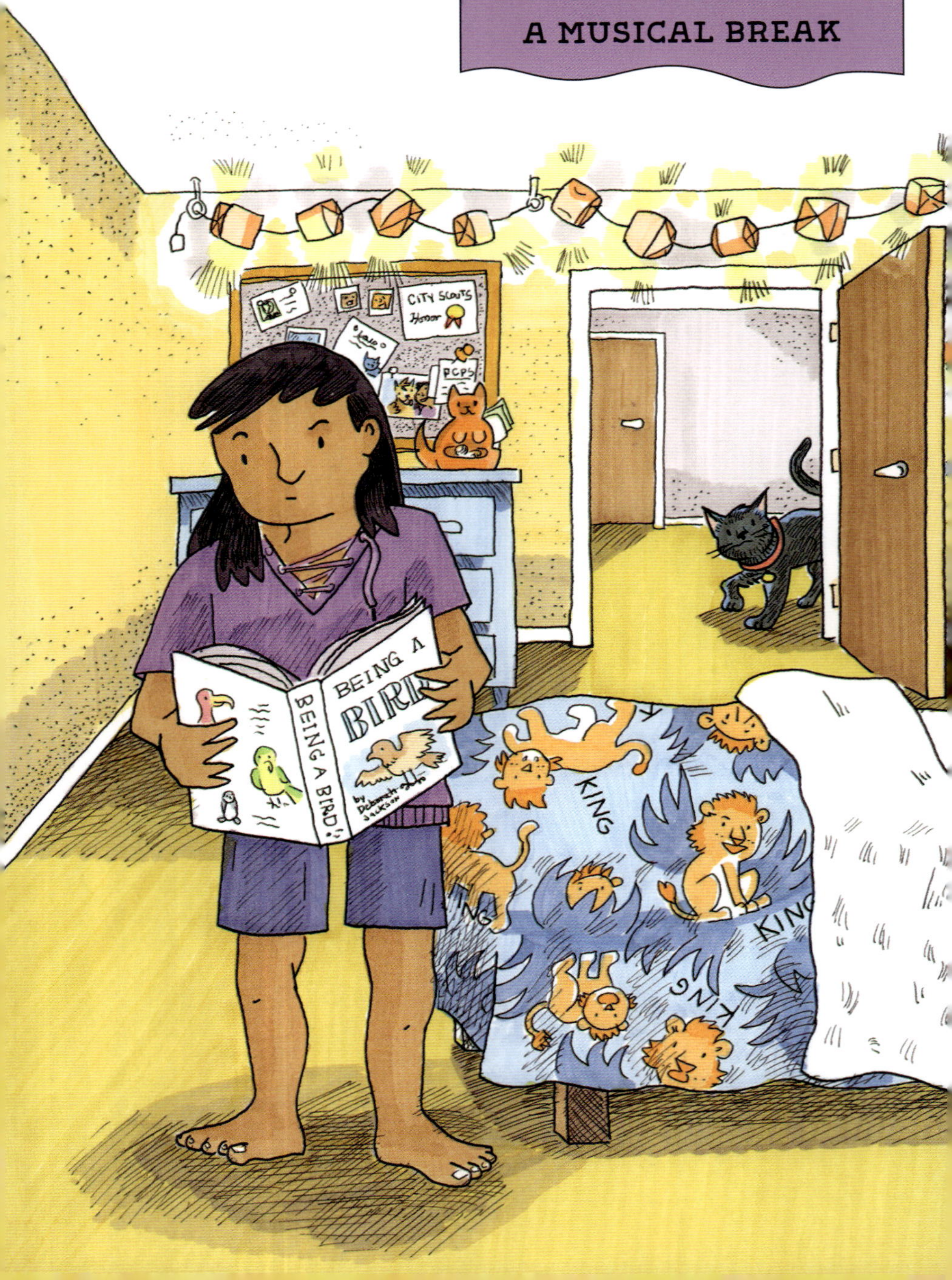

CITY SCOUTS
Honor
RCPS
BEING A
BEING A BIRD
KING

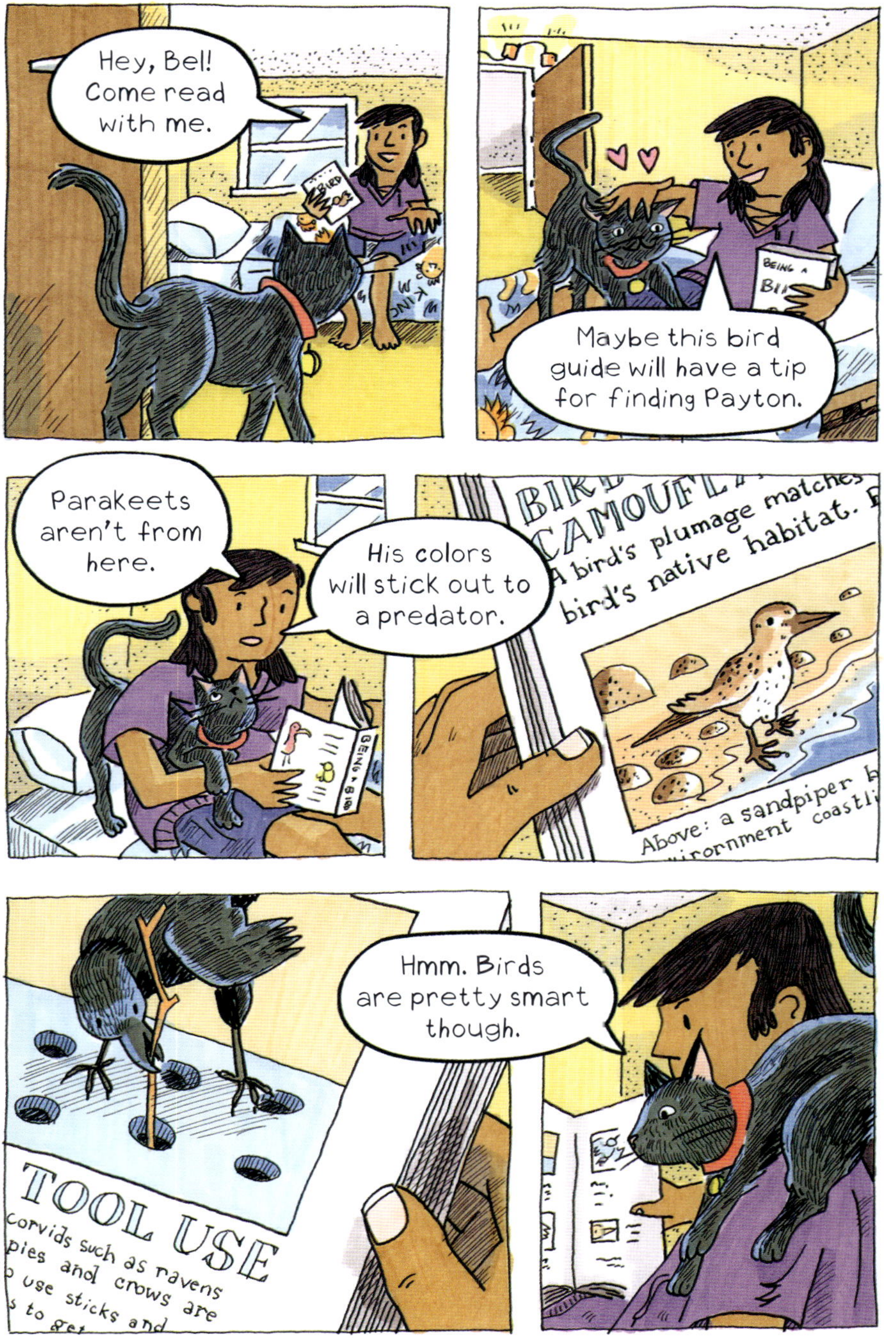
Hey, Bel! Come read with me.
Maybe this bird guide will have a tip for finding Payton.
Parakeets aren't from here.
His colors will stick out to a predator.
BEING A BIRD
A bird's plumage matches
bird's native habitat.
Above: a sandpiper
TOOL USE
corvids such as ravens
pies and crows are
use sticks and
Hmm. Birds are pretty smart though.

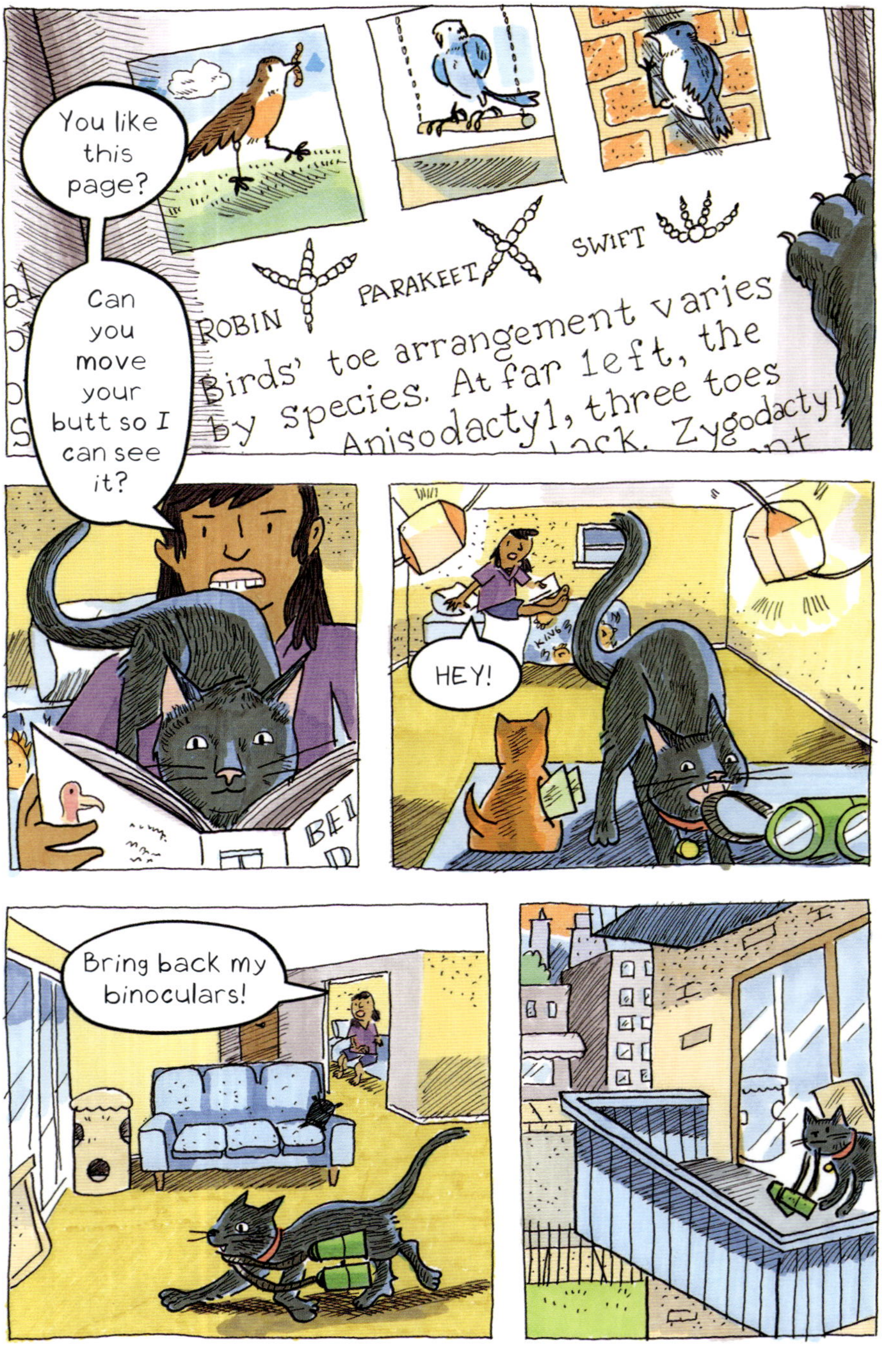
ROBIN
PARAKEET
SWIFT
Birds' toe arrangement varies
by species. At far left, the
Anisodactyl, three toes
...ack. Zygodactyl
You like this page?
Can you move your butt so I can see it?
HEY!
Bring back my binoculars!

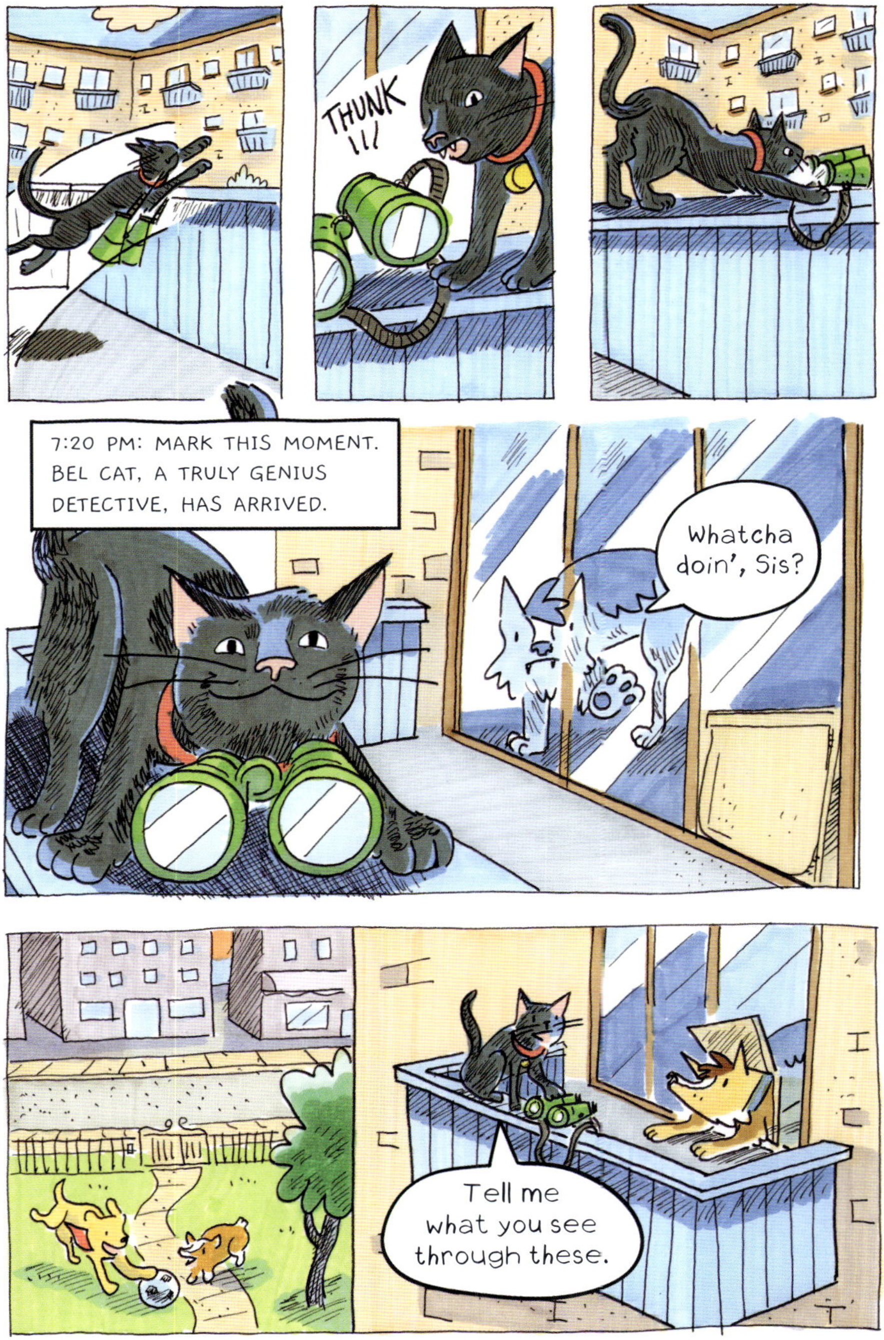
THUNK
7:20 PM: MARK THIS MOMENT. BEL CAT, A TRULY GENIUS DETECTIVE, HAS ARRIVED.
Whatcha doin', Sis?
Tell me what you see through these.

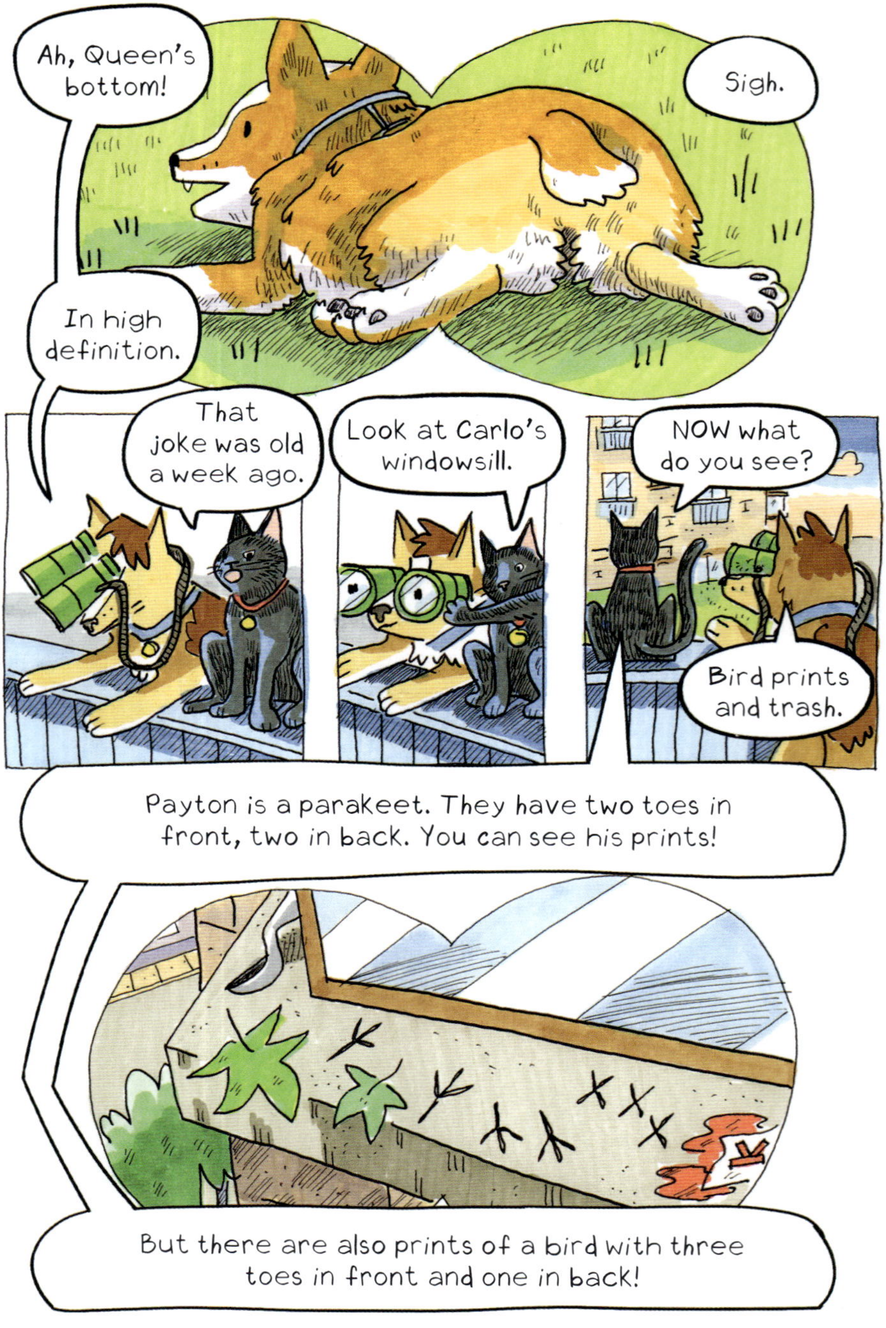
Ah, Queen's bottom!
Sigh.
In high definition.
That joke was old a week ago.
Look at Carlo's windowsill.
NOW what do you see?
Bird prints and trash.
Payton is a parakeet. They have two toes in front, two in back. You can see his prints!
But there are also prints of a bird with three toes in front and one in back!

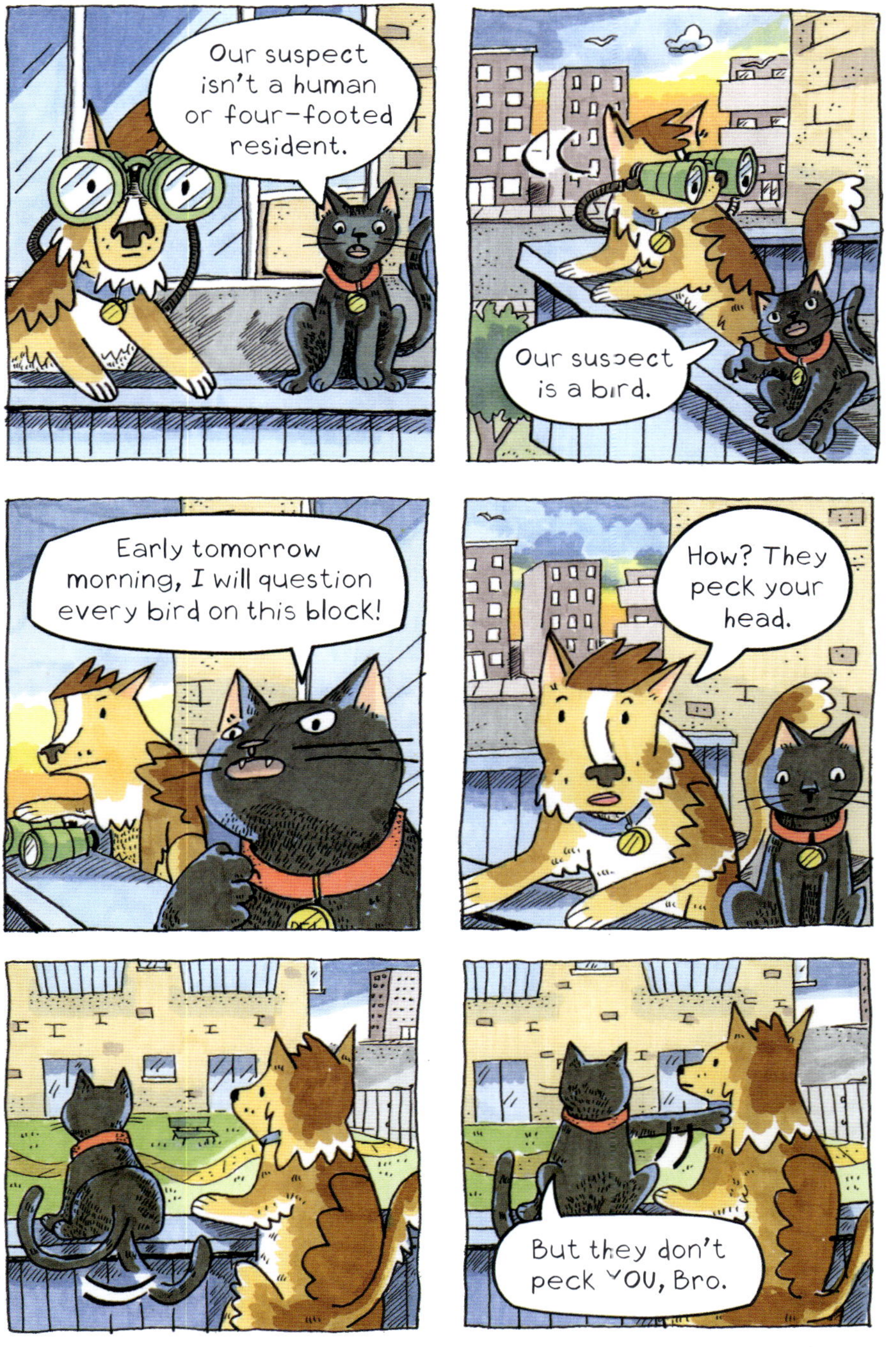
Our suspect isn't a human or four-footed resident.
Our suspect is a bird.
Early tomorrow morning, I will question every bird on this block!
How? They peck your head.
But they don't peck YOU, Bro.

JUNE 3, 8:15 AM: JOSEPHINE AND HER FAMILY GO WITH CARLO AND HALF A DOZEN OTHER BUILDING RESIDENTS TO SEARCH THE CITY FOR PAYTON.

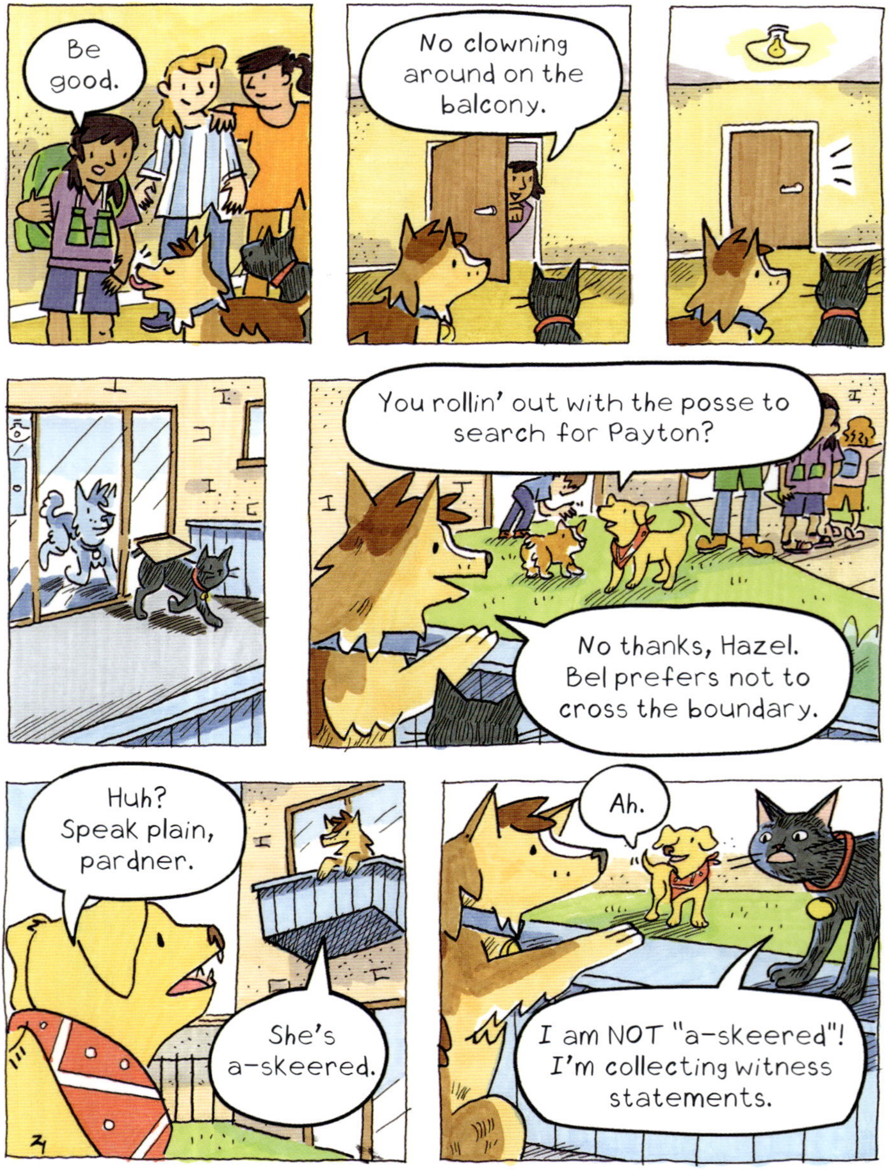

Be good.
No clowning around on the balcony.
You rollin' out with the posse to search for Payton?
No thanks, Hazel. Bel prefers not to cross the boundary.
Huh? Speak plain, pardner.
She's a-skeered.
Ah.
I am NOT "a-skeered"! I'm collecting witness statements.

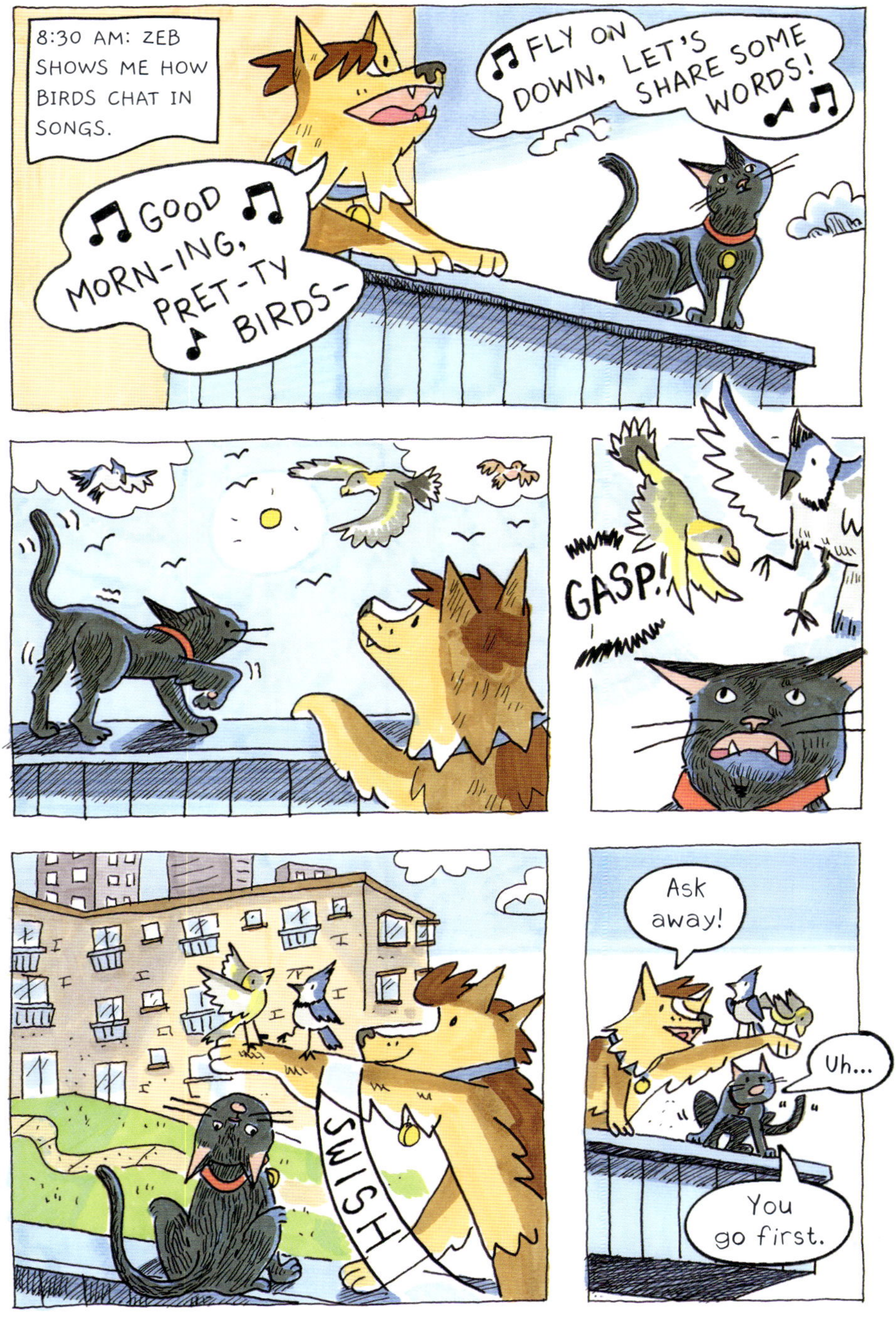
8:30 AM: ZEB SHOWS ME HOW BIRDS CHAT IN SONGS.
♫ GOOD ♫ MORN-ING, PRET-TY ♪ BIRDS-
♫ FLY ON DOWN, LET'S SHARE SOME WORDS! ♪ ♫
GASP!
SWISH
Ask away!
Uh...
You go first.

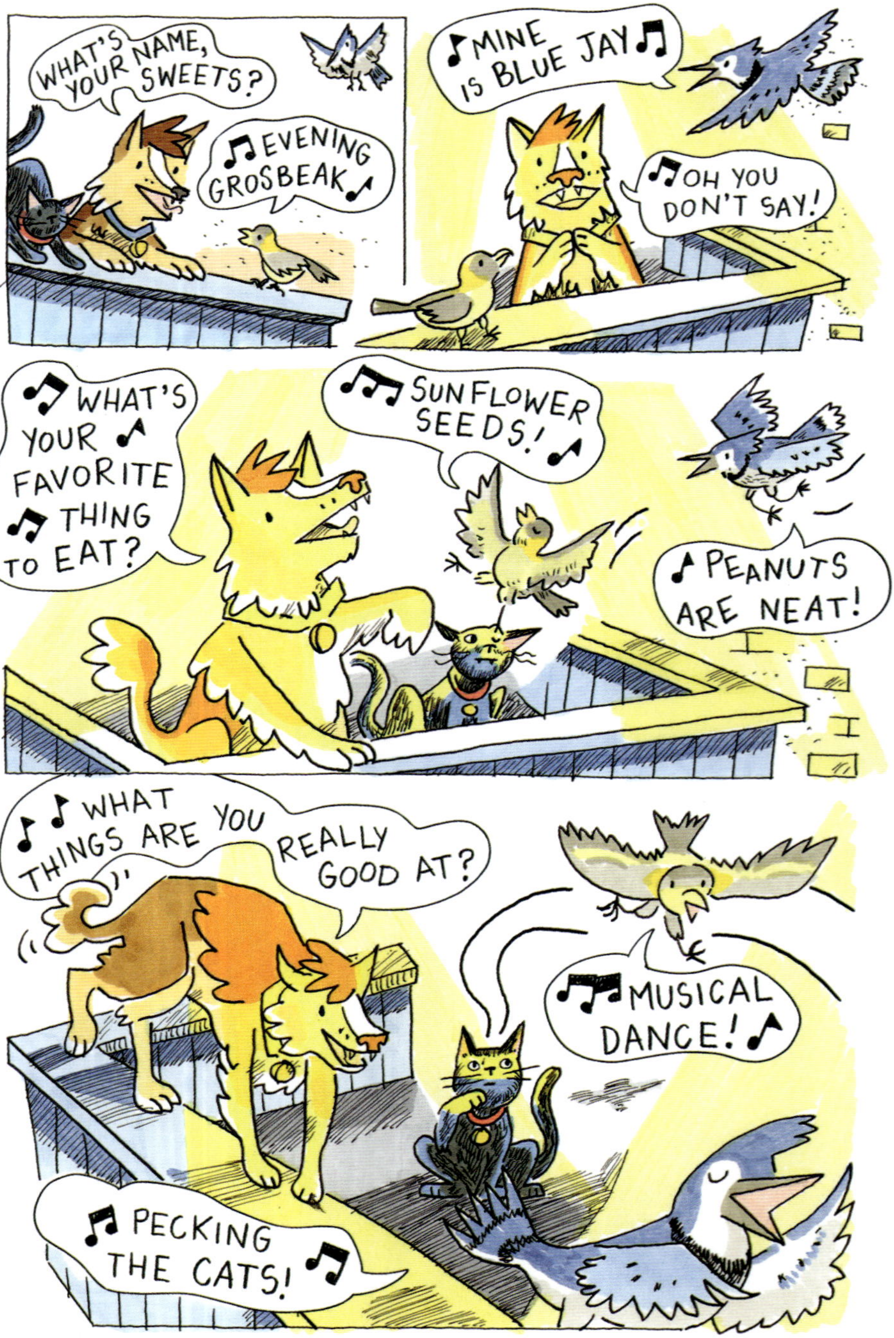
WHAT'S YOUR NAME, SWEETS?
♪ EVENING GROSBEAK ♪
♪ MINE IS BLUE JAY ♪
♪ OH YOU DON'T SAY!
♪ WHAT'S YOUR ♪ FAVORITE ♪ THING TO EAT?
♪ SUNFLOWER SEEDS! ♪
♪ PEANUTS ARE NEAT!
♪ ♪ WHAT THINGS ARE YOU REALLY GOOD AT?
♪ MUSICAL DANCE! ♪
♪ PECKING THE CATS! ♪

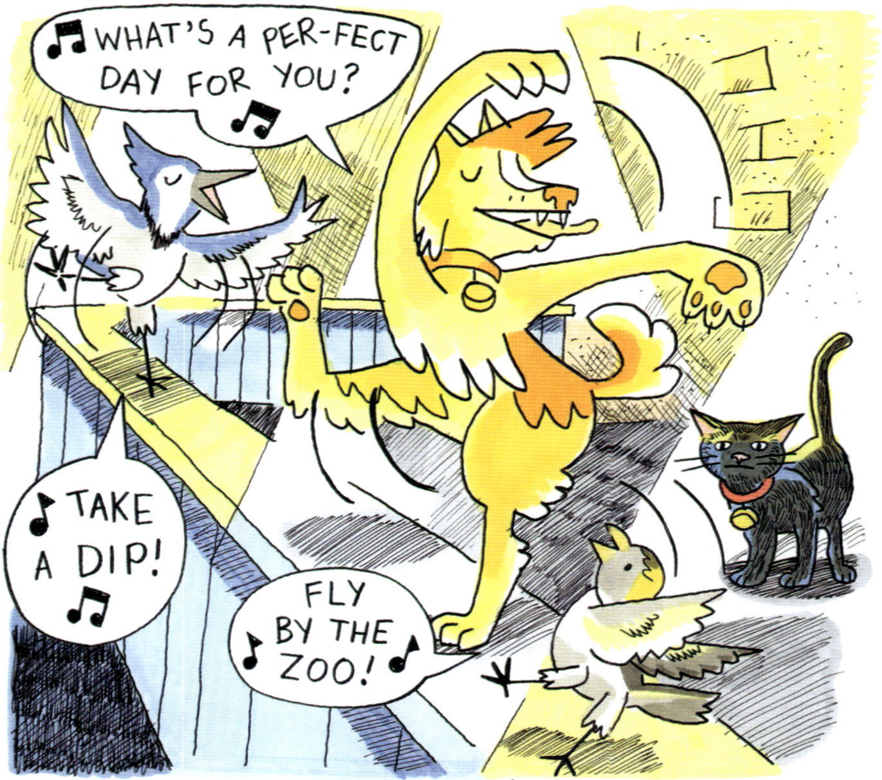
♫ WHAT'S A PER-FECT DAY FOR YOU? ♫
♪ TAKE A DIP! ♫
FLY ♪ BY THE ZOO! ♪

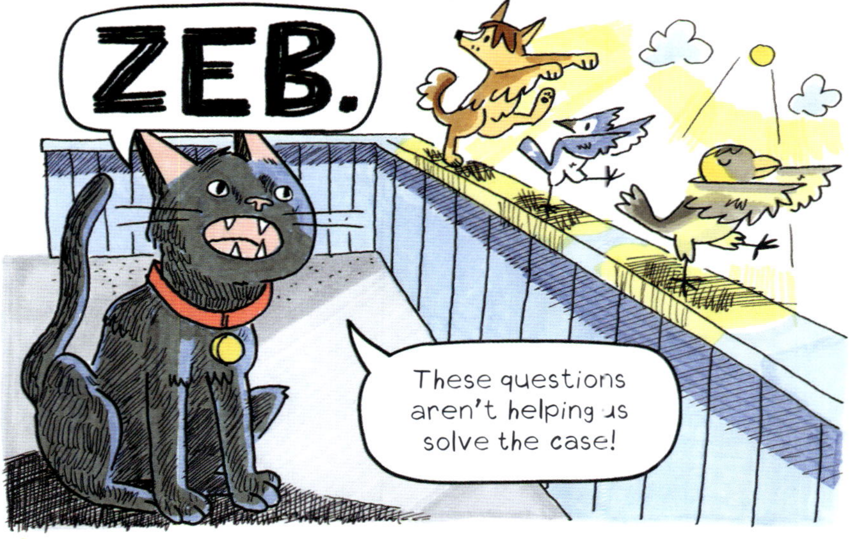
ZEB.
These questions aren't helping us solve the case!

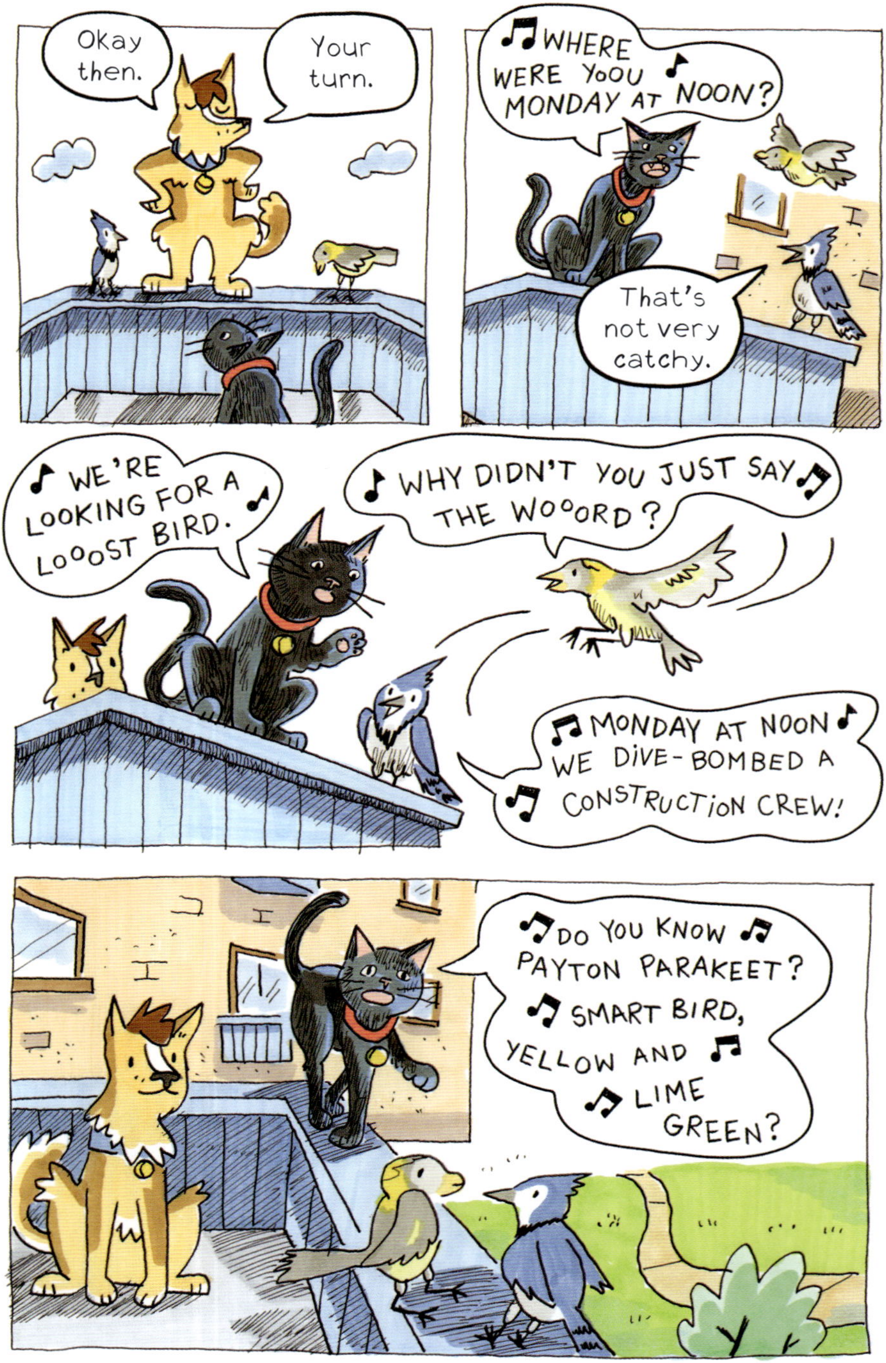

Okay then.
Your turn.
WHERE WERE YOOU MONDAY AT NOON?
That's not very catchy.
WE'RE LOOKING FOR A LOOOST BIRD.
WHY DIDN'T YOU JUST SAY THE WOOORD?
MONDAY AT NOON WE DIVE-BOMBED A CONSTRUCTION CREW!
DO YOU KNOW PAYTON PARAKEET? SMART BIRD, YELLOW AND LIME GREEN?

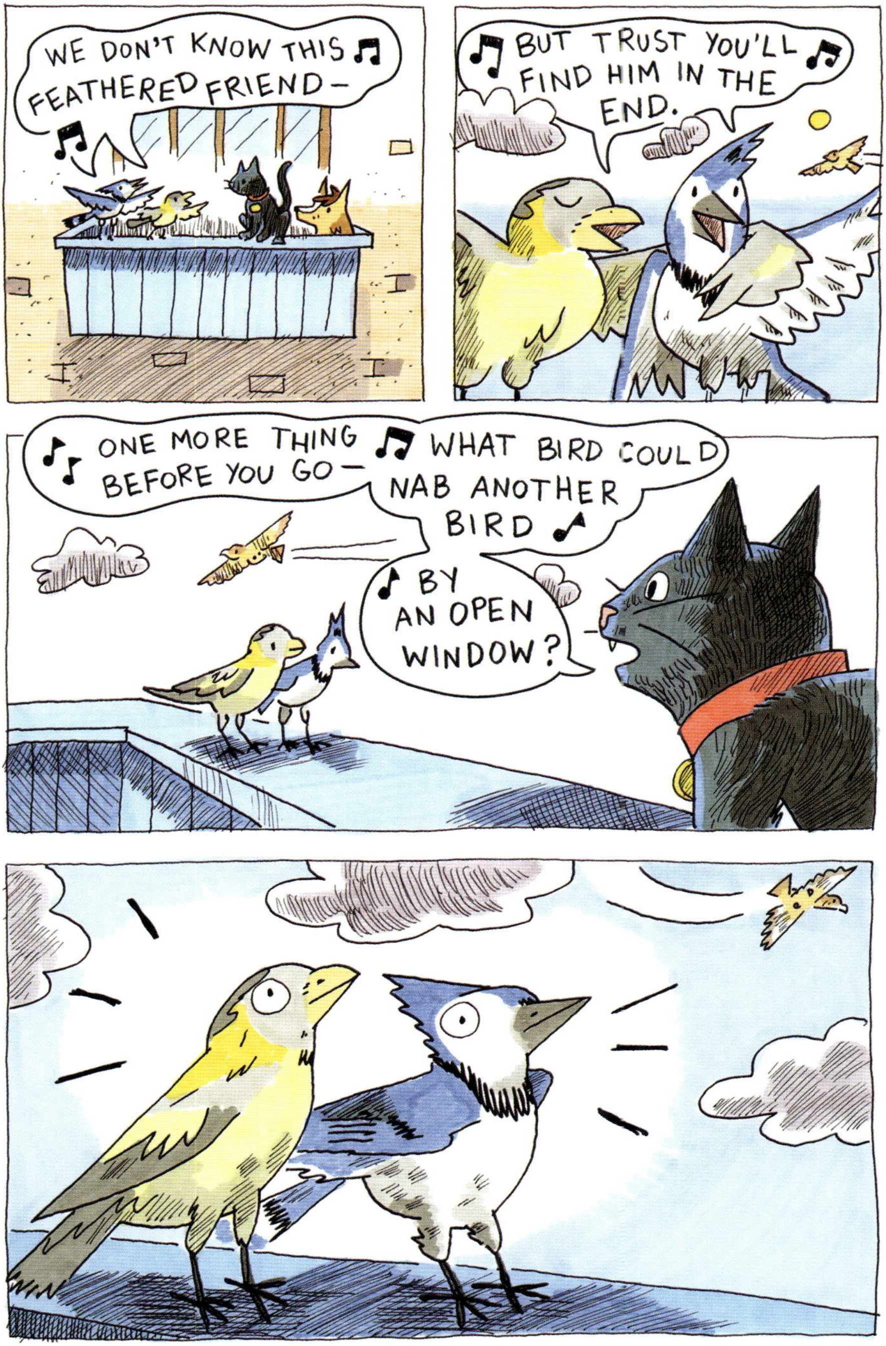
WE DON'T KNOW THIS FEATHERED FRIEND—
BUT TRUST YOU'LL FIND HIM IN THE END.
ONE MORE THING BEFORE YOU GO—
WHAT BIRD COULD NAB ANOTHER BIRD
BY AN OPEN WINDOW?

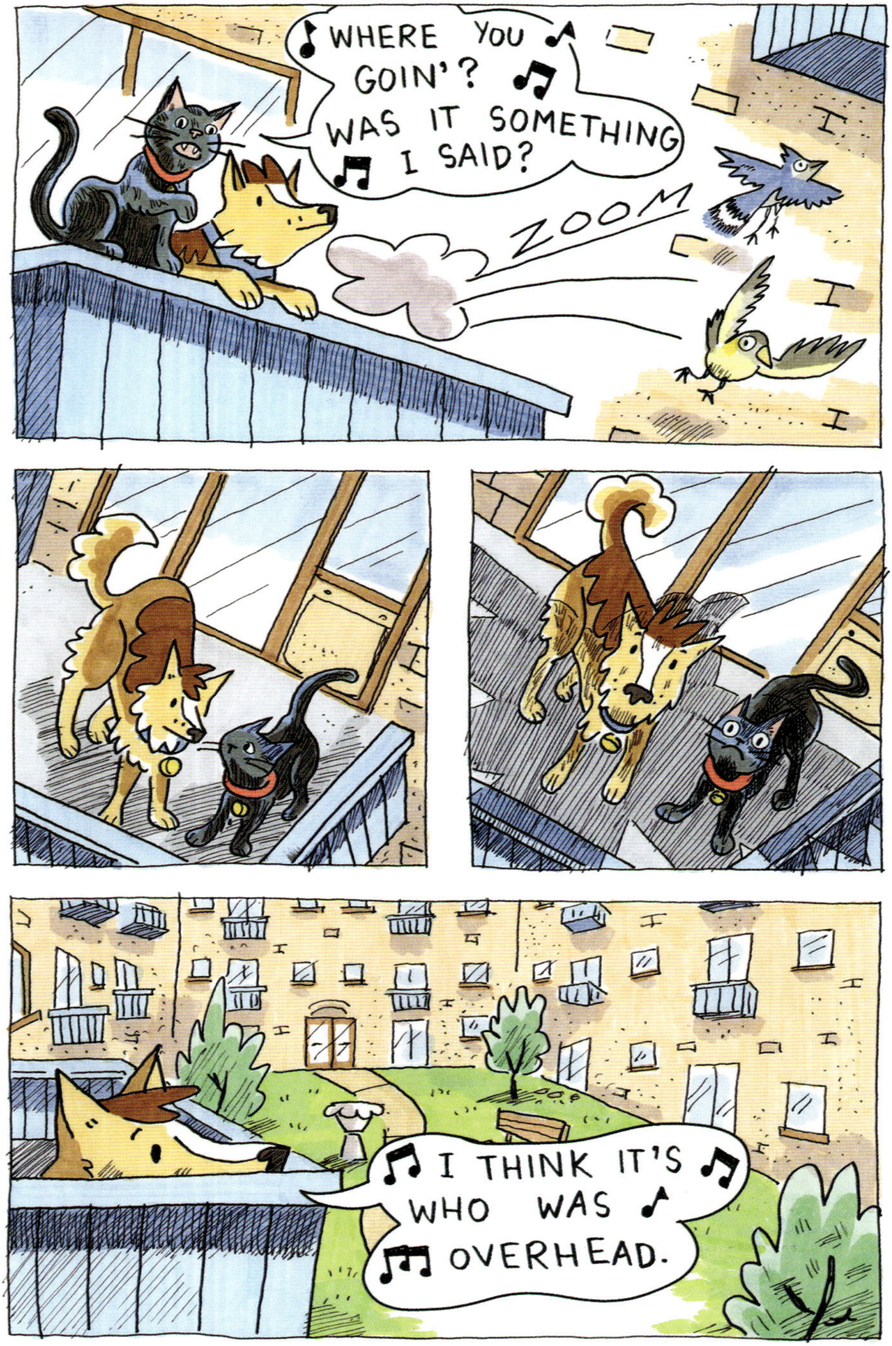
WHERE YOU GOIN'? WAS IT SOMETHING I SAID?
ZOOM
I THINK IT'S WHO WAS OVERHEAD.

CHAPTER 7
ZEB VANQUISHES A SUSPECT, GENTLY

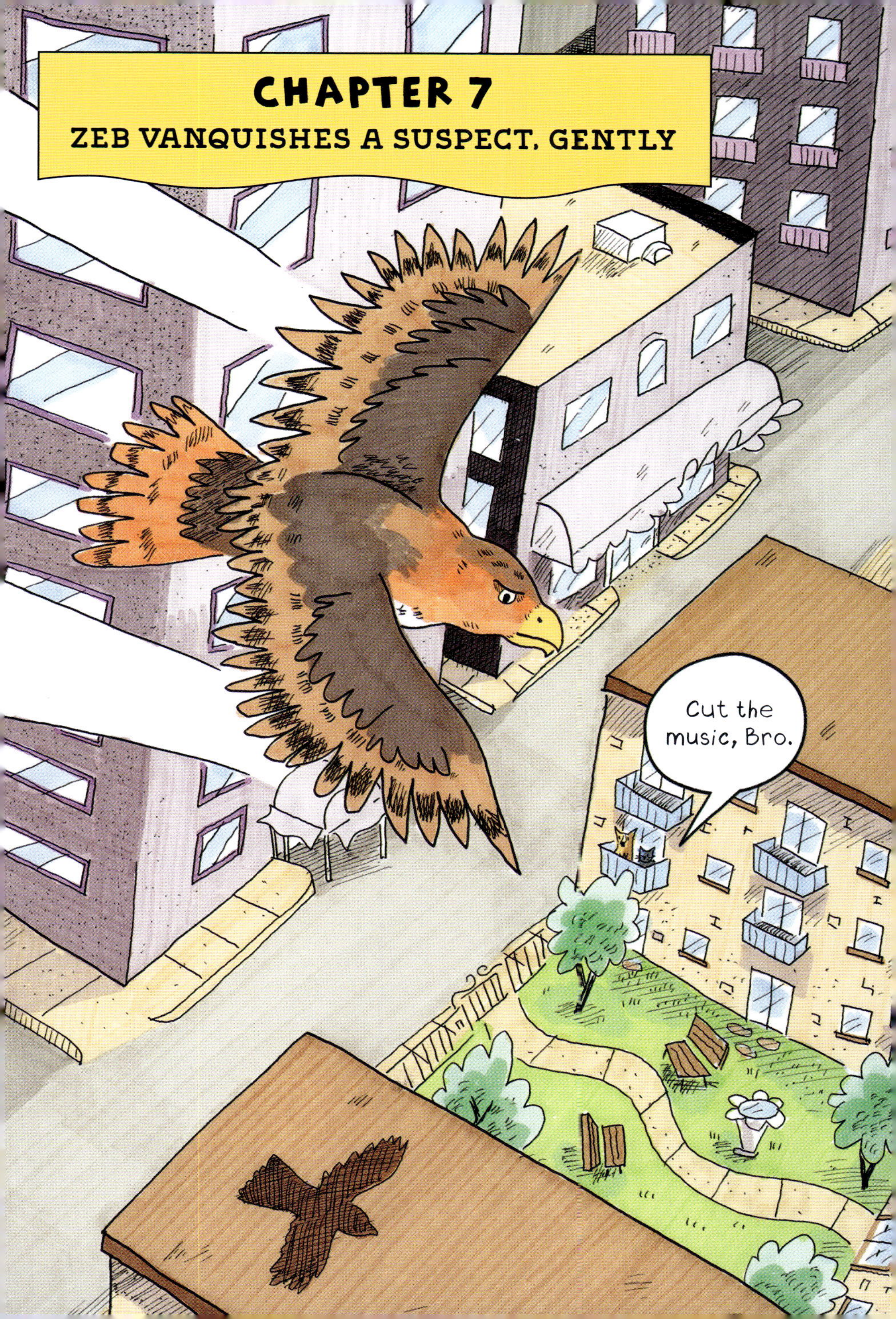
Cut the music, Bro.

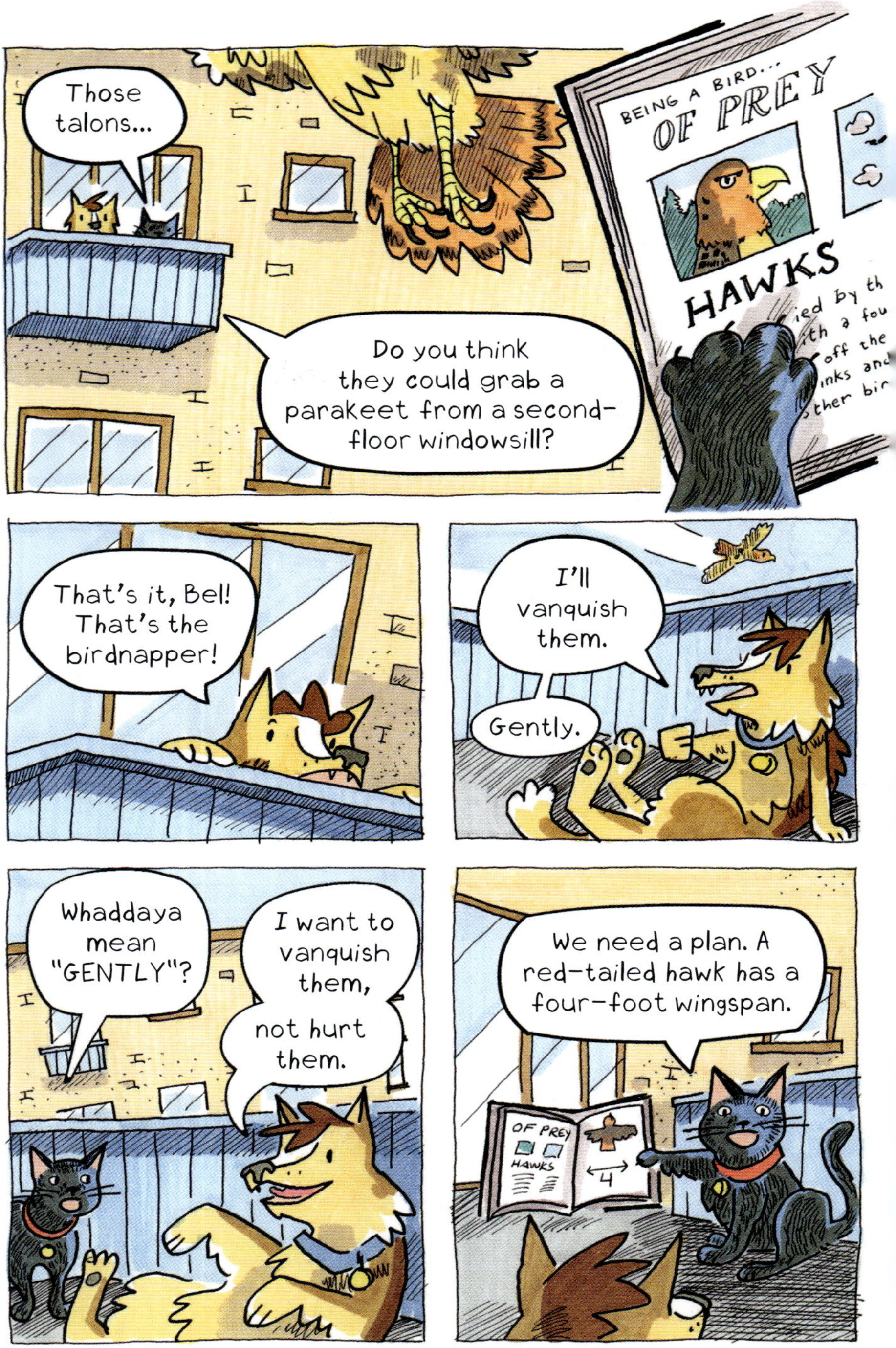
Those talons...
BEING A BIRD... OF PREY
HAWKS
Do you think they could grab a parakeet from a second-floor windowsill?
That's it, Bel! That's the birdnapper!
I'll vanquish them.
Gently.
Whaddaya mean "GENTLY"?
I want to vanquish them,
not hurt them.
We need a plan. A red-tailed hawk has a four-foot wingspan.
OF PREY
HAWKS
4

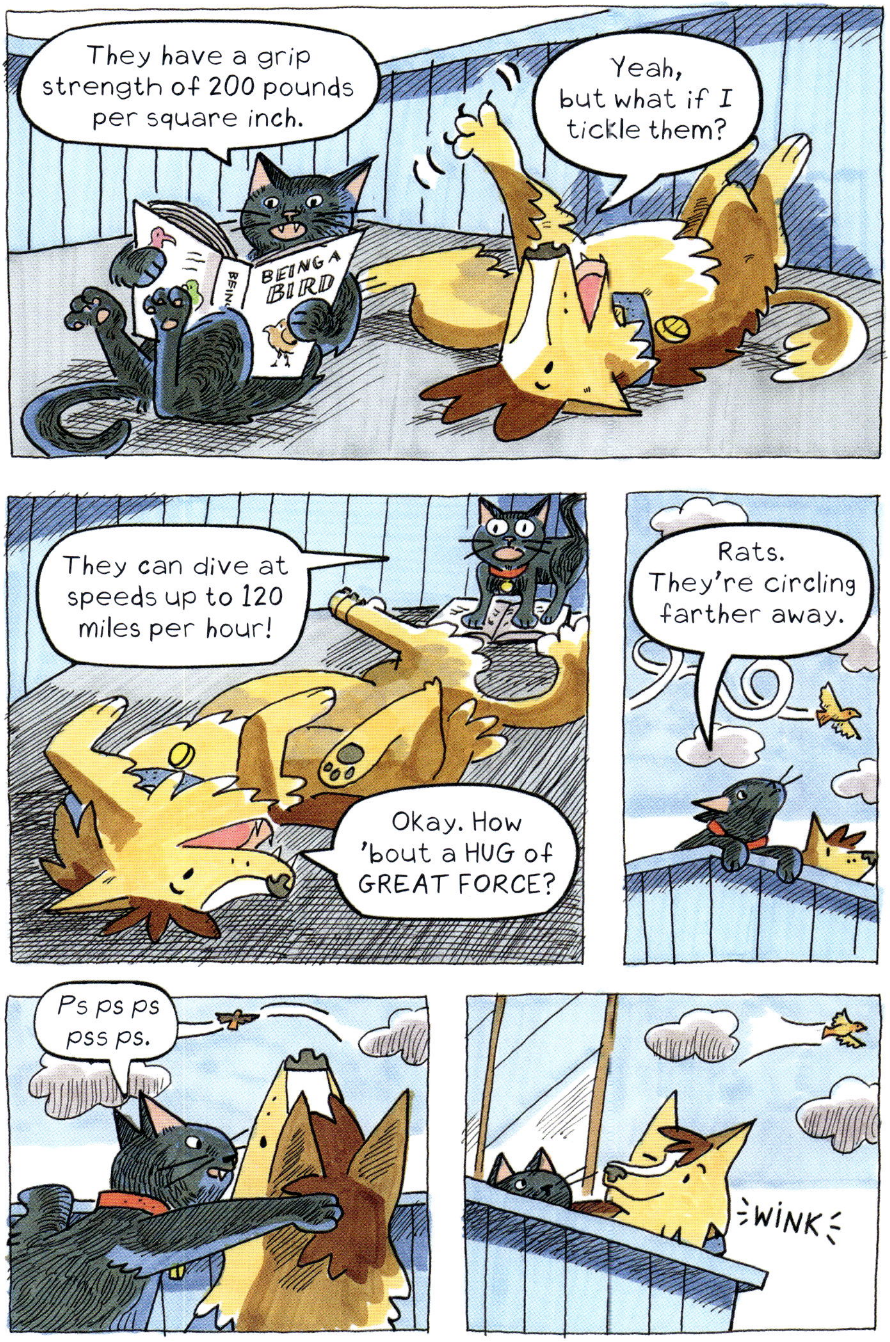
They have a grip strength of 200 pounds per square inch.
Yeah, but what if I tickle them?
BEING A BIRD
They can dive at speeds up to 120 miles per hour!
Okay. How 'bout a HUG of GREAT FORCE?
Rats. They're circling farther away.
Ps ps ps pss ps.
WINK

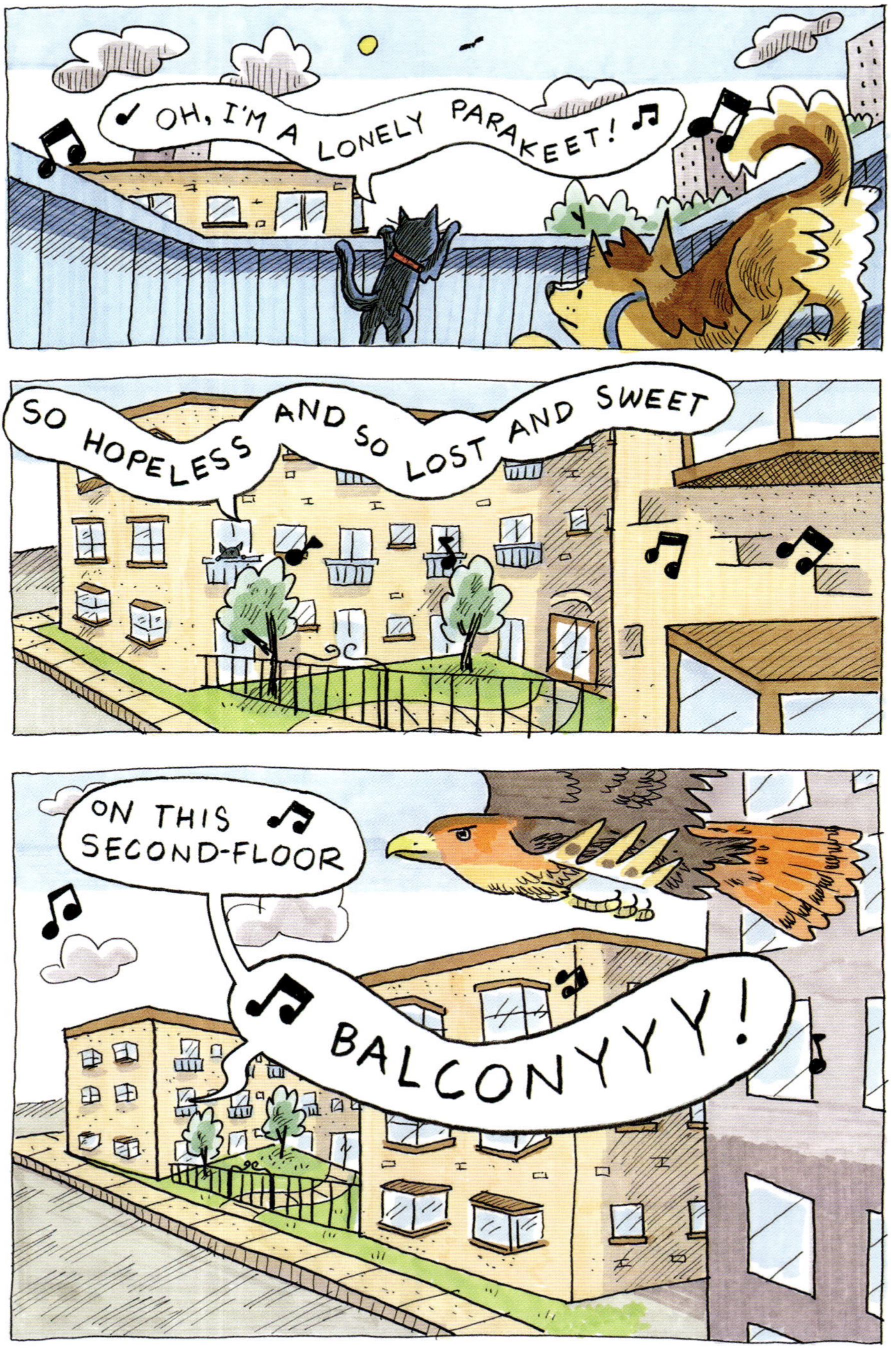
OH, I'M A LONELY PARAKEET!
SO HOPELESS AND SO LOST AND SWEET
ON THIS SECOND-FLOOR
BALCONYYY!

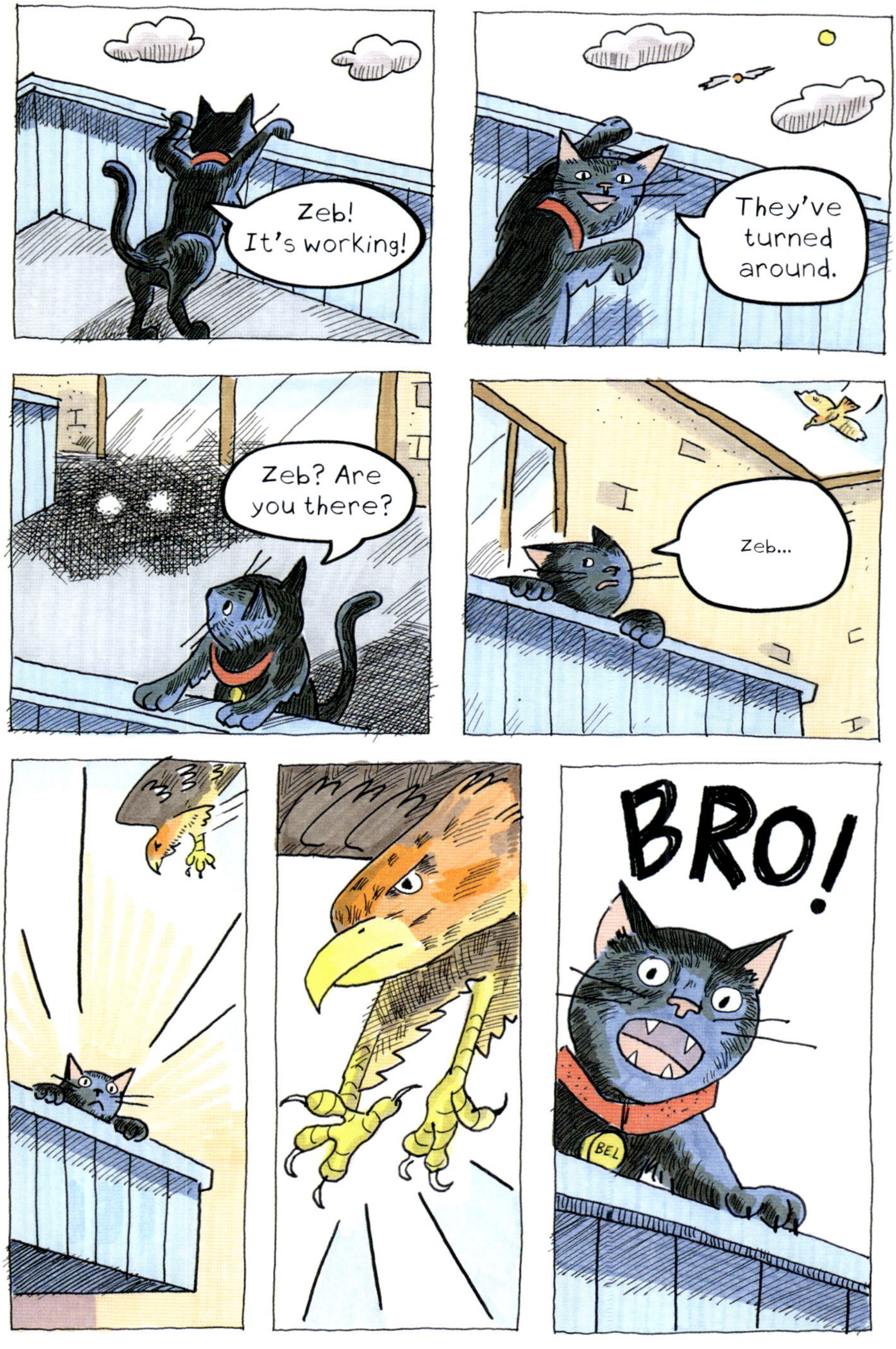
Zeb! It's working!
They've turned around.
Zeb? Are you there?
Zeb...
BRO!
BEL

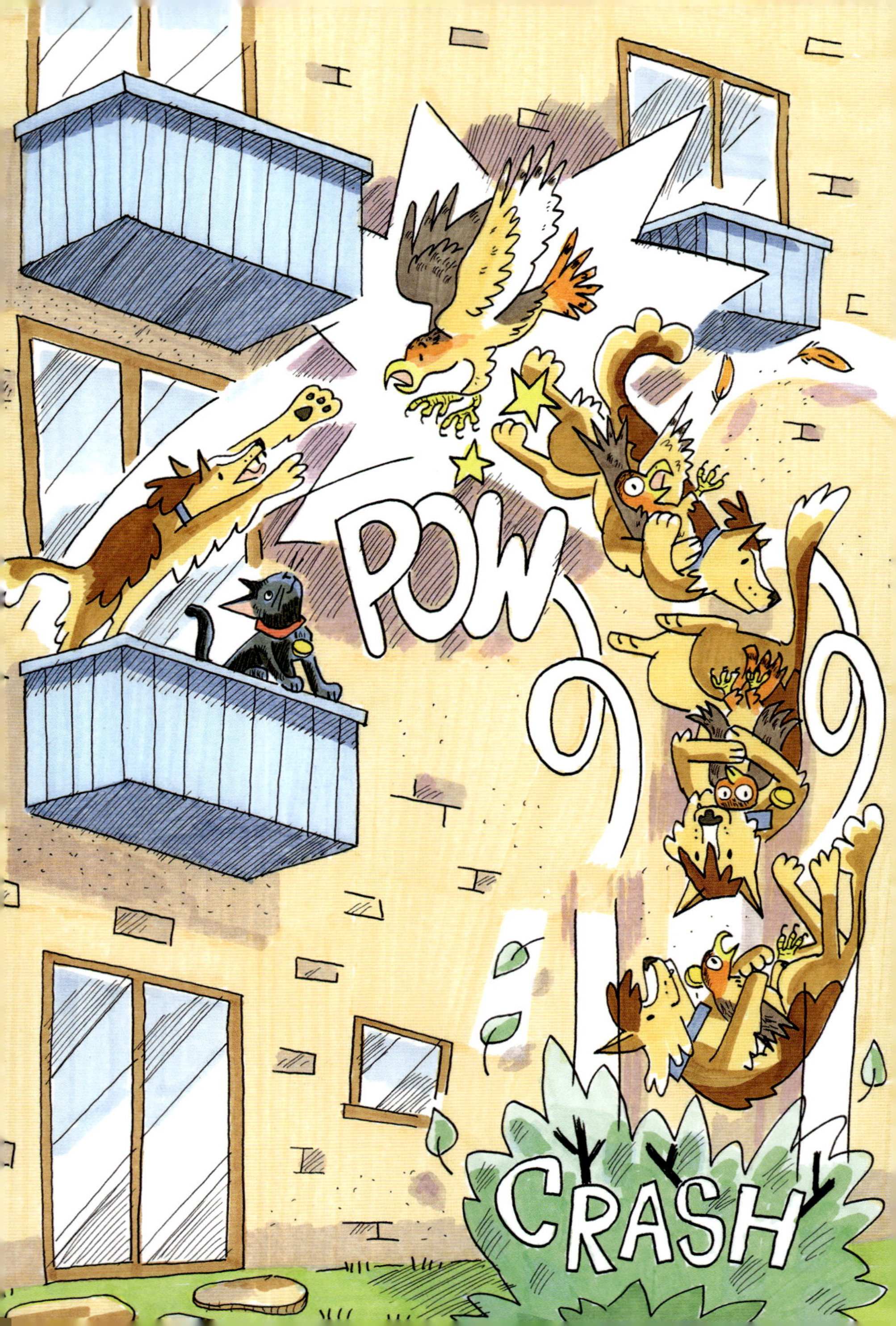
POW
CRASH

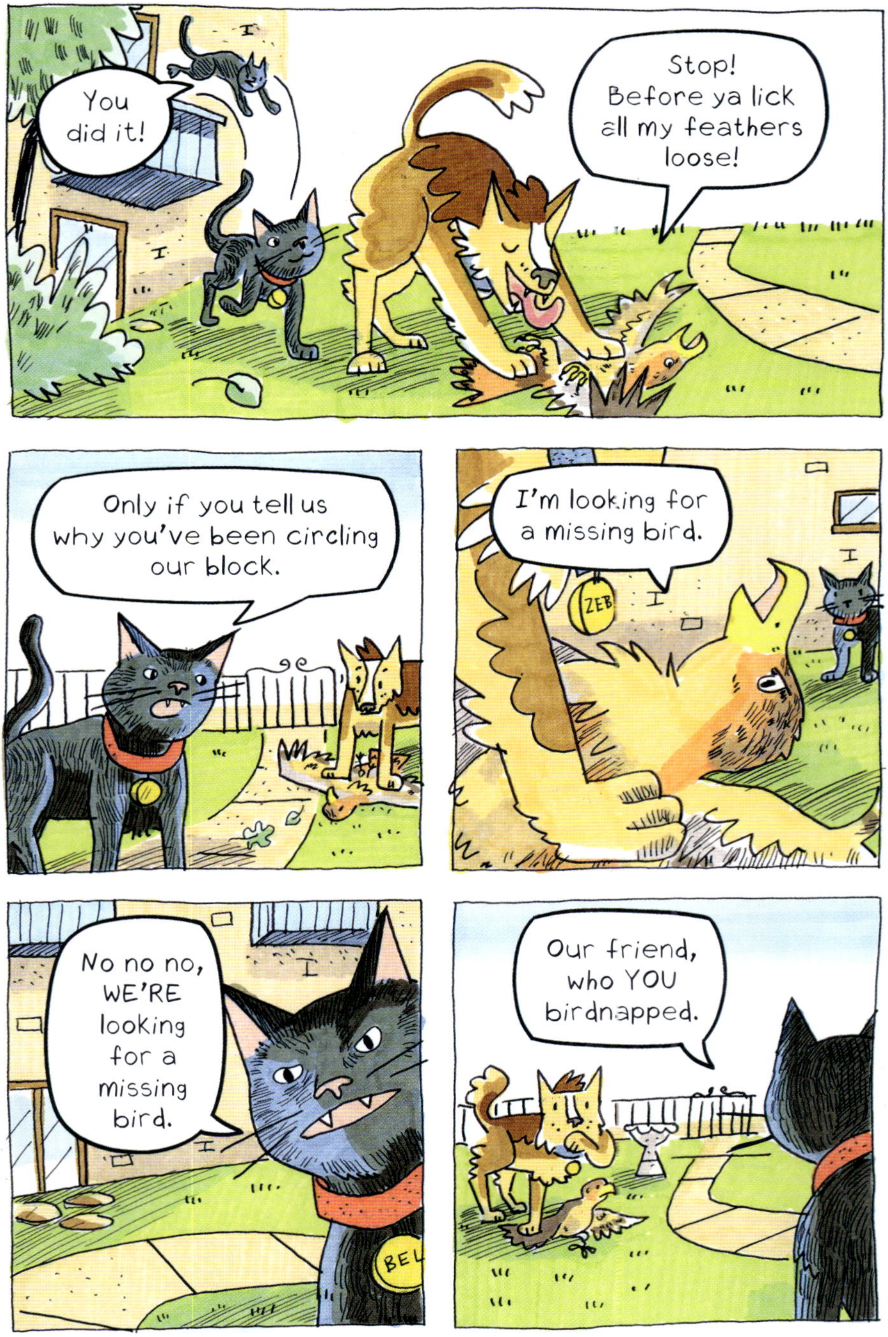
You did it!
Stop! Before ya lick all my feathers loose!
Only if you tell us why you've been circling our block.
I'm looking for a missing bird.
ZEB
No no no, WE'RE looking for a missing bird.
BEL
Our friend, who YOU birdnapped.

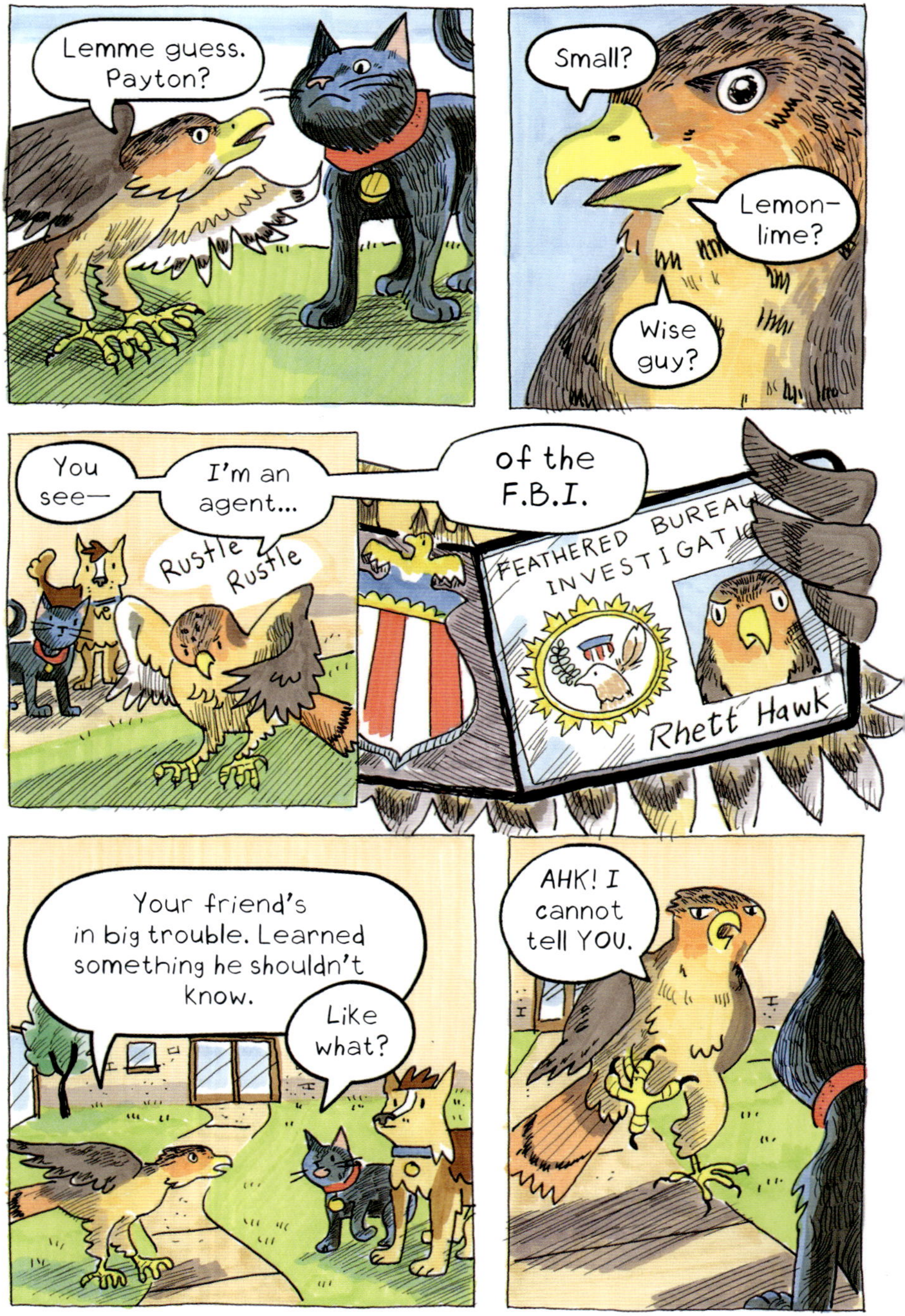
Lemme guess. Payton?
Small?
Lemon-lime?
Wise guy?
You see—
I'm an agent...
of the F.B.I.
Rustle Rustle
FEATHERED BUREAU INVESTIGATIO
Rhett Hawk
Your friend's in big trouble. Learned something he shouldn't know.
Like what?
AHK! I cannot tell YOU.

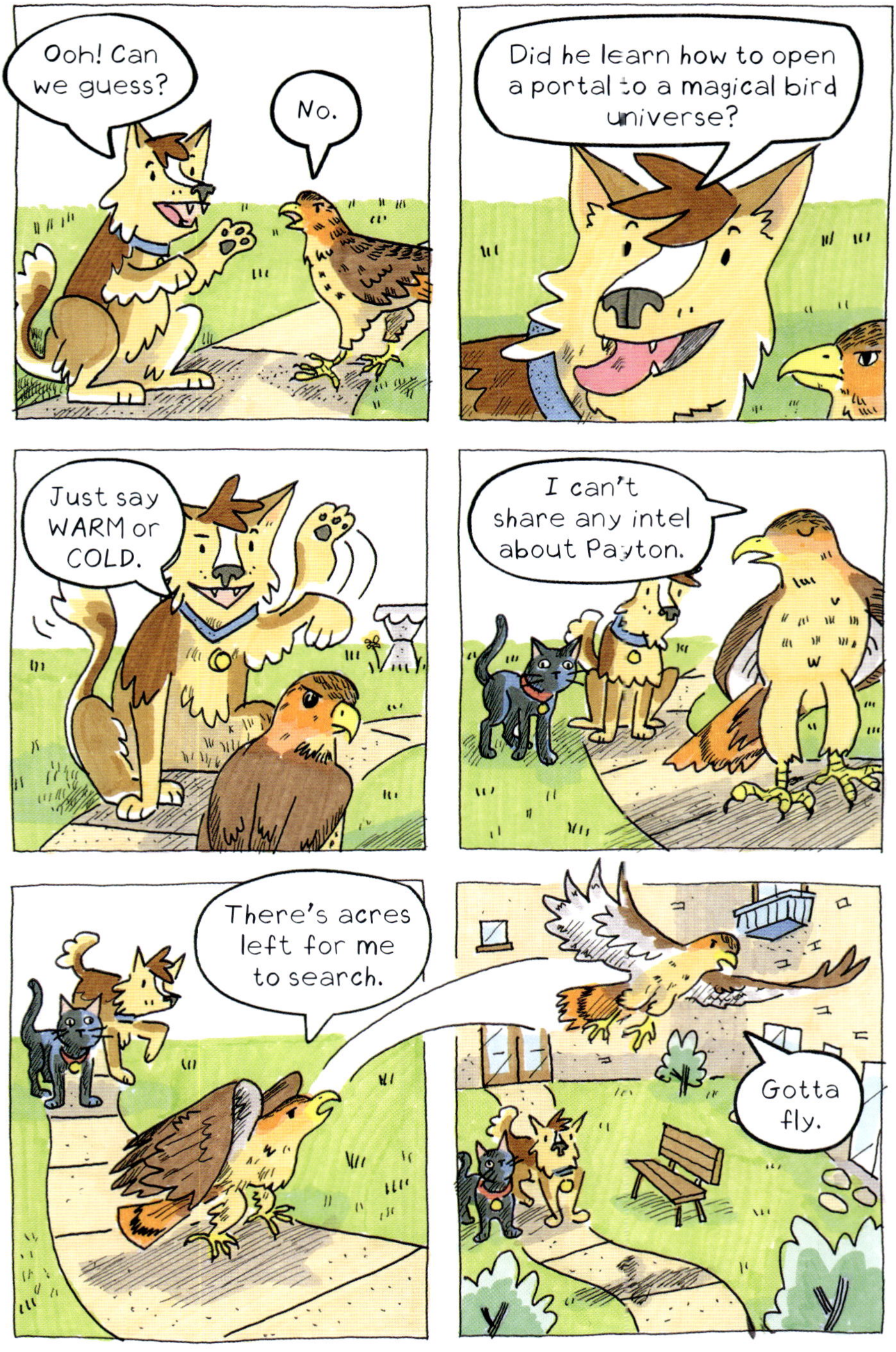
Ooh! Can we guess?
No.
Did he learn how to open a portal to a magical bird universe?
Just say WARM or COLD.
I can't share any intel about Payton.
There's acres left for me to search.
Gotta fly.

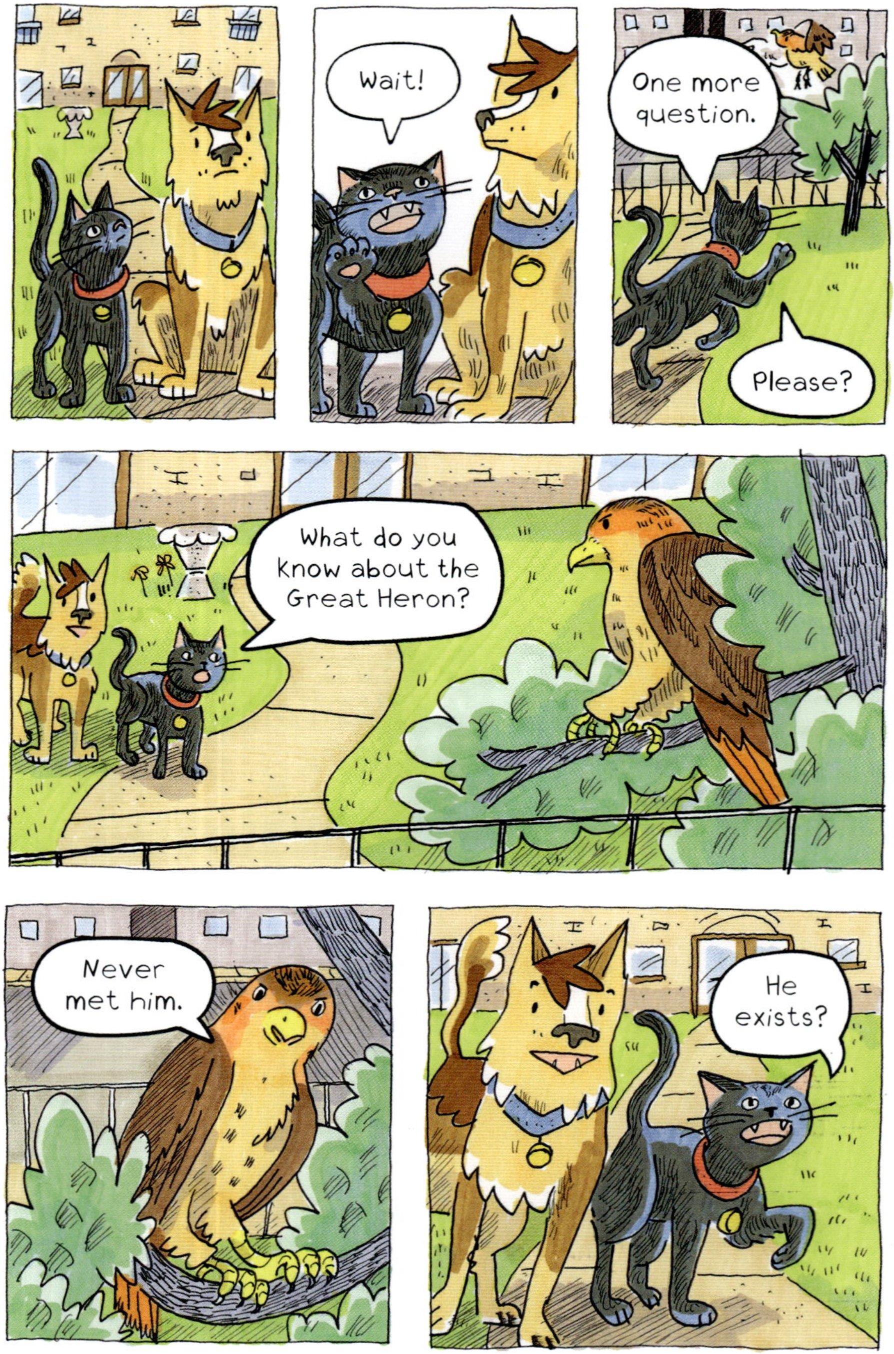
Wait!
One more question.
Please?
What do you know about the Great Heron?
Never met him.
He exists?

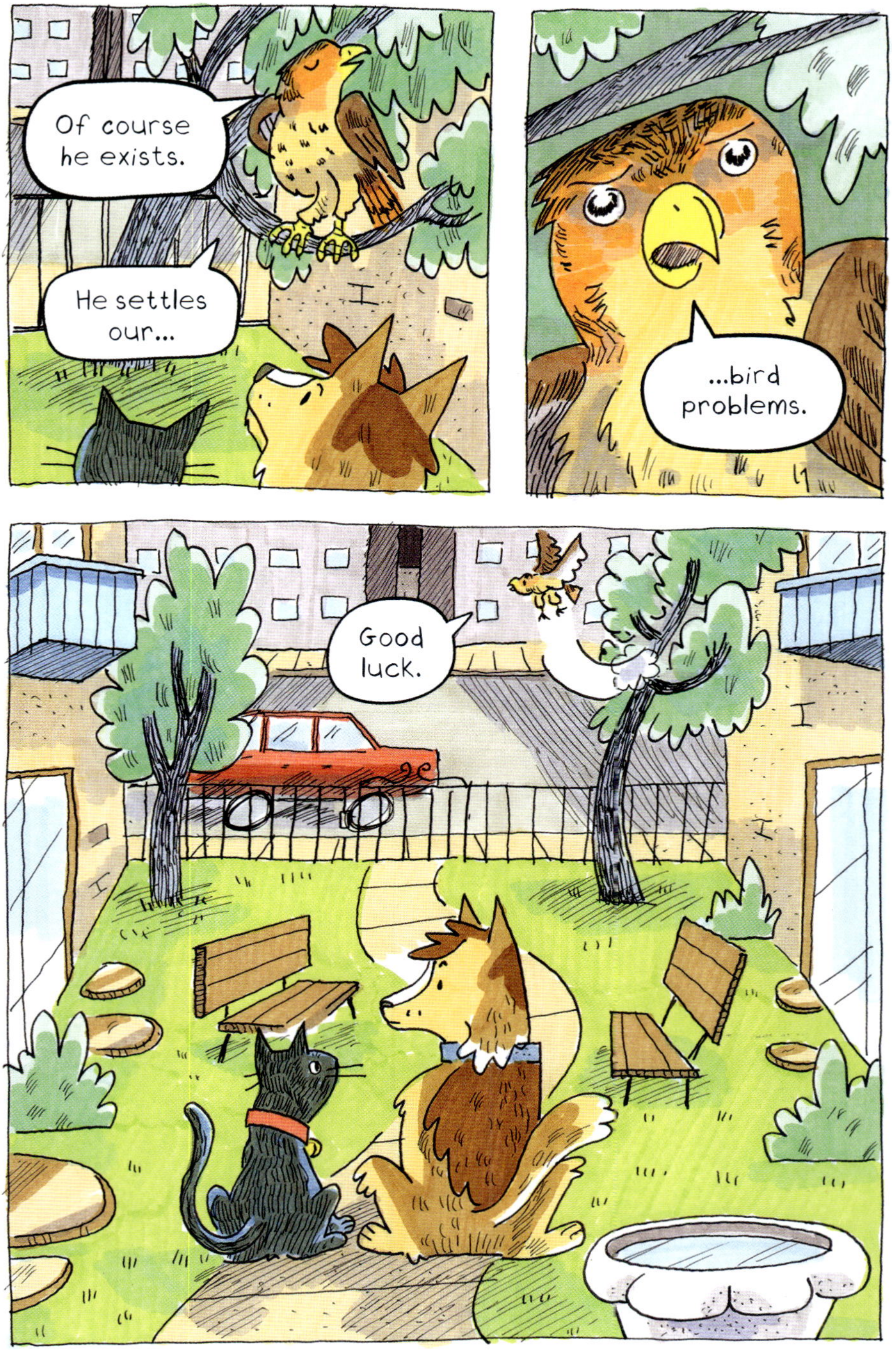
Of course he exists.
He settles our...
...bird problems.
Good luck.

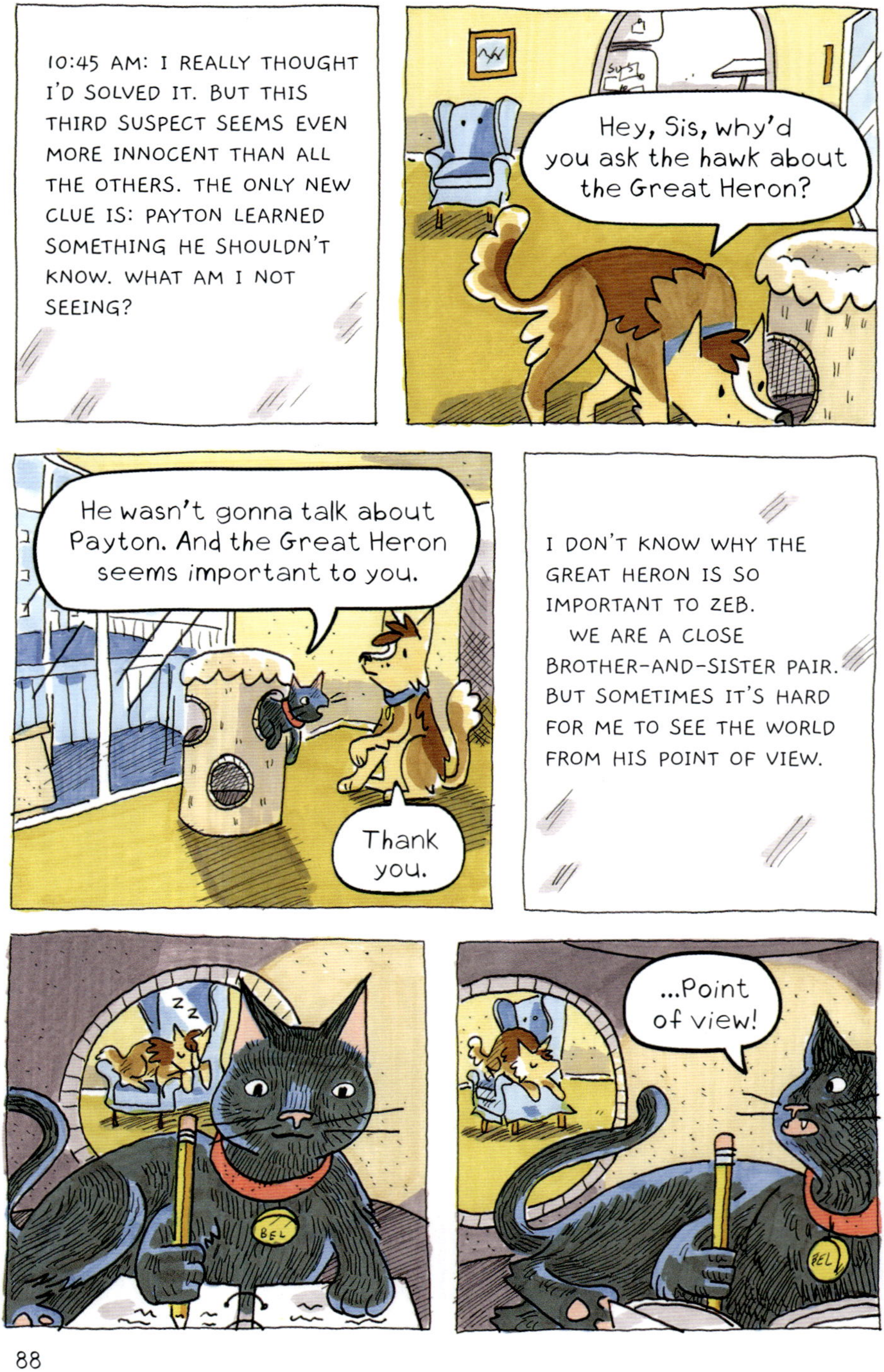
10:45 AM: I REALLY THOUGHT I'D SOLVED IT. BUT THIS THIRD SUSPECT SEEMS EVEN MORE INNOCENT THAN ALL THE OTHERS. THE ONLY NEW CLUE IS: PAYTON LEARNED SOMETHING HE SHOULDN'T KNOW. WHAT AM I NOT SEEING?
Hey, Sis, why'd you ask the hawk about the Great Heron?
He wasn't gonna talk about Payton. And the Great Heron seems important to you.
Thank you.
I DON'T KNOW WHY THE GREAT HERON IS SO IMPORTANT TO ZEB.
WE ARE A CLOSE BROTHER-AND-SISTER PAIR. BUT SOMETIMES IT'S HARD FOR ME TO SEE THE WORLD FROM HIS POINT OF VIEW.
ZZ
...Point of view!

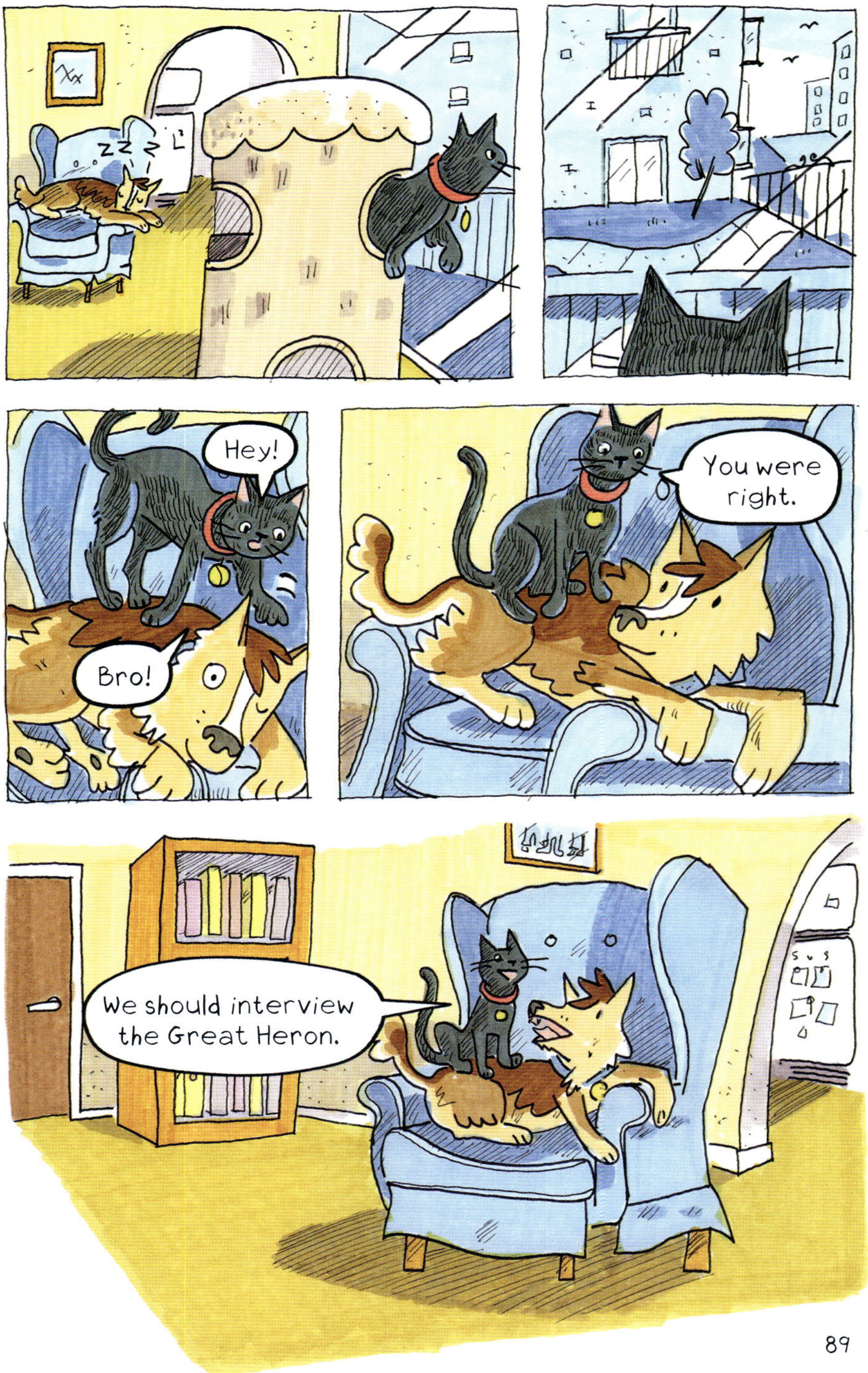
ZZZ
Hey!
Bro!
You were right.
We should interview the Great Heron.

CHAPTER 8
BOUNDARY-BREAKING BEL

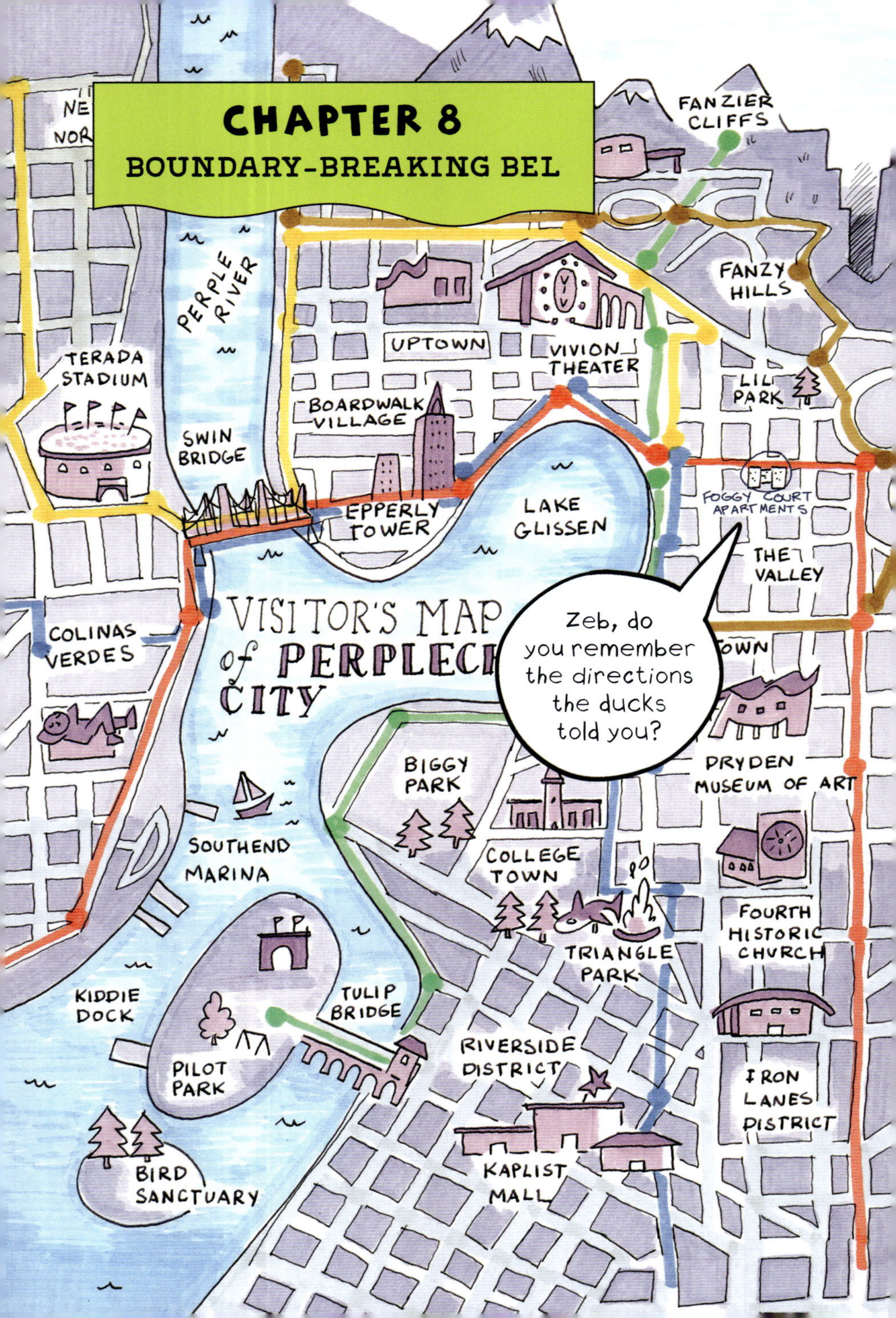
FANZIER CLIFFS
PERPLE RIVER
FANZY HILLS
UPTOWN
VIVION THEATER
TERADA STADIUM
LIL PARK
BOARDWALK VILLAGE
SWIN BRIDGE
EPPERLY TOWER
LAKE GLISSEN
FOGGY COURT APARTMENTS
THE VALLEY
VISITOR'S MAP
of PERPLEC
CITY
Zeb, do you remember the directions the ducks told you?
COLINAS VERDES
BIGGY PARK
DRYDEN MUSEUM OF ART
SOUTHEND MARINA
COLLEGE TOWN
FOURTH HISTORIC CHURCH
TRIANGLE PARK
KIDDIE DOCK
TULIP BRIDGE
RIVERSIDE DISTRICT
PILOT PARK
IRON LANES DISTRICT
KAPLIST MALL
BIRD SANCTUARY

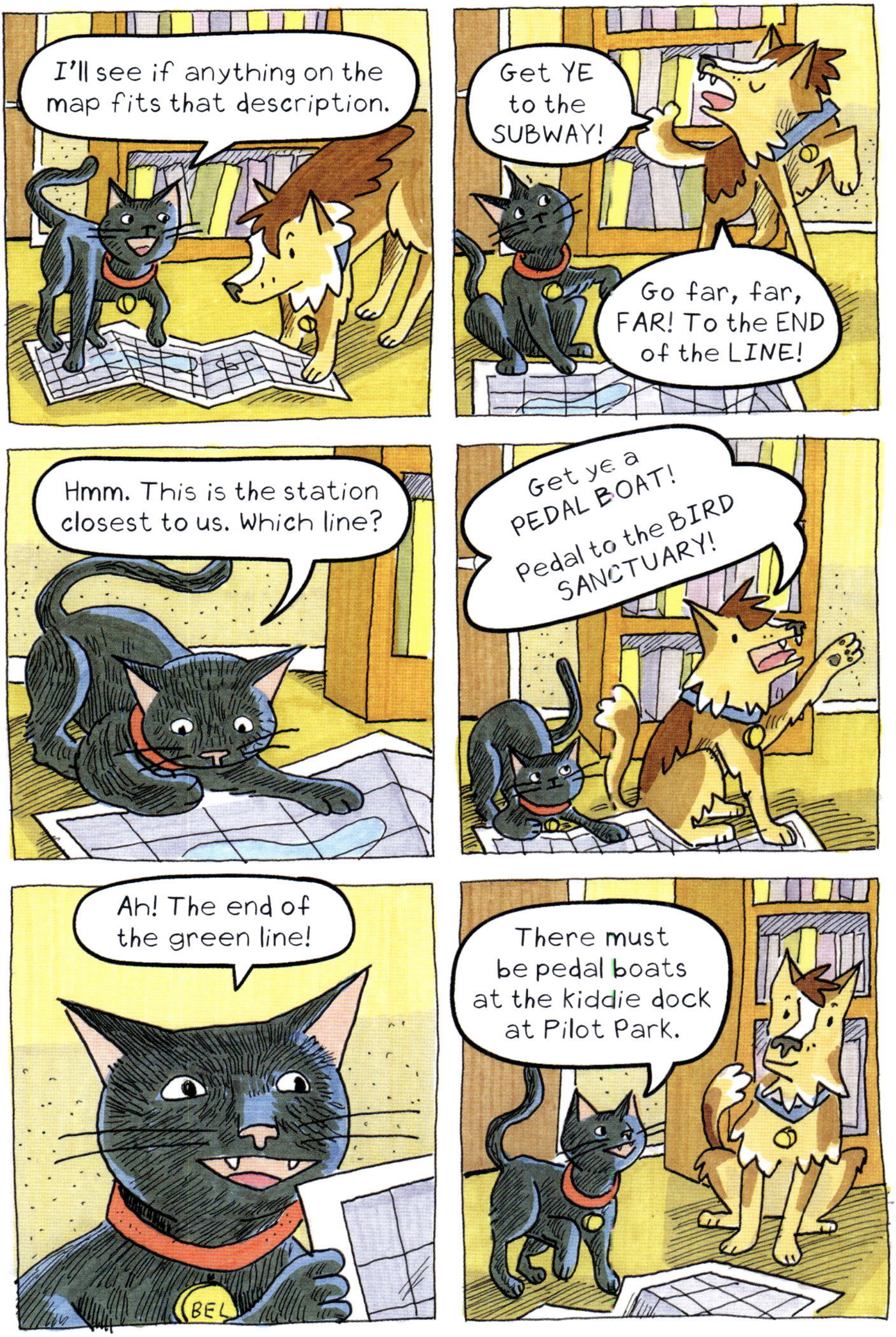
I'll see if anything on the map fits that description.
Get YE to the SUBWAY!
Go far, far, FAR! To the END of the LINE!
Hmm. This is the station closest to us. Which line?
Get ye a PEDAL BOAT!
Pedal to the BIRD SANCTUARY!
Ah! The end of the green line!
BEL
There must be pedal boats at the kiddie dock at Pilot Park.

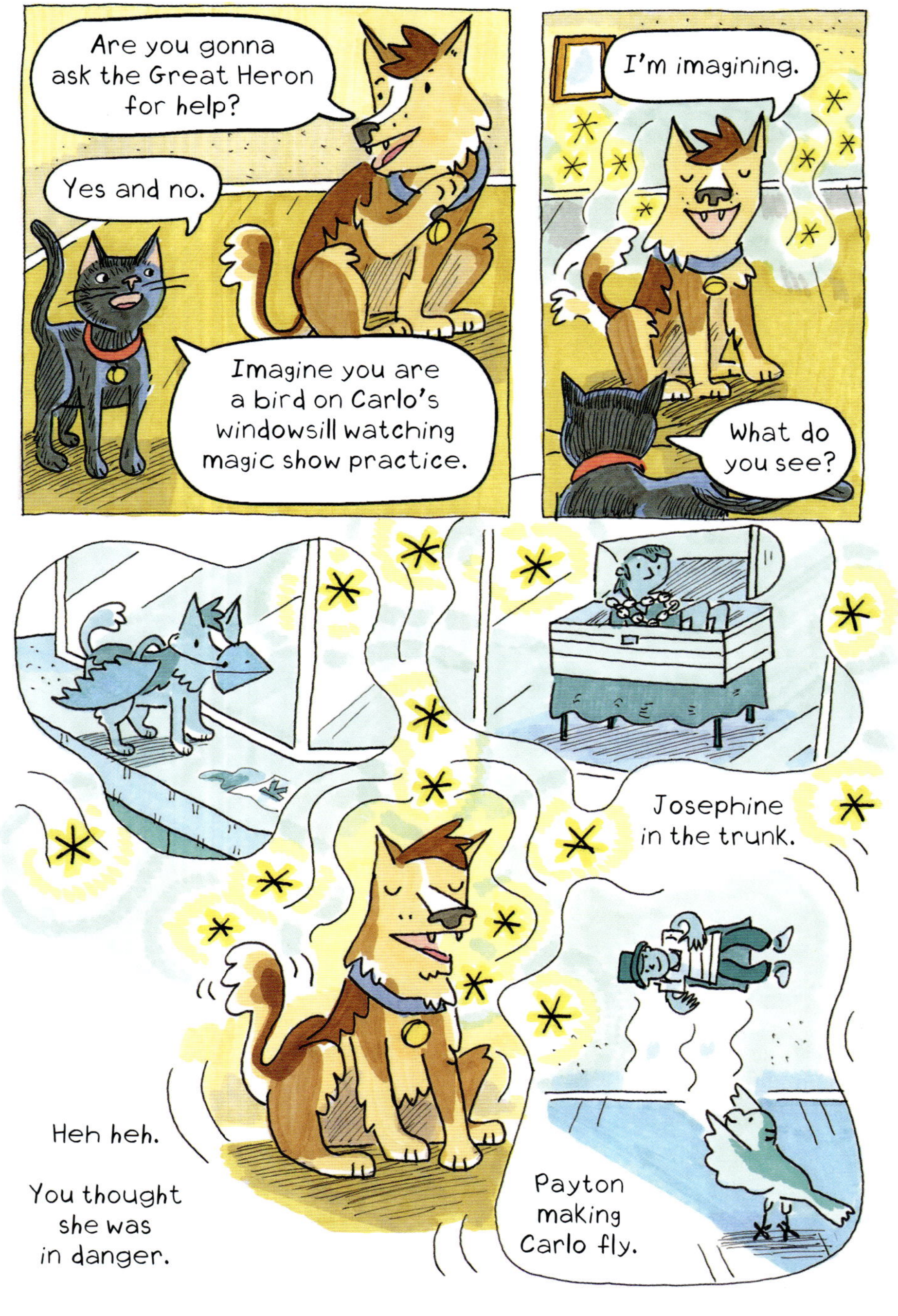
Are you gonna ask the Great Heron for help?
Yes and no.
Imagine you are a bird on Carlo's windowsill watching magic show practice.
I'm imagining.
What do you see?
Josephine in the trunk.
Heh heh.
You thought she was in danger.
Payton making Carlo fly.

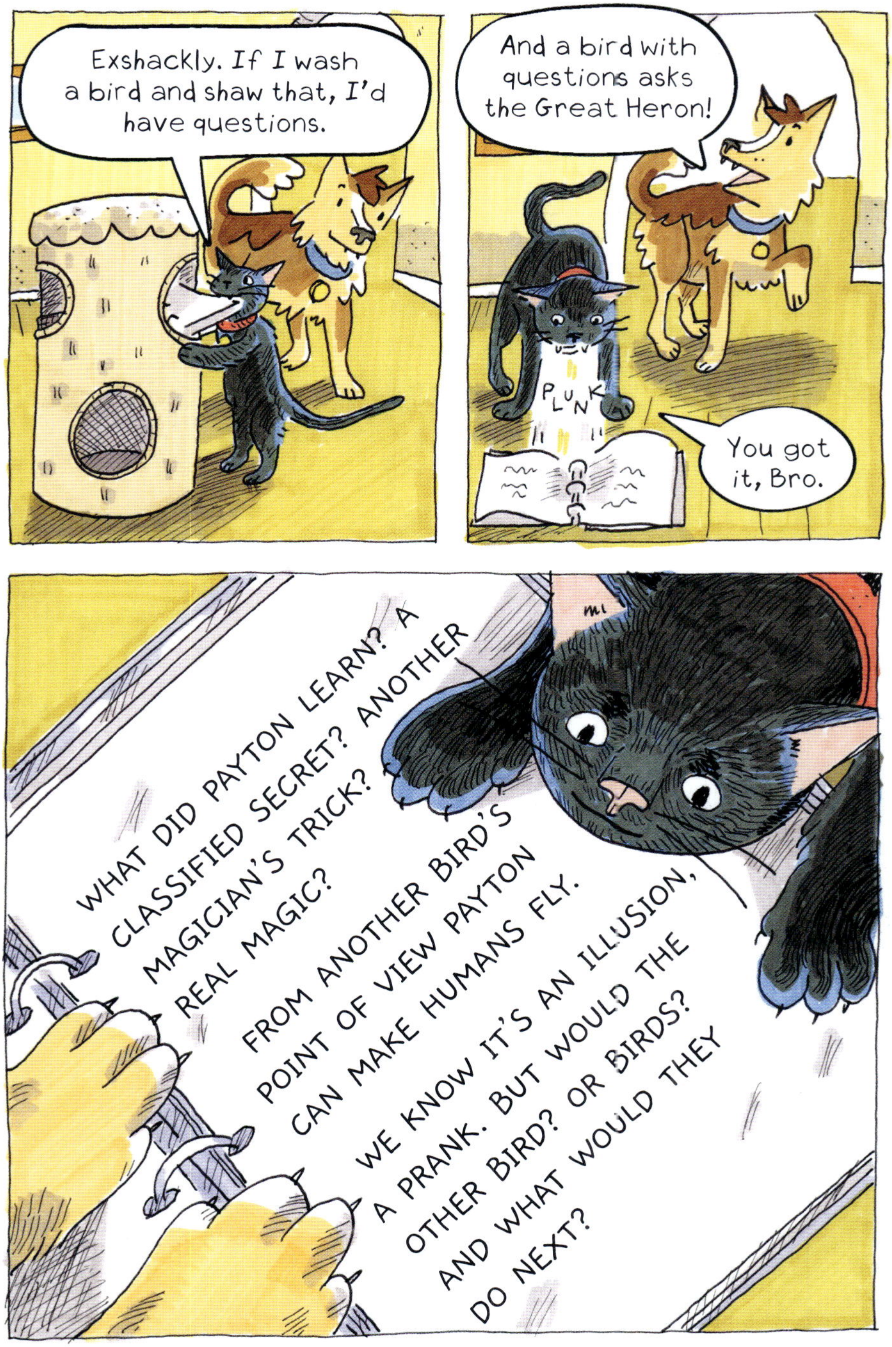
Exshackly. *If I* wash a bird and shaw that, *I'd* have questions.
And a bird with questions asks the Great Heron!
PLUNK
You got it, Bro.
WHAT DID PAYTON LEARN? A CLASSIFIED SECRET? ANOTHER MAGICIAN'S TRICK? REAL MAGIC?
FROM ANOTHER BIRD'S POINT OF VIEW PAYTON CAN MAKE HUMANS FLY.
WE KNOW IT'S AN ILLUSION, A PRANK. BUT WOULD THE OTHER BIRD? OR BIRDS? AND WHAT WOULD THEY DO NEXT?

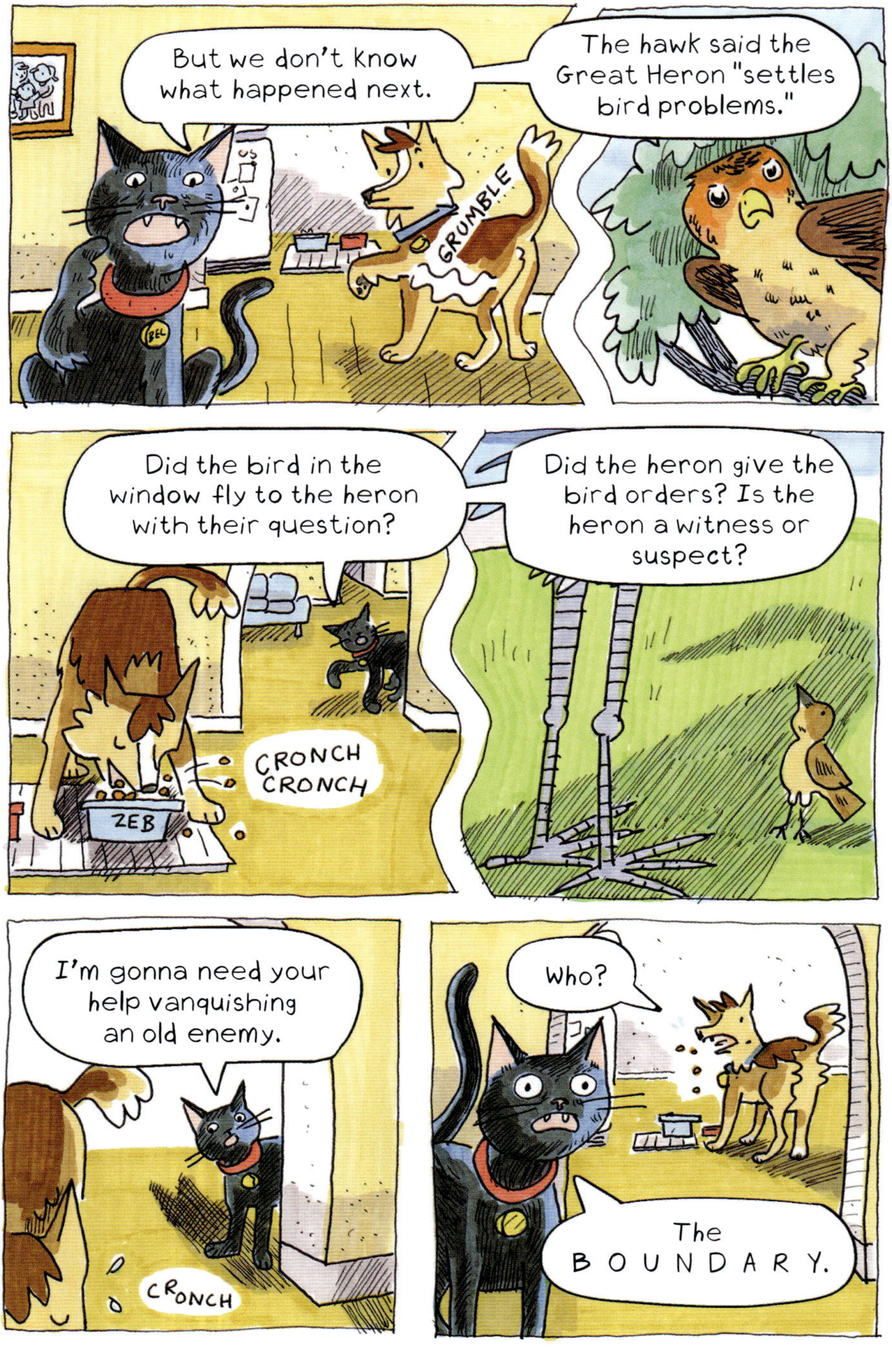

But we don't know what happened next.
GRUMBLE
The hawk said the Great Heron "settles bird problems."
Did the bird in the window fly to the heron with their question?
ZEB
CRONCH CRONCH
Did the heron give the bird orders? Is the heron a witness or suspect?
I'm gonna need your help vanquishing an old enemy.
CRONCH
Who?
The B O U N D A R Y.

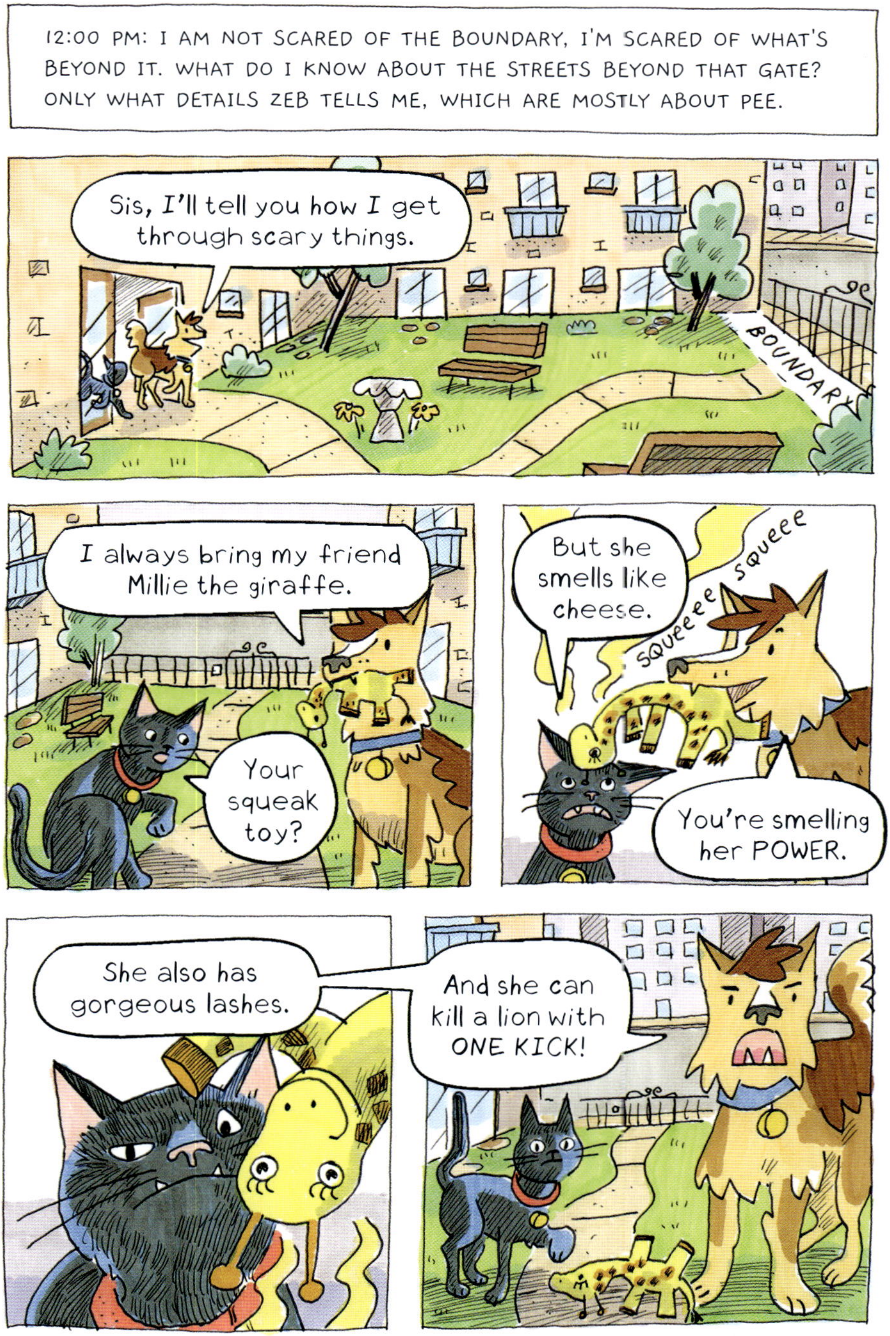
12:00 PM: I AM NOT SCARED OF THE BOUNDARY, I'M SCARED OF WHAT'S BEYOND IT. WHAT DO I KNOW ABOUT THE STREETS BEYOND THAT GATE? ONLY WHAT DETAILS ZEB TELLS ME, WHICH ARE MOSTLY ABOUT PEE.
Sis, I'll tell you how I get through scary things.
BOUNDARY
I always bring my friend Millie the giraffe.
Your squeak toy?
But she smells like cheese.
SQUEEEE SQUEEE
You're smelling her POWER.
She also has gorgeous lashes.
And she can kill a lion with ONE KICK!

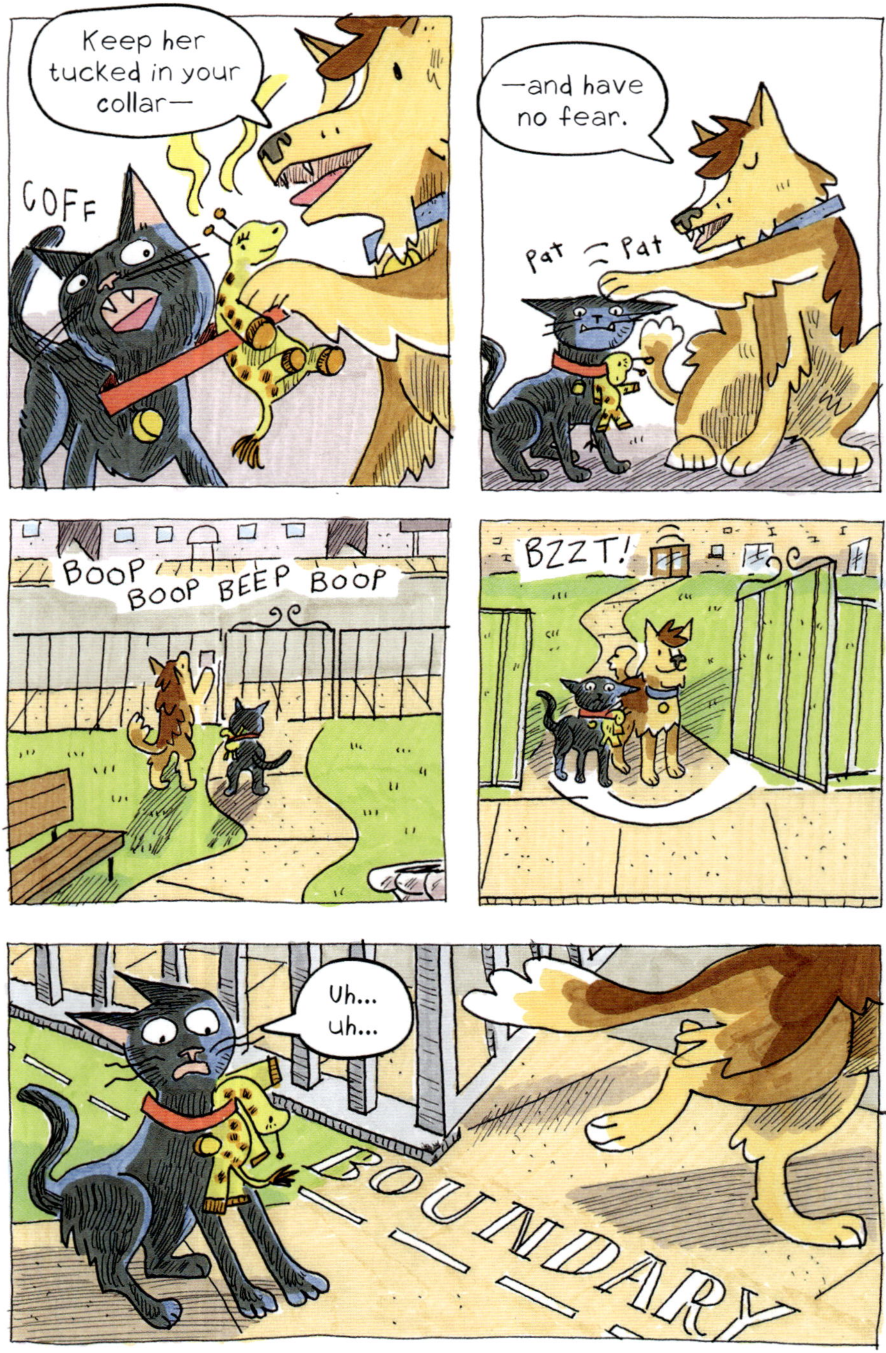
Keep her tucked in your collar—
COFF
—and have no fear.
Pat Pat
BOOP BOOP BEEP BOOP
BZZT!
Uh... uh...
BOUNDARY

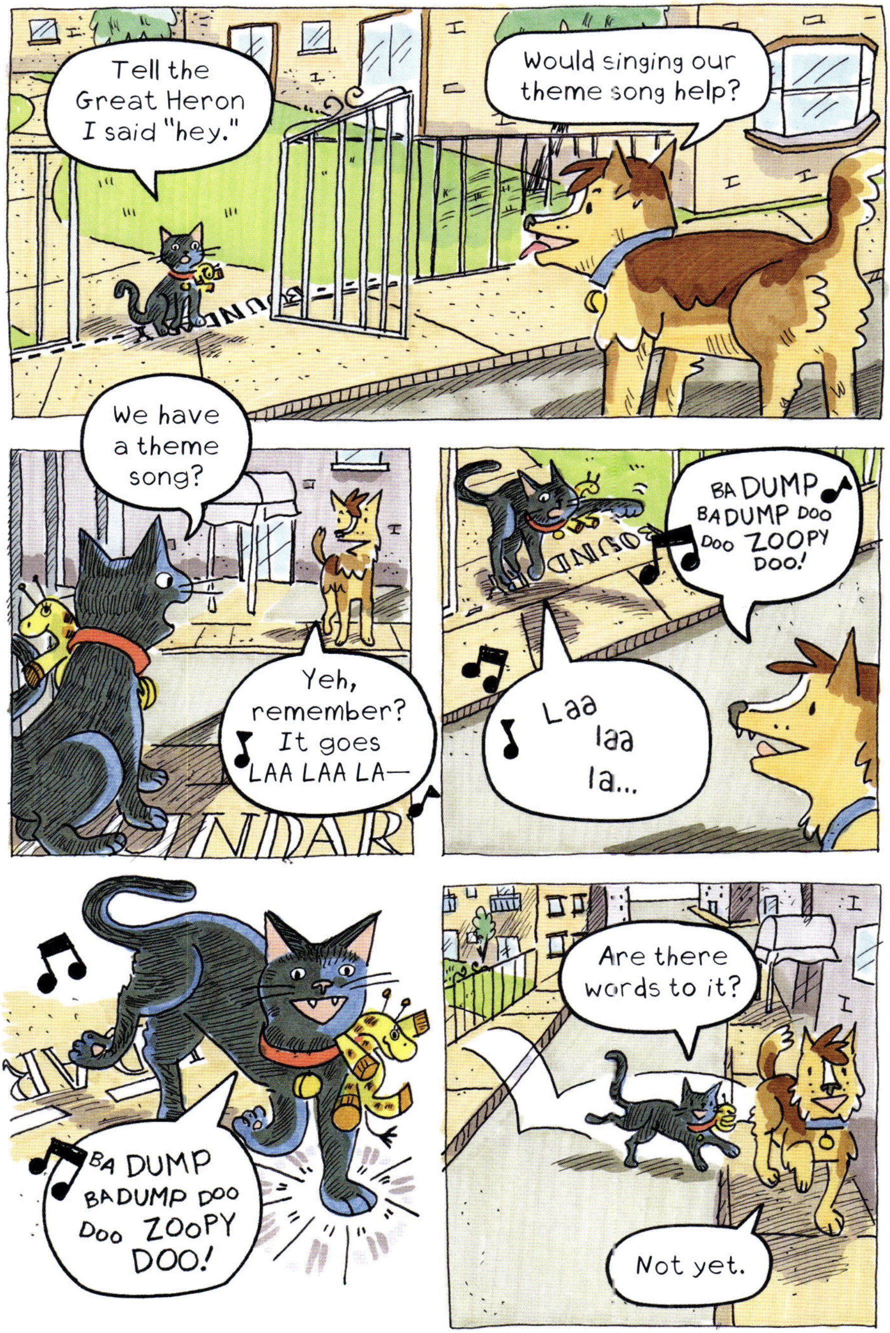
Tell the Great Heron I said "hey."
Would singing our theme song help?
We have a theme song?
Yeh, remember? It goes LAA LAA LA—
BA DUMP BADUMP DOO DOO ZOOPY DOO!
Laa laa la...
BA DUMP BADUMP DOO DOO ZOOPY DOO!
Are there words to it?
Not yet.

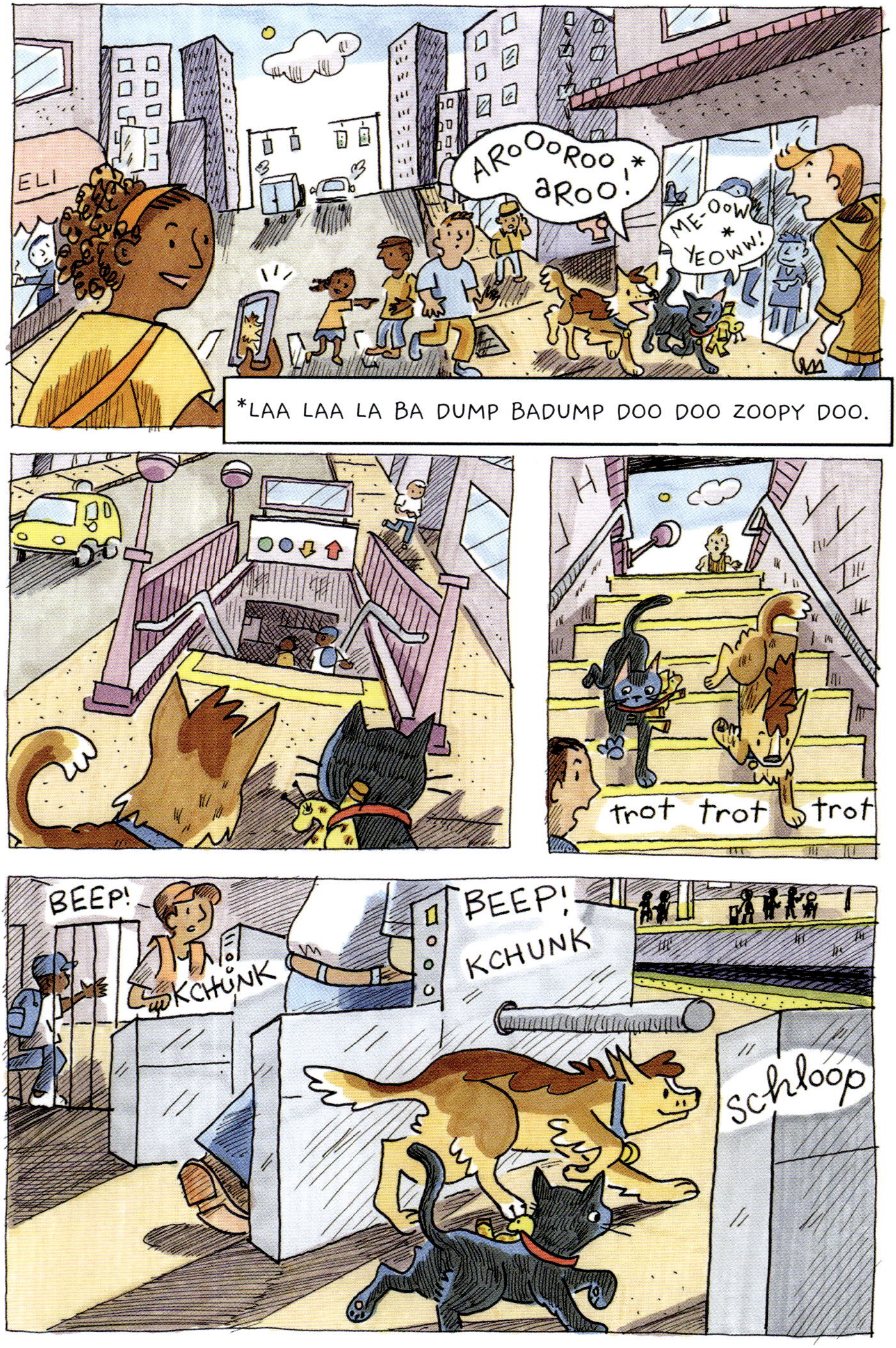
AROOOROO AROO!*
ME-OOW * YEOWW!
*LAA LAA LA BA DUMP BADUMP DOO DOO ZOOPY DOO.
trot trot trot
BEEP!
KCHUNK
BEEP!
KCHUNK
schloop

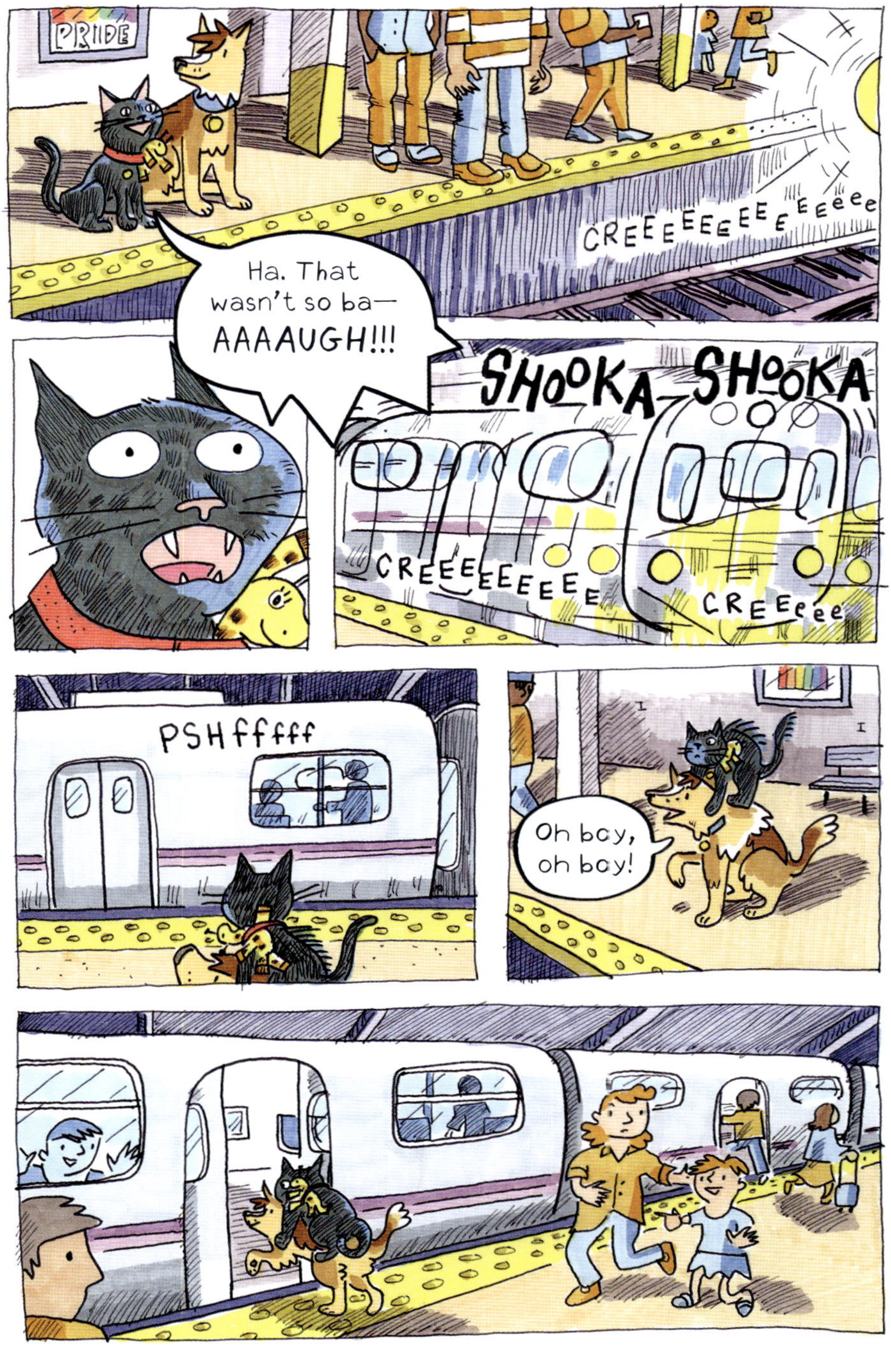
PRIDE
CREEEEEEEEEeeee
Ha. That wasn't so ba—AAAAUGH!!!
SHOOKA-SHOOKA
CREEEEEEEEEE
CREEeee
PSHffff
Oh boy, oh boy!

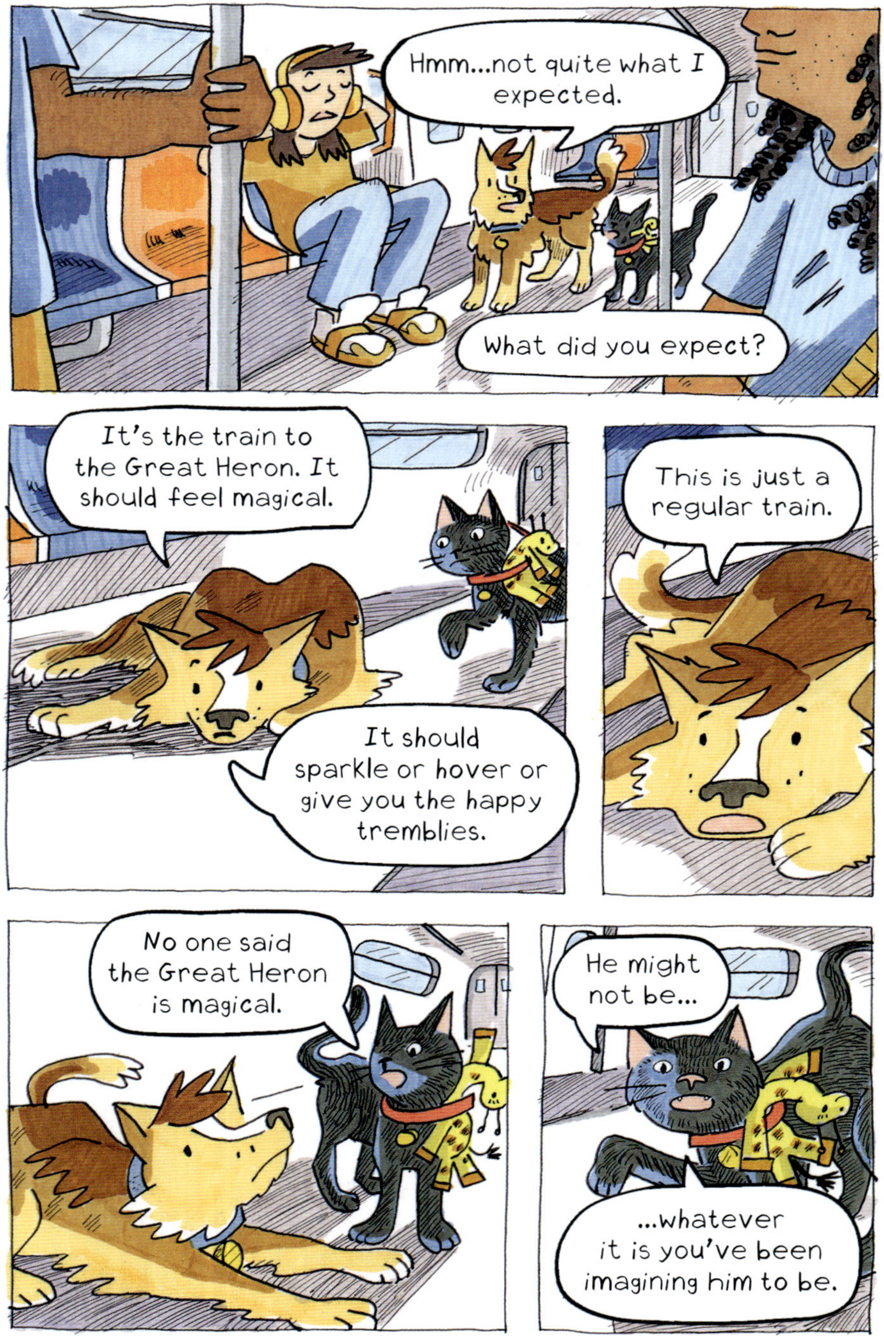
Hmm...not quite what I expected.
What did you expect?
It's the train to the Great Heron. It should feel magical.
It should sparkle or hover or give you the happy tremblies.
This is just a regular train.
No one said the Great Heron is magical.
He might not be...
...whatever it is you've been imagining him to be.

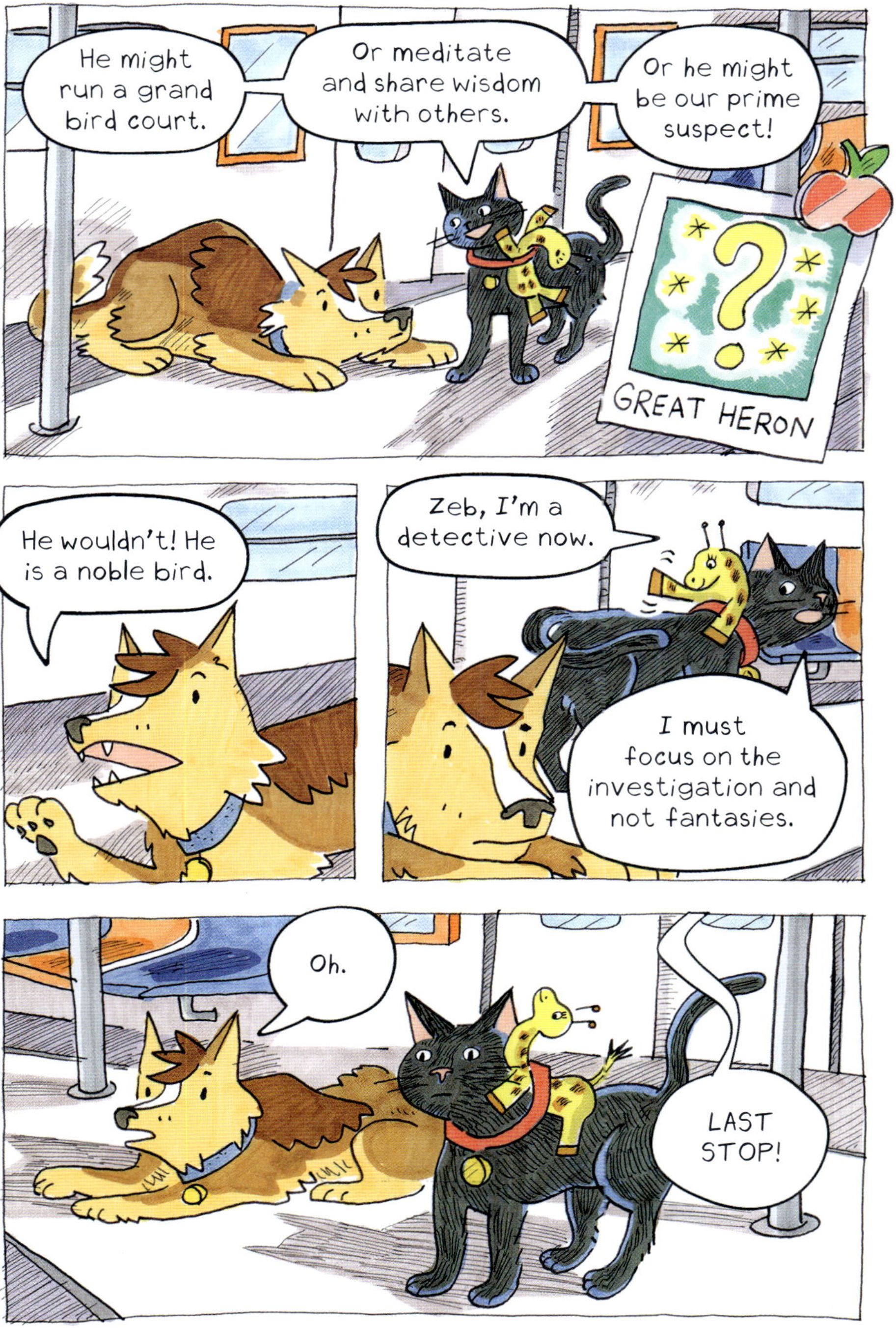
He might run a grand bird court.
Or meditate and share wisdom with others.
Or he might be our prime suspect!
GREAT HERON
He wouldn't! He is a noble bird.
Zeb, I'm a detective now.
I must focus on the investigation and not fantasies.
Oh.
LAST STOP!

CHAPTER 9
THE SANCTUARY

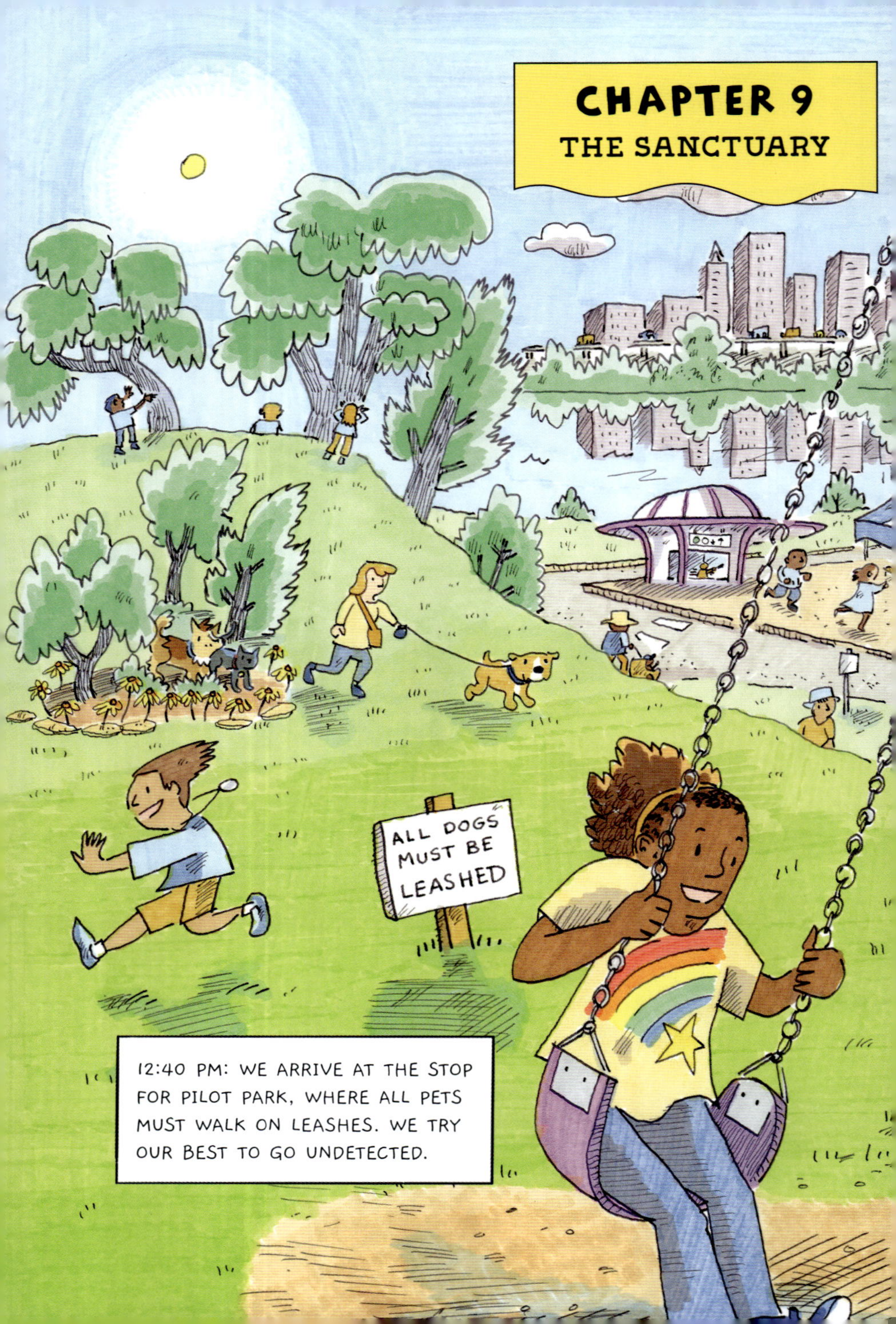
ALL DOGS MUST BE LEASHED
12:40 PM: WE ARRIVE AT THE STOP FOR PILOT PARK, WHERE ALL PETS MUST WALK ON LEASHES. WE TRY OUR BEST TO GO UNDETECTED.

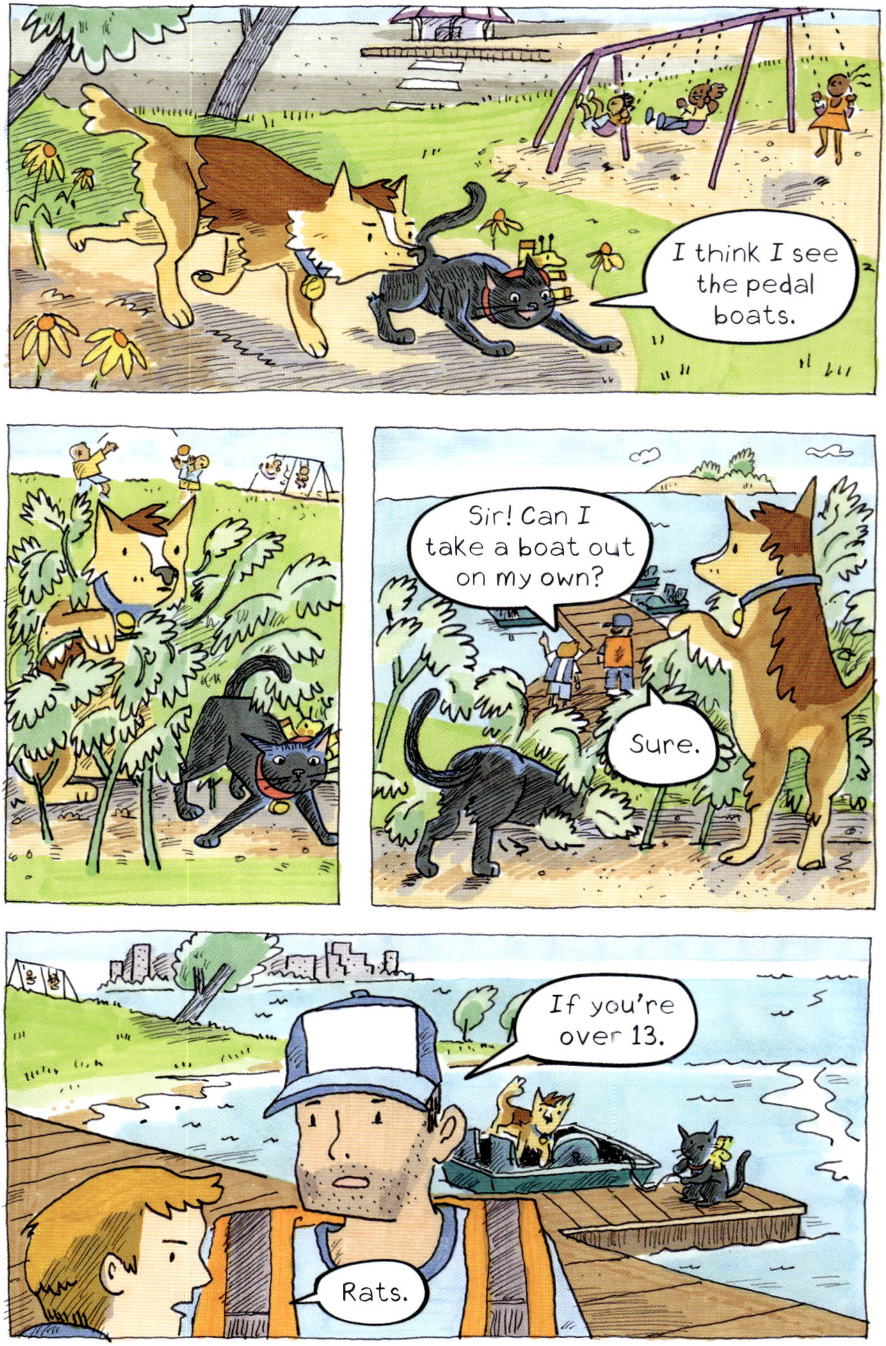
I think I see the pedal boats.
Sir! Can I take a boat out on my own?
Sure.
If you're over 13.
Rats.

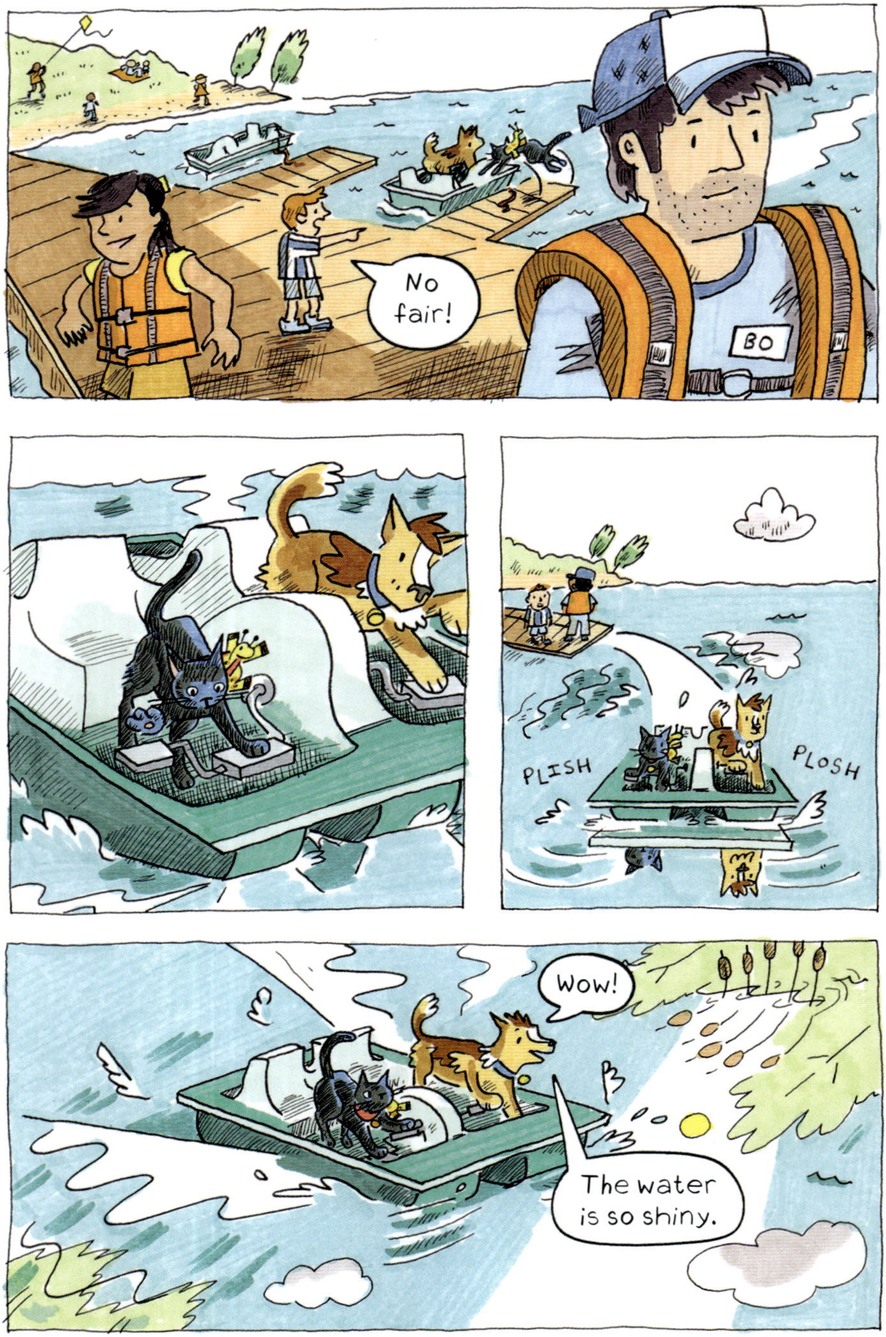

BO
No fair!
PLISH
PLOSH
Wow!
The water is so shiny.

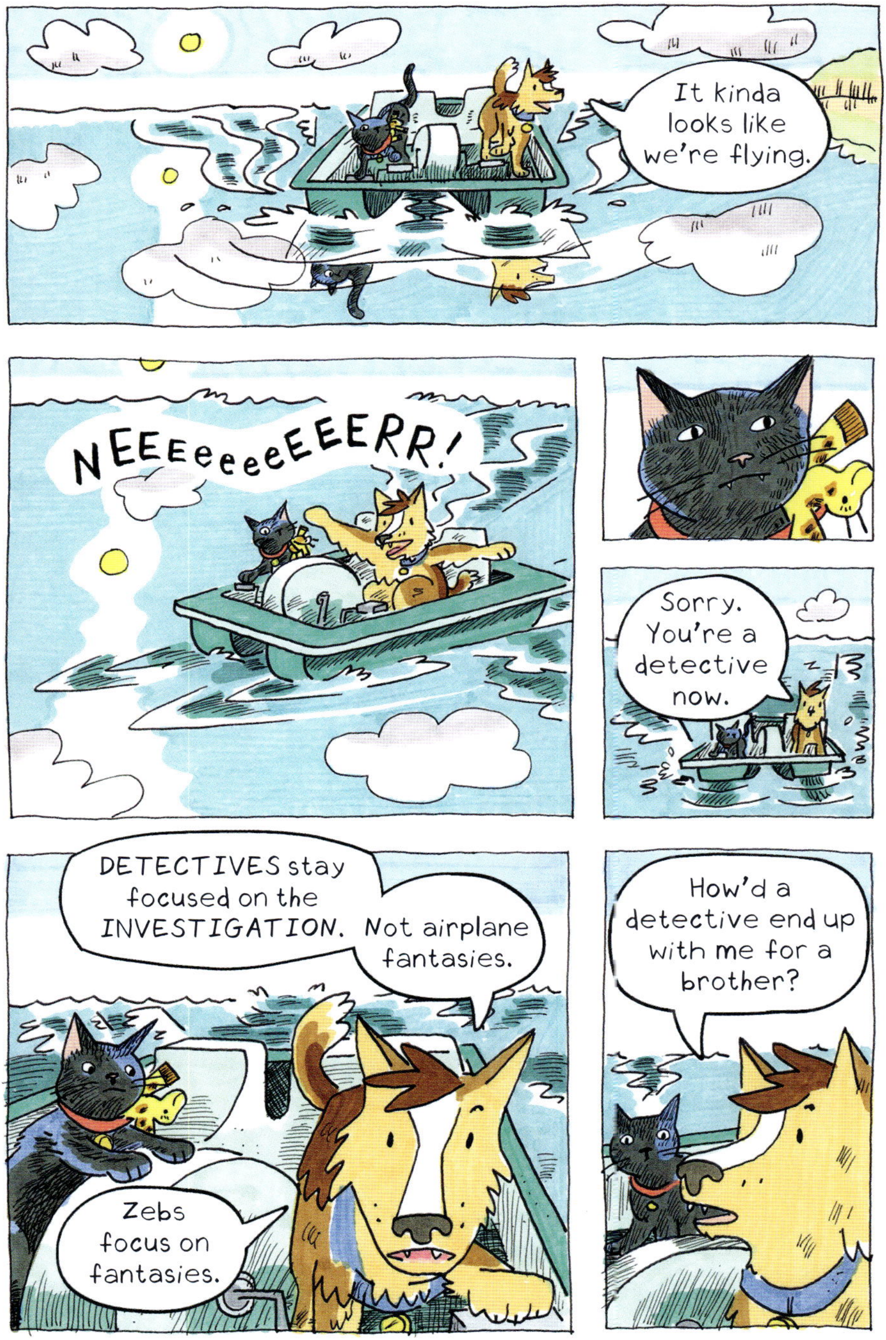
It kinda looks like we're flying.
NEEEeeeeEEERR!
Sorry. You're a detective now.
DETECTIVES stay focused on the INVESTIGATION.
Not airplane fantasies.
Zebs focus on fantasies.
How'd a detective end up with me for a brother?

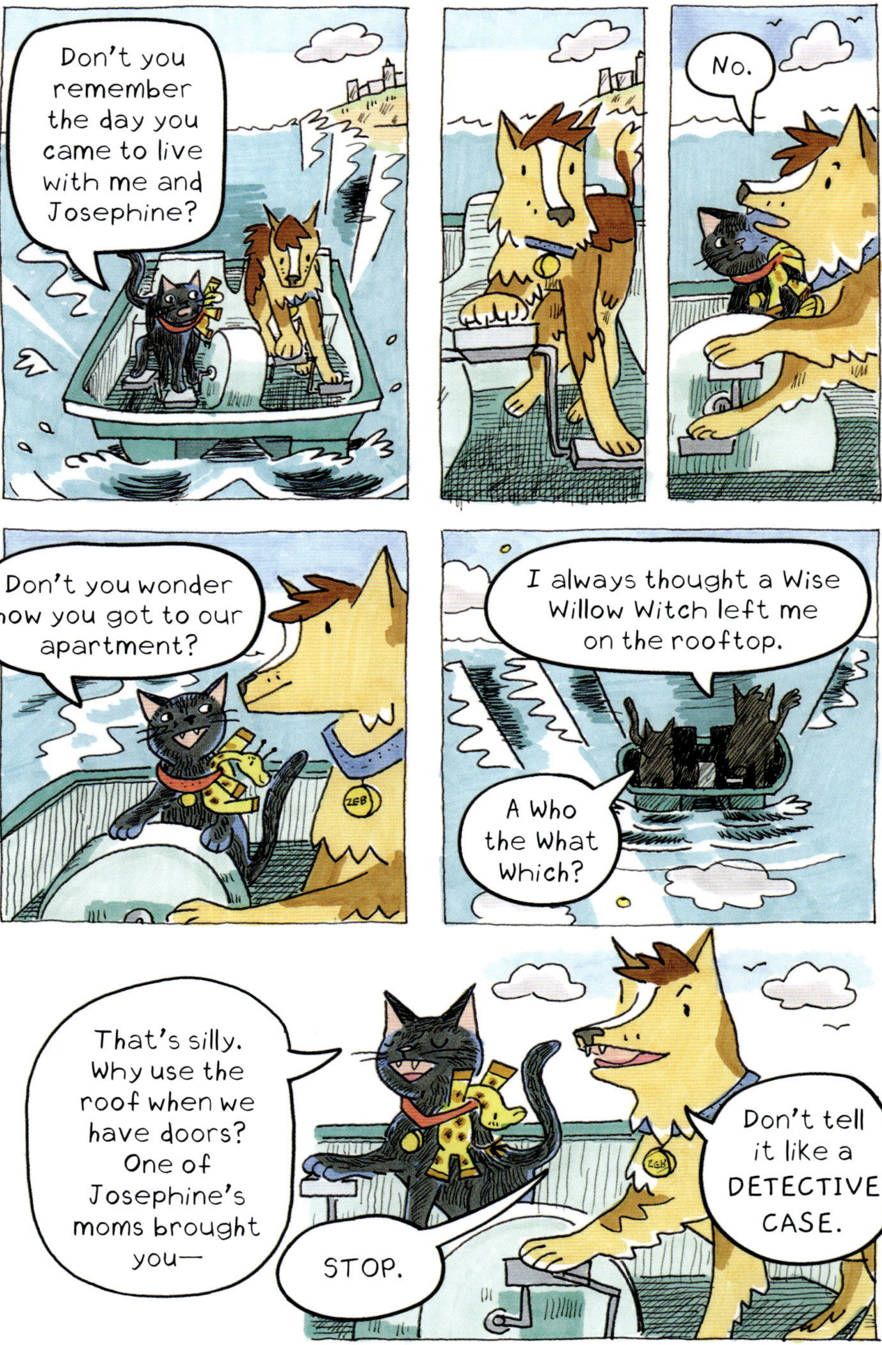
Don't you remember the day you came to live with me and Josephine?
No.
Don't you wonder how you got to our apartment?
I always thought a Wise Willow Witch left me on the rooftop.
A Who the What Which?
ZEB
That's silly. Why use the roof when we have doors? One of Josephine's moms brought you—
STOP.
Don't tell it like a DETECTIVE CASE.

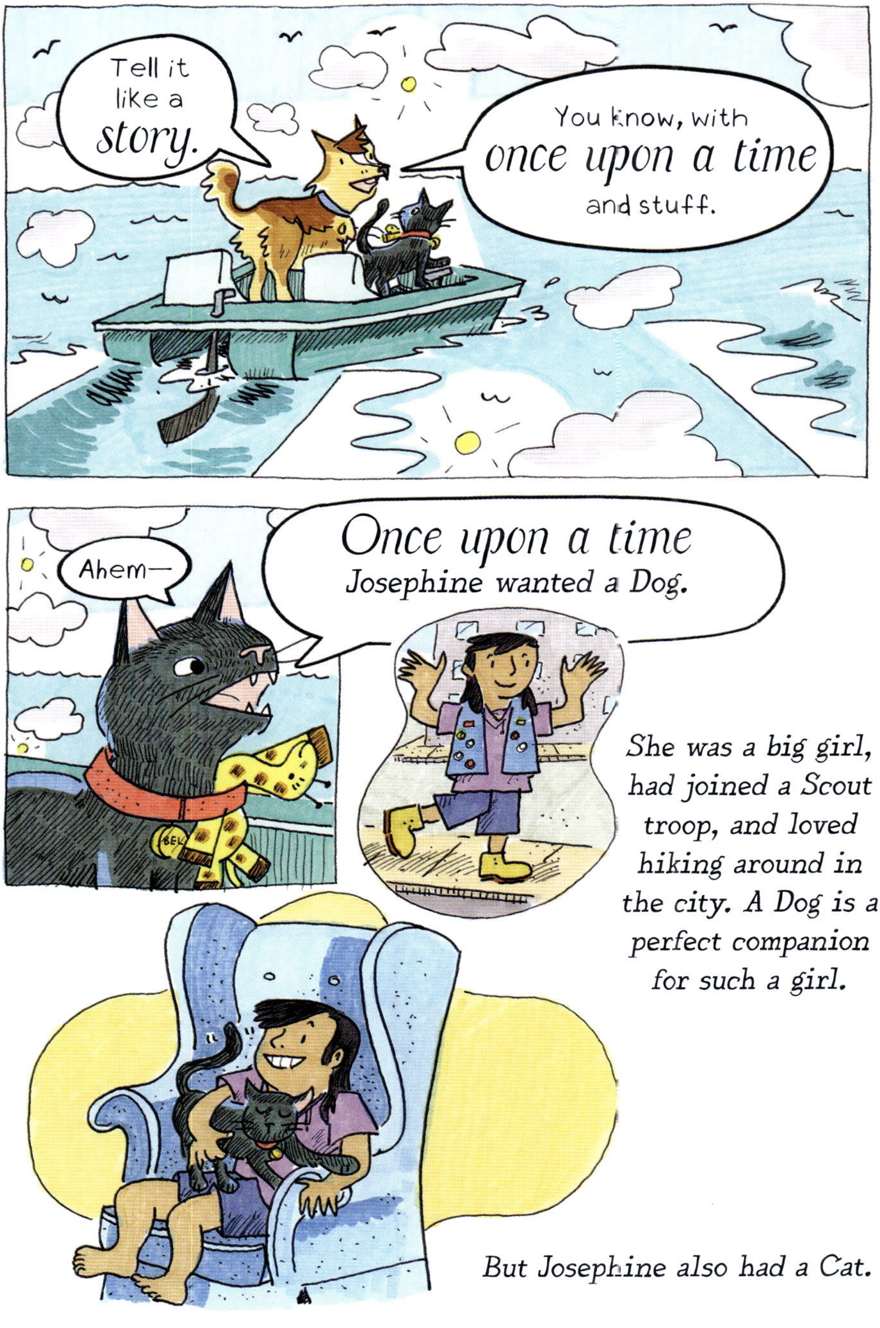
Tell it like a story.
You know, with once upon a time and stuff.
Ahem—
Once upon a time Josephine wanted a Dog.
She was a big girl, had joined a Scout troop, and loved hiking around in the city. A Dog is a perfect companion for such a girl.
But Josephine also had a Cat.

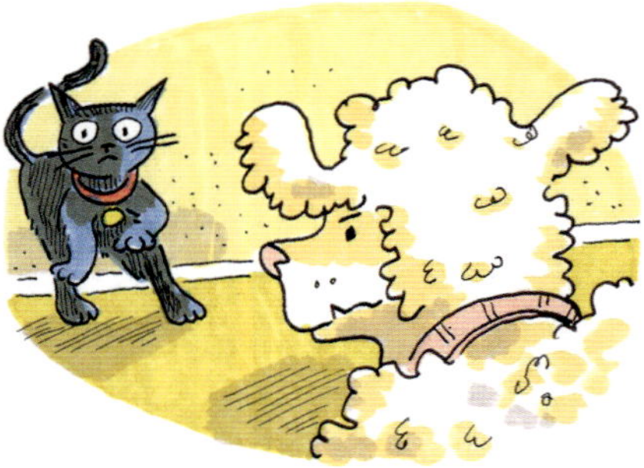

Every Dog they
brought home was no
match for this Cat.

The dogs called her
"kitty" and "furball" and
"puss puss" and chased her.
The Cat yowled and spat.

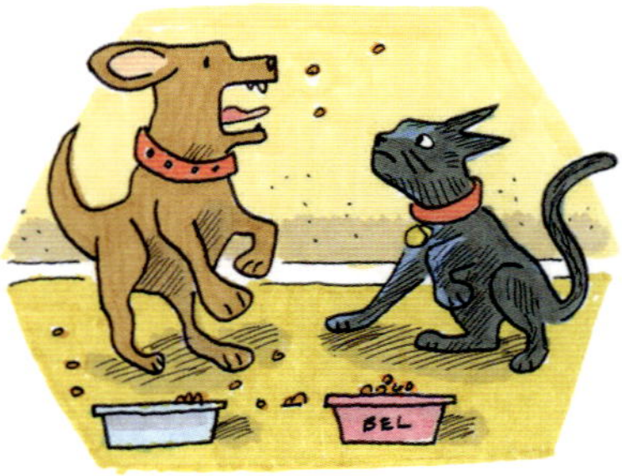
BEL

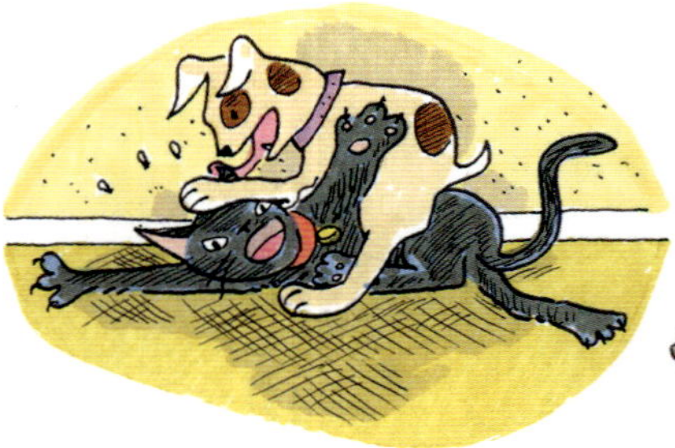

Each Dog went to live with
a different family—

—because pets must
Get Along, you know.

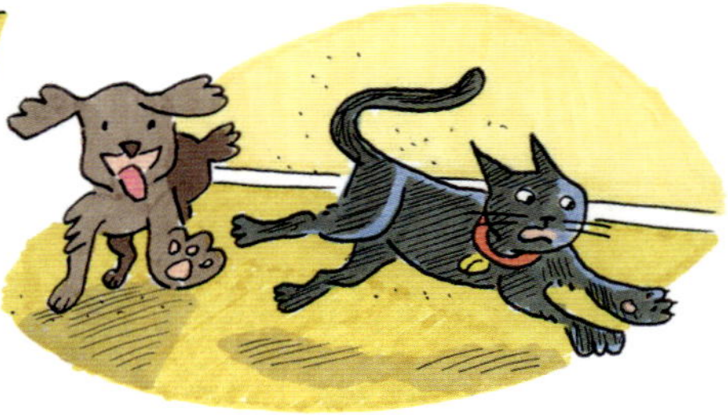

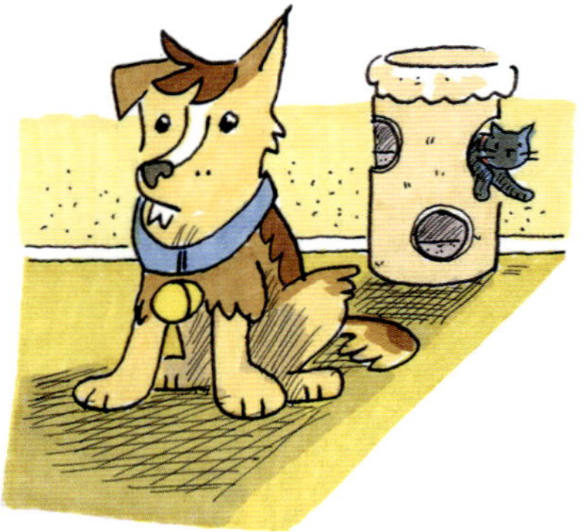

Until one day, a floppy
three-colored pup
arrived. And this Dog
was the best Dog
for the girl.

And for the Cat.

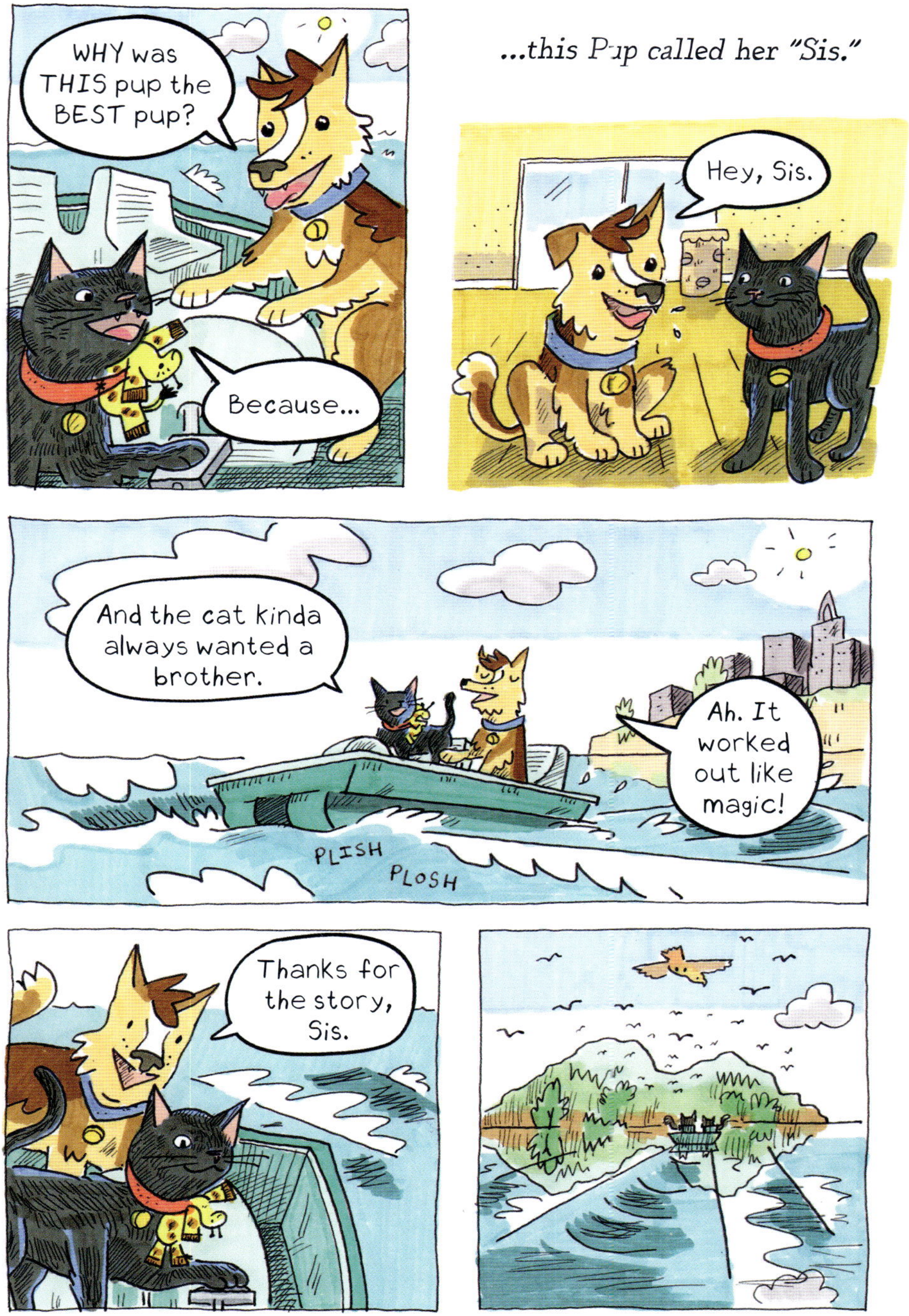
WHY was THIS pup the BEST pup?
Because...
...this Pup called her "Sis."
Hey, Sis.
And the cat kinda always wanted a brother.
Ah. It worked out like magic!
PLISH
PLOSH
Thanks for the story, Sis.

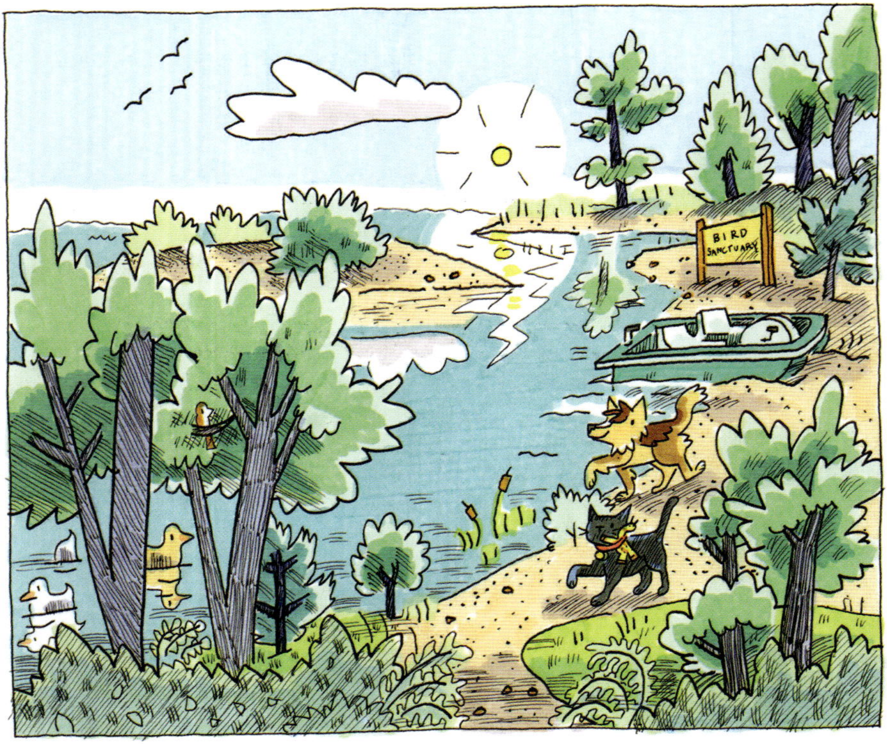
BIRD SANCTUARY

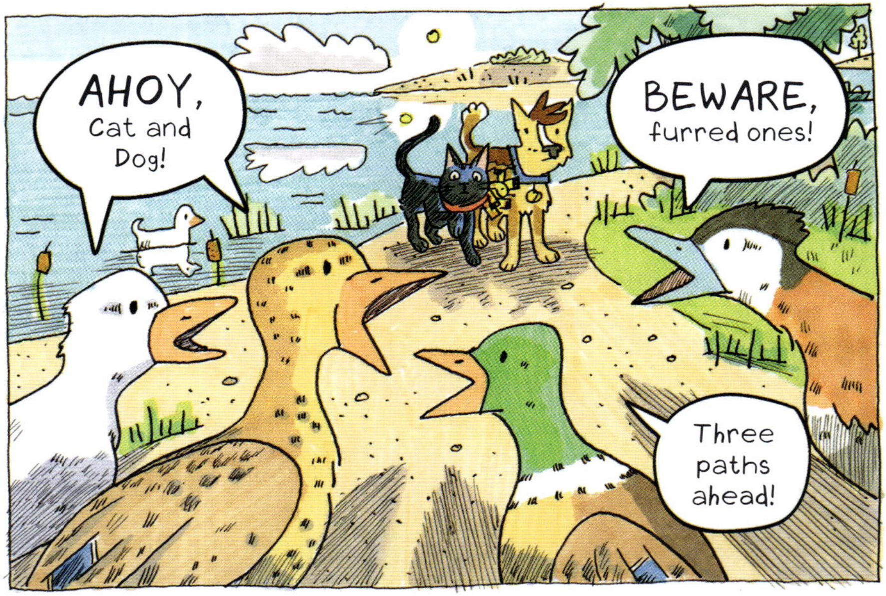
AHOY, Cat and Dog!
BEWARE, furred ones!
Three paths ahead!

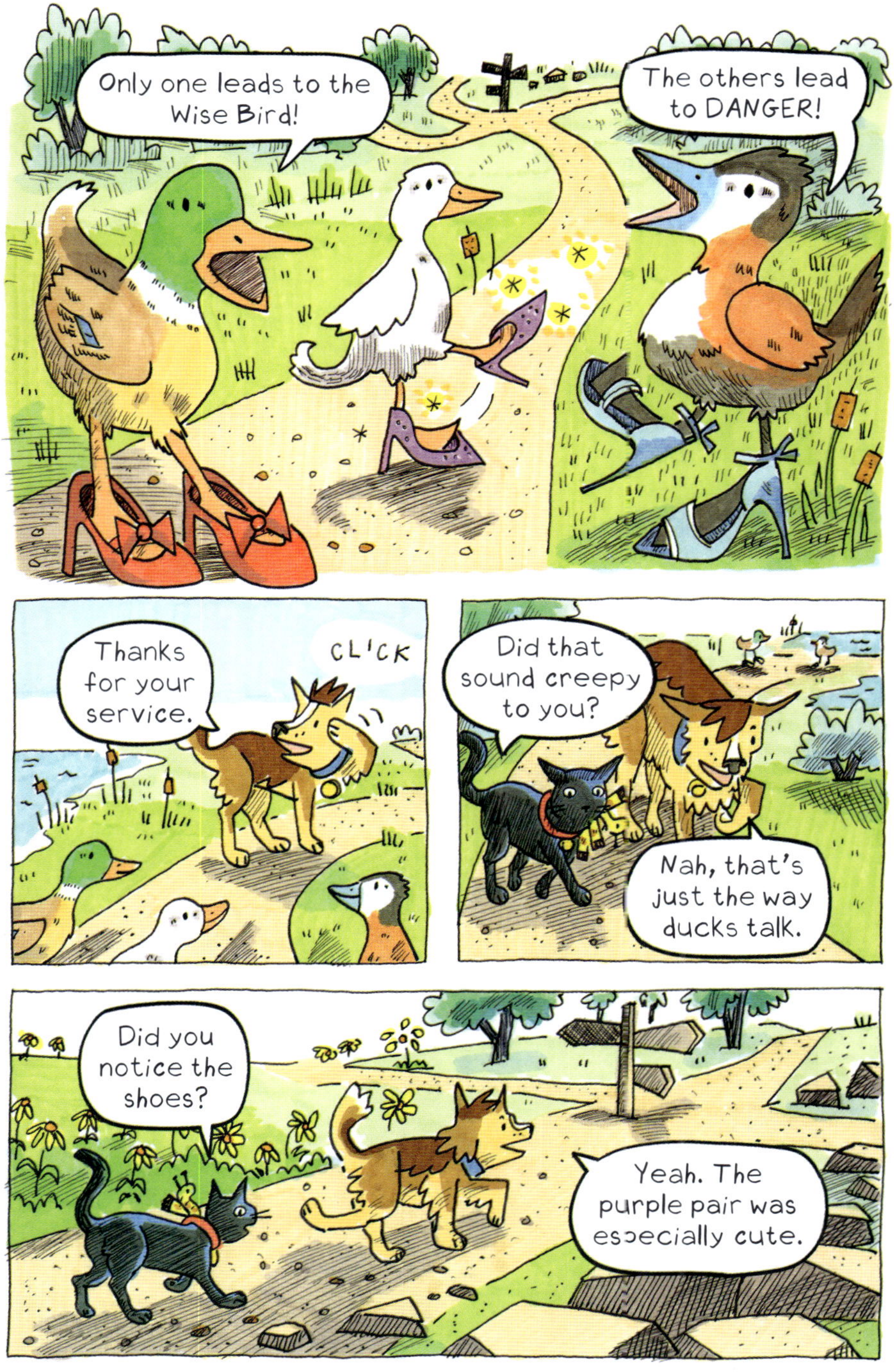
Only one leads to the Wise Bird!
The others lead to DANGER!
Thanks for your service.
CLICK
Did that sound creepy to you?
Nah, that's just the way ducks talk.
Did you notice the shoes?
Yeah. The purple pair was especially cute.

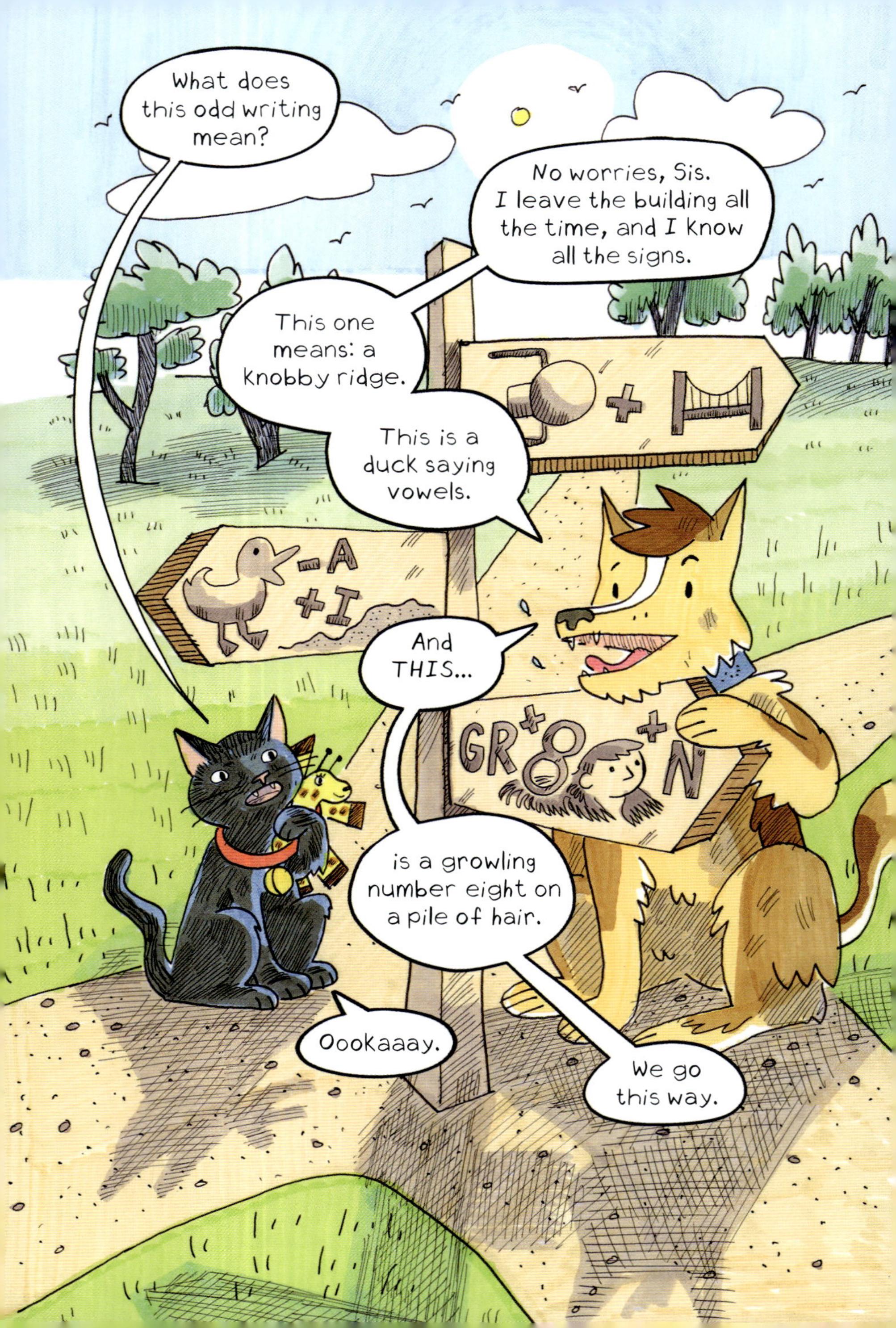

What does this odd writing mean?
No worries, Sis. I leave the building all the time, and I know all the signs.
This one means: a knobby ridge.
This is a duck saying vowels.
-A +I
And THIS...
GR+8+N
is a growling number eight on a pile of hair.
Oookaaay.
We go this way.

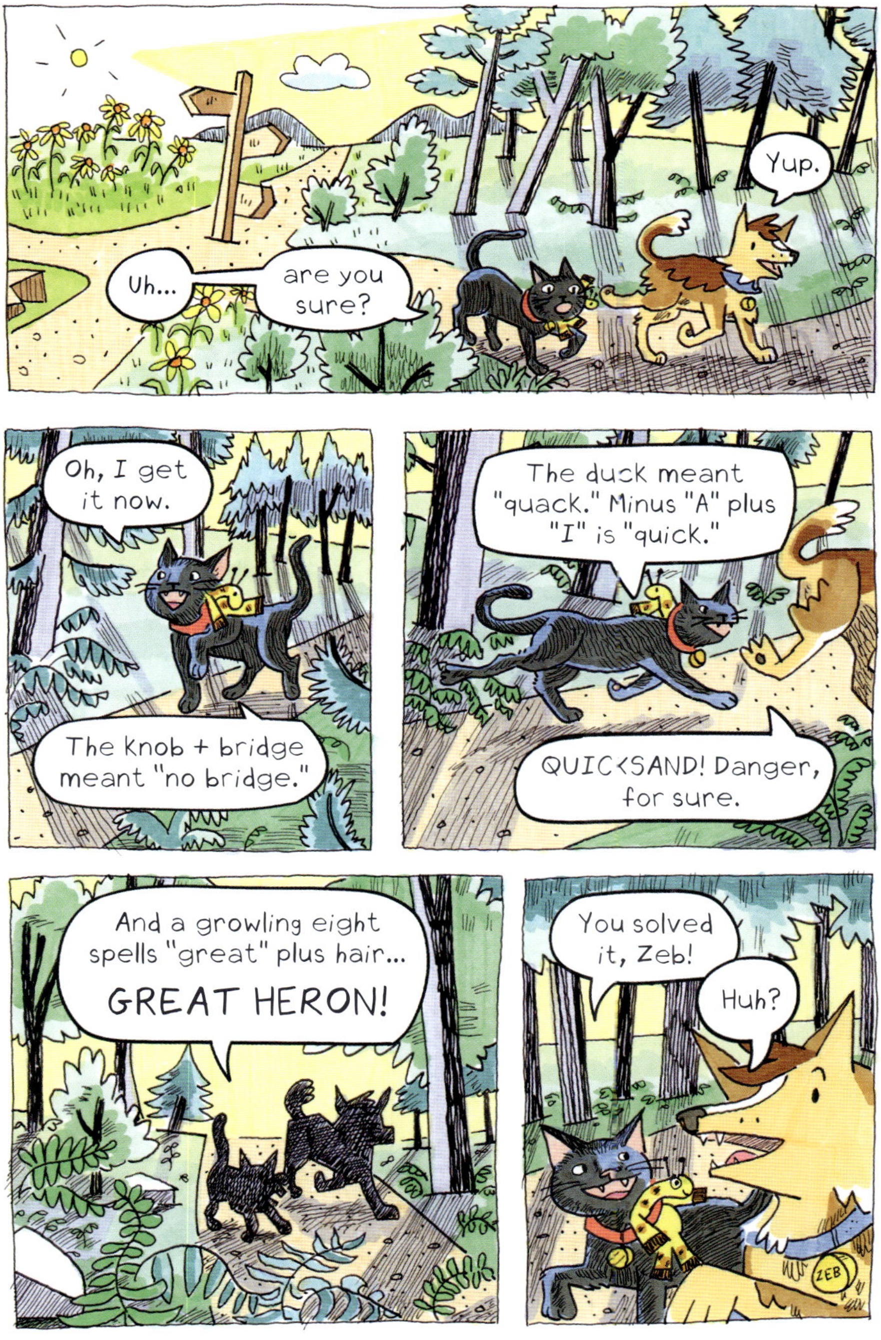
Yup.
Uh...
are you sure?
Oh, I get it now.
The knob + bridge meant "no bridge."
The duck meant "quack." Minus "A" plus "I" is "quick."
QUICKSAND! Danger, for sure.
And a growling eight spells "great" plus hair...
GREAT HERON!
You solved it, Zeb!
Huh?
ZEB

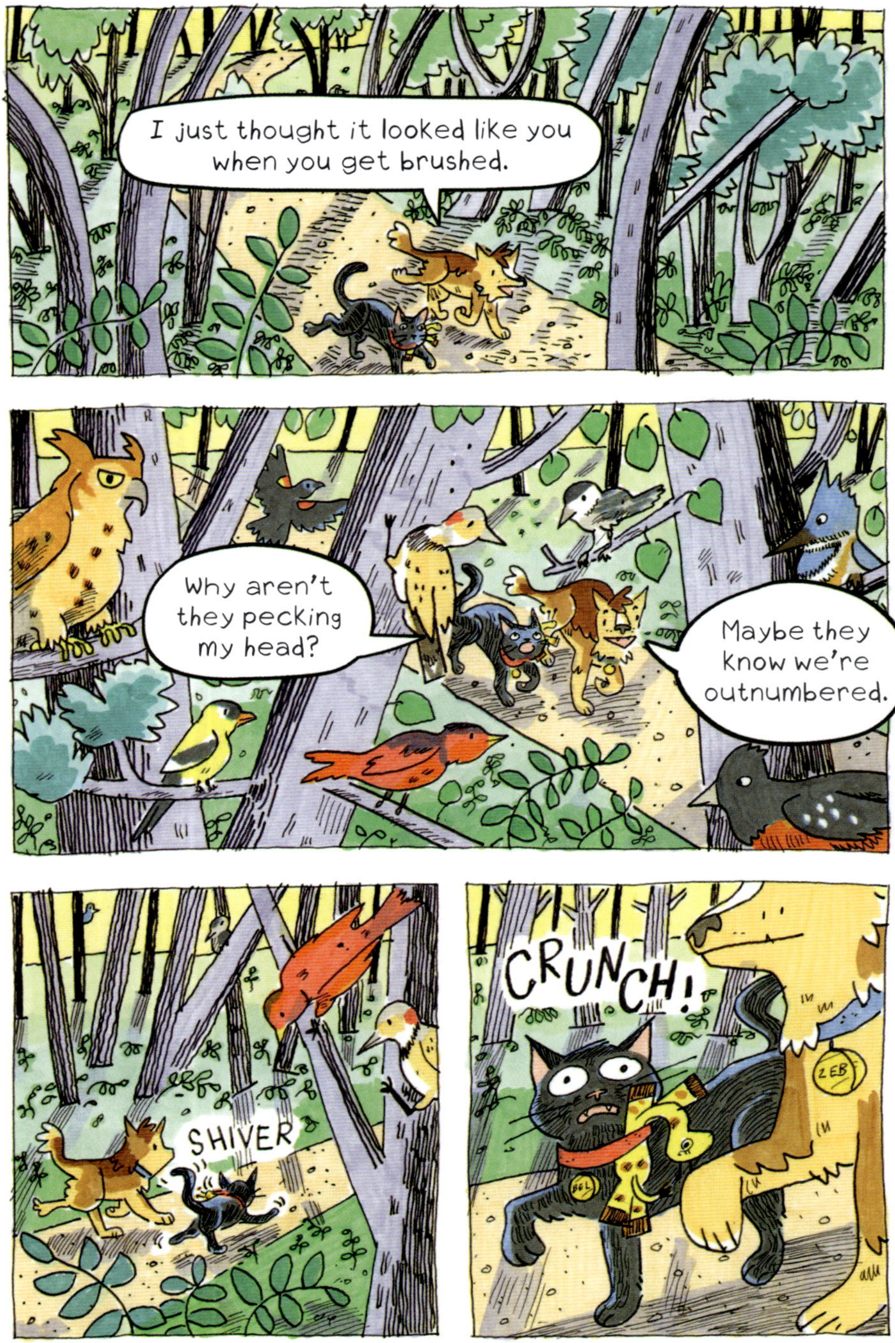
I just thought it looked like you when you get brushed.
Why aren't they pecking my head?
Maybe they know we're outnumbered.
SHIVER
CRUNCH!
ZEB

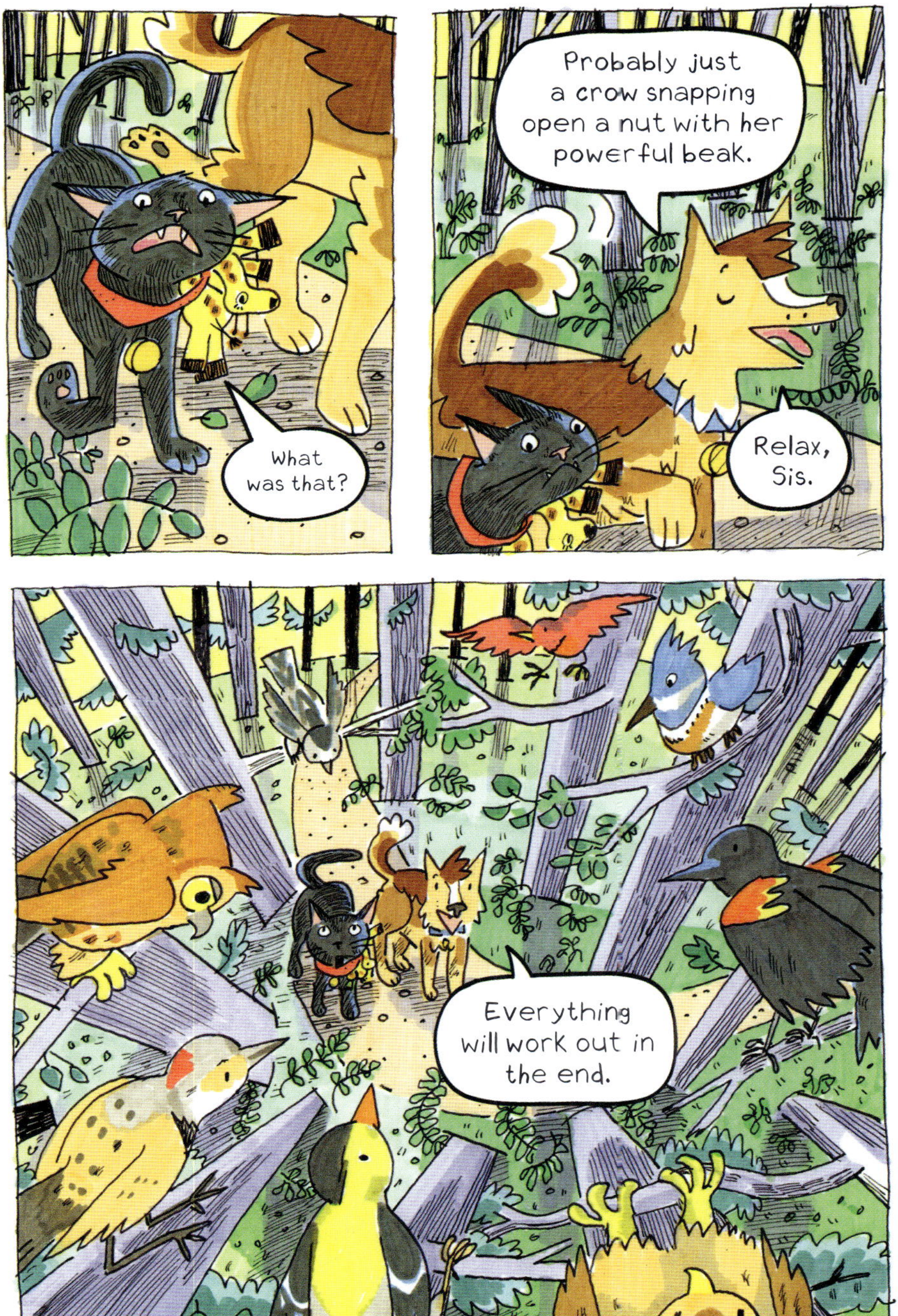
What was that?
Probably just a crow snapping open a nut with her powerful beak.
Relax, Sis.
Everything will work out in the end.

CHAPTER 10
A MEETING WITH GREATNESS

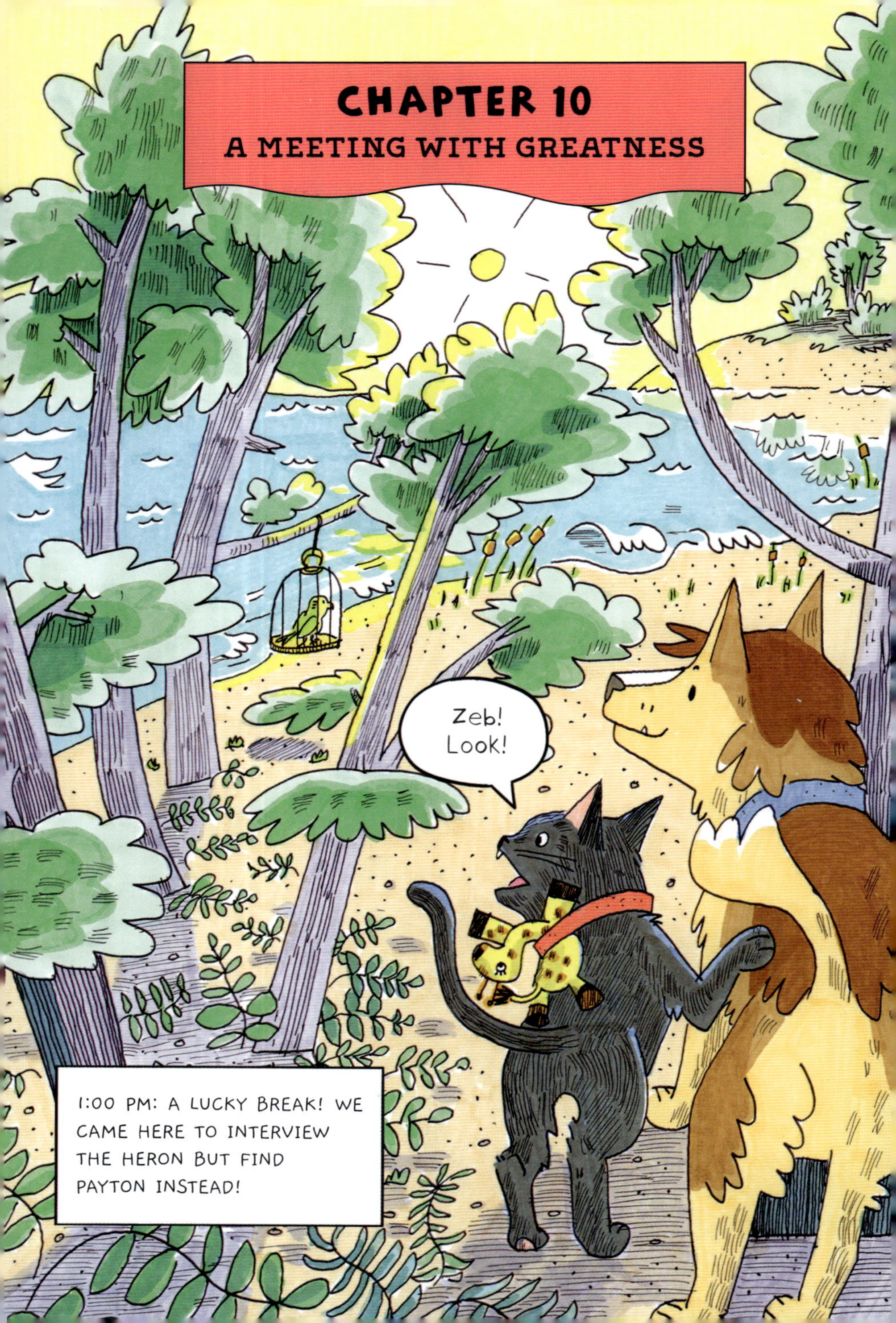
Zeb! Look!
1:00 PM: A LUCKY BREAK! WE CAME HERE TO INTERVIEW THE HERON BUT FIND PAYTON INSTEAD!

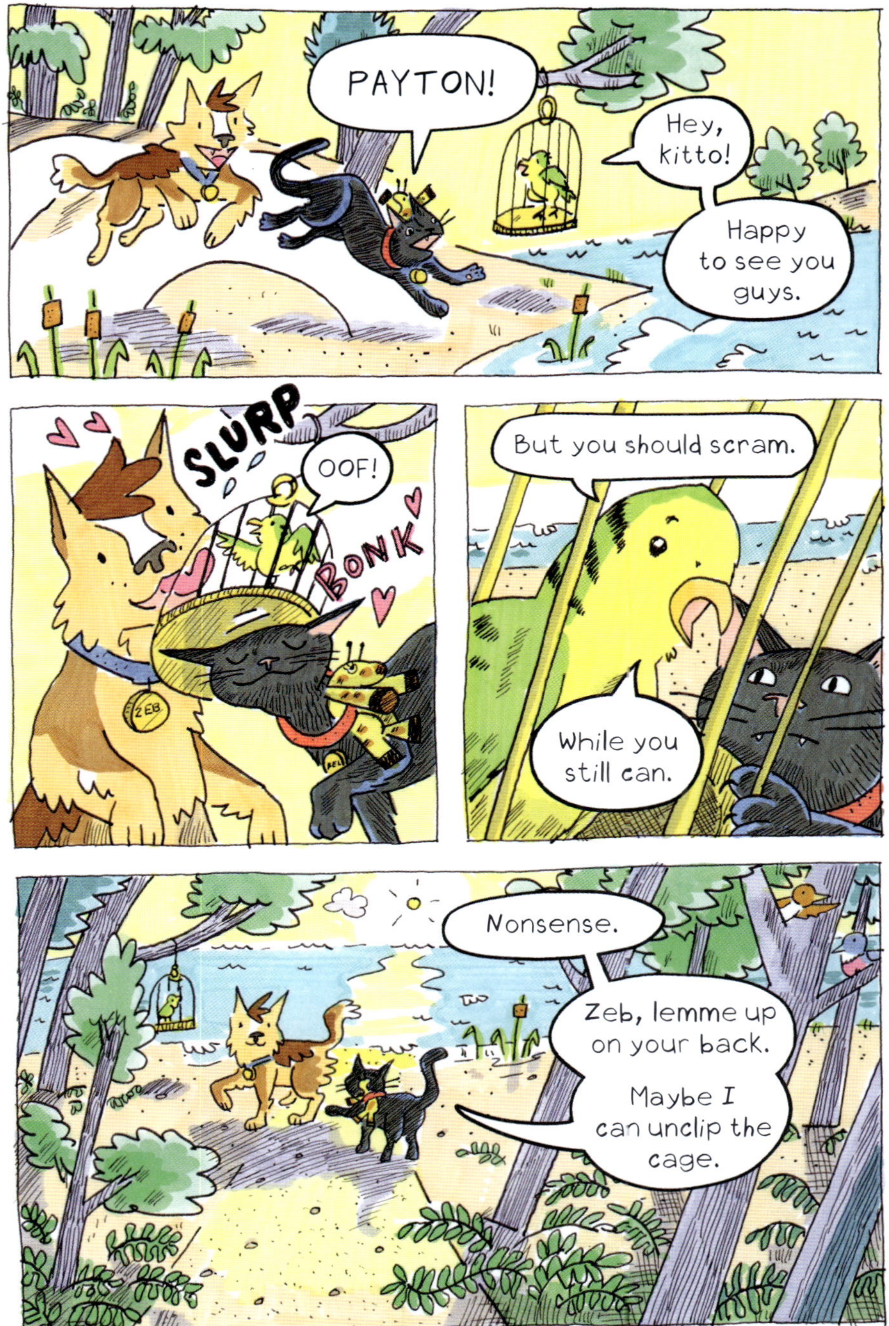
PAYTON!
Hey, kitto!
Happy to see you guys.
SLURP
OOF!
BONK
But you should scram.
While you still can.
ZEB
Nonsense.
Zeb, lemme up on your back.
Maybe I can unclip the cage.

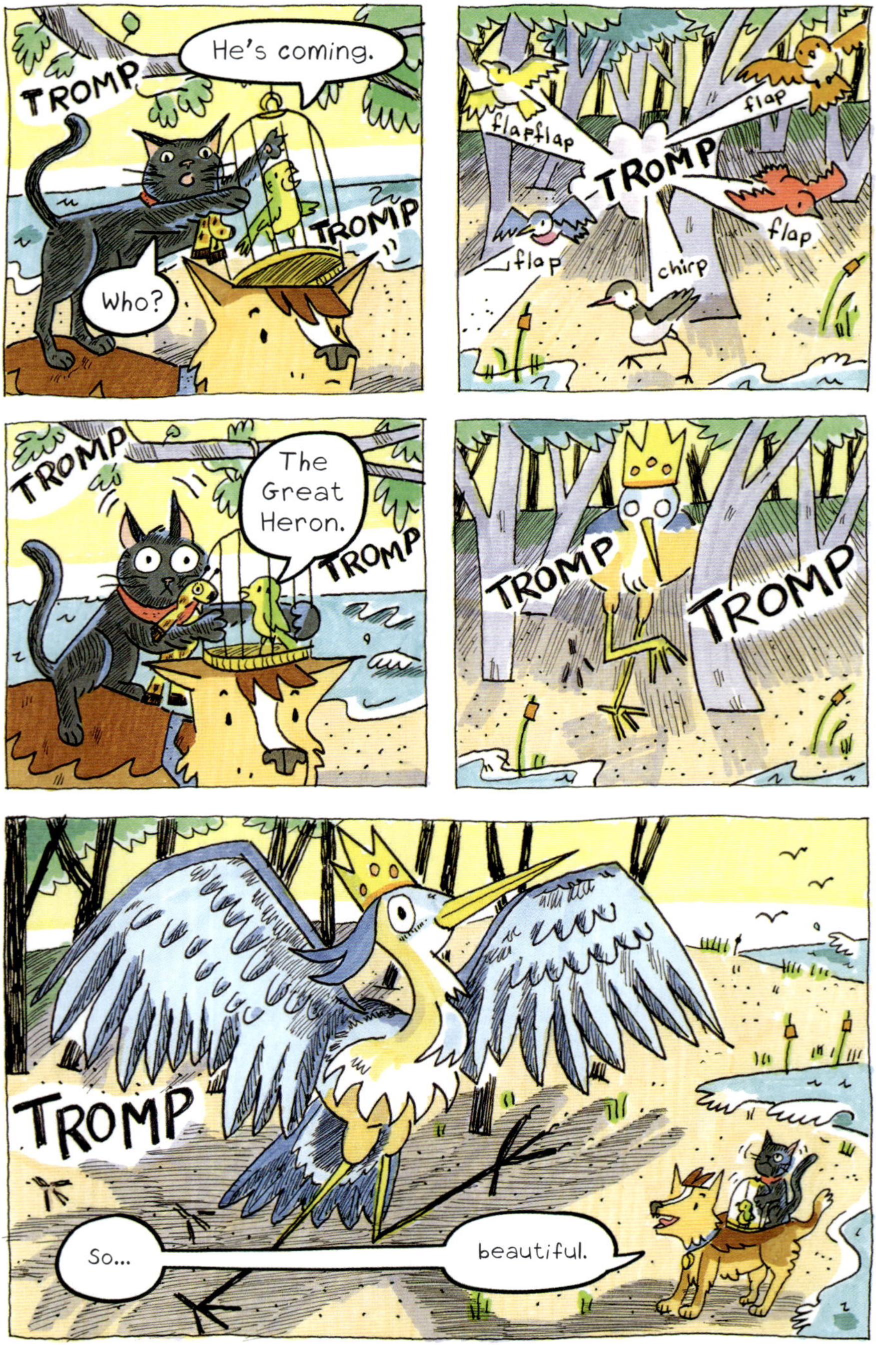
TROMP
He's coming.
TROMP
Who?
flapflap
flap
TROMP
flap
flap
chirp
TROMP
The Great Heron.
TROMP
TROMP
TROMP
TROMP
So...
beautiful.

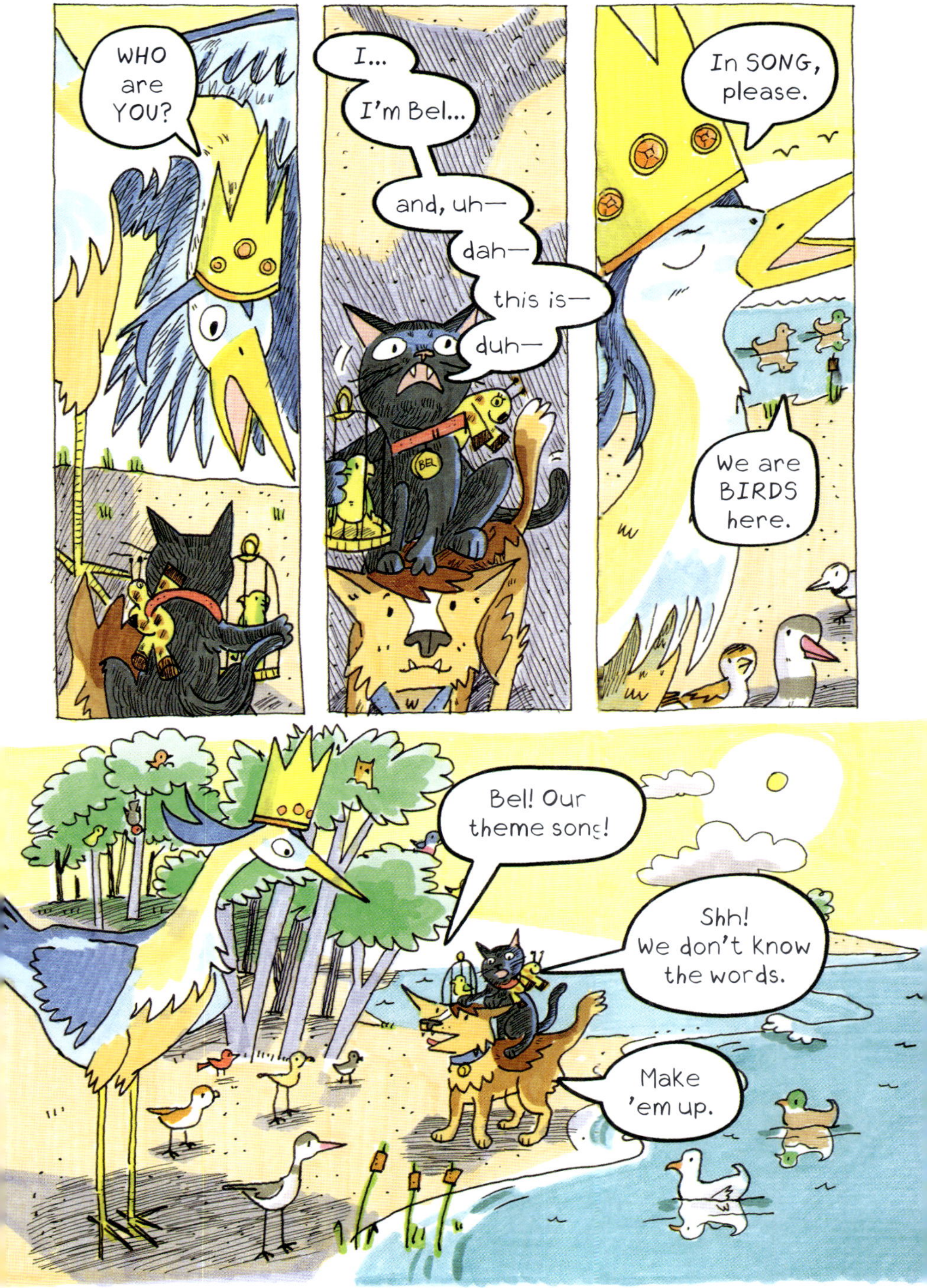
WHO are YOU?
I...
I'm Bel...
and, uh—
dah—
this is—
duh—
In SONG, please.
We are BIRDS here.
Bel! Our theme song!
Shh! We don't know the words.
Make 'em up.

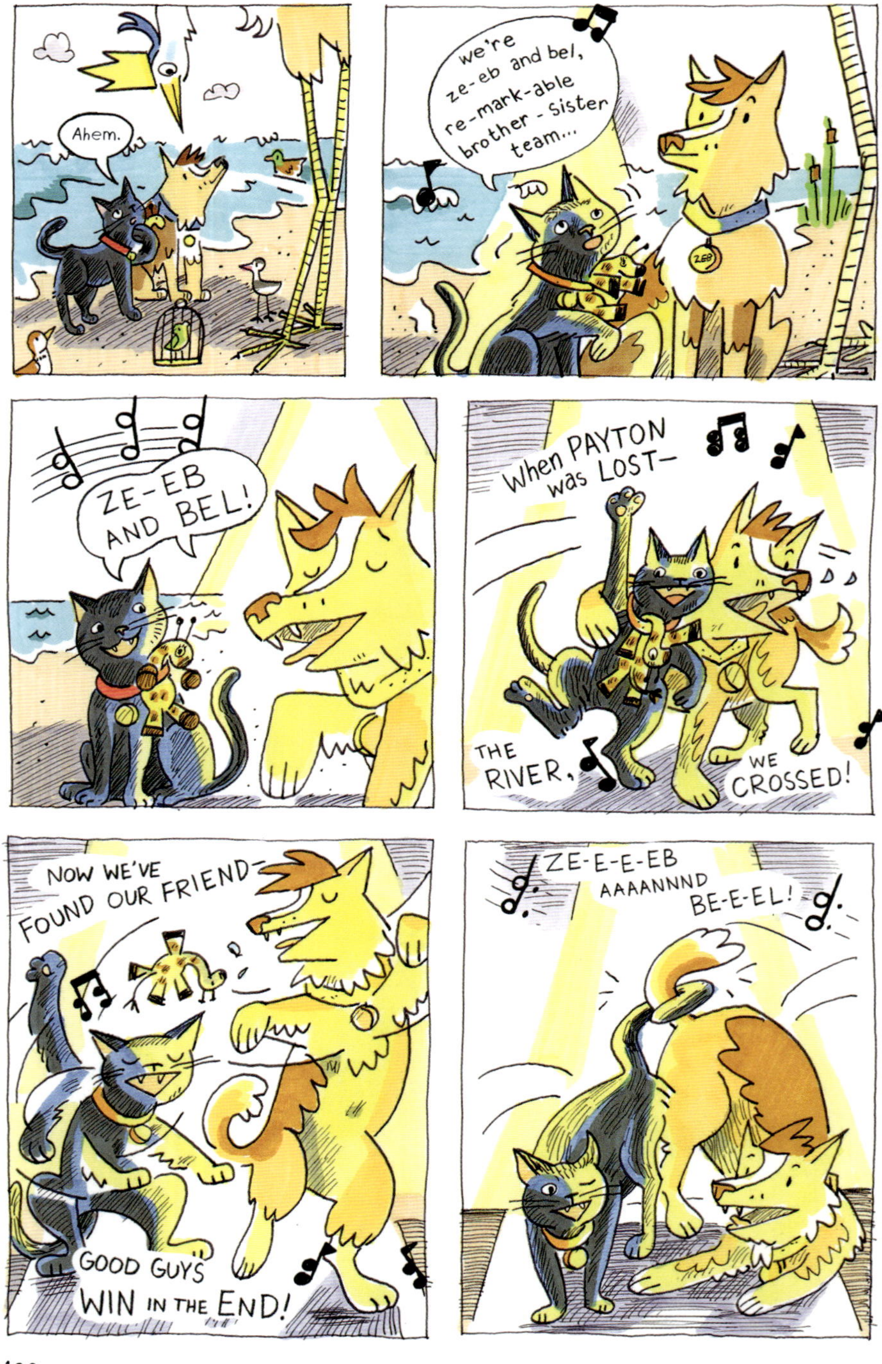
Ahem.
we're ze-eb and bel, re-mark-able brother-sister team...
ZEB
ZE-EB AND BEL!
When PAYTON was LOST—
THE RIVER,
WE CROSSED!
NOW WE'VE FOUND OUR FRIEND—
GOOD GUYS WIN IN THE END!
ZE-E-E-EB AAAANNND BE-E-EL!

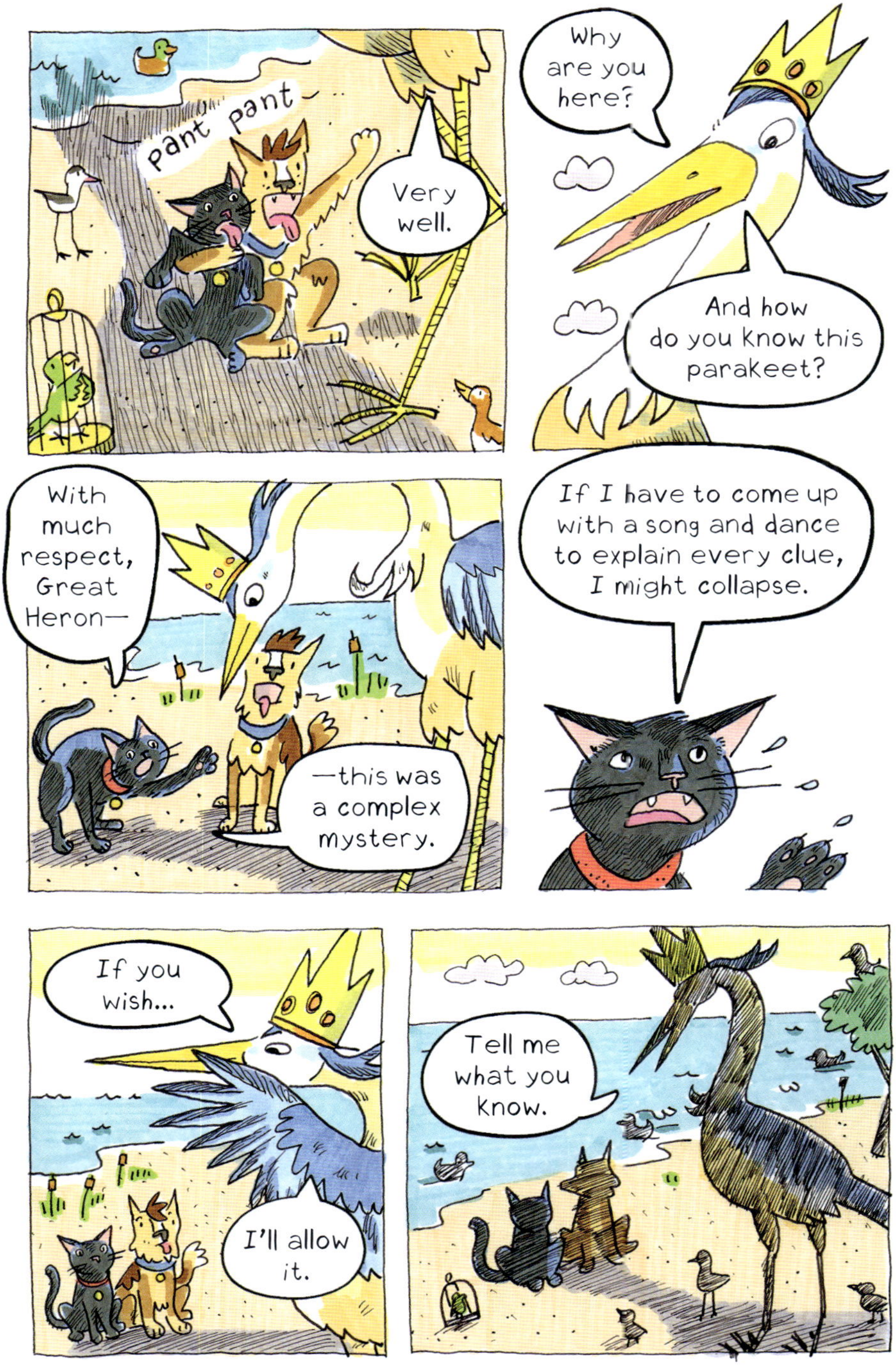
pant pant
Very well.
Why are you here?
And how do you know this parakeet?
With much respect, Great Heron—
—this was a complex mystery.
If I have to come up with a song and dance to explain every clue, I might collapse.
If you wish...
I'll allow it.
Tell me what you know.

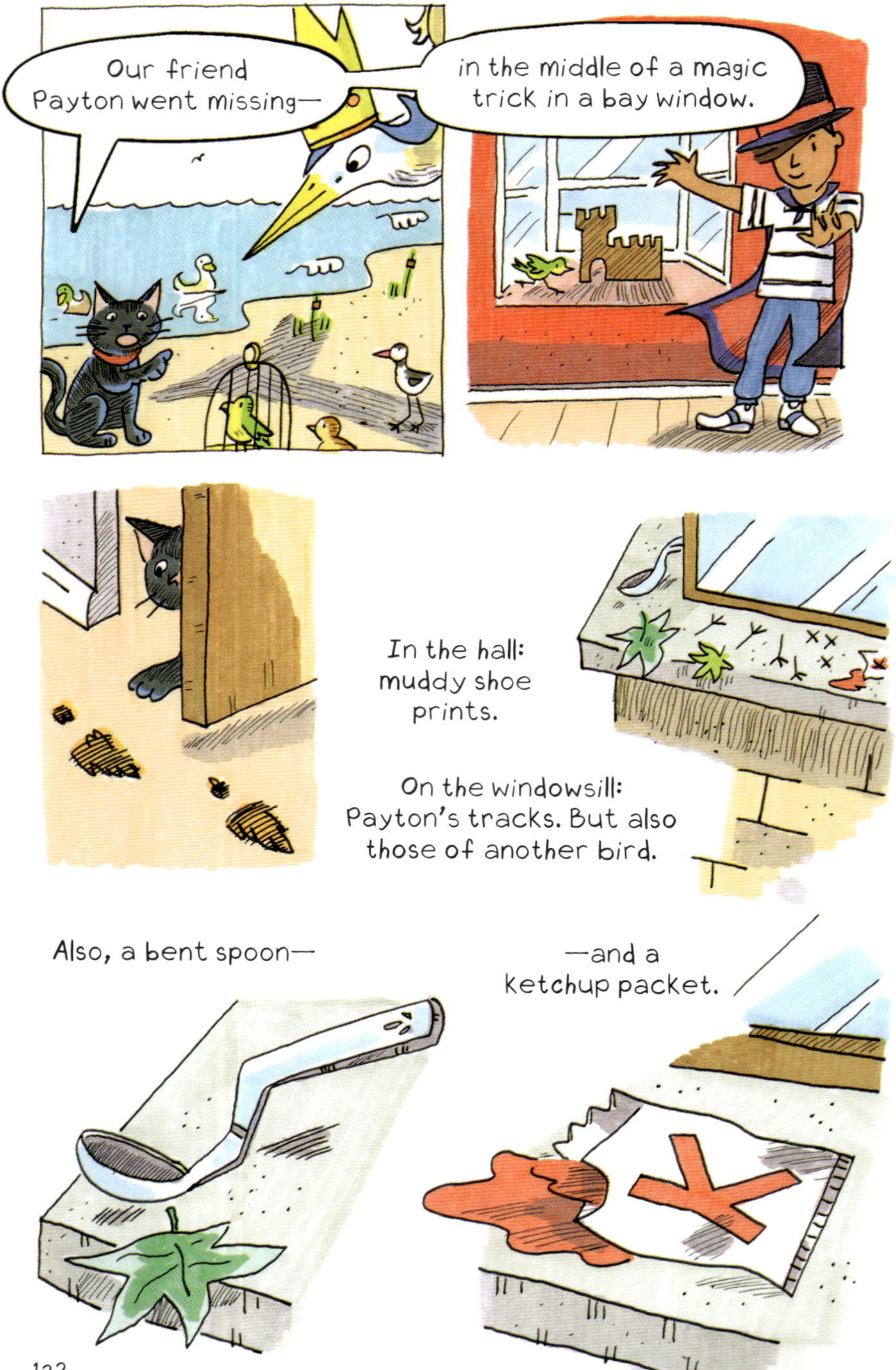
Our friend Payton went missing—
in the middle of a magic trick in a bay window.
In the hall: muddy shoe prints.
On the windowsill: Payton's tracks. But also those of another bird.
Also, a bent spoon—
—and a ketchup packet.

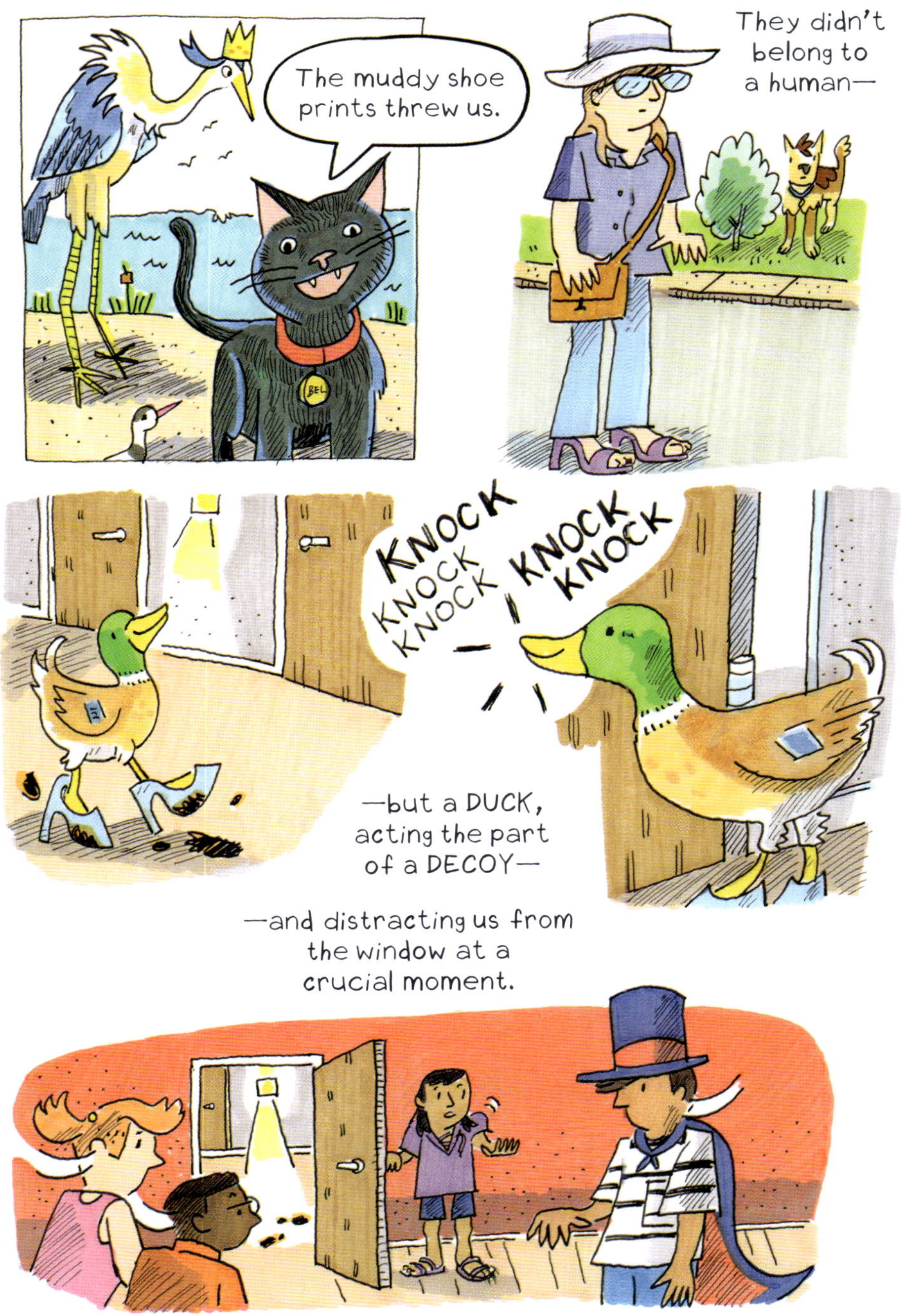
The muddy shoe prints threw us.
BEL
They didn't belong to a human—
KNOCK KNOCK KNOCK
KNOCK KNOCK
—but a DUCK, acting the part of a DECOY—
—and distracting us from the window at a crucial moment.

A bird on the windowsill
opened the window...

...and reached through
the ripped screen with
a french fry box,

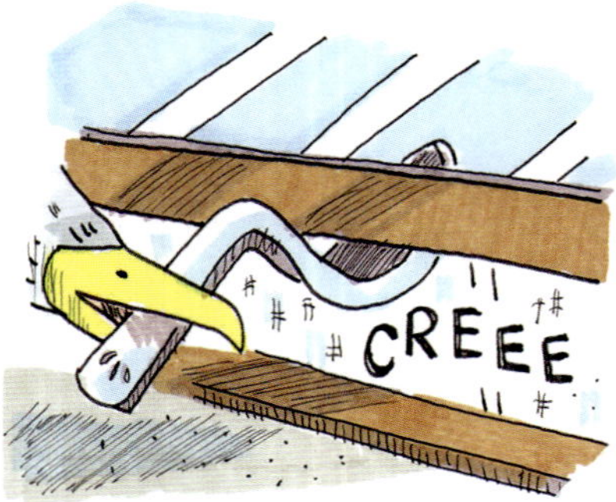
CREEE

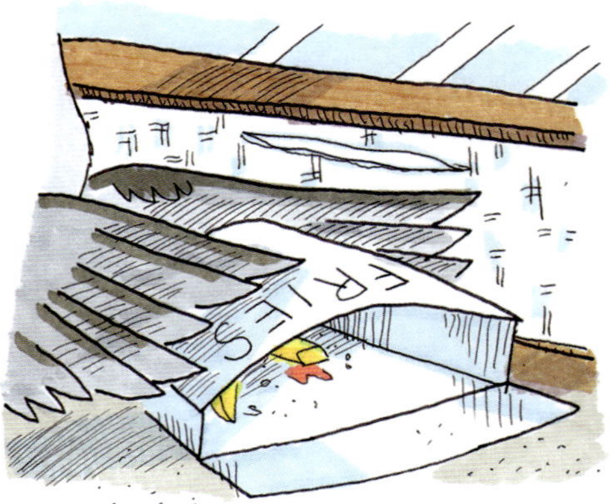
FRIES

setting up a MAGIC
TRAP of their own!

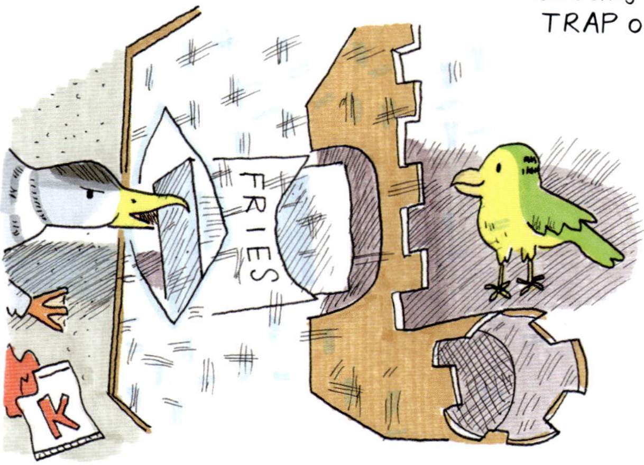
FRIES
K

Payton ran out
of the castle
into the box.
There must've
been a short
struggle on
the sill.

But by the time
the prop castle
collapsed in a
puff of smoke,

the bird was
carrying
Payton on
a flight to
the bird
sanctuary.

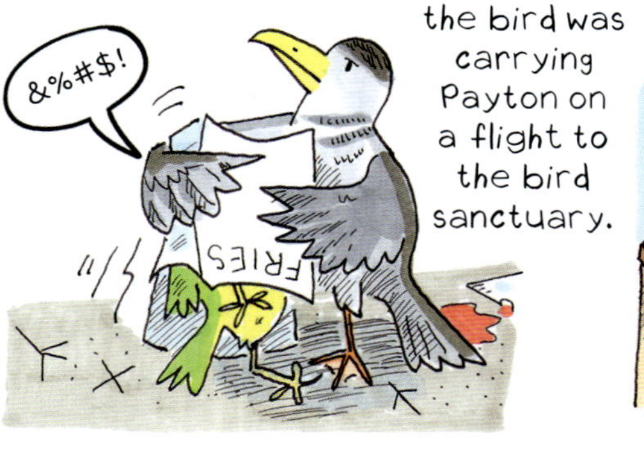
&%#$!
FRIES

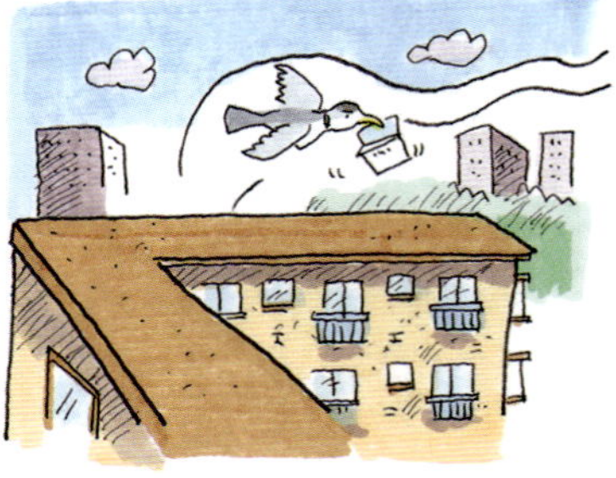

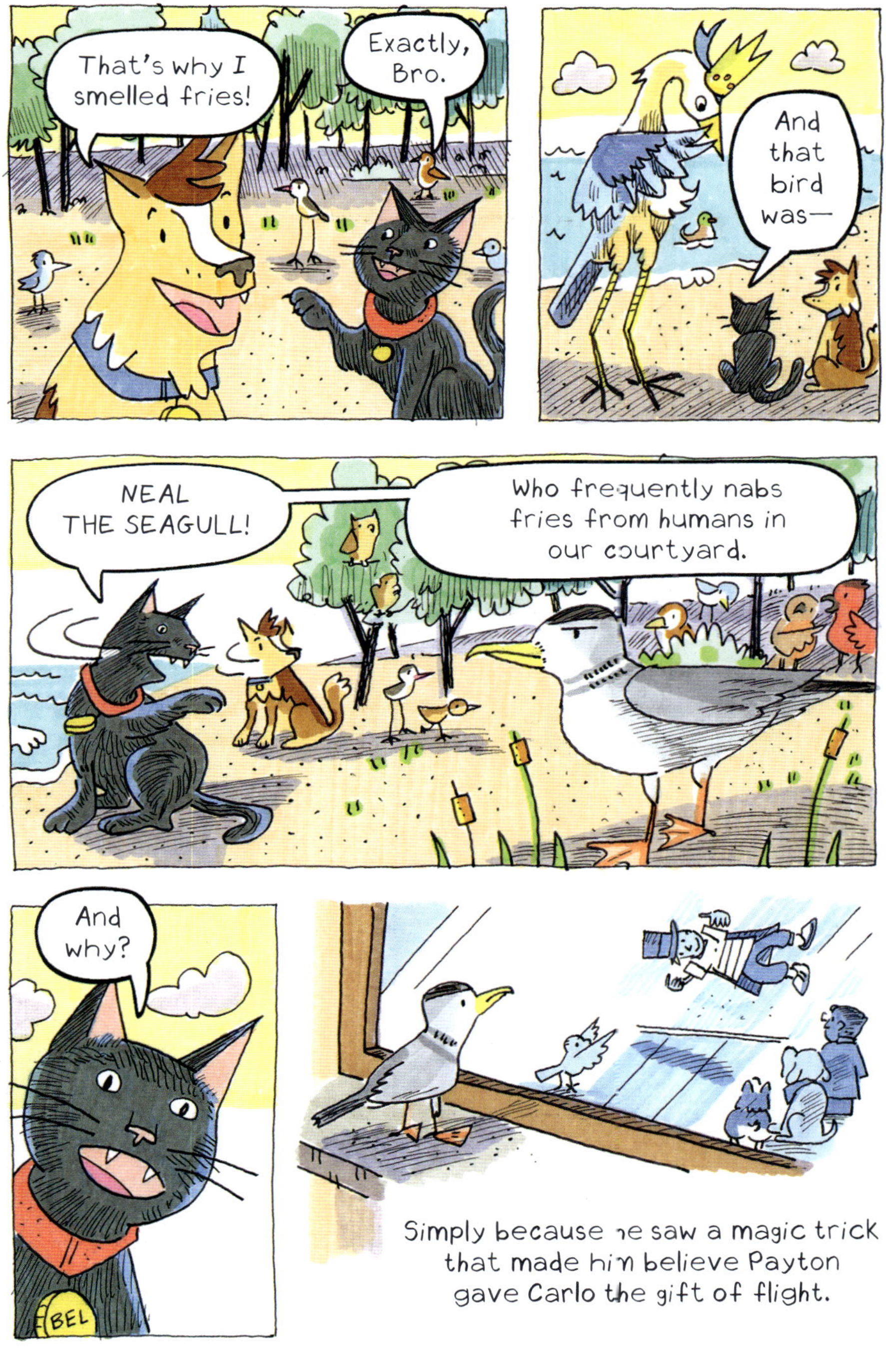

That's why I smelled fries!
Exactly, Bro.
And that bird was—
NEAL THE SEAGULL!
Who frequently nabs fries from humans in our courtyard.
And why?
BEL
Simply because he saw a magic trick that made him believe Payton gave Carlo the gift of flight.

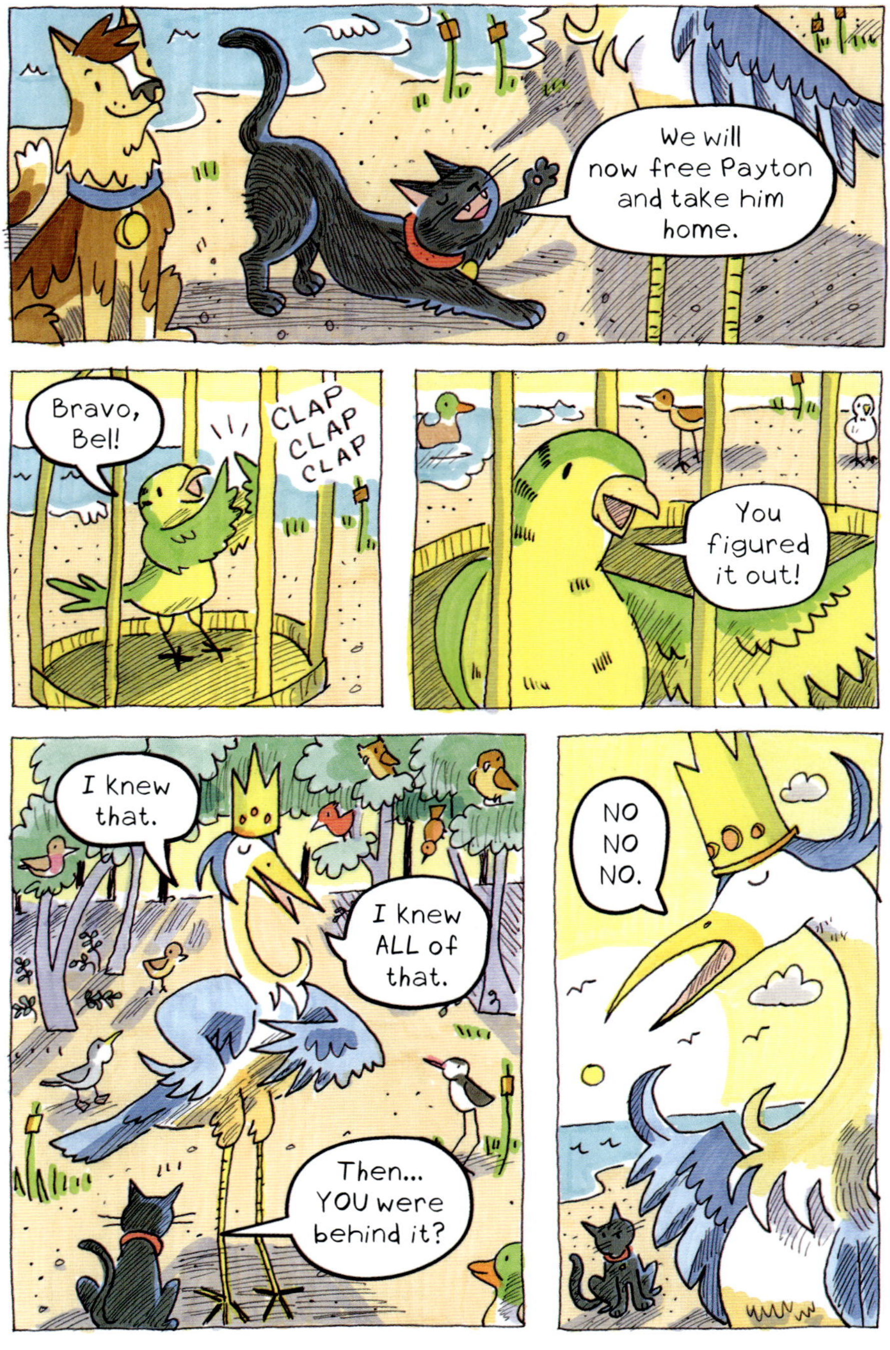
We will now free Payton and take him home.
Bravo, Bel!
CLAP CLAP CLAP
You figured it out!
I knew that.
I knew ALL of that.
Then... YOU were behind it?
NO NO NO.

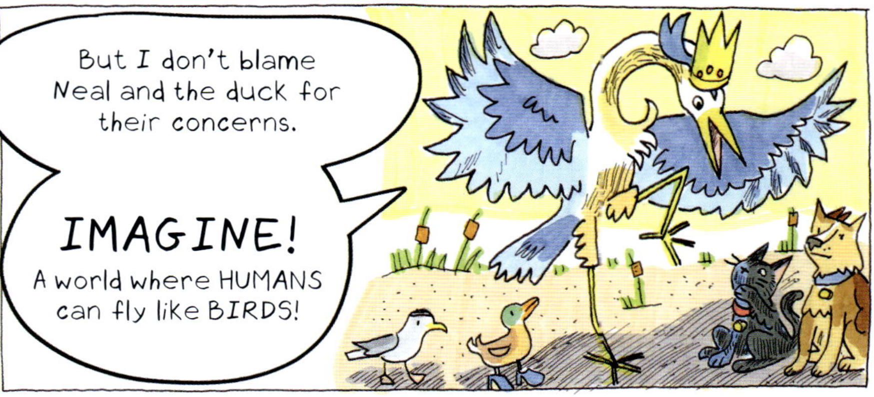
But I don't blame Neal and the duck for their concerns.
IMAGINE!
A world where HUMANS can fly like BIRDS!

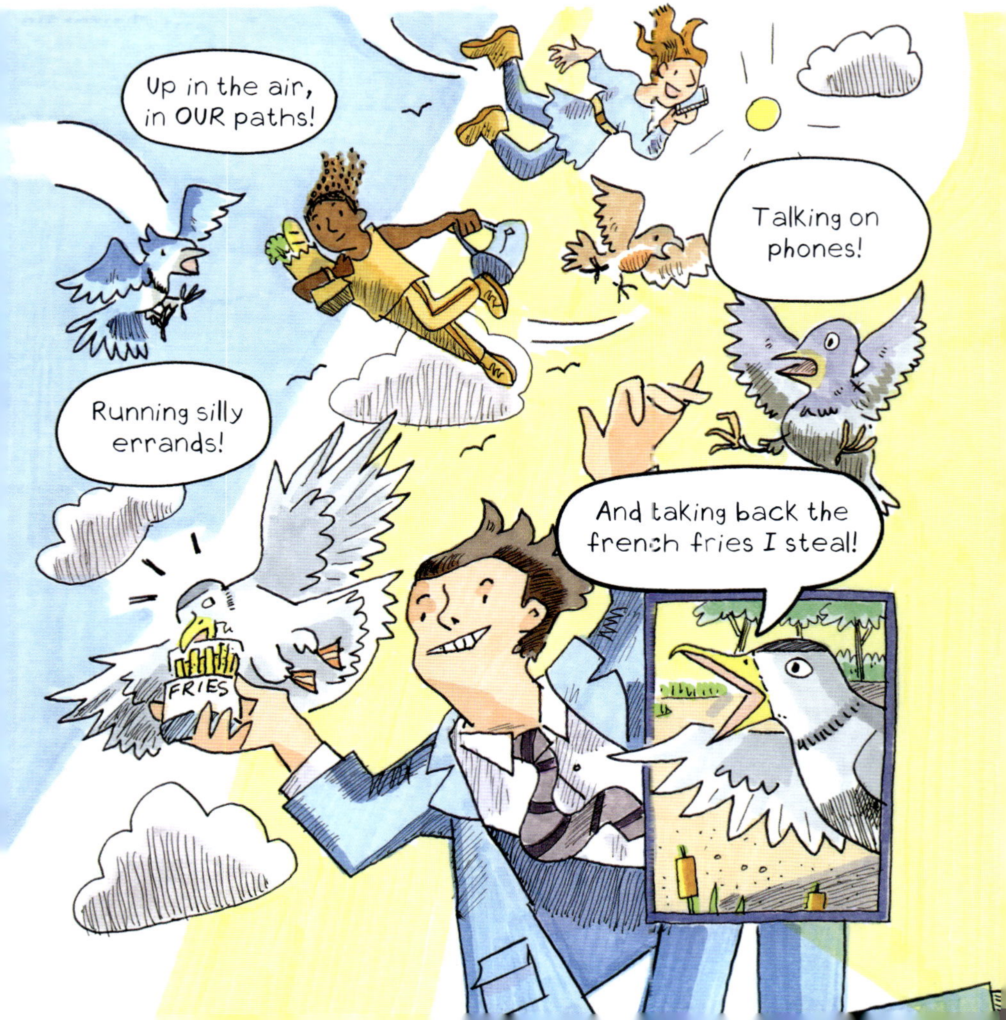
Up in the air, in OUR paths!
Talking on phones!
Running silly errands!
And taking back the french fries I steal!
FRIES

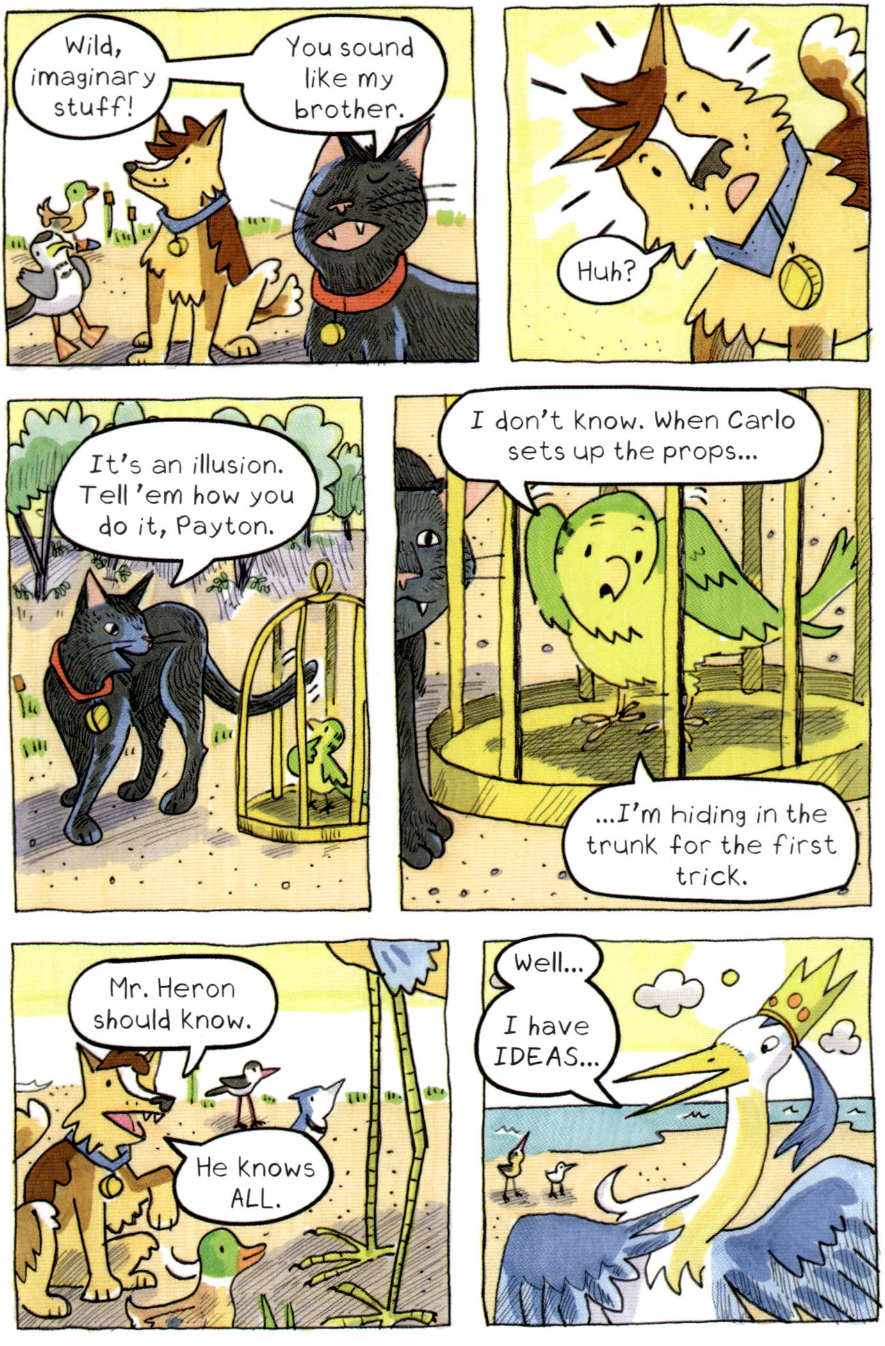
Wild, imaginary stuff!
You sound like my brother.
Huh?
It's an illusion. Tell 'em how you do it, Payton.
I don't know. When Carlo sets up the props...
...I'm hiding in the trunk for the first trick.
Mr. Heron should know.
He knows ALL.
Well...
I have IDEAS...

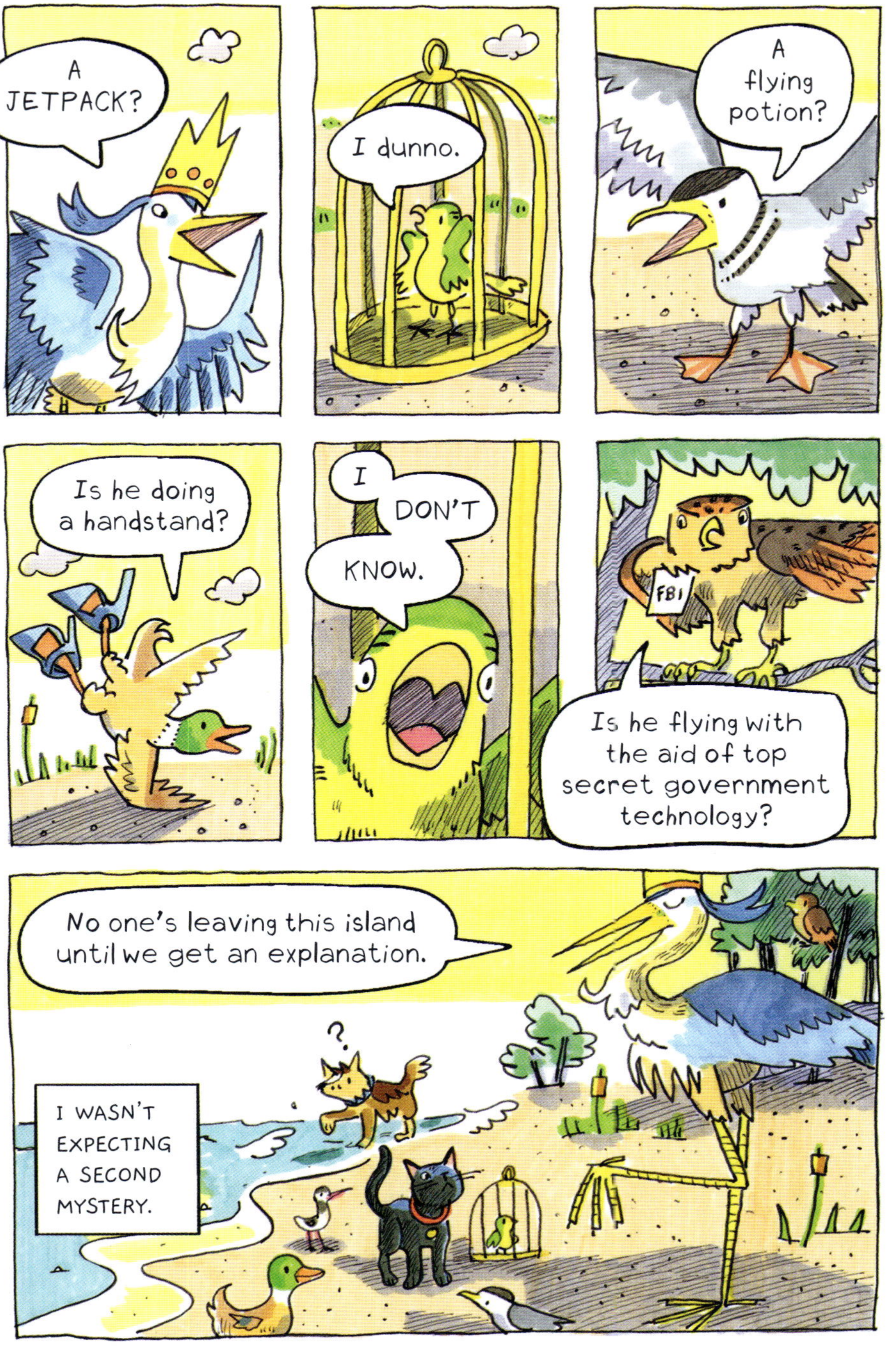
A JETPACK?
I dunno.
A flying potion?
Is he doing a handstand?
I DON'T KNOW.
FBI
Is he flying with the aid of top secret government technology?
No one's leaving this island until we get an explanation.
?
I WASN'T EXPECTING A SECOND MYSTERY.

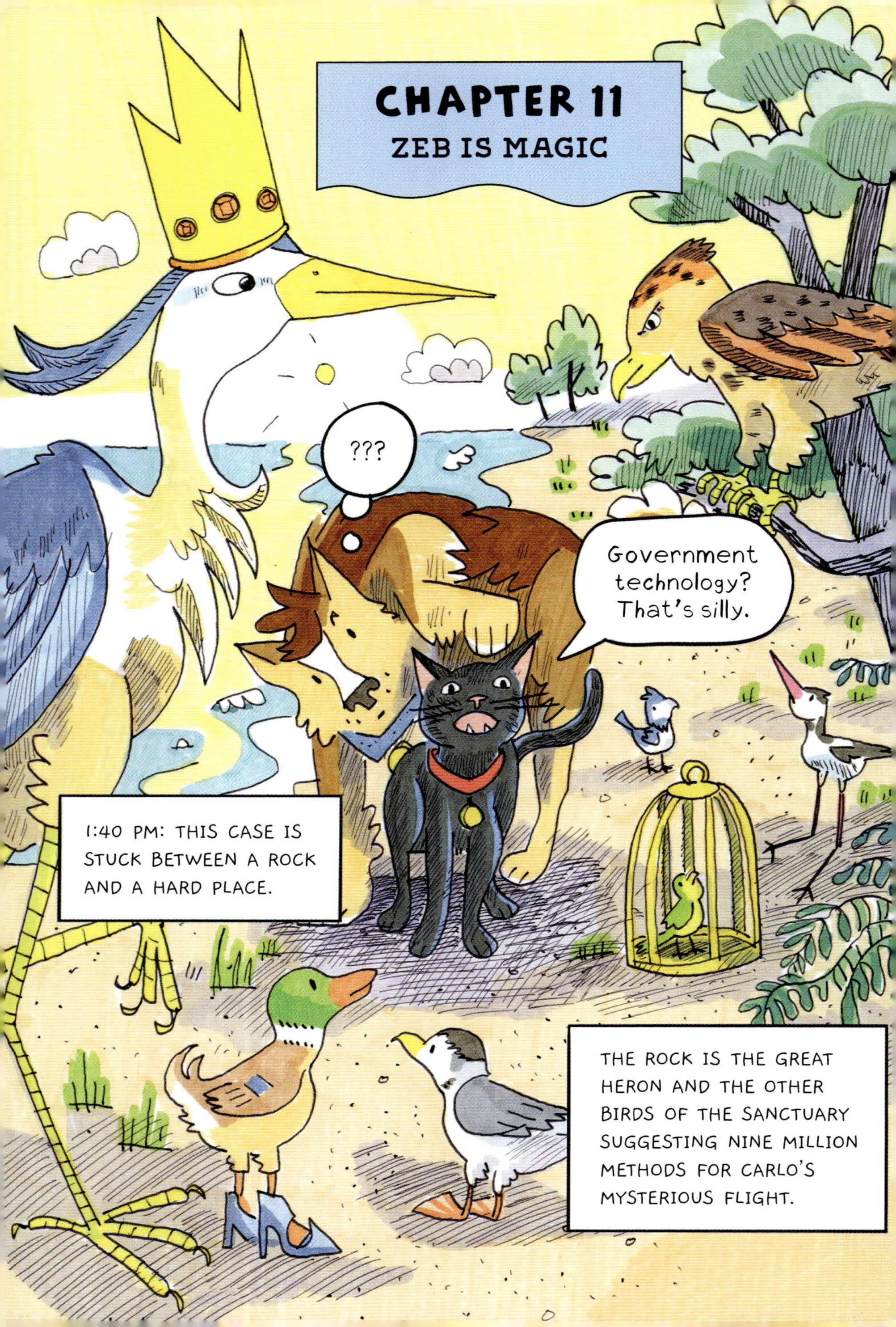
CHAPTER 11
ZEB IS MAGIC
???
Government technology? That's silly.
1:40 PM: THIS CASE IS STUCK BETWEEN A ROCK AND A HARD PLACE.
THE ROCK IS THE GREAT HERON AND THE OTHER BIRDS OF THE SANCTUARY SUGGESTING NINE MILLION METHODS FOR CARLO'S MYSTERIOUS FLIGHT.

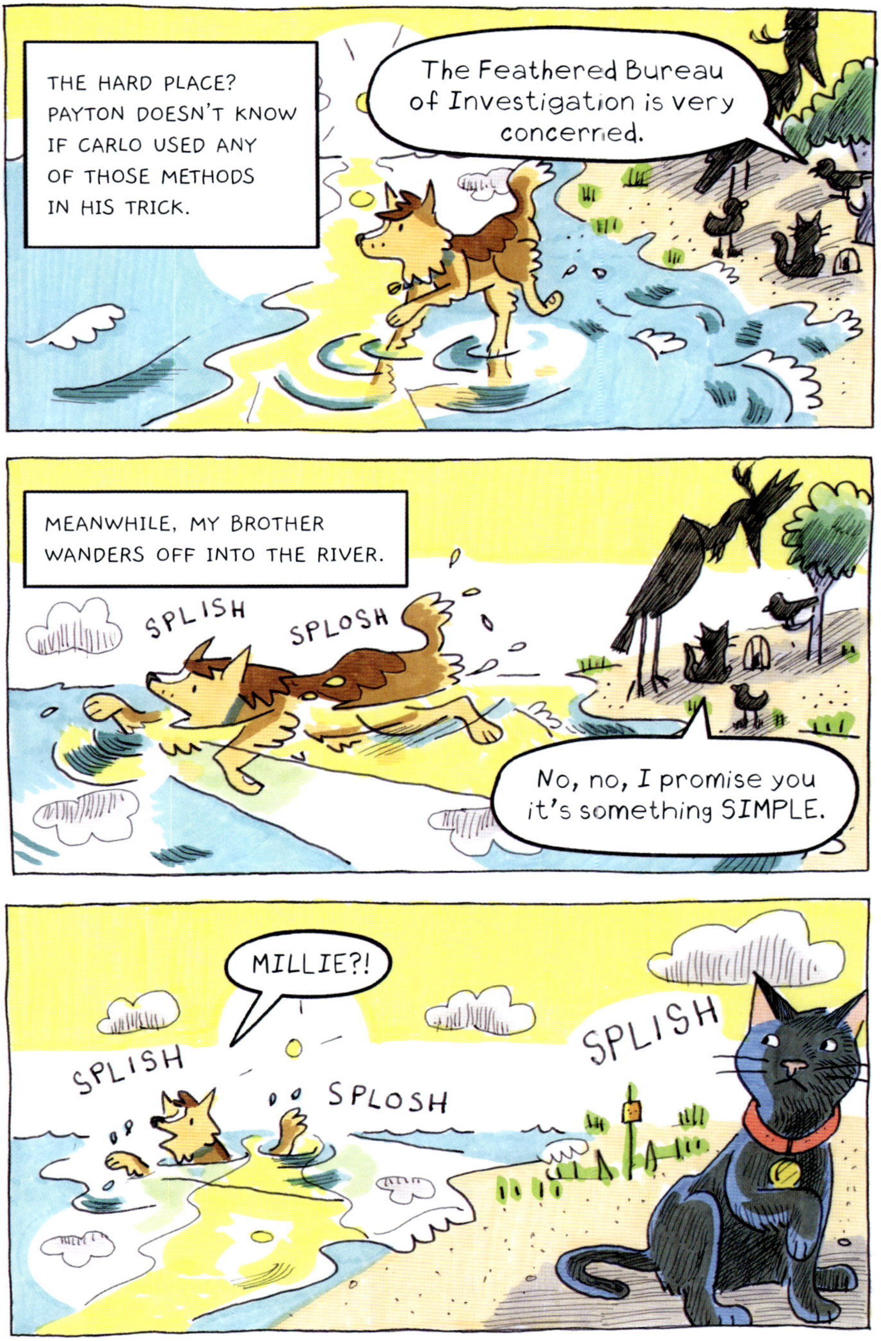
THE HARD PLACE? PAYTON DOESN'T KNOW IF CARLO USED ANY OF THOSE METHODS IN HIS TRICK.
The Feathered Bureau of Investigation is very concerned.
MEANWHILE, MY BROTHER WANDERS OFF INTO THE RIVER.
SPLISH
SPLOSH
No, no, I promise you it's something SIMPLE.
MILLIE?!
SPLISH
SPLOSH
SPLISH

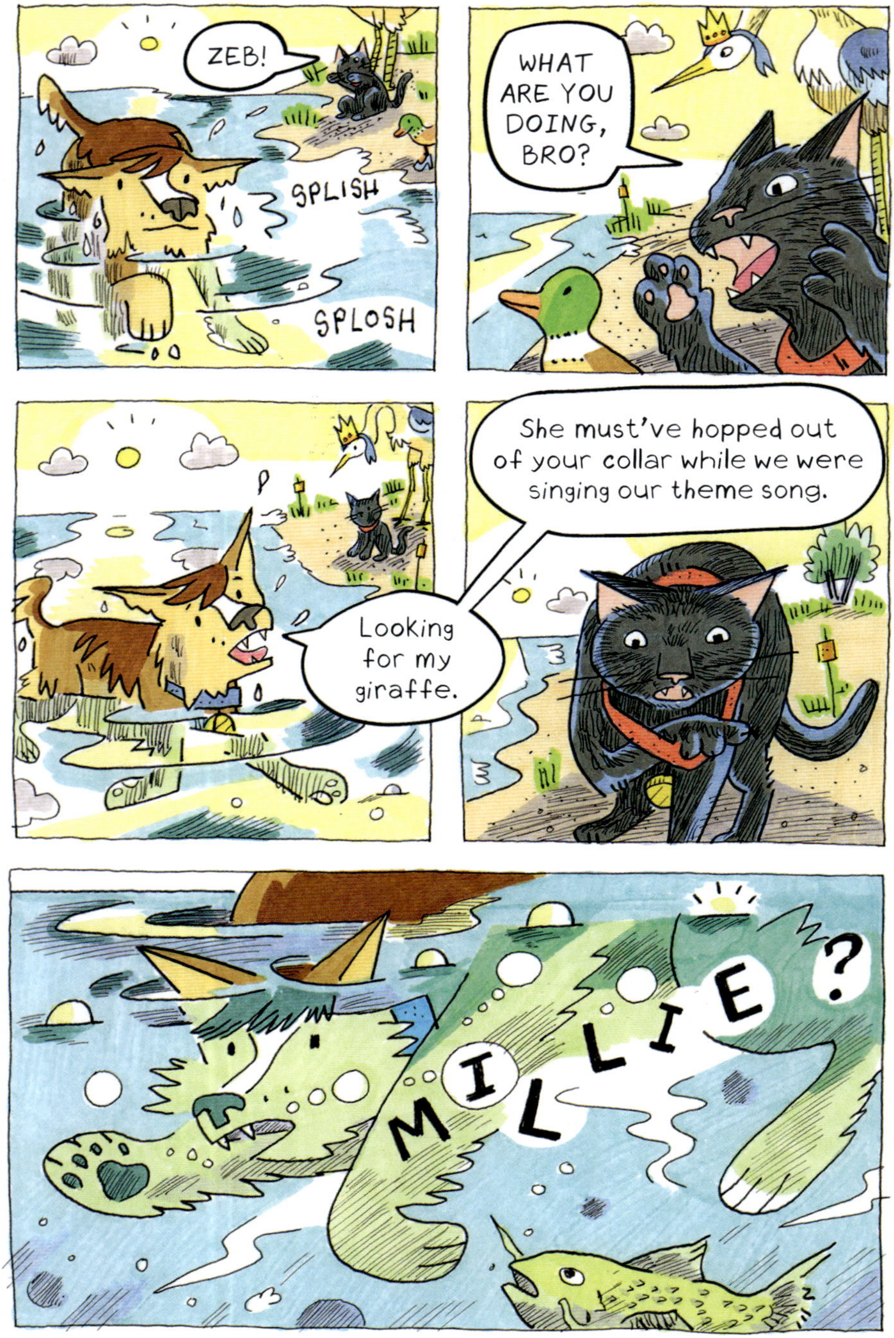
ZEB!
SPLISH
SPLOSH
WHAT ARE YOU DOING, BRO?
Looking for my giraffe.
She must've hopped out of your collar while we were singing our theme song.
MILLIE?

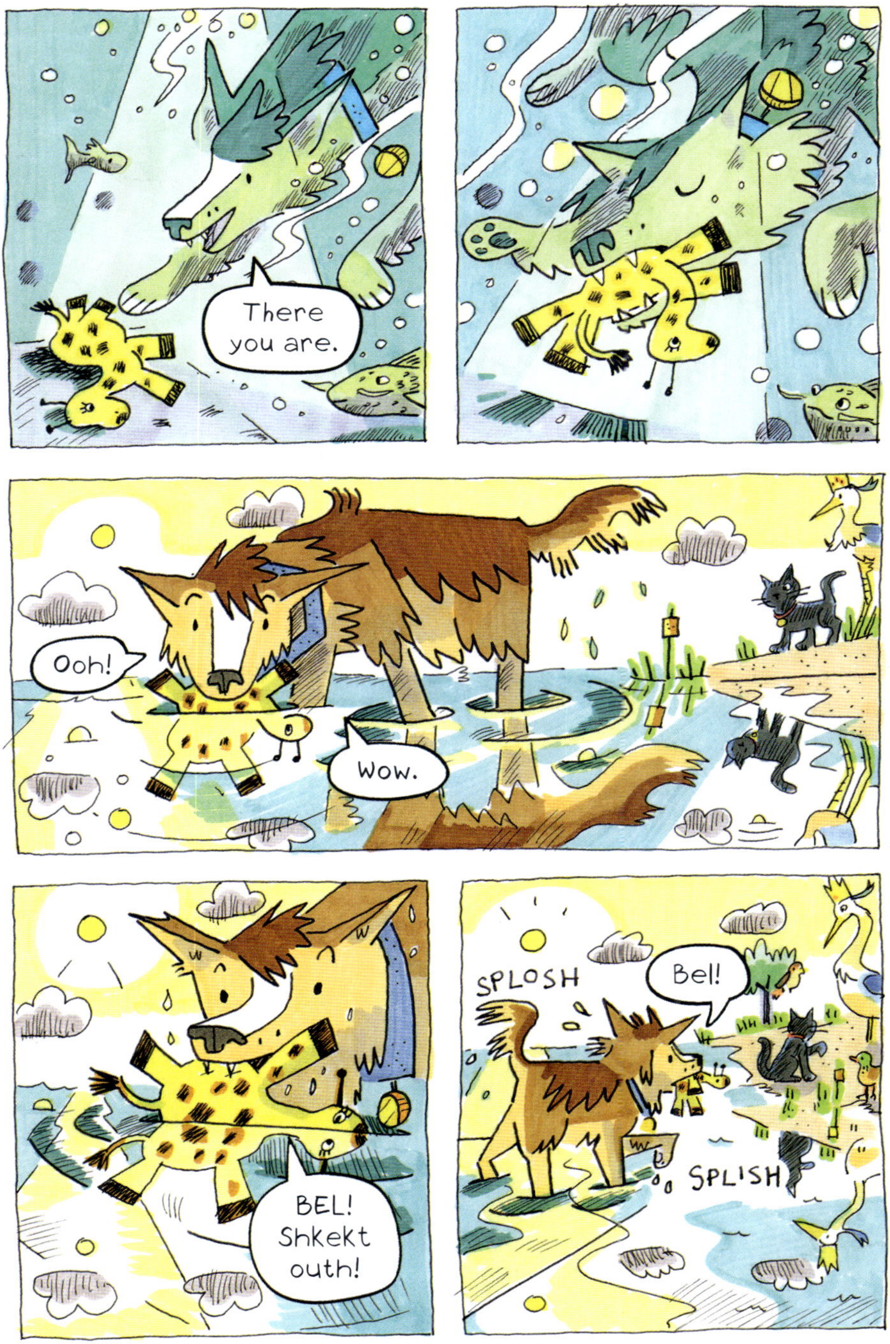
There you are.
Ooh!
Wow.
BEL! Shkekt outh!
SPLOSH
Bel!
SPLISH

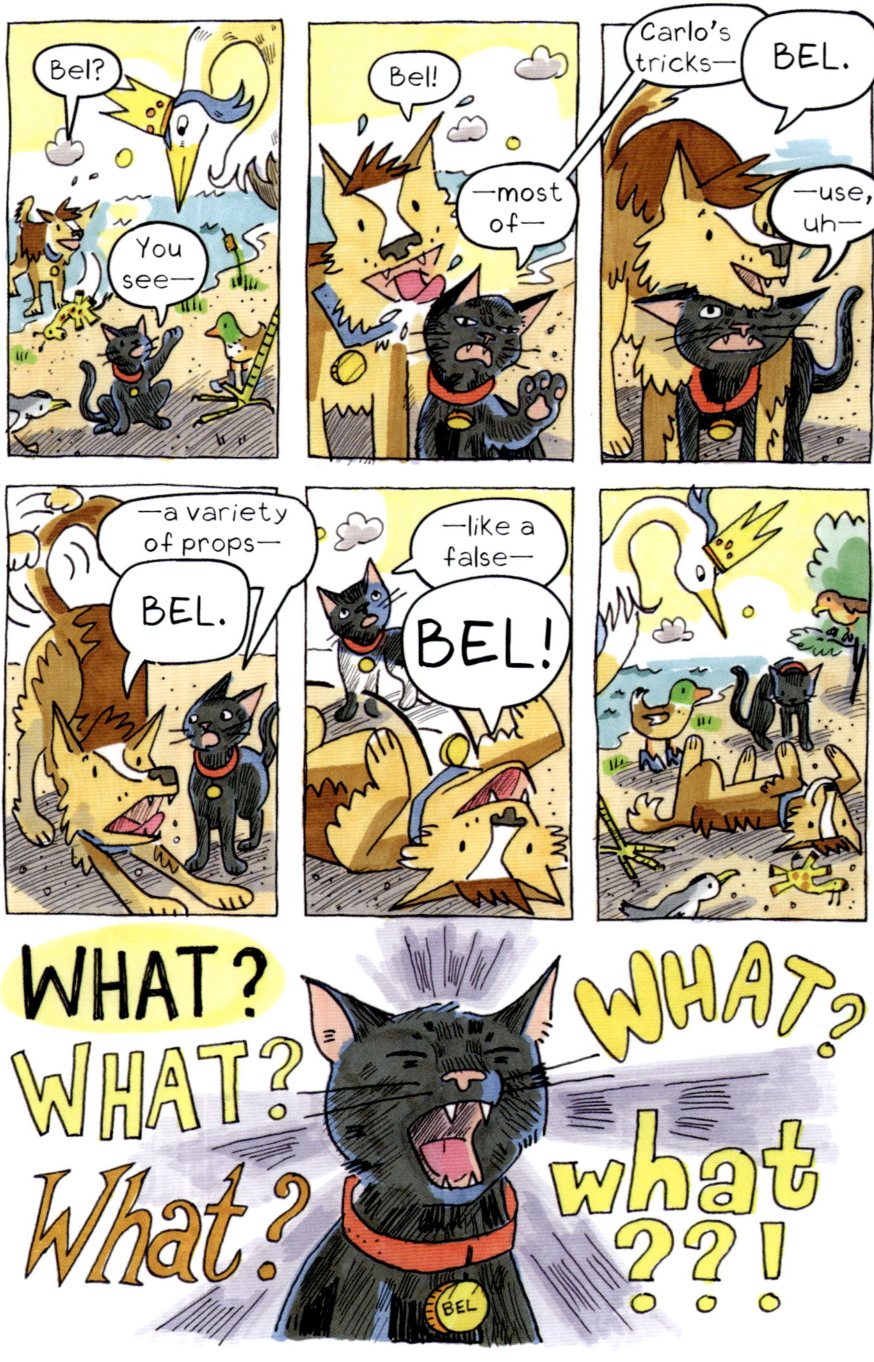
Bel?
You see—
Bel!
—most of—
Carlo's tricks—
BEL.
—use, uh—
—a variety of props—
BEL.
—like a false—
BEL!
WHAT?
WHAT?
What?
WHAT?
what ??!
BEL

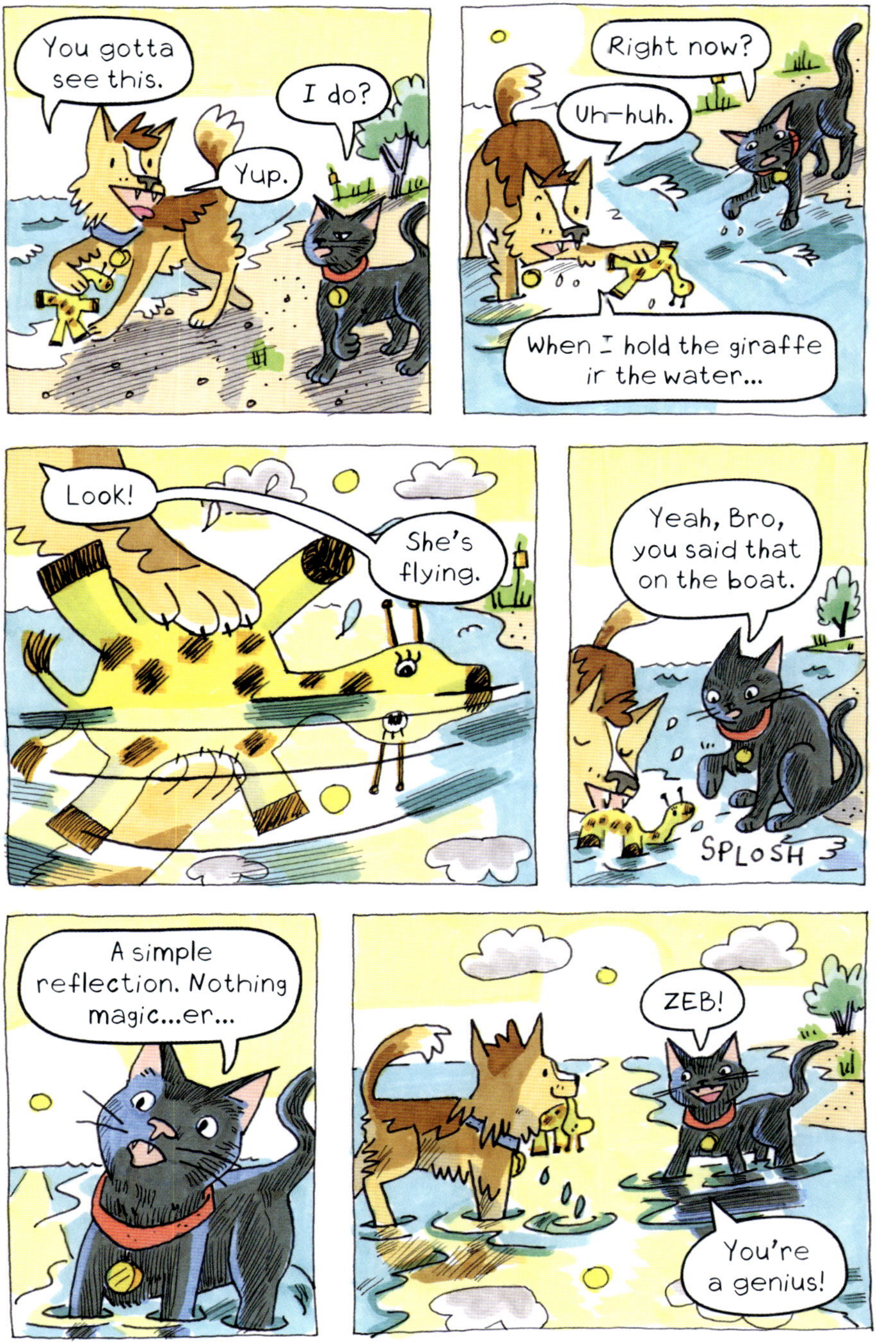

You gotta see this.
I do?
Yup.
Right now?
Uh-huh.
When I hold the giraffe ir the water...
Look!
She's flying.
Yeah, Bro, you said that on the boat.
SPLOSH
A simple reflection. Nothing magic...er...
ZEB!
You're a genius!

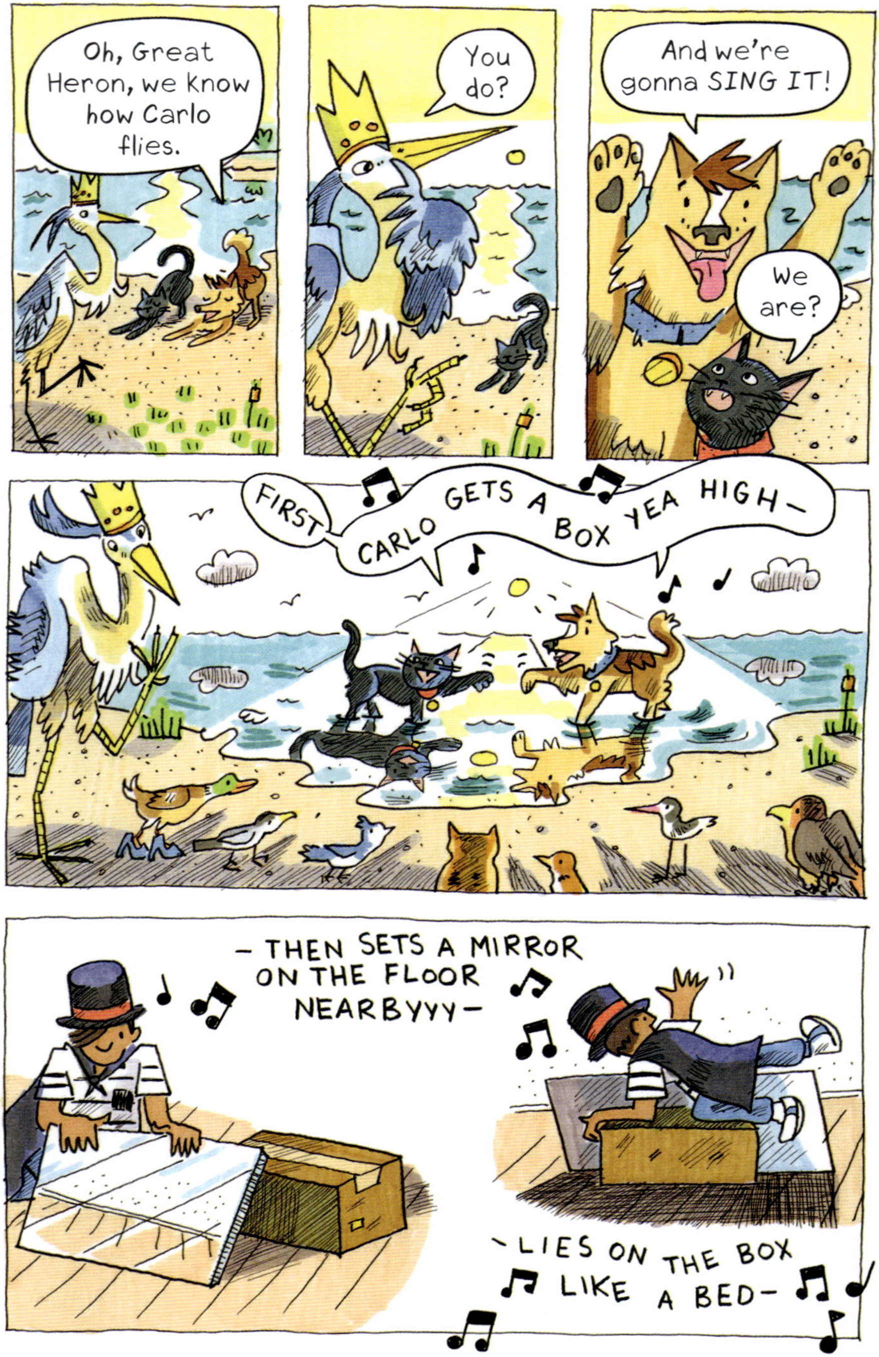
Oh, Great Heron, we know how Carlo flies.
You do?
And we're gonna SING IT!
We are?
FIRST
CARLO GETS A BOX YEA HIGH—
—THEN SETS A MIRROR ON THE FLOOR NEARBYYY—
—LIES ON THE BOX LIKE A BED—

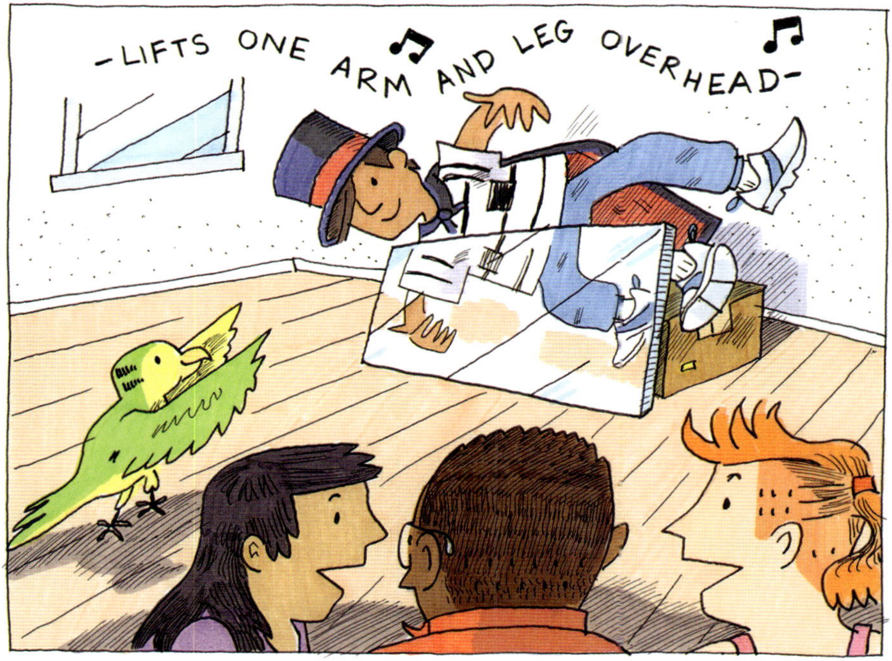
-LIFTS ONE ARM AND LEG OVERHEAD-

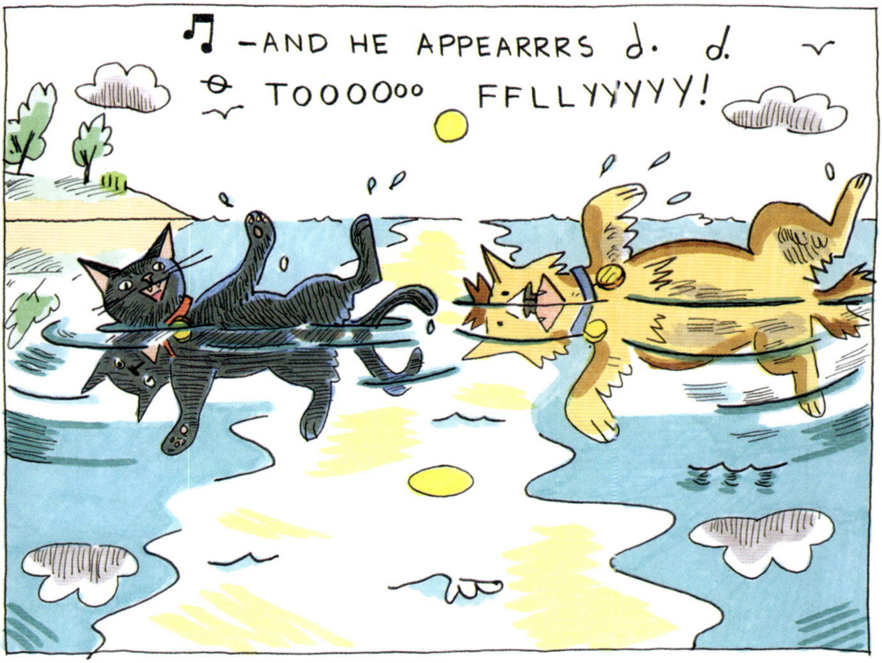
-AND HE APPEARRRS
TOOOOoo FFLLYYYYY!

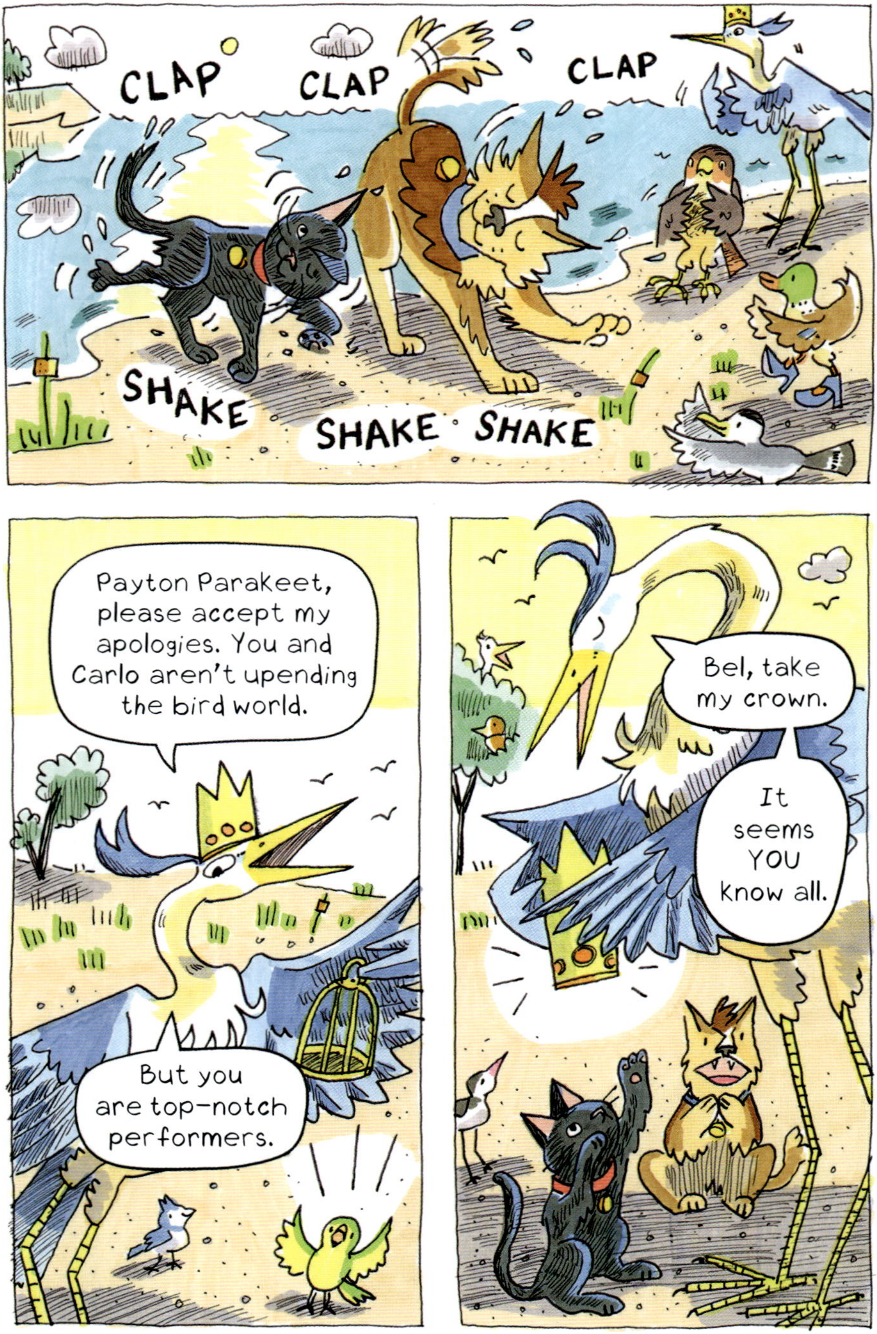
CLAP
CLAP
CLAP
SHAKE
SHAKE
SHAKE
Payton Parakeet, please accept my apologies. You and Carlo aren't upending the bird world.
But you are top-notch performers.
Bel, take my crown.
It seems YOU know all.

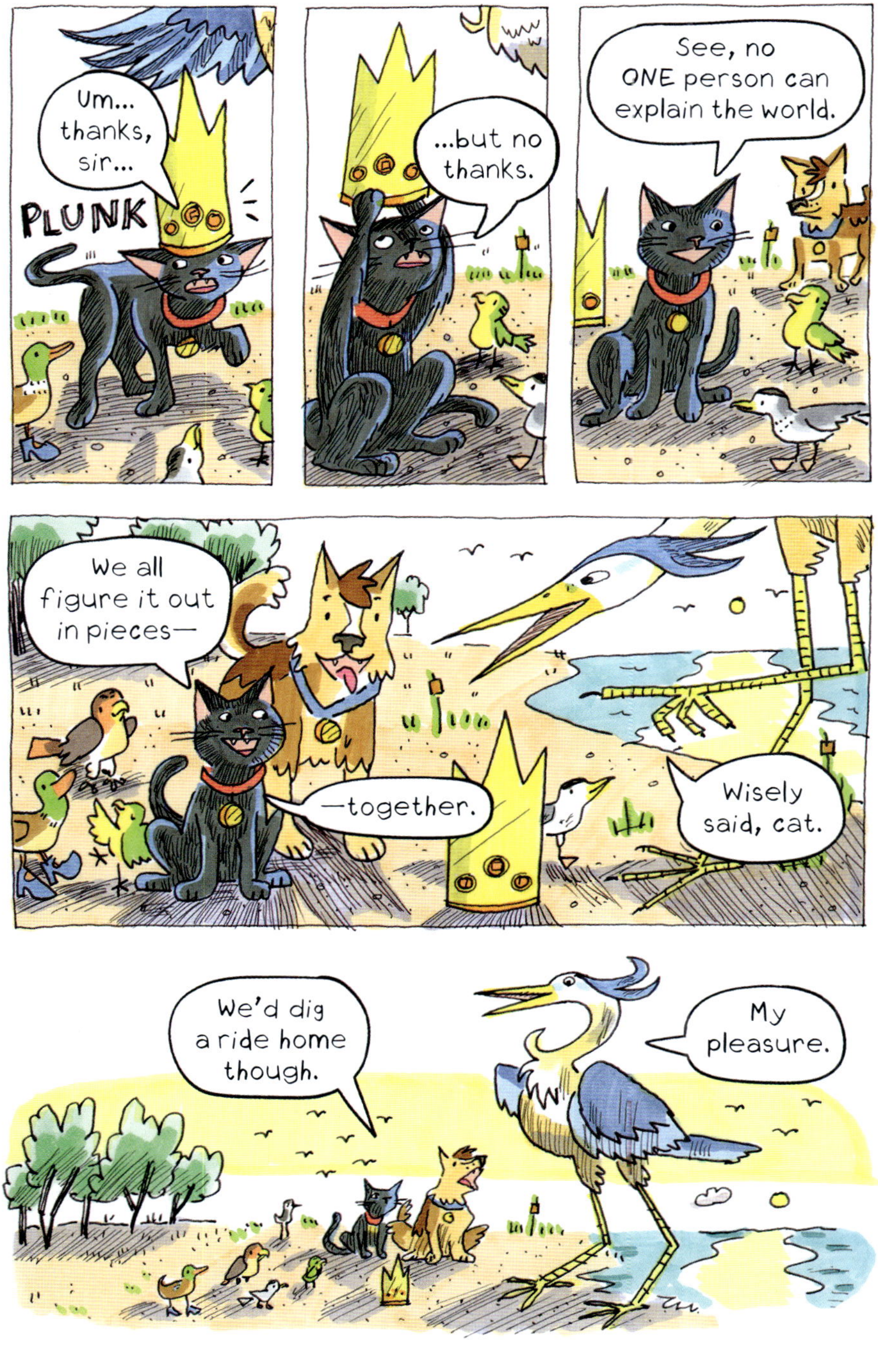

Um... thanks, sir...
PLUNK
...but no thanks.
See, no ONE person can explain the world.
We all figure it out in pieces—
—together.
Wisely said, cat.
We'd dig a ride home though.
My pleasure.

CHAPTER 12
A VERY NORMAL NEIGHBORHOOD

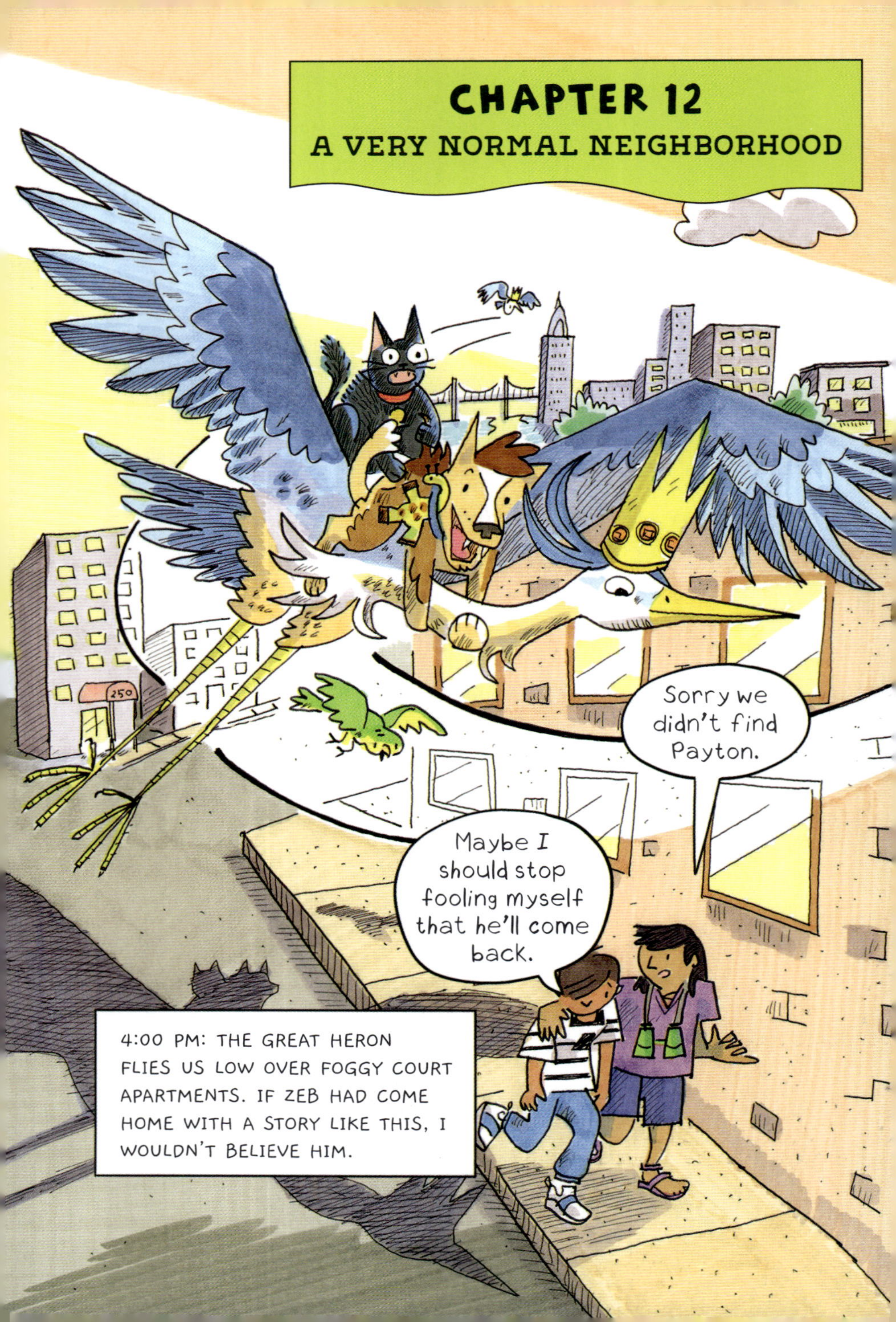
Sorry we didn't find Payton.
Maybe I should stop fooling myself that he'll come back.
4:00 PM: THE GREAT HERON FLIES US LOW OVER FOGGY COURT APARTMENTS. IF ZEB HAD COME HOME WITH A STORY LIKE THIS, I WOULDN'T BELIEVE HIM.
250

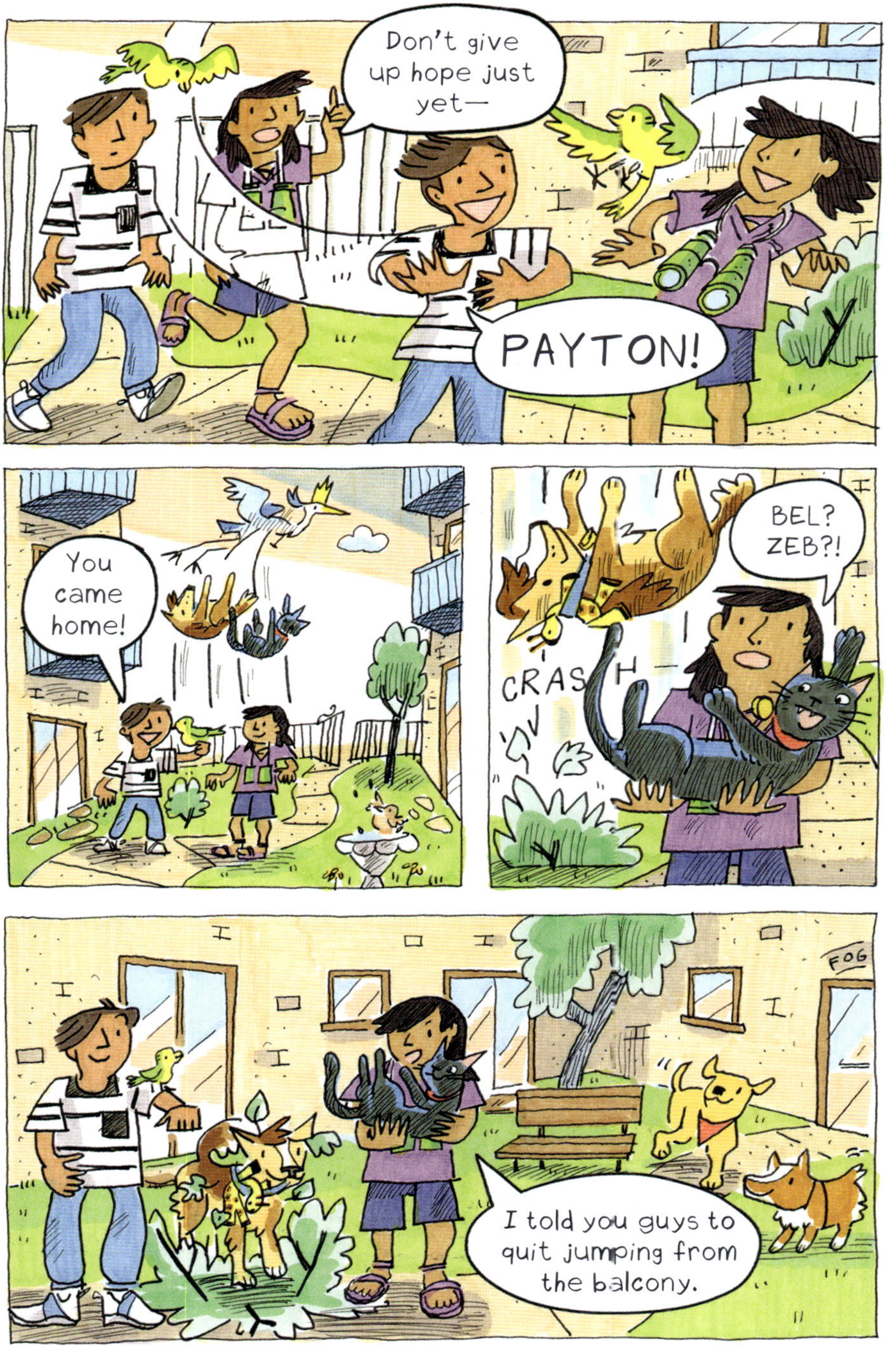
Don't give up hope just yet—
PAYTON!
You came home!
BEL? ZEB?!
CRASH
I told you guys to quit jumping from the balcony.
FOG

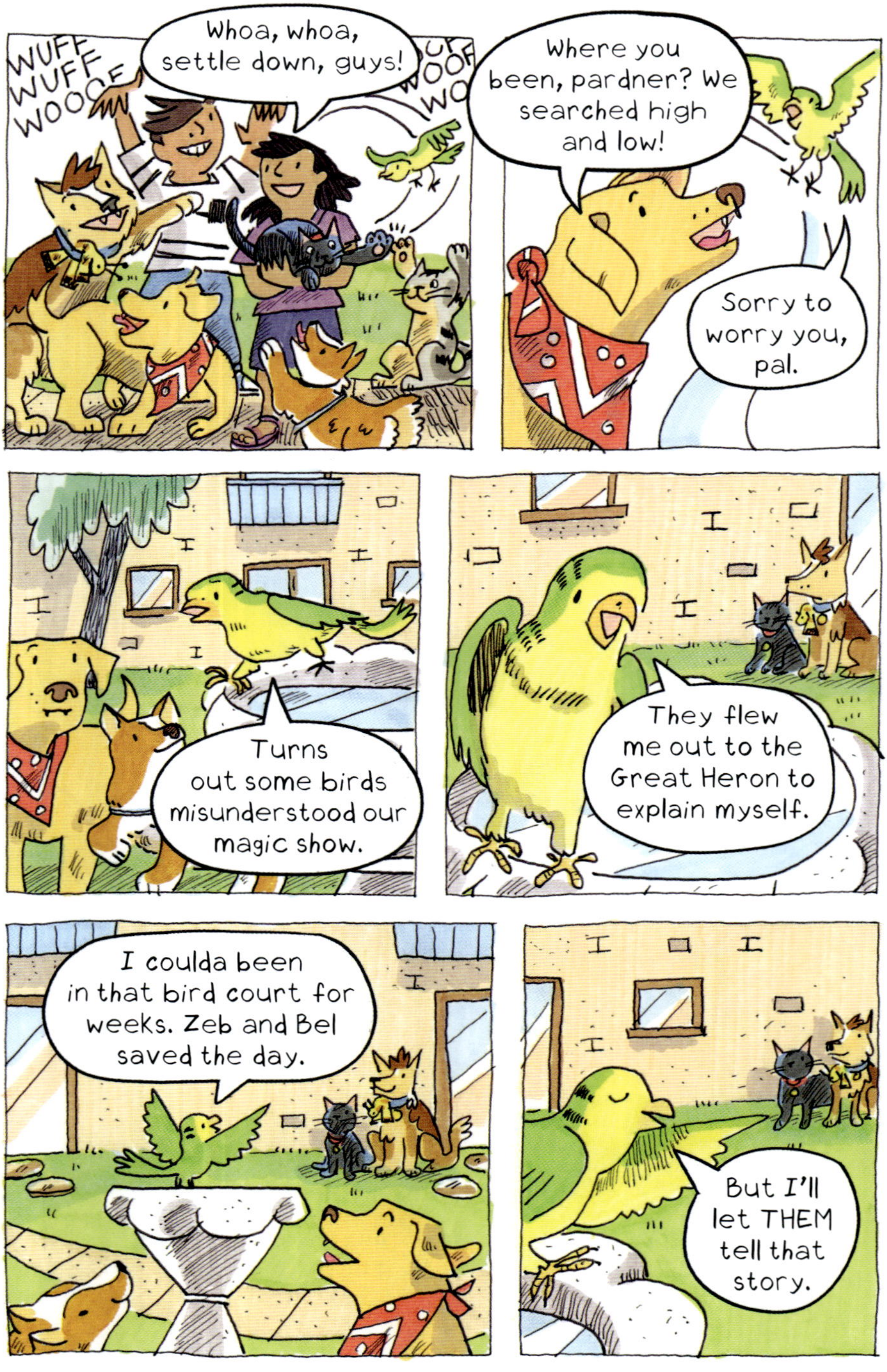

WUFF WUFF WOOOF
Whoa, whoa, settle down, guys!
WOOF
Where you been, pardner? We searched high and low!
Sorry to worry you, pal.
Turns out some birds misunderstood our magic show.
They flew me out to the Great Heron to explain myself.
I coulda been in that bird court for weeks. Zeb and Bel saved the day.
But I'll let THEM tell that story.

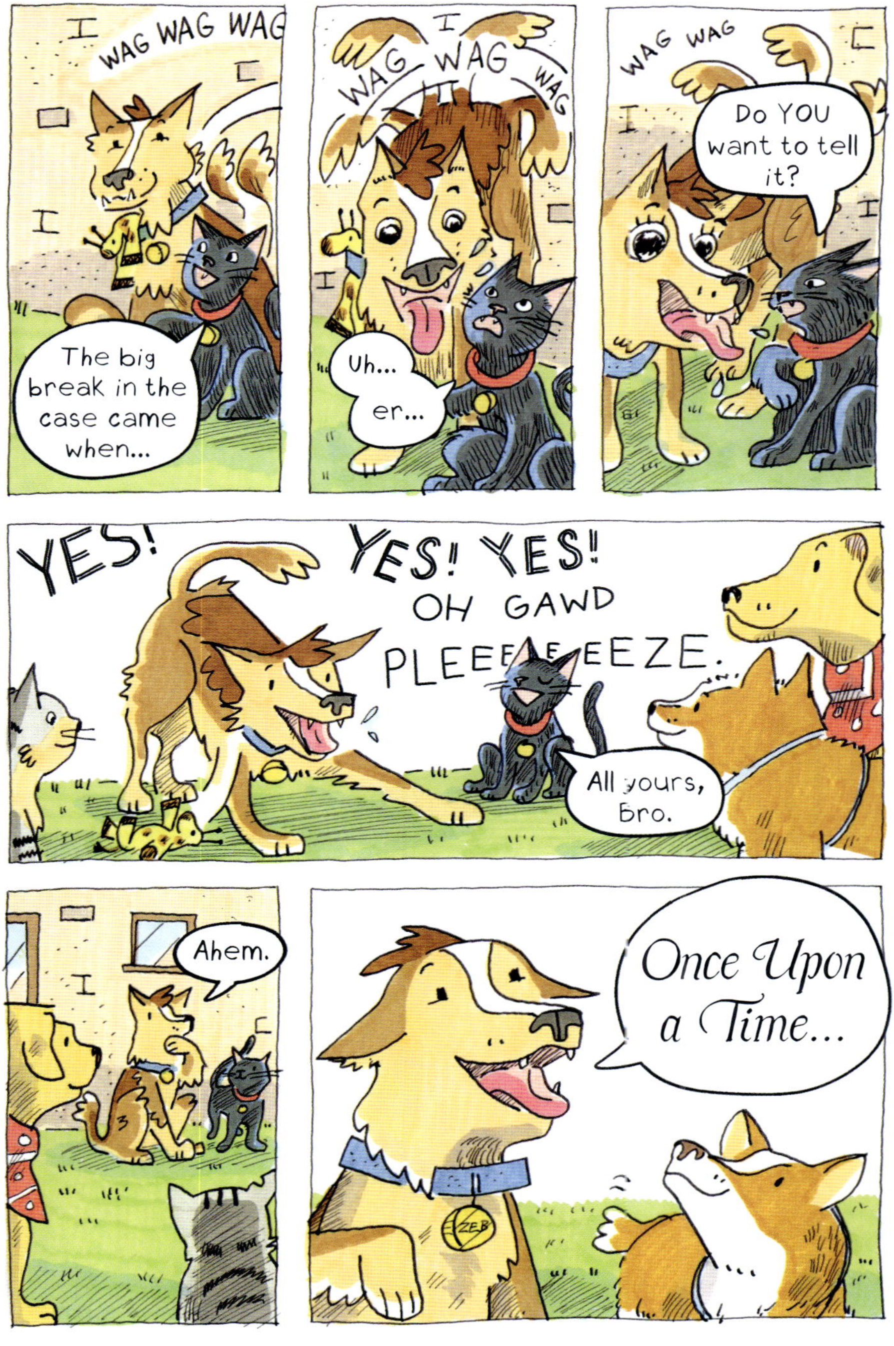
WAG WAG WAG
The big break in the case came when...
WAG WAG WAG
Uh... er...
WAG WAG
Do YOU want to tell it?
YES! YES! YES!
OH GAWD PLEEEEEEEZE.
All yours, Bro.
Ahem.
Once Upon a Time...

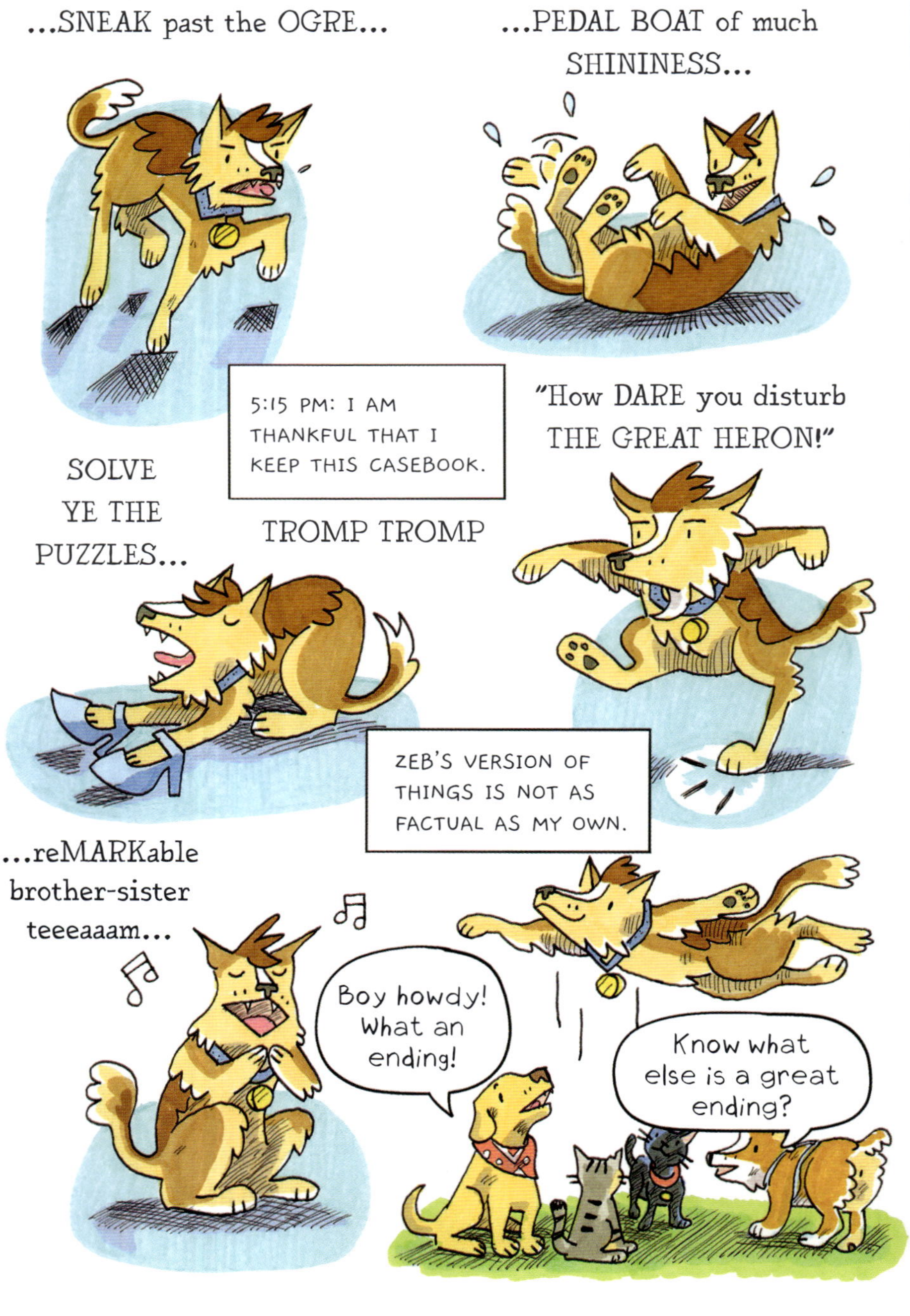
...SNEAK past the OGRE...
...PEDAL BOAT of much SHININESS...
SOLVE YE THE PUZZLES...
5:15 PM: I AM THANKFUL THAT I KEEP THIS CASEBOOK.
TROMP TROMP
"How DARE you disturb THE GREAT HERON!"
ZEB'S VERSION OF THINGS IS NOT AS FACTUAL AS MY OWN.
...reMARKable brother-sister teeeaaam...
Boy howdy! What an ending!
Know what else is a great ending?

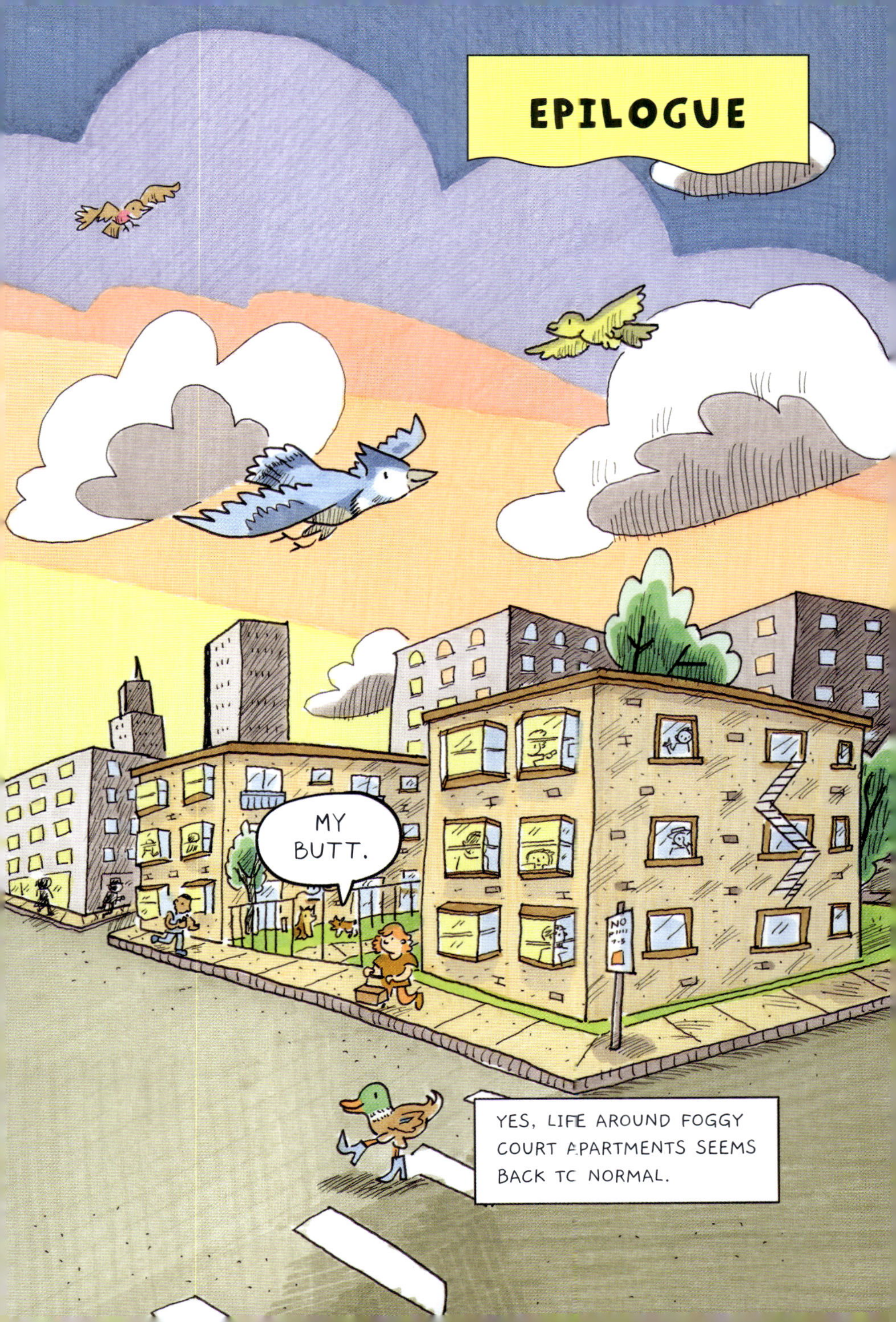
EPILOGUE
MY BUTT.
YES, LIFE AROUND FOGGY COURT APARTMENTS SEEMS BACK TO NORMAL.

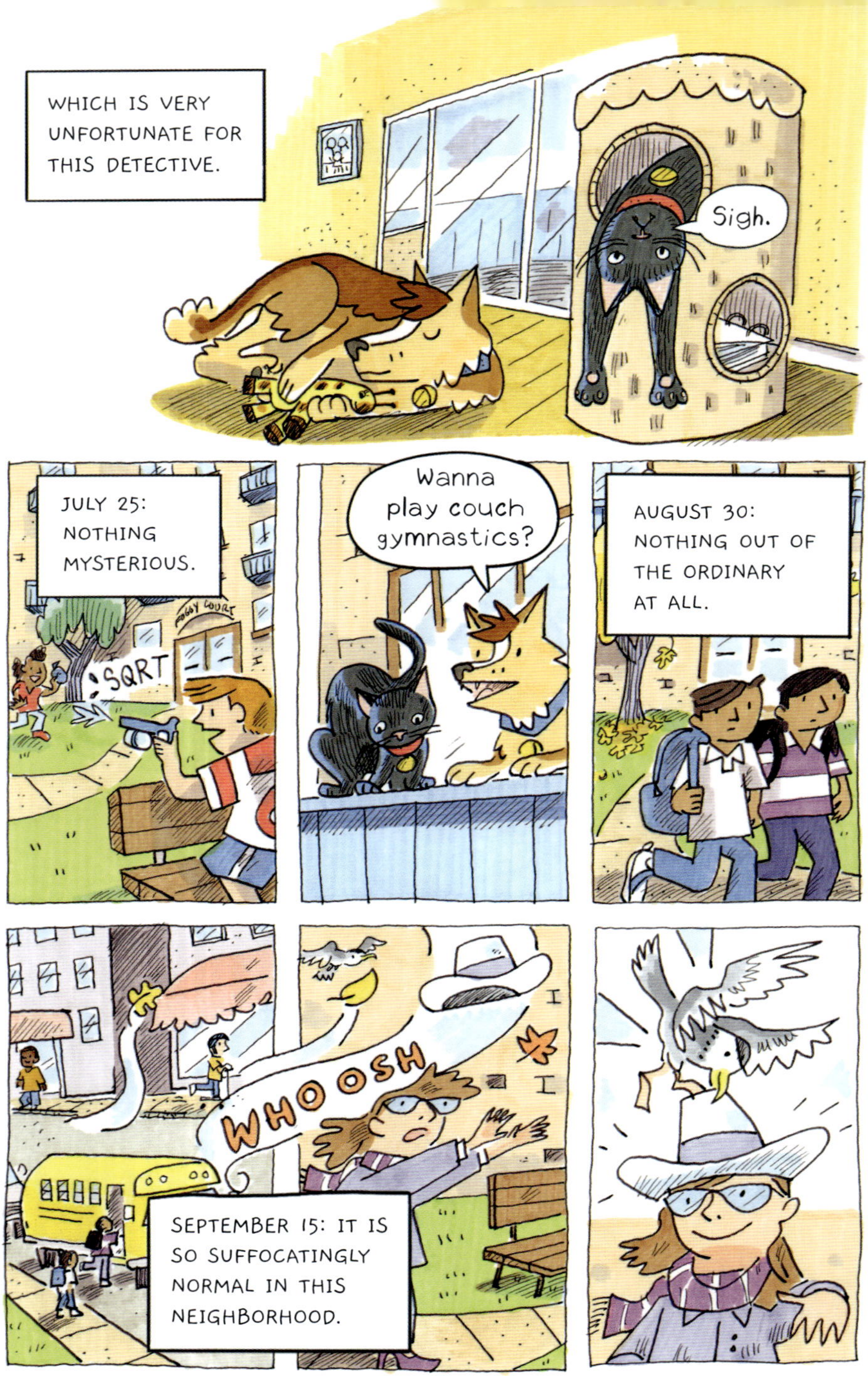
WHICH IS VERY UNFORTUNATE FOR THIS DETECTIVE.
Sigh.
JULY 25: NOTHING MYSTERIOUS.
FOGGY COURT
SQRT
Wanna play couch gymnastics?
AUGUST 30: NOTHING OUT OF THE ORDINARY AT ALL.
WHOOOSH
SEPTEMBER 15: IT IS SO SUFFOCATINGLY NORMAL IN THIS NEIGHBORHOOD.

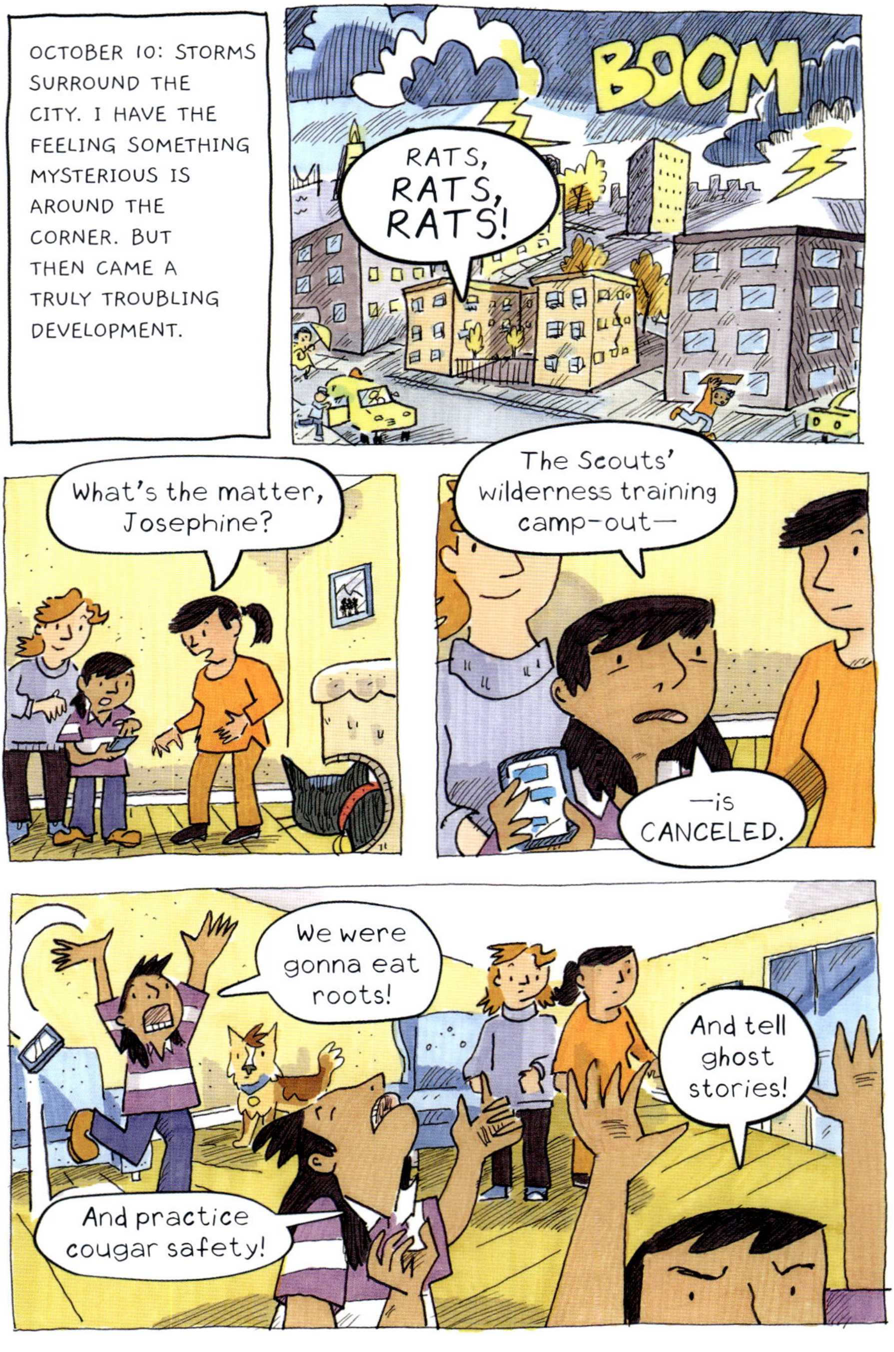
OCTOBER 10: STORMS SURROUND THE CITY. I HAVE THE FEELING SOMETHING MYSTERIOUS IS AROUND THE CORNER. BUT THEN CAME A TRULY TROUBLING DEVELOPMENT.
BOOM
RATS, RATS, RATS!
What's the matter, Josephine?
The Scouts' wilderness training camp-out—
—is CANCELED.
We were gonna eat roots!
And tell ghost stories!
And practice cougar safety!

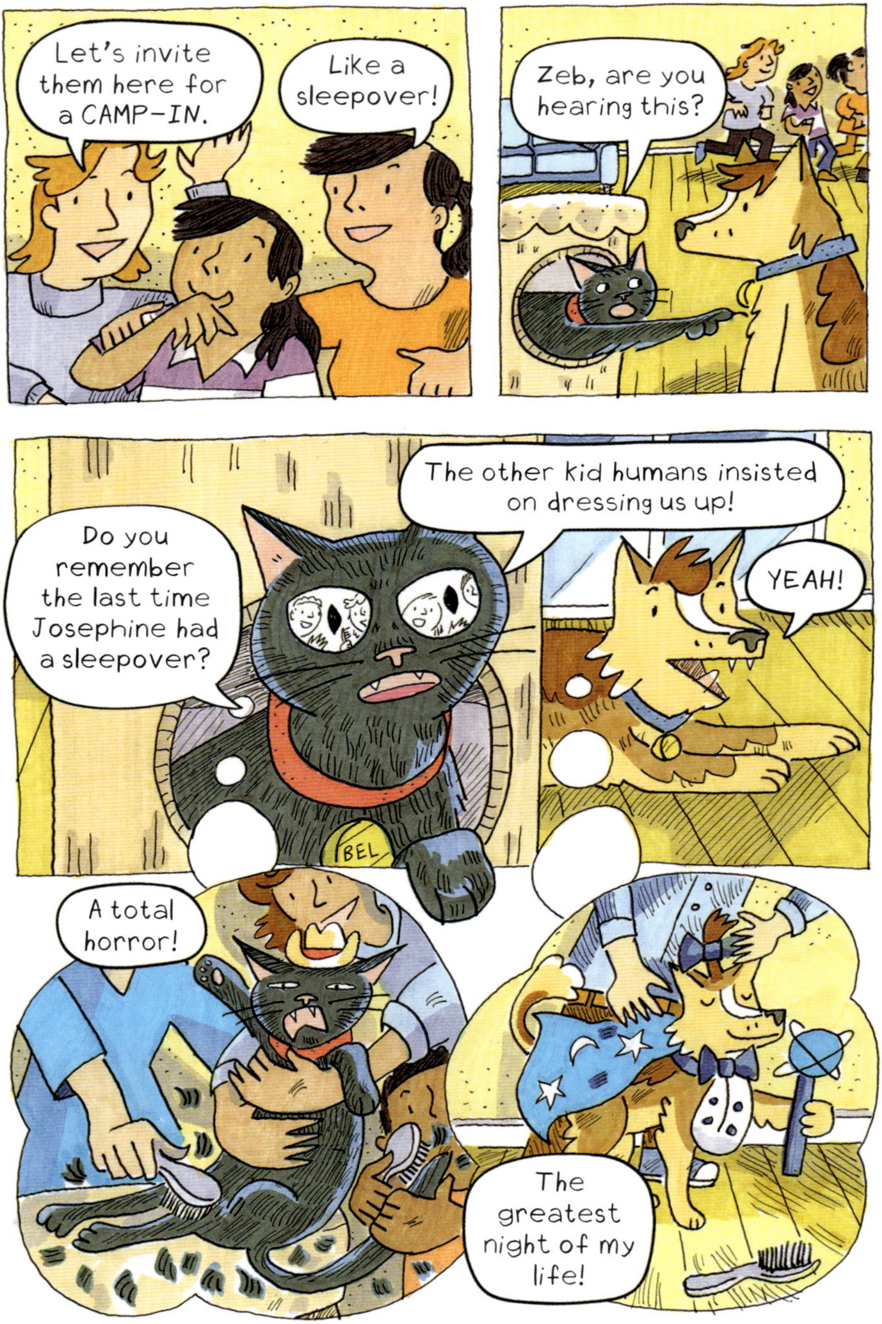
Let's invite them here for a CAMP-IN.
Like a sleepover!
Zeb, are you hearing this?
Do you remember the last time Josephine had a sleepover?
The other kid humans insisted on dressing us up!
YEAH!
BEL
A total horror!
The greatest night of my life!

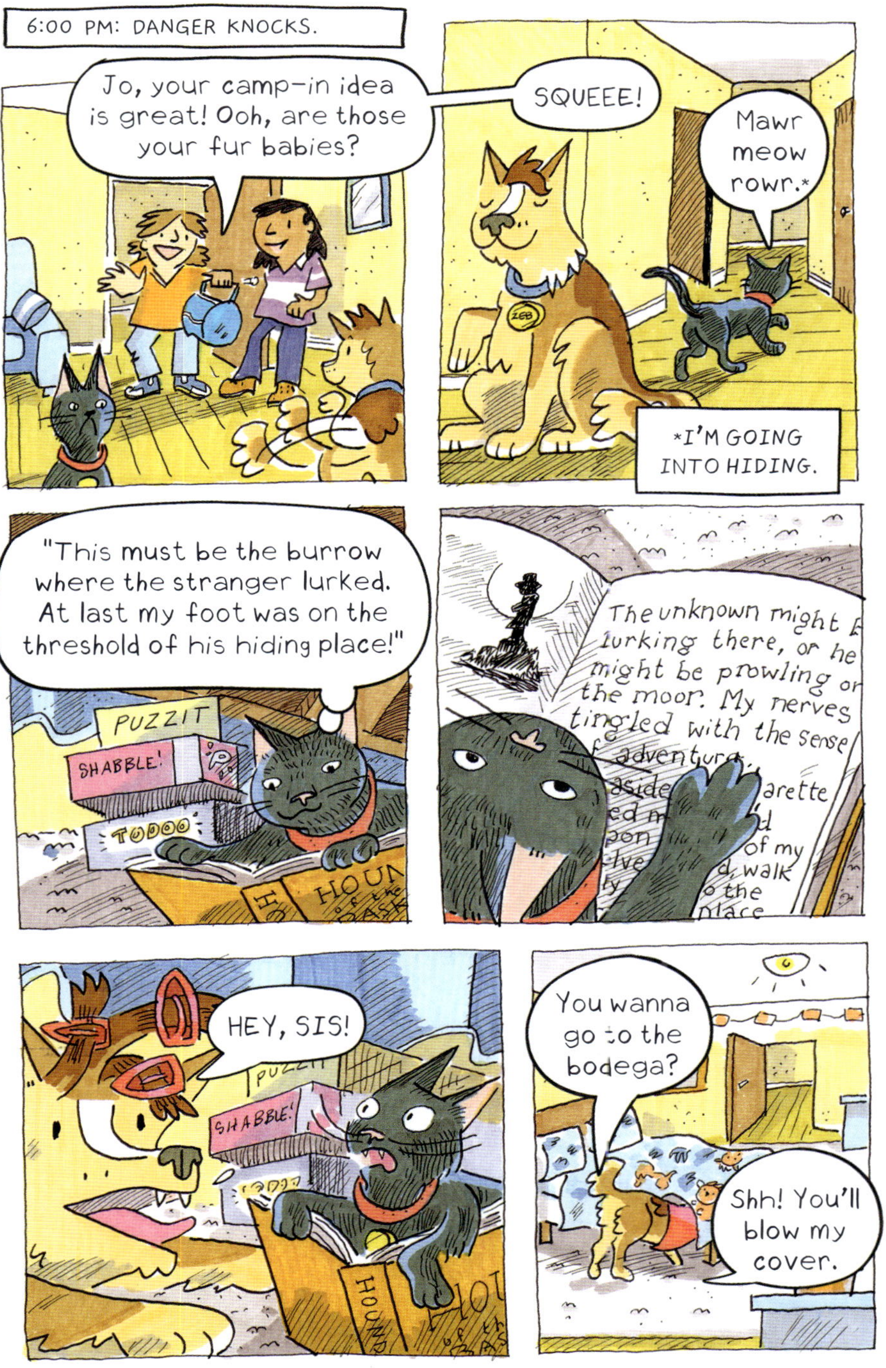
6:00 PM: DANGER KNOCKS.
Jo, your camp-in idea is great! Ooh, are those your fur babies?
SQUEEE!
ZEB
Mawr meow rowr.*
*I'M GOING INTO HIDING.
"This must be the burrow where the stranger lurked. At last my foot was on the threshold of his hiding place!"
PUZZIT
SHABBLE!
TODOO
HOUN
The unknown might
lurking there, or he
might be prowling or
the moor. My nerves
tingled with the sense
of my
walk
the
HEY, SIS!
SHABBLE!
HOUND
You wanna go to the bodega?
Shh! You'll blow my cover.

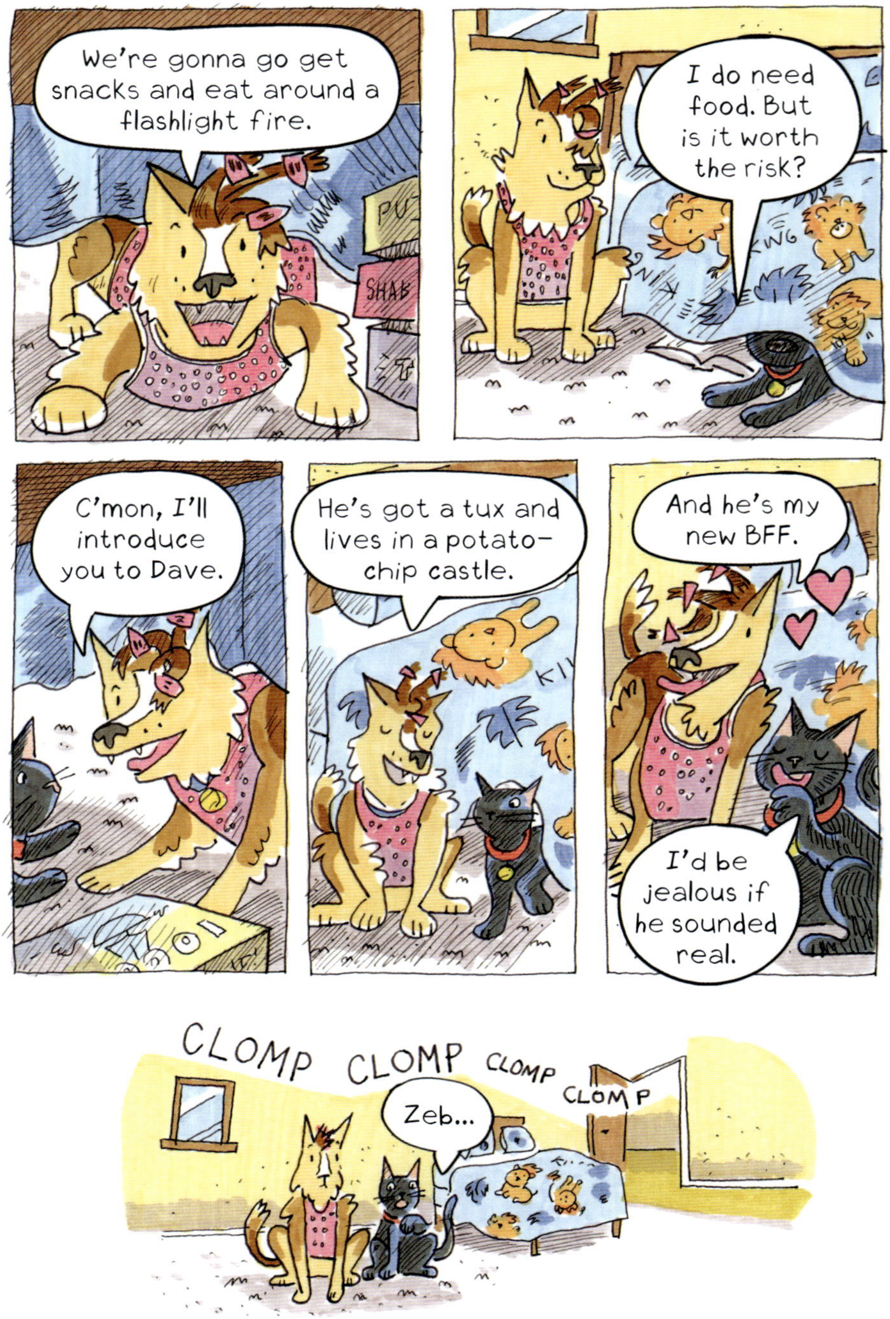
We're gonna go get snacks and eat around a flashlight fire.
I do need food. But is it worth the risk?
C'mon, I'll introduce you to Dave.
He's got a tux and lives in a potato-chip castle.
And he's my new BFF.
I'd be jealous if he sounded real.
CLOMP CLOMP CLOMP CLOMP
Zeb...

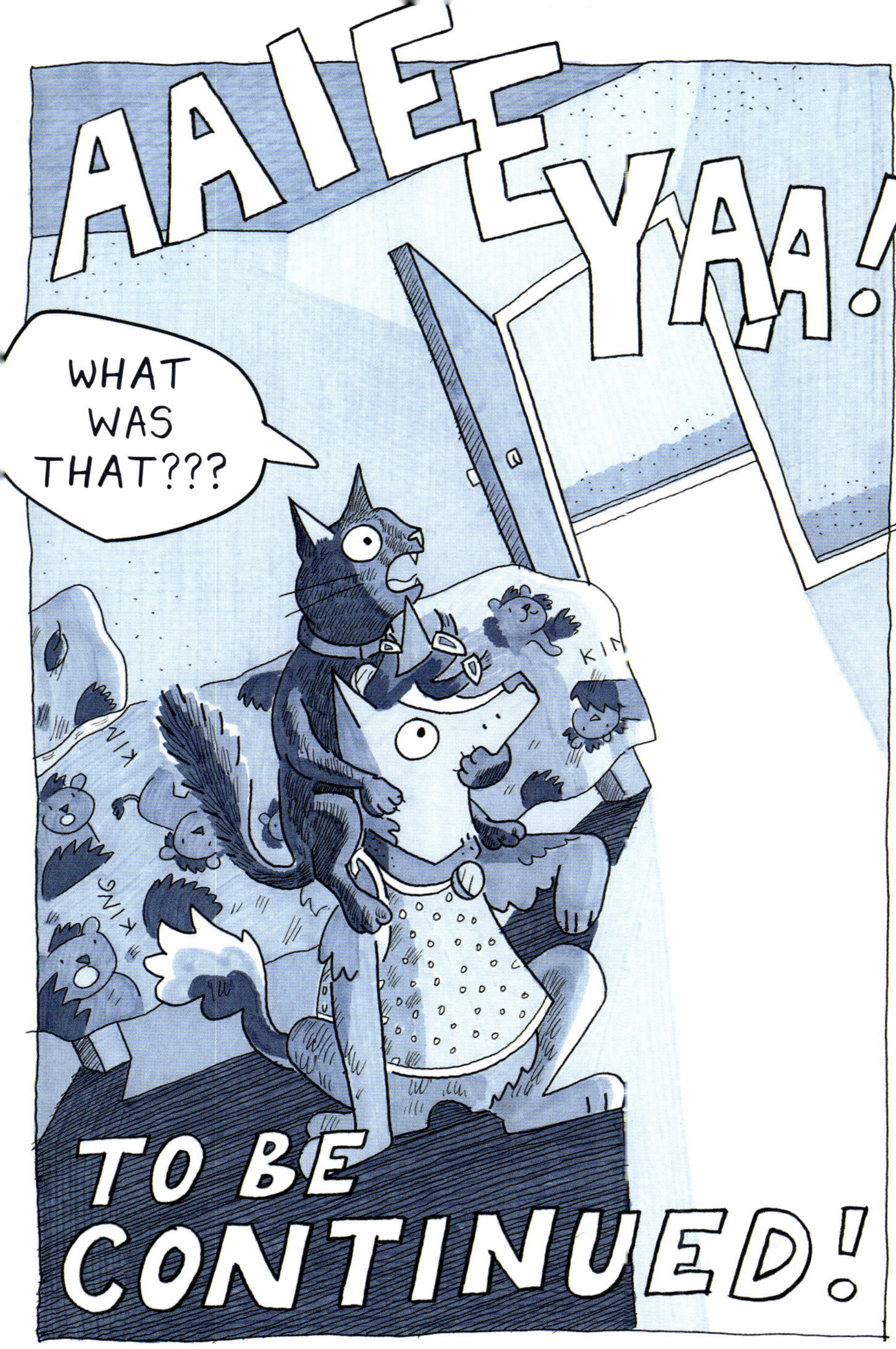
AAIEEEYAA!
WHAT WAS THAT???
KING
KING
KING
TO BE CONTINUED!

HOW TO DRAW BEL!

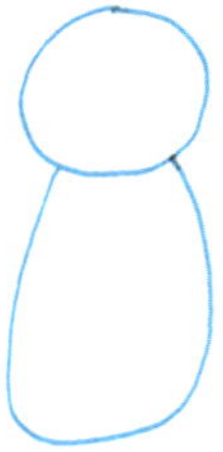

1. DRAW A CIRCLE AND ADD A BOTTLE SHAPE.

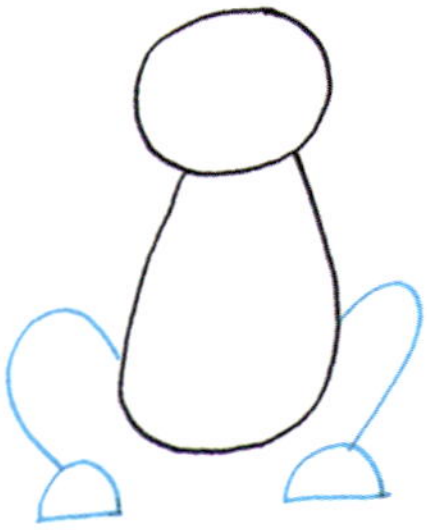

2. DRAW THE SITTING LEGS.

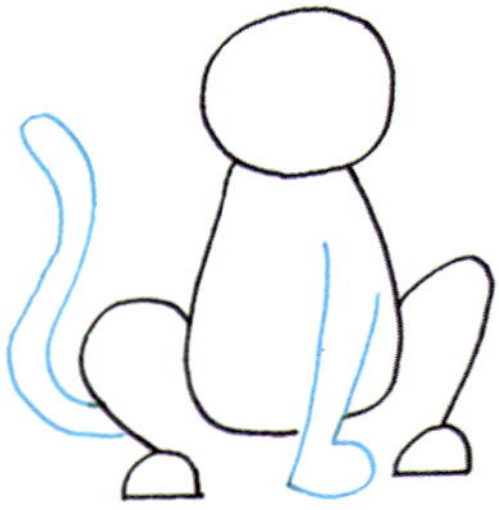

3. ADD A TAIL AND A FRONT LEG.

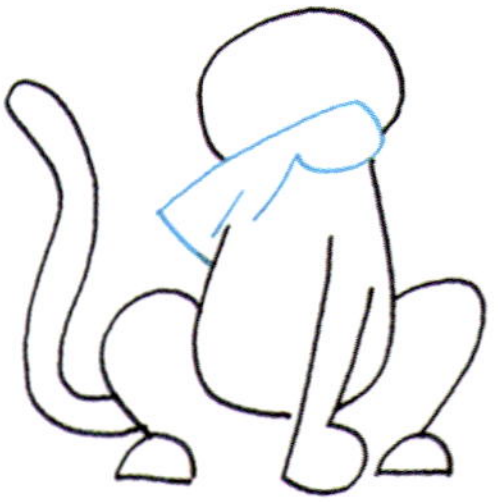

4. ADD THE PAW OF THOUGHT.

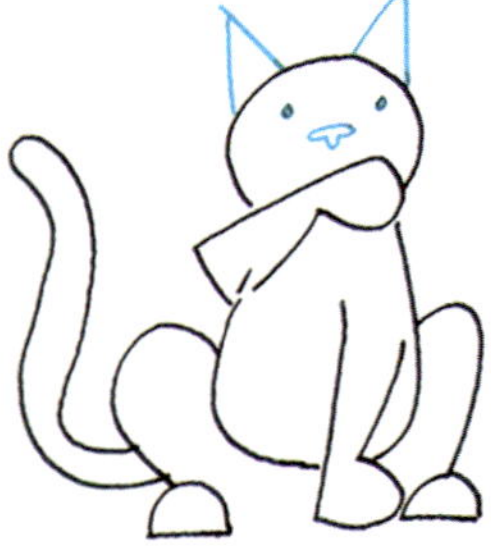

5. ADD EARS, PUPILS, AND NOSE.

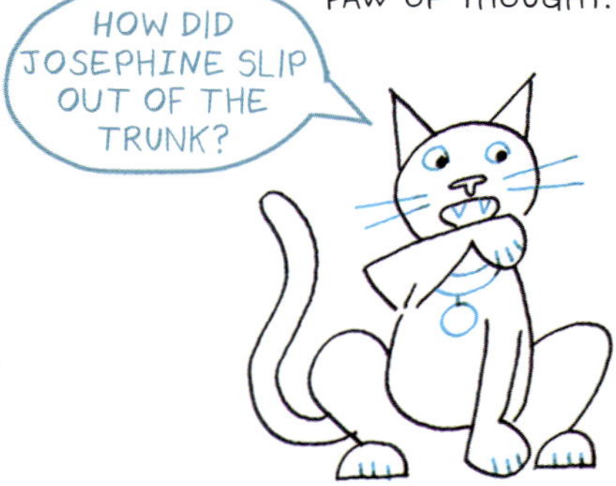
HOW DID JOSEPHINE SLIP OUT OF THE TRUNK?

6. ADD WHISKERS, COLLAR, AND EYE CIRCLES, AND GIVE HER SOMETHING TO THINK ABOUT.

HOW TO DRAW ZEB!

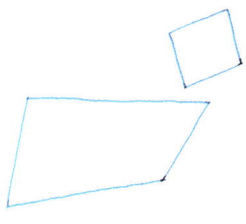

1. DRAW SQUARISH SHAPES.

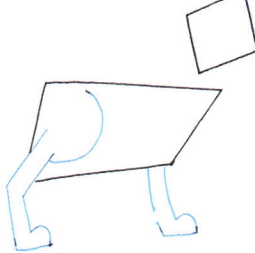

2. ADD THE STANDING LEGS.

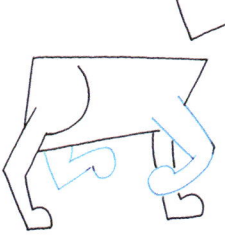

3. ADD THE PRANCY LEGS.

4. ADD THE EARS AND TAIL.

5. ADD EYES, NOSE, AND MOUTH.

DO GHOSTS FALL IN LOVE?

6. ADD FUR AND COLLAR, AND GIVE HIM SOMETHING TO DREAM ABOUT.

DID YOU SEE...

NEIL THE SEAGULL HANGING OUT ON THE WINDOWSILL IN CHAPTER 1
AND PEEKING IN ON THE MAGIC SHOW IN CHAPTER 2?

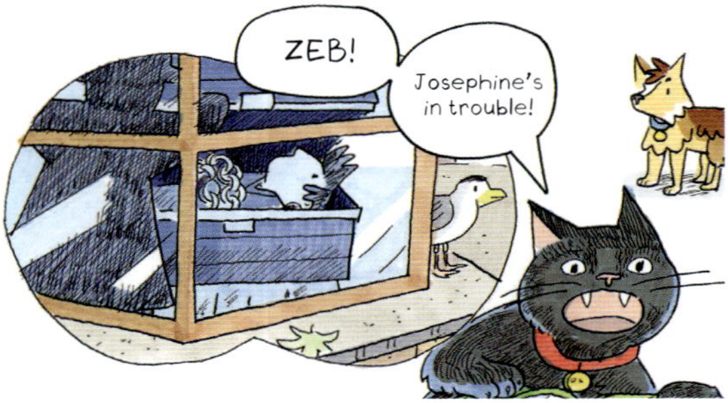
ZEB!
Josephine's in trouble!

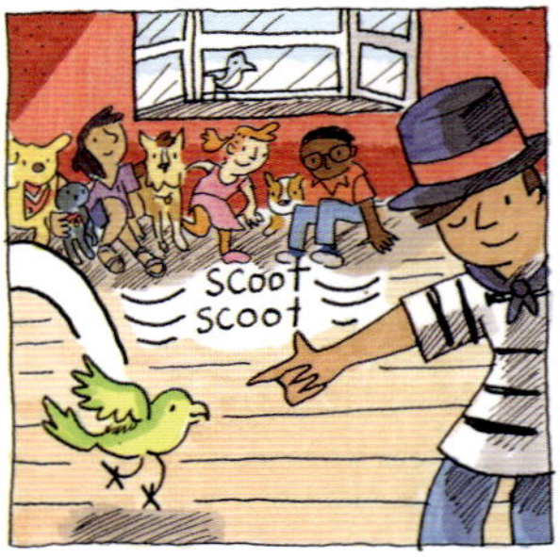
SCOOT SCOOT

THE BOX AND MIRROR THAT CARLO USED
FOR THE FLYING TRICK IN CHAPTERS 2 AND 3?

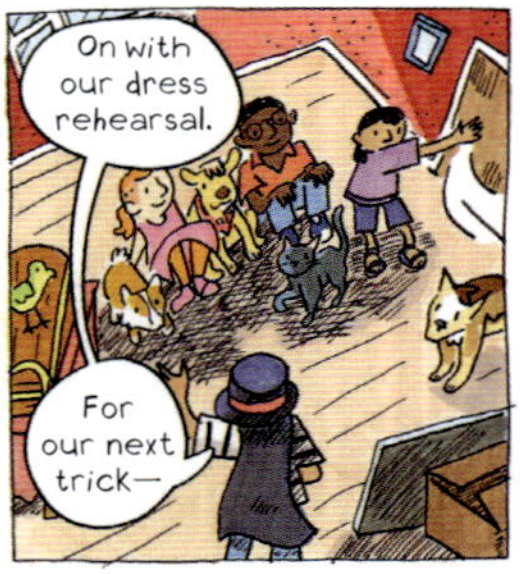
On with our dress rehearsal.
For our next trick—

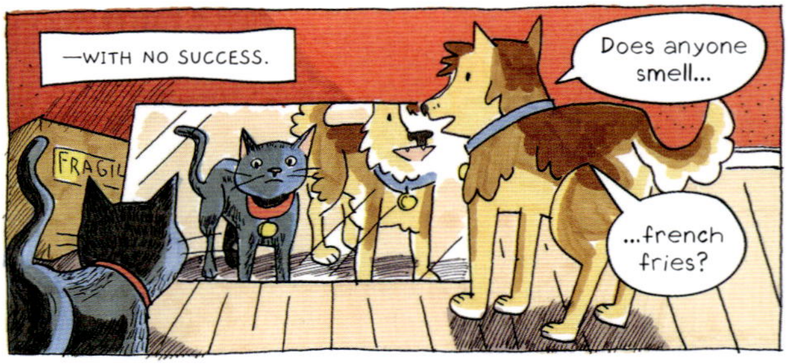
—WITH NO SUCCESS.
Does anyone smell...
...french fries?

THE DUCK IN HIGH HEELS
AT THE DISCOUNT STORE
IN CHAPTER 5?

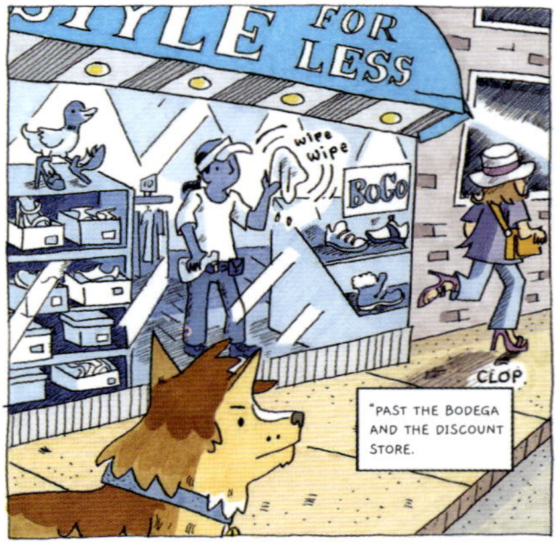
FOR LESS
wipe wipe
BoGo
CLOP.
*PAST THE BODEGA AND THE DISCOUNT STORE.

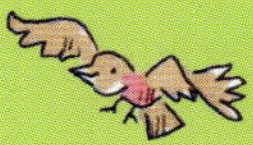

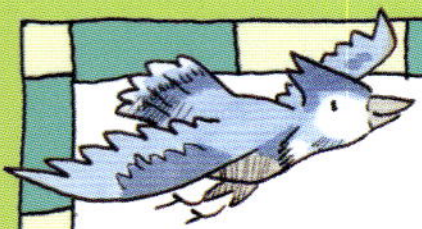

ACKNOWLEDGMENTS

Thank you to many people who helped make this book:

Editors Donna Bray and Rose Pleuler, who called this book a "happy place" and shared their photos of childhood pets. Agent Susan Hawk, who helped make Zeb and Bel not just pets, but pet sibling detectives who sing musical numbers. Art director Dana Fritts and designer Caitlin Stamper, who clue into drawn details that I overlook, and Caitlin Lonning, who caught so many details with an eagle eye. Creative writer and illustrator friends Krista, Scout, Mark, Serena, Shawn, Mariama, and many more, whose work I'm in awe of every day.

My brother David, who gives me a lifetime of wonderful sibling experiences to draw from, and my sister-in-law Kayo, who adds many more. My wife, Carol, who knows every line of *Rear Window*, and jokingly asked, "What if L. B. Jefferies was a dog?" My sister-in-law Martha, who gave me a Kaweco fountain pen used to draw this book. My nieces and nephew, who draw with me and ask the best questions for any investigation. My parents, who adopted every stray that showed up and patiently lived with a Sherlock Holmes–obsessed child.

Most important—thank you to kids who read comics. I get to meet you at book events and workshops. Your love of reading makes my day, every day.

Thank you.

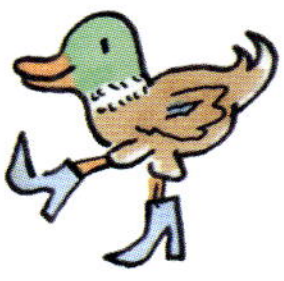

Don't miss this duo's next mystery!

ZEB AND BEL

NIGHT OF THE BODEGA CAT

HarperCollins Children's Books, a division of HarperCollins Publishers,
195 Broadway, New York, NY 10007

HarperCollins Publishers, Macken House, 39/40 Mayor Street Upper,
Dublin 1, D01 C9W8, Ireland

HarperAlley is an imprint of HarperCollins Publishers.
Zeb and Bel: A Case of Bird Problems • Copyright © 2026 by Rachel Elliott
All rights reserved. Manufactured in Johor, Malaysia.
No part of this book may be used or reproduced in any manner whatsoever without written permission except in the case of brief quotations embodied in critical articles and reviews. Without limiting the exclusive rights of any author, contributor, or the publisher of this publication, any unauthorized use of this publication to train generative artificial intelligence (AI) technologies is expressly prohibited. HarperCollins also exercises their rights under Article 4(3) of the Digital Single Market Directive 2019/790 and expressly reserves this publication from the text and data mining exception.
harpercollins.com

Library of Congress Control Number: 2025935459
ISBN 978-0-06-335429-6 (PBK) — ISBN 978-0-06-335430-2
Book design by Caitlin E. D. Stamper. Hand-lettered by Rachel Elliott.
25 26 27 28 29 PCA 10 9 8 7 6 5 4 3 2 1 • First Edition